Praise for
Nightlife

"Thomas Perry's terrific *Nightlife* begins with a harbinger of things to come—which is to say that this tight, transfixing crime story gets off to a bone-chilling start. . . . A lot of care and ingenuity have gone into the suspenseful chessboard plotting of this story. . . . *Nightlife* is especially devilish in its calculations about how best to move anonymously through the American landscape. . . . *Nightlife* connects with the reader. Extraordinary."
—*The New York Times*

"There are probably only half a dozen suspense writers now alive who can be depended upon to deliver high-voltage shocks, vivid, sympathetic characters, and compelling narratives each time they publish. Thomas Perry is one of them. *Nightlife*, his tale of a female serial killer who starts hunting the female police officer trying to catch her, is original and highly entertaining. I can't imagine any reader finishing this and thinking he or she didn't get his or her money's worth. And it's scary! I say that with deep admiration."
—STEPHEN KING

Books published by The Random House Publishing Group
are available at quantity discounts on bulk purchases for
premium, educational, fund-raising, and special sales use.
For details, please call 1-800-733-3000.

Nightlife

THOMAS PERRY

BALLANTINE BOOKS • NEW YORK

2007 Ballantine Books Mass Market Edition

Copyright © 2006 by Thomas Perry

Published in the United States by Ballantine Books, an imprint of The Random House Publishing Group, a division of Random House, Inc., New York.

BALLANTINE and colophon are registered trademarks of Random House, Inc.

Originally published in hardcover in the United States by Random House, an imprint of The Random House Publishing Group, a division of Random House, Inc., in 2006.

ISBN 978-0-345-49600-3

Cover images: Tony Greco

Printed in the United States of America

www.ballantinebooks.com

OPM 9 8 7 6 5 4 3 2 1

For Jo, Alix, and Isabel

1

Tanya stood in front of the full-length mirror on the bedroom wall and brushed her hair. She watched the other girl, in another room, wearing the same new blue skirt and tank top, using her left hand instead of her right to brush the long blond hair to a shine. Tanya had always secretly relished the existence of the other pretty girl who lived in the other room beyond the glass, like a fish in an aquarium. She loved the whole idea of a second girl who lived a second life.

In Wheatfield when she was little she had sometimes turned her mother's dresser so the mirror would be directly across from the full-length one on the closet door. She could make a whole long line of other girls, then kick her legs and look like the Rockettes, the nearest ones as big as she was, and the others smaller and smaller as their line stretched off into infinity.

She had dressed up in her mother's clothes sometimes, so she could change the girl in the mirror. She would be someone who had a good life, someone who was loved and cared for, someone who was beautiful and had everything she wanted.

She could invent things that the girl in the mirror could say, and practice them, whispering so the girl in the mirror would not be overheard. She would assume faces that were distant and just a little disapproving, and know that seeing them would make people frantic, trying to find ways to please her. She tried expressions designed to reward too, opening her eyes and mouth wide in a grateful smile that admitted no possibility of darker thoughts, nothing held back or hidden. Sometimes when she did that she would add a laugh at the end—not a small, forced sound, but a delighted laugh that made her eyes glisten and her white teeth show to their best advantage.

The alarm system's cool male electronic voice announced, "Kitchen . . . door": Dennis was finally home. This was it. Tanya stopped brushing her hair, slipped the brush into her purse, felt for the other handle and gripped it once, then released it.

She could hear Dennis's hard leather soles on the slate floor of the kitchen. There was no sound of his dropping his briefcase on the kitchen floor, so he had set it down gently: he had brought his laptop home again. He was planning to spend the evening working. "Tanya?" He was in the living room now.

She put her purse on the floor beside the dresser. "Up here."

She spent the next fifteen seconds considering him—turning him around and around in her mind and evaluating him. Women always said men had a hard outer shell but were soft and sweet and vulnerable inside, but she had found the opposite. They had a layer outside that was yielding and squeezable, but when you squeezed you began to feel the hardness beneath, like bone. She had squeezed him a lot in a short time, and she was already beginning to reach the hardness. He was getting ready to say no to her, to deny her things. Maybe he would even criticize her when the bills came and he could see everything added up. It was time.

Dennis's heavy shoes thumped on the carpeted stairway, coming closer. She already saw each step of the stairway in her mind, even though she had only been with Dennis Poole for a month, and all but a week of that had been spent in hotels. As he climbed step by step, she began to enumerate his unpleasant qualities. She didn't like his laugh. It was a quick staccato that made his voice go one octave higher, like a jackass's bray. A few times she had gotten up from her chaise next to him and gone into the hotel pool to cool her sun-warmed skin, come up from underwater, and seen him looking at other women in their bathing suits. He tipped waiters exactly fifteen percent and never a penny more, and was proud of it because it showed he could do the arithmetic in his head. He was not a sincerely appreciative lover. He pretended to care and be solicitous of her, but there was a practical quality about it. His concern was to please her, but it wasn't the right kind of concern. He wasn't a man unable to stop himself because he was enthralled. He was merely thinking about whether he was pleasing her enough to keep her.

Dennis had reached the top of the stairs. As she turned to look at him, her detachment was complete. He was a forty-two-year-old man with a soft belly and thinning hair who spent his days selling computer equipment to other men like himself. He was nothing. She smiled beautifully, stepped into his embrace, and kissed him slowly, languorously. "Hello, cowboy," she whispered.

He laughed as she had expected. "I could get used to coming home like this and finding you waiting for me." He looked more serious. "You know, I'm glad you were here for another reason. I think we need to talk about some things."

"Sure. We can talk, but first, don't you want to get comfortable? I should think you'd be tired after sitting in that office all day." She knew that tone of voice. Anyone could tell he was getting ready to be cheap with her, to start complaining about money. She pulled back and said, "I'll bet you're sick of wearing that suit. Why don't you get out of it, relax, and soak in the tub?" She looked down at his tie as she loosened it, not into his eyes. "Maybe I'll join you."

"Good idea." He took his suit coat off and his tie, while Tanya went into the bathroom and turned on the water. The oversized Jacuzzi tub had jets that bubbled, so she turned them on too.

Dennis Poole was naked now, and he put his arms around her. She tolerated his embrace for a few seconds, then wriggled away and whispered seductively, "Wait."

She went back out to the bedroom and walked to the dresser, where she had left her purse. She waited until she heard him turn off the water faucet, so the only sound was the steady burble of the jets. She quietly walked into the bathroom.

He was lying in the tub with his head cushioned by a folded towel, looking self-absorbed and distant as the bubbles massaged his skin. Tanya reached into her purse, took out the pistol, held it about a foot from his head, and squeezed. The report was a bright, sharp bang that echoed against the tile walls and made her ears ring. She turned away from the sight of his corpse, the red blood draining into the bath, and stopped being Tanya Starling.

2

Hugo Poole's rubber-soled shoes made almost no sound as he walked along the sidewalk outside the CBS Studio Center's iron railings, past the soundstages on his way up Radford Street from Ventura Boulevard. He never would have set up a night meeting in the Valley, so far from the old downtown movie theater he used for an office, but he had often found that it was worth making small concessions just to learn what the other side wanted to do. There was no single precaution that would always work, and the least effective was never taking a risk. As soon as caution turned predictable, it became the biggest risk of all.

Still, he wished he could stay right here. He liked being near a television studio, because these complexes were usually on the itineraries of the people who heard voices telling them that God wanted them to punish a few actors. That ensured that there would always be plenty of jumpy security guards. He would have preferred to meet Steve Rao right here outside the gate, under the tall security lights.

Hugo Poole walked on beside the railing, now moving into the dimly lighted eucalyptus-lined blocks beside the big parking structure, and then he stopped at Valleyheart Street. He crossed the street to the city's chain-link fence and looked through it to the place where the concrete bed of the Tujunga Wash met the concrete bed of the Los Angeles River. On this hot midsummer night, the only water was the runoff from automatic lawn sprinklers, a steady trickle confined to a foot-deep groove a man could step across that ran down the center of each bed. In the rainy season this place became the confluence of two turbulent brown floods crashing together at thirty miles an hour and rushing south toward the Pacific.

Hugo Poole looked to his left, up the scenic walkway above the river toward the iron gate at Laurel Canyon that was designed to look like a big toad. At this hour nobody wanted to go for a walk above a concrete riverbed. He waited for the minute hand of his watch to reach the hour. Then he took out the key he had received in the mail. He unlocked the padlock on the gate above the wash, and slipped inside. Steve Rao's people had knocked off the city padlock and put on their own, then sent him the key to open it. Hugo Poole took a moment to close the gate. He reached into his pocket, took out his own lock, and placed it on the gate. He stuck Rao's key into Rao's lock, tossed them both down the hill into the bushes, and walked on.

He descended the sloping gravel driveway that the city had cut so its maintenance people could come down once a year to remove the tangle of dried brush and shopping carts from the concrete waterway before the rains. He reached the bottom, took a few steps onto the pavement of the river, and stopped to look around. He could hear the distant whisper of cars flashing along the Ventura Freeway a few blocks away, and a constant dribble of water dripping out of a storm drain and running down the wall a few feet from him.

Hugo Poole's eyes adjusted to the darkness and picked out four silhouettes in the deeper shadow across the wash. They floated toward him, and Poole tried to pick out Steve Rao's short, strutting body, but couldn't.

The one who separated from the others was too tall to be
Steve Rao. "What are you doing here?" the voice said. It was
young, with a trace of Spanglish inflection.

It was the wrong question. Somebody Steve Rao had sent
would know why Hugo was here.

Hugo Poole said, "I'm not here to hurt you. That's all you
need to know about me."

The heads of the four shapes turned to one another in quiet
consultation, and Hugo Poole prepared himself, waiting for
them to spread out. There was a sudden, sharp blow to his
skull that made a red flare explode in his vision and knocked
his head to the side. He spun to see the two new shapes just
as they threw their shoulders into him. His head snapped
back and his spine was strained as they dug in and brought
him down on the concrete.

They seemed to have expected him to give up, but he
began to bring his knees into play as he grappled with them.
They tried to hold him down on the pavement, but Hugo
Poole fought silently and patiently, first separating them,
then twisting his torso to jab a heavy elbow into a face. He
heard a crack, a howl of pain, and felt his opponent fall away.
He rolled to the other side to clutch the second assailant, and
delivered a palm strike that bounced the back of the man's
head off the pavement. The man lay still.

Hugo Poole was up on his feet again, sidestepping away
from the two motionless bodies. The other four had made it
only halfway across the riverbed toward him, and now they
stopped with the shallow trench full of water separating them
from Hugo Poole.

Poole put his head down and charged at the one who had
spoken earlier. The young man hesitated, then looked at his
companions, who showed no inclination to help him. They
backed away, not from Hugo Poole but from their companion, as though if they could dissociate themselves from his
fate, they would not share it. As Hugo Poole leapt the trench,
the young man spun on his heel and ran about a hundred feet
before he turned to see if he was safe.

The other three interpreted his flight as permission to run

too. They dashed to the far wall where the shadows were deepest, and then moved off into the darkness down the river-bed. Hugo Poole turned to see that the two who had been on the ground were rapidly recovering. One was helping the other to his feet, and then they hobbled off together up the in-clined driveway toward the street.

Hugo Poole stood in the dim concrete riverbed and caught his breath. The right knee of his pants had a small tear in it; the elbow of his suit coat felt damp, so he looked at that too. It had a dark splash of blood on it from the first man's nose. He sighed: this was turning into an irritating evening, and it was still early.

Then Hugo Poole saw a new light. It began as a vague im-pression in his mind that there must be clouds moving away from the moon. Then the light brightened and the impression changed. The light was coming from somewhere down the channel. The wall opposite him began to glow, and then the light separated into two smaller, more focused circles.

A set of headlights appeared around an elbow bend in the channel and came toward him. He was aware that it might be a police patrol car, or the animal control people checking on the coyotes that used the concrete riverbeds to travel across the city at night. Either way, it would be best to stay still. It was especially important not to move if it was Steve Rao.

Hugo Poole stood and watched as the ghostly vehicle drew nearer, its headlights brightening until it pulled up beside him and stopped. Now that the headlights were shining past him, he saw that it was a black Hummer with tinted win-dows. Someone in the passenger seat used a powerful flash-light to sweep the walls of the channel and the bushes and hiding places up above at street level.

The flashlight went out, the passenger door opened, and a large man with wavy dark hair got out. He wore a light-weight black sport coat and pants of a color that looked gray in the near darkness. The driver got out, and Hugo Poole could see that he was wearing a sport coat too. Almost cer-tainly the coats were intended to hide the bulges of firearms. The driver stood with his back against the door of the Hummer and kept guard while the other man approached Hugo Poole.

The man said, "Sir, are you Mr. Poole?"

"Yes."

"Can you put your arms out from your sides for me, please?"

Hugo Poole complied, and stood with his feet apart so his legs could be checked next. He waited, staring into the distance as the man patted him down expertly, then stepped back. "Thank you very much, sir."

Hugo Poole said, "You're an off-duty cop, aren't you?"

He didn't deny it. "I'm a friend of Steve's."

Hugo nodded and watched the driver open the back door of the Hummer. Steve Rao was perched on the edge of the high seat when the door opened. He was wearing black jeans and a black T-shirt with a dark windbreaker, as though he were out to commit a burglary. His shoes were half light and half dark, like bowling shoes. He slid to the end of the Hummer's back seat and then jumped down, smiling.

He looked proud of himself, his eyes and teeth reflecting the distant light from above. "Hugo, my man. Thanks for coming. I hope it wasn't too inconvenient."

"You saw?"

Steve Rao looked very serious. "I didn't have anything to do with them, I swear to God."

"I didn't think you did," said Hugo Poole.

"It's terrible," said Steve Rao. "This isn't even gang territory. The city really has to do something."

"I'll write a letter to the *Times*."

Steve Rao's grin returned. "You're still pretty mean, though, aren't you? You can handle yourself against these young kids even now."

Hugo Poole did not smile.

Steve Rao gestured toward the two men beside his black Hummer. "These two guys are my solution to that foolishness. You won't see me rolling around on dirty cement beating the shit out of no gang of kids. I learned that much."

"I'll be honest with you, Steve. This night is beginning to

wear on my patience. Why did you want to meet me in a place like this?"

"It's safe and secure."

"It's safe and secure up there on the corner of Ventura and Laurel Canyon, and you can get a cup of coffee in Du Par's," said Hugo. "What is it you want?"

Steve Rao began to walk. Hugo followed for about two hundred feet, and stopped. Steve Rao noticed, so he stopped too, and spoke. "I've been around for a while now. You know that?"

"I've noticed you for about five years," said Hugo Poole.

"I haven't been lying around all that time."

"I've noticed that too."

"I've been busy. I've been talking to people, making deals, making friends."

"No flies on you," said Hugo Poole.

"It's worked out. I've gotten big." It was a strange thing for a man Hugo Poole judged was about five feet five to say. "It's time to make a deal with you too." He glared at Hugo Poole. "I've put it off for longer than I should have."

"I'm listening."

"I want ten thousand a month from you."

"In exchange for what?"

"For being able to do whatever you want. For not having to worry. You can go on forever, just like you have been, and nobody will bother you."

"Nobody bothers me now."

Steve Rao stopped and pointed back at the Hummer, where the two off-duty cops were sitting. "See those guys?"

Hugo Poole gave his second sigh of the evening. "Steve, how old are you?"

"Twenty-four."

"When you're a young guy, just starting out, you have to consider the possibility that the people who were here before you were born aren't all dumb."

"What do you mean?"

"You should look around and say, 'What are people already doing that works? What are people not doing, even though it's an obvious thing to do? And why aren't they?' "

Steve Rao glared at him again, then resumed walking. "A lot of people are doing this. People have sold protection for a hundred years."

"Street gangs. They shake down a few Korean grocery stores, a couple of small liquor stores. They ask for just enough so the payoff is cheaper than buying a new front window. The game lasts a few months, until all the gang boys are in jail for something else or dead. Grown-ups don't do this in L.A. And they don't use off-duty cops for bodyguards."

"Why are you saying this shit?" Steve was quickly beginning to feel the heat around his neck cooking into anger. "It's all shit! Half the rock stars in town have hired cops with them wherever they go."

"I'm telling you this because I want to do you a big favor," said Hugo Poole. "That works great for musicians. Cops have to carry guns off-duty, so nobody has to make any guesses."

"That's right," said Steve Rao. "So don't even think about trying to get out of this. I might as well be made out of steel. Anybody opens up anywhere near me, my cops will drill his ass for him. They got my back. Nobody can do anything to me."

"That's probably true," said Hugo Poole. "But what can you do to anybody else?"

"Anything," said Steve Rao, but he sounded uncertain.

Hugo Poole said, "Off-duty cops will keep people from killing you if they can, just like they do for rock stars. But they won't let even the biggest rock stars grease somebody else."

"We have an understanding."

"They understand you better than you understand them."

"They're mine. I bought them."

"You're paying cops money to stay a few feet from you. They can see you make deals, they can hear what you say. When they've seen and heard enough, they're going to arrest you and all of the people who do business with you."

"You're full of shit."

"Steve, these guys know the system. They know that if they get in trouble, you won't be able to do them any good. The only people who can help them are other cops." He paused.

"You aren't going to collect any money from anybody, Steve, because you can't hurt anybody in front of two cops. You just put yourself out of business."

"Hugo, I always heard you were supposed to be the smartest man in L.A. But this is pitiful," said Steve Rao. He took a small semiautomatic pistol from his jacket. He didn't point it at Hugo, just shifted it to his belt. "I want your ten grand tomorrow by five, and then once a month. Be on time."

"Ask me how I knew they were cops."

"All right. How did you know?"

"They're wearing microphones," said Hugo Poole. "See you, Steve." Hugo Poole walked down the concrete riverbed, away from Steve Rao.

"You don't walk away from me," said Steve Rao. "You wait until I walk away from you." His voice sounded strained and thin, as though his throat were dry.

Hugo Poole walked on, his pace the same smart stride he always used on the street that kept his head up and his eyes on the world in front of him and let him scan the sights beside him. He had decided that it would be best not to return to the street by the same path he had used to come down here, so he walked on for what he judged to be an extra two blocks before he came to the next ramp built for the flood maintenance people. At the top of the path he had to climb an eight-foot chain-link fence, something he hated to do, but since his suit was beyond repair, he supposed he could hardly ruin it twice.

He swung himself over, dropped to the ground, then walked back up to Radford. Just as he was coming out of the dimly lighted, quiet street toward Ventura Boulevard, he heard the distant pops of four shots in rapid succession, then seven more. They seemed to echo from the direction of the river. As he walked along, he considered the eleven shots. Eleven was a bad number for Steve Rao. The magazines for pistols like Steve Rao's held no more than ten in a single stack.

3

Hugo Poole parked in front of the Hundred Proof Bar and slipped a twenty-dollar bill to the bouncer outside the door in exchange for protecting his car from the tow trucks. The frightening late-night clientele of the Hundred Proof would keep the hot-wire artists away. As he walked along Sheldrake Avenue toward the Empire Theater he looked respectable but tired, like the bartender of an intermittently violent nightclub. He wanted to get this suit off. He would get a shower, put on a clean shirt and a new suit, and feel right again. Hugo Poole never wore a tie, because during his formative years he had watched a fight in which a man had been choked out with his Windsor knot.

He walked under the big, ornate marquee that announced EMPIRE THEATER CLOSED FOR RENOVATION. He stepped into the alcove across the terrazzo inlay of 1920s bathing beauties and stopped beside the ticket booth in front. He stared up and down Sheldrake Avenue. Hugo Poole did not simply glance: he took his time, his eyes narrowed to impart sharpness and definition to distant shapes. When he decided he had outlasted any possible duckers-behind-corners or walkers-the-other-way, he took a full turn and stopped with his back against the door to be absolutely sure he had not been followed. He had not. Hugo Poole unlocked the door to the movie theater, opened it, slipped inside, closed it, and tugged it once to be sure it had locked behind him.

He turned. The dim pink glow of the light inside the candy

display case let him see the gilded plaster-cast sconces and the ancient painted murals of women who seemed half nymph and half movie star getting out of long antique limousines. Behind them, aimed upward in the sky, were beams from big spotlights. He heard a noise and turned to the carpeted stairway across the lobby that led up toward the balcony.

"Evening, Hugo." Otto Collins and Mike Garcia came into the lobby from upstairs. They had been waking up the building, doing the evening walk-around, turning on lights and unlocking the inner doors.

"Hello, guys," Hugo Poole said. He was not about to forget that the easiest way for somebody to kill him was to pay these two to do it here in the theater, but he had already studied them and acquitted them for tonight. Every night he looked at them for signs that they were going to betray him.

Hugo Poole was not watching for nervous twitches and smiling, sweaty upper lips. These were men. They worked for Hugo Poole, and they could be expected to behave with a certain amount of self-possession. What he was looking for was the opposite: excessive self-control. He had seen it come upon serious men when they were contemplating risky behavior. He knew that on the day when he was going to die Mike and Otto would grow cold and distant.

Hugo Poole knew that he was reputed to be a deep thinker, and it was a useful myth to cultivate. He was only premeditative, but to many people that made him seem clairvoyant. He made his way upstairs to the carpeted upper hallway, past the door marked PROJECTION ROOM, opened a wooden door that seemed to be a part of the paneled wall, and went inside.

Hugo walked to his desk and sat down, then glanced at his watch. It had taken him forty-five minutes to get back here from the Valley, and he judged that to be enough time. He consulted the telephone book on the corner of his desk, picked up his telephone, and called the police precinct station in North Hollywood.

He said, "This is G. David Hunter. I'm an attorney under retainer for Steven Rao, R-A-O. He hasn't shown up where he was expected this evening. Could you please check to see whether he has been taken into custody tonight?" He listened for a moment, then said, "Shot dead? You did say 'dead'? I'm shocked. When did this happen?" He listened for a few more seconds, then said, "Thank you. No doubt you'll be hearing from me in the future. The body? I'm not sure. Let me talk to the family. I'll have to get back to you. Good night."

He sat back, stared at the wall, and thought about this evening. He supposed he might have to anticipate some sort of retaliation from the two cops who'd had to shoot Steve Rao. They were certainly smart enough to know why Rao had turned on them. Hugo would have to postpone a few of the schemes he had been prospering on—removing small numbers of items from cargo containers at the harbor and replacing them with stones to keep the weights constant, having women pose as hookers so Otto and Mike could be the vice squad who burst in to confiscate wallets—and substitute a few that seemed a bit less flagrant.

He searched his memory for ideas that were safer. He had recently seen a television program in which a crowd of middle-class people stood in line carrying old possessions so that a team of antique dealers could appraise them. He had noticed that some not particularly prepossessing articles were assigned very high prices.

He had also noticed that in almost every case, the more scarred and damaged an item was, the more likely the experts were to revere it. He had become fascinated by the way the antique dealers talked. No matter what obsolete and arcane castoff the expert was appraising, he could always talk about "the collectors" of that very item.

There was no doubt in Hugo Poole's mind that there were ways to make money from his discovery. How could he not make money off people who were willing to haul a five-hundred-pound sideboard to a television studio and then stand in line for hours to have some guy with a fake accent look at it?

There was a rap on the door. Hugo Poole automatically crouched low and moved to the left, where the steel filing cabinets full of books and papers would stop a bullet. He eyed the Colt Commander .45 that he kept duct-taped to the back of the cabinet against his day of doom. It was just possible that Steve Rao's untimely death was not being taken well by somebody. Hugo Poole waited a moment, but nobody kicked in the door.

"Who is it?" he called.

"Just me. Otto."

"Come in."

Otto said, "There's a call for you on the house phone down there, Hugo. It's a woman who says she's your aunt."

Hugo squinted at Otto for a second, then stood up and hurried past him to the stairwell. It was unusual for anyone to call in on the Empire Theater's telephone number, and during the daytime there was usually nobody here to answer it. When Hugo, Otto, and Mike were here, they were usually asleep.

He went to the small office off the lobby near the candy counter and picked up the telephone. "Hugo Poole here." He listened. "Hi, Aunt Ellen. How are you? What? Dennis? Oh, my God." He closed his eyes and listened for a few seconds. Then he rubbed his forehead. "I'm so sorry, Aunt Ellen. I never imagined that anything like this could happen to Dennis."

4

Joe Pitt looked up at the chandelier. There were a few hundred tear-shaped crystal pieces like diamond earrings hanging above him, the light that came off them bright white with glints of rainbows. It was like heaven up there.

He looked down again at the green felt surface of the table, gathered his cards, and glanced at them. It was not heaven down here. Three of clubs, six of diamonds, four of spades, ten of diamonds, nine of hearts.

Joe Pitt watched his four opponents pick up their cards. Jerry Whang's tell was that he always blinked once when he picked up a really good hand. It was as though he were closing the shutters of his mind, because when he opened his eyes again, he revealed nothing more. There was the blink.

Stella Korb picked up her cards and looked sick. She'd had a Botox injection today to deaden the muscles under her facial skin, but it didn't change her eyes. The new guy that Pitt thought of as the Kid, who had the repulsive habit of wearing a baseball cap indoors, retained the same dumb look after seeing his cards.

Delores Harkness squeezed her cards open with her thumb, closed them again to look around, then thumbed them open once more to be sure she had seen what she had seen.

She opened with a single twenty-five-dollar chip, patiently trying to keep all of the others in as long as she could before she started murdering the last optimists. She succeeded, each of them tossing in a chip until it came to Joe Pitt. He set his cards down. "Have a good evening, everyone. I'm out."

Billy the dealer swept Pitt's cards away. "See you, Joe." Pitt stepped off, heading past the crowds of gamblers toward the front door of the card club. He walked outside, sniffed the night air, looked around himself, and listened. Just beyond the far side of the parking lot he could see headlights flashing past on the freeway and he could hear the constant swish of tires on the pavement. For once he had managed to lose all of the money he had allowed himself for the evening and not go to the cashier's window with a credit card. He supposed that was a kind of half victory, like getting into a crash and having the car still run well enough to get him home. Then why didn't he feel better?

He stared at the aisle of the big parking lot where he had left his car and sensed that something was not right. His right hand moved reflexively to pat his left side once, a gesture that was so habitual that most observers would have missed it. He was still permitted to carry his pistol in a shoulder rig under his sport coat: for the rest of his life there would be the chance that someone who had gotten to know him during his twenty years as an investigator for the D.A.'s office would finally get around to killing him.

He opened his coat and stepped forward, away from the lighted front of the casino. Joe Pitt had a willingness to pay attention to vague sensations, and when he sensed that something was threatening he went toward it.

He had built his reputation by solving murders, and he had done it by moving toward whatever didn't feel right. Offices closed on weekends, but every day on the calendar the killer was a killer, and Joe Pitt was working his way toward him. Any suspect who had not understood it that way had found himself at a severe disadvantage. It wasn't some theoretical entity called the State of California that was after him; it was Joe Pitt.

He selected a row of cars three spaces to the left of his car, and began to walk up the aisle. It took a moment before he saw the heads in the car parked beside his. As he walked his angle changed, and he could see more: there was a male driver in front, and a second man sitting in the back seat. Maybe it was a rich guy with a chauffeur, and maybe it was an easy way of putting two shooters into position to fire at him.

Joe Pitt stopped beside a car, pretended to unlock it, then went low, as though he had gotten into the driver's seat. He stayed low and scurried along the spaces between parked cars until he was beside the car where the two men waited. He stood up slightly behind the passenger, with his gun in his hand close to the open window.

The passenger looked at him. "Hello, Joe."

Joe Pitt's hand tightened on the gun. "Hello, Hugo."

"You know my friend Otto?"

"Of course. How are you, Otto? Congratulations on your early release."

"Thanks," said Otto. "It's nice to be out. And yourself?"

"I'm fine, thanks. What's up, Hugo?"

Hugo Poole looked up at him. "I need to talk to you. If you

feel safer doing it inside the casino, I'll send Otto in to arrange for a private space."

"I'm not afraid of you. I'm just not interested." He put his gun away.

"It's worth money to you."

"I have money, thanks," said Joe Pitt.

"You have a weakness for women and a gambling problem, and nobody's got enough money for those. Three different guys have come to me in the past year or so to sell me that information. I only paid the first one, but I remembered it. We don't have time to bullshit each other. Tonight when I found out I needed you I knew where you would be."

"The gambling isn't a problem. It's the losing. What do you think you need me for?"

"Will you get in so we can talk? You're safe with us." Hugo Poole pushed open the door and then slid to the other side. Joe Pitt hesitated, then got in beside him. Otto Collins drove the car up the aisle and out to the street.

Pitt said, "I know that a few times when I needed information, you arranged for somebody to miraculously turn up to give it to me. I got the solution to something that was puzzling me, and you got—whatever it was that you got. That may have made me forget to add your name to a list of menaces to the public welfare. But life isn't the same now."

"You're the same, I'm the same. What's different?"

"I'm retired from the district attorney's office. I'm out. I can't affect the outcome of some investigation. Whatever it is that you want, I'm not in the position to give it to you."

"You're a private detective now. You're getting famous."

"Everybody's got to do something. But I don't do anything for money that can send me to jail."

"I assumed that. You wouldn't last long enough to get to the front of the chow line. If it were anything illegal, I wouldn't waste your time with it," said Hugo Poole.

"So what do you want?"

"Yesterday my cousin Dennis got shot to death in Portland."

"What for? Was he working for you?"

"No. He's never worked for me. I haven't even seen him in about four or five years."

"So what was he into?"

Hugo Poole frowned. "Nothing. Dennis wasn't into anything. He was a computer salesman."

Pitt's face was expressionless.

"Dennis was a straight businessman. He had a store up in Portland and a warehouse, and he sold computer stuff wholesale and over the Internet. He was good at it. He made money. I want to know what gets a guy like that killed."

"That's what you want? You want me to find out what happened?"

Hugo Poole held up his hands. "I can't just leave this to a bunch of shitkicker cops in Oregon. I need somebody on this who knows what's what."

"Portland isn't a small town, Hugo. They have homicide detectives who can handle an investigation," said Pitt. "And I don't think an outsider has much chance of finding anything they won't. It's their city."

"It's not just their city I'm worried about. I need someone who will be able to make the connections between what went on there and what goes on here."

Pitt's eyes settled on Hugo's face. "You think your cousin's killing had something to do with you?"

"Dennis may have had some enemies of his own. He may even have been into something that I don't know about. But until somebody proves that, the only reason anybody had to shoot Dennis was that he was related to me."

"What do you think I can do for you?"

"Fly up there. Cops all over the country know who you are, and the cases you solved when you were the D.A.'s investigator. They'll hear your name and think you can help them find out who killed Dennis. So I want you to do it. I'll pay you a lot of money."

Pitt stared at him, unblinking. "Then what if it is about you? I'm not interested in being paid to go up there and steer a police investigation away from you."

"You wouldn't. I can keep myself out of trouble without any help from you. If the investigation starts pointing back in the direction of L.A., you'll be able to tell them where to look. Even if it's toward me."

Pitt said, "Then you'll need time to clean up your act, won't you? Or have you already started phasing down your operations?"

"Tonight I'm clearing up loose ends so you can go after this guy without tripping over my feet. I'm pulling my feet out of the way."

"If I get into this, I'm not going to point the finger at some guy so you can kill him."

"I want you to help the cops find the killer—the real one, not some poor bastard they decide to pin it on. If you do that much for me, then you did your job."

"How much are you offering?"

"A hundred thousand plus expenses if you agree to make a serious effort. Another hundred when they get the guy."

"You must really feel guilty."

"If you won't take the job because it's my money, then say it."

"No, I'm like a doctor," said Joe Pitt. "If you've got a heartbeat, I'll work on you until it stops or your bank account runs dry."

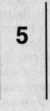

5

Joe Pitt followed Sergeant Catherine Hobbes up the driveway of what had been Dennis Poole's house. He couldn't help letting his eyes spend more time looking at her than was practical. He estimated that she was about thirty, but it was hard to be sure. She had a rounded athletic little body, but she had tried to blur the contours with a masculine gray pantsuit, and she had tried to harden her pretty face by pulling her strawberry-blond hair into a bun and wearing little makeup. Joe Pitt watched her step over the POLICE LINE—DO NOT CROSS tape, climb the steps to the door, where she ignored the big sticker that said CRIME SCENE—DO NOT ENTER, and unlock the door.

"Nice place," he said.

"I hate this kind of house. It's pretentious—way too big for the lot it's on, and everything inside it was made to be looked at, not used."

He said, "I wasn't asking you to move in with me. I just meant it looks expensive."

"It's that, all right." She stared past him as she swung the door open, and stepped inside to hold it so he had to go in ahead of her.

Catherine Hobbes had been surprised to see how fine Pitt's features were, and how alert and intelligent his eyes looked. But for her there wasn't anything endearing about his attractiveness. He talked with the kind of easy familiarity that meant he was aware that he had an advantage with women.

She was irritated at Joe Pitt already, but she was determined to be polite to him. She had orders, and she was not about to get in trouble just because he was arrogant. If she could tolerate him long enough, she could learn something. He was a well-known investigator who had, in his prime, solved a number of murders. If she had to endure his banter to learn what he knew, then she would do it. "There isn't any sign of forced entry here. The other doors are bolted from the inside."

Pitt looked around. As a concession to the rainy Portland climate there was a small foyer with a black-and-white marble floor and a long wooden seat for changing boots, a coat rack above it, and an umbrella stand. Beyond that the thick carpet began, and everything in sight was beige or white.

"Where did he get shot?"

"Upstairs in the master suite. I'll show you." She went to the long straight staircase, and they climbed to the landing.

Pitt walked into Dennis Poole's bedroom, which was big enough for four bedrooms. He surveyed the furnishings. On the wall there was a plasma television about six feet wide, and below it on a cabinet a set of videocassette recorders and DVD players. There was a big desk with more computer equipment on it than anybody needed. There were shelves with so many books and magazines on them that they reminded Pitt that he hadn't seen any evidence of a book downstairs. The bed looked like the oversized king in a good hotel suite. "Was he in debt to pay for all of this?"

"We haven't found any debt yet. Considering his income, the house isn't at all extravagant," she said. "He bought it about a year after his divorce, when he was twenty-eight. That was fourteen years ago. He lived alone, and he cleared three to four hundred thousand a year. There's no sign of expensive hobbies or collections, no trace of drugs in his blood or the house, no history of gambling."

"Anything missing?"

"He lived alone, so we haven't got anybody who really knows. There are no dust spots where things have been removed, or marks on the walls from missing paintings or anything. We took a couple of people from his office through the house, and neither of them could remember seeing anything here that's gone." She held him in the corner of her eye. "Maybe you can tell me." Instantly she wished she had not said it.

He looked around him as though he had not heard. "Where was the body?"

"In the bathtub." She led him into the bathroom. It was big too, with an enormous black tub and a room-sized glass-walled shower with showerheads on three sides and a slate seat along one wall. Most of the surfaces were covered with fingerprint dust. "One shot to the head."

He looked down at the tub, then moved his face close to examine the blood-spatter pattern on the wall above it. "And you're sure he didn't just pop himself?"

"The gun wasn't found with him. Anyway, the angle was wrong."

"How?"

"Sort of like this." She pointed her index finger at her own head. "See? The angle is too high. You can't get a gun up there and point slightly downward, and why would you?"

Joe Pitt nodded and walked farther into the bathroom, examining the shower and the sinks without touching anything. "Was he taking a bath or did they just shove him in there to keep the job from getting messy?"

"He was naked. There was soap in the tub, and a towel under his head like a pillow."

Pitt left the bathroom and stared at the bedroom again. "I assume your people didn't find anything in the rest of the house."

"It's all just like what you saw on the way up here. The rooms look like no one's ever used them. It's white couches that nobody ever sat in, and glass tabletops without so much as a fingerprint. The kitchen is beautiful, but there's hardly anything in the refrigerator but drinks. He ate out three meals a day."

"He seems to have lived up here."

"That's how I see it," she said. "The television gets something like two hundred and fifty channels, about fifty of them sports. He could sit up here forever watching one game after another, and never go downstairs except for more beer."

"Who dusted the white couches and washed the windows?"

"He had a contract with Mighty Maids. They have a whole crew of women come in at once, clean the hell out of everything, and go away. That was how his body got found. His crew came twice a week during business hours, when he was usually at work. They had a key, but they also had an alibi—people who saw them cleaning houses at the time of death. They came in yesterday and there he was."

Joe Pitt stood in the center of the room and slowly turned all the way around, studying every detail. "Have you pieced together the sequence?"

She nodded. "He left work earlier than usual, but didn't have to tell anybody why, because he was the boss. He was wearing a dark gray suit that day. He was home by four, set his briefcase down in the kitchen, and came up here. He took off the suit and tie and hung them up in here." She walked to the huge walk-in closet and pushed the door open so Pitt could see the neat row of coats and trousers hanging along the pole. At least four were shades of gray. "They're in the lab, of course. Next he threw his shirt, socks, and underwear in the hamper, went into the bathroom, ran the water in the tub, and got in."

"So he was still doing everything voluntarily—no chance of force?"

"There are no abrasions or contusions on him to show a struggle, and there was no water splashed around when the maids found him. At some point, the killer probably slipped in, approached him from behind, held the gun a foot from his head, and fired once. The entry wound is behind the right ear. The neighbors on both sides and across the street were still at work, and nobody else in the neighborhood remembers hearing a shot."

"You figure it was intended to be a faked suicide at first?"

"I think so, but it was botched. Maybe Mr. Poole heard the guy at the last instant and flinched. Maybe the killer just got too eager and fired early."

"Was the gun Poole's? Did he have one that's missing?"

"He didn't have any firearms registered to him."

Pitt looked down at his feet. "This isn't going to be easy, is it?"

"No," said Catherine Hobbes. "He seems to have been secure and prosperous. He had no enemies anybody knows about. He just came back from vacation a couple of weeks ago, and the people at work said he seemed happy and relaxed."

"What about women?"

"What about them?"

"Did he like them? Did he like one in particular?"

"That's one of the things that's been worrying me. The trace evidence people found some long, straight blond hairs. There were two on suits of his, a few on the carpet in here, one on a bathrobe. The women on the Mighty Maids crew are all black or Hispanic."

"Any blondes at his company?"

"Two, but the hair isn't a match for either one. Nobody seems to remember seeing him with a blond woman lately. There are no female relatives who live in town, and his mother says none have long, straight blond hair."

"This blond woman seems like the most promising thing I've heard," said Pitt. "She could have been married. That would give Poole a reason to try to keep the relationship quiet, and a good motive for the husband to kill him."

"We've been concentrating on her, and we've found nothing yet. On the other hand, we do have one odd thing that turned up unexpectedly."

"What?"

"You."

"I don't feel like an odd thing."

She shrugged. "I got an order from my captain that I'd be cooperating with an expert from Los Angeles, a former D.A.'s investigator who will help with the case. I looked you up on Google and found lots of articles about you, mostly in the *Los Angeles Times,* but in national magazines too. Pictures of you and everything."

"Anything interesting?"

"You're retired from the D.A.'s office—honorably, it said—and now you make a gazillion dollars a year doing private investigation. At that point, I was ready to invite you over for a home-cooked dinner and a shot at meeting my parents. Then I talked to my captain and found out you were working for the cousin."

"You lost interest?"

"Let's say the nature of my interest changed."

"It doesn't have to," said Pitt. "I'm not here to do anything wrong, and I really do make a gazillion dollars."

"You're working for a bad guy," said Hobbes. "Lips that have touched Hugo Poole's ass will never touch mine."

"Your ass?"

"My anything," she said.

Joe Pitt nodded. "So up here, when a known criminal asks you to investigate his relative's murder, you say no?"

"We don't actually consult him. When there's a murder we go after the killer, whether anybody wants us to or not." She patted his arm and said with mock sympathy, "It's not you, Joe. It's me. I just don't like people taking money from a crook to keep him out of a murder investigation."

"I wasn't hired to do that," he said. "Hugo Poole agrees with you. He thinks the killing is a reprisal for something he did down in L.A. If you want to pursue that, he'll try to help you. But it's not what happened."

"You don't know that."

"If it's a reprisal, they wouldn't try to make it look like a suicide. They'd make it as big and ugly as they could, and make damned sure Hugo knew why."

Joe Pitt stalked around the room, looking at things. "This place has been cleaned up. I asked you before if something was missing, and you didn't know. I know now what it is. It's the mess."

"But he wasn't messy," she said. "Downstairs each room looks like a department store window."

"Because he didn't live down there. He lived up here, in this suite. But there's nothing random, nothing out of its place up here. I know it wouldn't look like a room in a fraternity house, but this isn't the way it looked when he died, either. It's been sanitized. The only person who would have done that is the killer."

"You think the killer took the time to go through this whole suite wiping off prints and picking up fibers?"

"Yes, I do," he said. "But I think that what the shooter didn't want us to know about wasn't his prints. I think he was removing signs of the blond woman. The killer came in and shot Poole—one round, no struggle. At that point, he could have exited without much risk of leaving anything of himself. But instead he straightened the suite, put everything away, vacuumed the carpets. He missed a couple of blond hairs on the floor and stuck to Poole's clothes."

"The blond hairs on the suit don't mean somebody cleaned the place. Maybe that's all there were."

"You said the Mighty Maids were all black or Hispanic, and they cleaned the hell out of this place twice every week. That takes hours of hard work, a lot of it on their hands and knees. So where are the fibers from their uniforms? Where are the dark hairs?"

"Oh, God," said Hobbes. He was right. Damn him. "What if she was what it was about?"

"Could be. Maybe some other man came here to take her—or take her back."

"I've got to find that girl."

6

The girl felt some sadness, but she was satisfied. She had thoroughly experienced Dennis Poole, so she was not disappointed in herself. She was proud of herself for overcoming her shyness and fear in the hotel bar in Aspen, and being the first to speak. That alone was an accomplishment. She had found something about him appealing—his tall, slightly awkward body, the clothes he wore that seemed to be right out of the box, as though he had never worn anything all year but a business suit. She had sat in the bar at a small table near the window that looked out on the mountains, then feigned surprise to find him sitting nearby and said, "What a wonderful sky. I love the color of the sky just after sundown." How could he not reply?

After she had talked to him for a few minutes, she had found that she almost instantly knew what to say to him and how to say it. There had never been more than a few moments when she had needed to doubt herself. She had listened to him carefully, begun to accumulate a small trove of facts about who he was and what he liked, and then made herself the woman that he wanted. He owned a small, dull business and he was on vacation, so she became a perfect vacation companion. She was the lively girl who was always happy, always on the edge of laughter, ready to go to the next place just to see what was there.

She had experimented with liking him—pretended to find him more interesting than he was, better looking than he was—and found that after a couple of days she actually did like him. She looked back on it now and missed him. She remembered the cool, clear nights of early summer, when they walked out on the balcony of his suite and looked up at the stars and there seemed to be about three times as many as usual.

As she drove along the gently curving highway, she said aloud to the image of Dennis, "At least we had a good time." Her face felt so right when she said it that she held the expression, and flipped down the sun visor to look at her reflection in the makeup mirror.

Perfect. The full lips pouted, the sparkly blue eyes were wistful and wise. She revised the words slightly. "At least we had fun." The way the row of small white teeth touched the lower lip to say "fun" was worth going for.

She flipped the visor back up and returned her eyes to the road. The darker hair she had given herself made her look a bit more serious than she had looked as Tanya, too sophisticated to bleach her hair platinum blond. She liked the subtle reddish highlights.

She felt good today. There was something hopeful about driving south, away from rain and toward warmth and sunshine and flowers. She had saved enough money from the month with Dennis Poole to be happy for a while. As soon as she had met him, she had begun pointing a finger at expensive, shiny things in stores and wishing aloud. She had loved it when he had bought them for her, and had rewarded him with affection.

Sometimes she would be about to leave him for the spa or the pool and ask him to give her some money for tips or drinks. A couple of times she had taken money from his wallet while he was asleep. After he had persuaded her to visit him at his house in Portland, she had come with only one suitcase, let him talk her into staying longer, and got his permission to pay for the extra clothes she would need by borrowing one of his credit cards. Dennis had been a satisfying experience, but Dennis was over.

Who to be now? Being a brunette made her feel sedate, understated, aristocratic. Her new name should be something old-fashioned, even biblical, but Anglo-Saxon—no Catholic saints, and nothing faux French. Sarah would be good, or Rebecca. No, both were too common. Rachel. That was just about right.

She had always favored names that sounded like rich people's names, but nothing too heavy-handed. She didn't want to call herself a name that was also the name of a company: it would be hard to pass as a Ford or a Pillsbury. She thought about her new self for a few minutes, and decided that she should have roots in New England. Maybe a place-name. Stamford? No. Sturbridge. That felt right: Rachel Sturbridge—how do you do?

Rachel Sturbridge held the car to the south, and began to wonder where to stop. San Francisco was the next city she had heard about along the way, so she decided to aim for it and stop to see if it felt right. She drove half the night and reached the city at three A.M., then parked the car in a big structure near Union Square. She made her way downhill to the square, then walked around staring at the big buildings, the quiet, lighted entrances to hotels and the dark display windows of stores. She loved seeing a city late at night, after all of the superficial busyness and crowding and knotted traffic had been stripped away. She decided that she would stay. Then she returned to the parking structure and slept in the back seat of her car until people began starting the cars near hers and driving off.

In the morning Rachel used her Tanya Starling identification to rent a small furnished house, then added the name of Tanya's roommate, Rachel Sturbridge, to the lease. That afternoon she rented a post office box in both names, then placed a fictitious-business-name statement in the ad section of the *Chronicle*. It said that Rachel Sturbridge and T. Star-

ling were doing business as Singular Aspects, and gave the
post office box as the address. She went to City Hall and
bought a business license for Singular Aspects, which she
said on the form produced a "mail-order newsletter for alternative lifestyles." She was pleased with the fact that the description was utterly meaningless.

Before the banks closed at six she managed to start a Singular Aspects bank account with the two women as signato-
ries and a deposit of four thousand dollars. At the end of each
day for the next two days she made another cash deposit.
When the balance reached twelve thousand dollars, she made
out an application for a business credit card in the name of
Singular Aspects. She flirted a little bit with the manager on
duty, a young man named Bill, and he took the application
without asking any embarrassing questions.

Dennis Poole had been dead three days. On the way home
that night she bought the Portland newspapers at a newsstand and searched for stories about what the police were
doing, but there was no mention of an investigation. There
was only a short obituary that said his death had been declared a homicide. Since there was no mention of a woman,
she supposed that meant her part in the episode was over,
and decided that in the future she would remember only the
good parts.

The next morning Rachel went to a copy center and selected a pack of ten sheets of heavy white paper with high
rag content and a blank CD. She paid for them at the counter,
rented a computer, and went to a Web site that she had found
once before. It was a fan site devoted to every aspect of the
life of the actress Renee Stipple Penrose. There were pictures
of her parents' home in Barnstable, Connecticut, including
some taken by a camera aimed through the windows, pictures of her elementary school and her high school, and—
because there was a controversy about her real birth date—a
clear and sharp image of her birth certificate.

Rachel copied the image to the computer and removed the
original names and dates without altering the signatures or
seals. She copied the blank birth certificate onto the CD for
future use, and put the CD into her purse. Then she selected

a matching type font and filled in the form to record the birth of Rachel Martha Sturbridge twenty-five years ago, and printed the new certificate onto one of her sheets of official-looking paper.

Rachel still had a driver's license she had obtained in Illinois as Tanya Starling. Now she found a matching type font, typed her new name a few times, and printed it out on a sheet of thin white paper.

When she was in her house that night she patiently scratched the old name off the license with a razor blade. She took the printout with the name Rachel Martha Sturbridge on it, cut it out in a narrow strip, placed it in the groove on the license she had created with the blade, and used a drop of clear glue to hold it there. In the morning, when it was dry, she placed a laminating sheet over the front of the license, and trimmed it carefully.

Two days later she went to the Department of Motor Vehicles office, flashed her Illinois license and her birth certificate, took a written test, and received a new California driver's license in the name Rachel Martha Sturbridge. She was so pleased that on the way home she joined the Auto Club and applied for a library card.

She let a week pass before she placed an ad in the *Chronicle* and sold Tanya Starling's car for fifteen thousand dollars. She deposited the check in the Singular Aspects account so Rachel Sturbridge would be able to write checks against it. Then she bought a six-year-old Nissan for five thousand in cash. The whole process of changing names was like watching a candle burn down and begin to gutter, and using its flame to light a new one before it went out.

She had made the change now, and it was time to think about the future. She needed to keep working at building her savings. Her goal was that someday she would be rich, and she knew that even though she was only at the beginning of the process, her progress was going to consist of hundreds of small decisions. For now, she had to keep her expenses under control and devote most of her time to finding the next man.

It had always seemed to her that the best kind of man wanted the sort of woman who went to plays and concerts and art exhibits, so she began to read the Datebook section of the paper and then buy tickets to events. While she was there she scanned the crowds for men who did not already have women attached to them. She liked being out, but even when she saw the right sort of man in the lobby before a play or a concert—or, more often, caught one looking at her—the event would be imminent, they both would have to find their way to widely separated seats, and the lights would go out. A few times, when she had seen a promising prospect, she had even stayed in the lobby afterward and given him a chance to find her. He never did.

Sometimes, late at night, she would go to the girl in the mirror and help her become Rachel Sturbridge. For her expeditions into high culture she had developed a rapt expression to indicate artistic appreciation. If she listened to a piece of classical music it might include a satisfied nod or a slightly troubled look around the eyes, as though she were comparing the performance with an invisible score. But her best new look was a serene, smooth-faced expression that was at once benevolent and superior, the habitual demeanor of a just queen.

She decided to try expensive restaurants in the Union Square district. One evening she sat in the bar at Postrio having a martini before dinner, her coat on the stool beside her. She liked the bar because it served as a long, narrow anteroom, where every customer had to pass by on the way to the staircase leading down into the restaurant. There was a grill at the far end of the bar, where three chefs dodged flames under a big copper hood, and there were a few booths along the wall, where patrons ate informal versions of the food served downstairs. The French doors across from the bar opened into the lobby of the Prescott Hotel, and new people entered every few minutes. She watched for unaccompanied men, dismissed several, and then saw one who looked right.

Rachel smiled to herself as she sipped her martini, feeling the icy glass on her lips and then the fire of the vodka warming her as it moved down her throat. She pretended not to see him. He stood for a moment talking with the maître d', then stepped into the bar.

She turned her head and looked up, her face assuming its new regal expression. The man was tall, wearing a navy blue sport jacket and a pair of gray pants. It was one of the uniforms all men wore when they weren't actually working, and it would have been difficult for most women to evaluate him, but Rachel Sturbridge had become a shrewd appraiser. The coat was a good cut, the fabric was finely woven wool, and the tie was tasteful and expensive. He had come in through the French doors, not the street entrance, so he was undoubtedly staying at the hotel. Shoes and watches were the best indicators, but she could not see either just yet in this light. He surveyed the bar, looking for a seat.

She caught his eye. "Nobody is sitting here." She indicated the bar stool next to hers. She took the coat onto her lap.

"Are you sure you don't mind?"

"No," she said. "It's all yours."

He grinned, sat down, and said, "Thank you. If you're waiting for someone to meet you or something, I'll be happy to give it up when he comes."

"No need," said Rachel Sturbridge. "I'm alone."

He ordered a Macallan single-malt scotch, which showed he had some standards, but he wanted the twelve-year-old instead of the eighteen, which meant he wasn't showing off. He turned to her. "Can I get you another martini?"

"No, thank you," she said. "I just started this one."

She decided he was probably the sort of man Rachel Sturbridge would like. He was tall and manly looking, and he was friendly in his manner but polite, and he hadn't leaned over her to talk, the way some men did when they met an attractive woman.

He sipped his drink and looked straight ahead. She sensed that if she wanted to talk to a gentleman like him, she would have to give him a signal that she was willing. "I like this place, don't you?"

He appeared mildly surprised, as though he wasn't quite sure that she had intended her question for him. When he turned and she met his eyes, he seemed pleased. "So far, I like it very much. I haven't been here before, but I've heard good things." He glanced at his watch, and the gesture gave

Rachel Sturbridge two competing sensations. The indication that he might be bored made her stomach feel hollow, but her heart's tempo picked up when she recognized the watch, a Patek Philippe that sold for around six thousand dollars. She was relieved when he added, "It's pretty crowded. I didn't have a reservation, but they said they'd try to fit me in. It's nine now. I have to hope somebody cancels."

The young maître d' appeared beside Rachel and said, "Miss Sturbridge, we can seat you now."

Rachel smiled. She had favors to dispense. "Come along. You can share my table."

The man was delighted. "Well, thank you." The maître d' returned to his podium and the hostess arrived just as they were going about the awkward business of getting down from adjacent bar stools. Rachel noted that he quickly slipped off his, stood back, and held her hand to keep her from falling. They both left their barely touched drinks, but the hostess gave an invisible signal to a passing waiter, who snatched them up and followed.

The dining room at the bottom of the stairs was bright, lit by large bowl-shaped ceiling fixtures, and the light was re-flected up from bright linen tablecloths. In the light, Rachel's companion looked a bit more attractive but a bit older, and she revised her estimate from forty to fifty. While they were getting settled at a table near the far side of the room, she held her compact in her palm to see what the lighting was doing to her, but quickly verified that her makeup had kept her from losing her color, and the new brown hair shone ex-actly as she had intended. She slipped the compact back into her purse.

He said, "I'm David Larson, and I thank you for your gra-cious invitation. I was kicking myself for coming without a reservation, and I find that it worked out better this way. I may never call for a reservation again." She detected a faint accent, but couldn't quite place it—the South?

She liked it that he was confident enough to give an exag-gerated compliment, and she liked the way his blue eyes transmitted sincerity without awkwardness. She decided to encourage him. "My name is Rachel Sturbridge, and it's a pleasure to have your company." She delivered her words with a condescending ease, like an actress stopping on the red carpet outside a movie premiere to speak to a camera.

Larson said, "Usually I have my assistant make all my reservations from home, but this time I didn't have much notice. It was one of those times to throw some clothes in a bag and head for the airport."

"Where is 'home'?"

"Austin," he said. "How about you?"

"At the moment, I'm living in San Francisco," she said. "I've only been here a short time." If he was from Austin, the safe place to be from was the Northeast. "Originally I'm a Connecticut girl."

They had to devote some attention to the menu, because the waiter had begun to hover nearby. Larson ordered salmon, and Rachel decided her first compliment to him would be to order the same entrée, the same salad.

He ordered a good bottle of wine without any consultation that would have forced her to acknowledge his extravagance, and she liked that. When the waiter had departed again, he said, "What brought you to San Francisco?"

"Business," she said.

"What sort of business are you in?"

She devoted a half second to the thought that she should have said it was a vacation. He was obviously a businessman, and now she was going to have to talk about a subject he knew. All she could do was try to sound sensible. "I'm trying to start a magazine. This is a good place to do that. There are plenty of artistic people who will work cheap on the speculation that when the magazine takes off, so will they. There are almost too many good technical and business types who used to work for deceased Internet companies. There are lots of printers and good shipping facilities."

"What about the rents?"

"They're expensive, but not like New York, and I can work out of my apartment and my post office box for a long time before I need to expand," she said.

"I can tell you're a practical businesswoman," said Larson.

"And I know a little about that. What's the title of your magazine?"

"I'm calling it *Singular Aspects*. It's going to be about alternative lifestyles."

"What does that mean?"

"It means nothing and everything. Americans love to think they're special. Every last one of them, no matter how much of a conformist he is, wants to believe he's a maverick, an innovator. What people want to believe is what they'll buy, and lifestyle is everything. So I can do clothes, furniture, houses, music, books, movies, art, food, relationships, and say it's about them. It doesn't take much of a pitch to get them to buy an attractive version of themselves. They already like themselves."

"And you think San Francisco is a good place to do this?"

"Not just a good place," she said. "The very best place. More huge fads have come out of San Francisco than anywhere, block for block. This was the place to be a beatnik in the fifties. Practically the whole hippie movement in the sixties came from the corner of Haight and Ashbury. The food-worship fad came from restaurants like Chez Panisse in Berkeley in the seventies. The computer revolution came from just down the road in the eighties. It's wave after wave. Not only will fad watchers pay for the latest from here, but advertisers will pay to be part of the next wave before it leaves here."

He laughed. "Well, that's just great. I like everything about it, and I think it's a good bet to succeed." He stared at her for a few seconds. "I think it's the best idea I've heard this trip."

She saw her chance to move the conversation onto him. "You've heard others?"

"Well, yes," he said. "I feel so comfortable talking to you that I keep forgetting that we don't actually know each other yet." He took out his wallet—she caught a thick sheaf of green bills and a platinum card—and slid a business card out with his thumb, then handed it to her.

There was a logo with a pair of longhorns, and a business address in Austin for David Larson Ventures. She held it out for him to take back, but he said, "No, please hold on to it."

She slipped it into her purse. "So what are David Larson's ventures?"

"Oh, I make investments."

"In what?"

"Young companies, mostly start-ups. Anything where I can evaluate the product, the market, the competition, and the costs. I came to meet some people and hear some pitches."

Rachel Sturbridge let the topic drop to see whether he was going to be a bore who didn't talk about anything but business. Instead he talked about other restaurants he knew in the Bay Area, an art exhibition he wanted to see while he was in the city, a book he had read on the airplane.

She silently cursed the waiter when he delivered the check. She had not had enough time. When she reached for the check, Larson's big hand was on the little tray, covering it. He said, "Please. I already know you're the kind of person who likes to pay her own way, but you would be doing me a kindness to let me have it. You did a great favor to let me join you, and it's all I can do in return."

"Well, all right." When the waiter took his card and went away, she said, "Thank you."

She pretended not to pay any attention to the check after that, but she had found that the way people treated servers could be an early indication of unpleasant qualities. She excused herself to go to the ladies' room at the right moment and looked down at it over his shoulder. He was a generous tipper. When she returned, she said, "I would like to take you out for an after-dinner drink. There's a place near here that's quiet."

He seemed taken aback. "I would be absolutely delighted." He stood up, then said, "How near?"

"Two hundred feet." They walked down the street to the bar of the Pan Pacific hotel, just off the huge white marble lobby. They sat at a table and ordered drinks. He said, "I gave you my business card. Have you had any cards printed yet?"

"No," she said. "I haven't hired my designer yet, and I want to be sure everything has the right look."

He produced another card of his and a pen and set them on

the table in front of her. "Then please write a number where I can reach you."

She hesitated, then wrote the phone number at her house. They had their drink, but before either of them had finished it, she said, "I've got to get up early and meet with a photographer to look at his portfolio." He put her in a taxi in front of the hotel, and she went back to her house feeling pleased with herself for timing her exit to pique his interest.

The next day she got up early and walked to a newsstand on Market Street to buy the Portland *Oregonian,* then had a cup of coffee and a bagel while she searched it for new information about Dennis Poole. She found no mention of him, and she walked home feeling relieved. She turned the television to the local morning news for company while she read the *San Francisco Chronicle,* but didn't bother to turn it off when the news was replaced by reruns of a situation comedy. At eleven, her telephone rang for the first time. Nobody had her number except David Larson, so she hurriedly muted the television set before she answered it, smiled to herself, and said, "Singular Aspects."

The second dinner with David was at the Dining Room at the Ritz-Carlton on Nob Hill, and it went better than the first for Rachel Sturbridge. Just after their entrées were served, he said, "You know, I've been thinking. I would like to buy a half interest in your magazine."

She smiled and shook her head. "There is no magazine yet. How can I sell it?"

"That's why I'm offering now. I'm betting you're going to be so successful that it will be too expensive to buy in later. I bring you capital and business knowledge, and you bring me the idea, the talent, and the effort. That's how start-ups work."

"That's very flattering," she said. "But let's not be in a rush."

"Why the delay?"

"I'm going to ask for fifty billion dollars, and I need to give you time to raise it."

He laughed and touched her hand. "That's it," he said. "That's why I'm willing to bet on you. I wanted to make you the offer before I left for Austin, but that doesn't mean I need the answer by then."

"When are you going back?"

He looked unhappy, as though he had been dreading the subject. "On Friday. I hate to do it, but I have a meeting that afternoon, and I've already postponed it once."

"That's only two days."

"One, really. I leave early Friday morning."

"Is it that important?"

"Yes, I'm afraid so. People are coming from New York and London."

She couldn't let him go this way. She knew that he had been enjoying his time with her, and that she was rapidly making an impression on him. But he was a rich man in his fifties. He had met a great many attractive women by now, and he probably met more every month. She had not yet had time to reach the point where she would not simply fade into his memory with all of the others. She had to do something quickly. "Then you'll have to go. But can I take you out for a farewell dinner tomorrow night?"

He looked surprised. "Thank you. I'd love that. But it shouldn't sound so final. You and I are going to be partners, just as soon as I raise that fifty billion."

The third dinner was at the Fairmont. Once they were past the lobby, with its high, vaulted ceiling and marble columns, David seemed to relax. There was a quiet, comfortable quality to their conversation. He told her stories about his childhood in Texas, his business associates, his friends. When the waiter asked whether they would like anything else, Rachel said, "No, thank you." He asked, "Would you like to charge it to your room?" She said, "Yes."

David met her eyes, and she shrugged. "Another cat out of the bag."

He said, "You're staying here?"

"I reserved a suite when I made the reservation. The view from the tower rooms is one of the best in the city. I thought it might be a nice way to be sure you didn't forget me as soon as you got back to Texas."

"Not likely," he said.

She had prepared herself in advance for a night of closing her eyes tight and enduring, but she was pleasantly surprised. He was a gentle, considerate lover with an easy, appreciative disposition that made her feel less self-conscious. When they were not making love he was a cheerful, affectionate companion.

Late that evening after he fell asleep, she lay awake considering the best way to make use of him. She had been wise to resist the temptation to sell him a half interest in her imaginary magazine. She had been very close to yielding. He seemed accustomed to risky investments, and he would probably forgive her when she faked an attempt at a magazine and didn't return any money. But she could afford to let her bet stay on the table. She was beginning to think that maybe the way to get her money was the way lots of other women had done it. Maybe she should marry it.

The next morning they said good-bye in the room. He called a cab to take him to the Prescott to check out and then to the airport. Rachel took a second cab back to her house. She put his business card on her refrigerator with a magnet and waited.

On the third day, a FedEx package arrived. Inside was a velvet box. She opened it, and found a white-gold pendant with a single large diamond. The velvet box said Van Cleef & Arpels, but that was only a box. She took off the shade of her reading lamp and held the diamond close to the bulb. She could tell it was a good stone, about three carats, and very bright. It must have cost him at least ten thousand dollars, and possibly much more.

Looking at the light sparkling in the facets of the diamond made her feel lucky. It had probably been dangerous to get involved with another man so soon after Dennis Poole, but there had seemed to be nobody looking for her, so she had begun to look for a new man.

Men were a difficult way to make a living. All any of them really wanted was sex. It made them easy to attract and easy to play for a little money, but not necessarily easy to control. They got jealous and watchful, and at times the sex could be troublesome, too. At least with David it wasn't unpleasant or especially demanding. She took his card off her refrigerator, went to the telephone, and dialed the private number he had written on the back. When he answered, she said, "You certainly know how to keep a girl's attention, don't you?"

A week later David was in San Francisco again. He called her from the airport, then picked her up at her house and drove to a hotel in Carmel that consisted of a group of luxurious cabins on a wooded cliff above the ocean. They had dinner in the restaurant in the central building, watching the waves crash against the rocks below, then walked along the path through the pines to their cabin, and sat on the couch before the stone fireplace, listening to the crackling of the wood fire.

After a time, he said, "I've been thinking a lot about you."

"Good," she said. She leaned close and kissed him softly.

"I've even been trying to find ways to help you get your magazine started."

"You're sweet." She kissed him again.

"While I was doing it I found out a couple of things that made me curious."

"What kind of things?" She turned her body on the couch to face him. She could feel the hairs on her scalp rising. It wasn't exactly fear, but an intense anticipation.

"Well, you said you had never been married."

"That's right."

"I'm wondering if you changed your name at some point."

She kept her eyes on his face. "You've hired somebody to investigate me?"

He smiled. "Now, please don't get mad at me. It's a normal thing to do if you're thinking of making an investment in a start-up. I have a standing account at the Averill Agency in Dallas. Whenever I'm about to make a seed-money investment, they routinely do a quick rundown on the principal players, just to be sure none of them has a tail and a pitchfork. It's no different from asking your mechanic to take a look at a car you're buying."

Rachel leaned forward, her eyes searching his. "And?"

"As you know, they didn't find any problems, because there are no problems. But they did have trouble finding out

much else about you. They said that either you'd had a marriage at some point that you forgot to mention, or maybe had
petitioned for a name change."

She stared at him coldly, sensing the urge to make him suffer. "Rachel Sturbridge isn't the name I was born with. My
family was well-off and respected, but it looked good only
from the outside. From the inside, it wasn't a group you
would want to belong to. There wasn't a lot of love." She
paused, as though bravely controlling her emotions. "What
there was, was a lot of cruelty. After I grew up I spent years
trying to get over it, and on the advice of my therapist, I sev-
ered the connection completely. Being really free of them
meant using a different name, so I do. You're the only person
I've ever had to explain this to."

He was embarrassed at his mistake. "Rachel, I'm sorry. I
just cared so much about you that I couldn't know enough."

She stood up.

He looked horrified. "Please. I never imagined that talking to you about it would bring back bad memories. Stay
with me."

"I'm tired, and I'm going to sleep now. We can talk in the
morning." David had carried both of their suitcases into one
of the bedrooms when he'd unloaded the car. Now she went
into that room, took hers into the other bedroom, and quietly
closed the door.

When she awoke in the morning she knew that two things
were going to happen. One was that David Larson was going
to buy her a big present. The other was that she was going
back to San Francisco. She went into the bathroom, stood in
front of the mirror, and began to pull herself together. "I'm
heartbroken," she told the girl in the mirror. It was well said.
She would use it.

During the time while he was in Austin she had allowed
herself to grow overconfident. She had formed plans that
carried them both years into the future. She had pictured
them spending time in Europe together—maybe in the Greek
islands, which looked beautiful and warm in the magazines,
or Provence, which sounded in articles as though it existed
solely to serve food and wine to people like her. She was sure

David had accumulated enough money already. It seemed to her that the only reason he still traveled around chasing investments was that he'd had nothing better to do until he'd met Rachel Sturbridge. She could have made those years wonderful for him. But that was before he had betrayed her.

She watched herself in the mirror as she said, "I'm heartbroken" again. She meant it. He had told his stupid private detectives to pry into her private life looking for incriminating information, and she was just lucky they had not found anything. It had been a cold, calculating thing to do. Men always wanted you to do impulsive, risky things because you let your passion for them get too strong to resist. They wanted you to trust them completely, holding nothing at all back to protect yourself. But then, after your body and soul had gotten to be things they had, rather than things they wanted, they announced that they had reserved the right to be suspicious and cautious about you.

When David knocked and asked if she would go to breakfast with him, she called through the closed door, "No, you go ahead."

Rachel spent the next hour working efficiently and methodically to make herself beautiful. She had started beautician's school the summer she had turned sixteen, and had learned some cosmetology and hairdressing before she had missed a tuition payment. But she had learned her most valuable tricks years before that, in the long succession of beauty pageants her mother had entered her in beginning at age four. She had been born with good skin and small, symmetrical features, and she had a quick, practiced hand with a brush, eyeliner, and mascara.

She was good at dressing herself because she had a hard, objective eye. That was something else the pageant circuit had done for her. She could look at herself the way a contest judge would, with no sentimentality and no mercy. She accentuated her figure's best points and hid the flaws. She tried all three dresses she had brought, chose the one that would give him the most haunting memory of her body, and put on spike heels.

Rachel packed her suitcase, stood it upright on its wheels,

and extended the handle. Then she went to the living room, arranged herself on the small couch, turned on the television set, and waited. David returned about an hour after that.

When he opened the door and saw her, she could tell her effect was what she had intended. He stopped at the door and simply stared for a moment, then took a couple of deep breaths and walked toward her. "Rachel," he said. "I need to talk to you. I'm really very sorry. I never imagined I was going to hurt your feelings or remind you of anything that caused you pain."

She raised her face to him. Her eyes were cold, as though she were looking at him from a great distance.

He said, "I brought you a little something." He took a velvet jewelry box from his coat pocket and held it out to her. "Will you please forgive me?"

Seeing another jewelry box nettled her, partly because it showed he thought she was childish enough to be mollified by it, and partly because she wanted whatever lay inside the box. Her expression didn't change. "I waited here for you only because I felt that I should say something to you for the sake of clarity. If you'll remember, I never asked you to invest in my business."

"I never meant to imply—"

"Please let me finish. I won't be long." She glared at him, holding him in silence for a breath before she continued. "It was a purely personal relationship, from my point of view. I never offered you anything or asked you for anything. When you asked questions about my business I answered them. When you offered to invest, I repeatedly refused your money. You called in detectives anyway and had me investigated. Well, that was a deal breaker. I'm leaving now. I want you to tear up my telephone number and forget my address."

"But Rachel." He tried to sit beside her, but she recoiled and stood up. He held out his hands. "Can't we talk about this?"

"No. We can't. If you want to do something for me you can order your detectives to shred whatever files they have on me. Beyond that, I have no further interest in anything you do or say." She turned, walked to the bedroom, grasped the handle on her suitcase, and pulled it to the door on its wheels.

David Larson stood up, looking pained. "Please don't go, Rachel. It was a terrible mistake. I'm trying to make it up to you." As he raised his arms in supplication, he noticed the velvet box in his hand, and held it out. "This was for you. Won't you at least take a look at it?"

"No, I won't. Good-bye." She pushed the door open, dragged her suitcase out, and let the door swing shut behind her. She went down the steps and up the paved drive to the main lodge, and had the concierge call her a cab.

On the long drive to San Francisco she contemplated what she had done, and decided that leaving David Larson had been her only possible choice. She couldn't continue the relationship after he'd had her investigated. If she stayed, he would have the detectives resume their poking and prying. It was quite possible that they would find out that she had once been Tanya Starling, and maybe even that she had known Dennis Poole. It was also a bit late to allow him to buy into her imaginary magazine, and then make the money disappear on imaginary expenses. Now that the detectives had been called in, she couldn't even continue to play him for gifts and support.

Her only possible move had been to sever any connection with him. The paradox was that his having her investigated had made her want to kill him, and the only thing that was preventing her from doing it was that he'd had her investigated. Before his body could cool, his detectives would be there to give the police a whole dossier on her.

The next afternoon at one, there was a knock on her door. She looked out the window to decide whether to answer, and saw it was the Federal Express man. She opened the door, signed for the thick envelope, and took it inside to open it.

The envelope contained three items. The first was the typed report that David Larson had received from the Averill Detective Agency in Dallas, Texas, saying that there wasn't much about Rachel Sturbridge to know. The second was a file folder, stamped AVERILL AGENCY: CONFIDENTIAL. It had *Sturbridge, Rachel* on the tab, and contained about twenty

pages of handwritten notes describing things checked unsuc-
cessfully, credit reports on Rachel Sturbridge that had yielded
virtually no information, a copy of her business license, and
some photographs. There were pictures of her coming and
going from her house, as well as a few close-ups of her face
made from blowups of more distant shots.

The third item in the package was a note from David
Larson. It said, "You asked that I destroy the background
check. These are the only copies. Please accept my apolo-
gies. David."

Rachel searched the kitchen drawers until she found some
matches. She took the note, the file, and the report out to the
tiny square of concrete below her back steps, then made a
small bonfire. She looked at each piece as she added it to the
flames.

The detectives had been called off, and she was watching
the collection of incriminating information burn up, page by
page. She was confident that David was feeling contrite and
apologetic, not suspicious of her. But this wasn't enough.
She looked at the rented house, then down the hill at the city.
She picked up a stick to stir the ashes and make sure there
was nothing left of the paper. She would have to disappear.

7

The videotape was grainy and
distorted, and the colors seemed faded. It had been taken
through a plastic dome that covered the video camera in the
hotel hallway. The shot angled down from the ceiling. A

white-haired couple walked under it and up the hallway to the elevator alcove. A few seconds later, a man appeared, coming from the direction of the elevators. "That's him. That's my cousin Dennis," Hugo Poole said.

A thin blond woman caught up to Dennis while he stood at the door of his hotel room.

"Look at the hair," said Sergeant Hobbes.

"It's just about the right length," Joe Pitt said.

On the monitor, Dennis slid a key card out of his wallet. The woman stood facing Dennis, talking to him, waiting for him to push the card into the lock and turn the handle. Hugo Poole waited impatiently for the girl to show her face. Dennis Poole opened the door to let the girl in ahead of him. "Turn around, for Christ's sake," Hugo said. "Turn around!"

The girl half-turned to go inside, and Detective Hobbes froze the tape. The blond woman was held in place, her image quivering slightly, a band of static moving upward from the bottom of the screen, disappearing, then reappearing at the bottom. Her face was attractive but not distinctive—just small, regular features. She seemed to be one of those women whose eyelashes and brows were light, so that her eyes disappeared into her face until she put on her makeup each morning.

Detective Hobbes turned to look down at Hugo Poole, her expression controlled. "Well, Mr. Poole? Have you seen her before?"

"Never." He kept staring at the girl's image, scowling.

Joe Pitt asked, "How did you get this tape?"

"Dennis Poole had been on vacation until two weeks before he died," said Hobbes. "His credit card slips gave us the hotel in Aspen where he had been staying. We asked the hotel for their security tapes, and I went down to watch them. The ones from early in his stay were all erased, but a few of the later ones survived. This is the clearest, I'm afraid."

"Do you know who she is yet?" asked Pitt.

"Her name is Tanya Starling. She was registered at the hotel for two days before he arrived. After he had been there for about three days she canceled her room and moved in with him."

"Did the hotel have a home address for her?"

"Yes," she said. "An apartment in Chicago. The phone number was out of service, so we asked the Chicago police to find out whether the number had been changed, but the whole account was closed. They checked with the company that manages the place and found she had moved out before she left for Colorado. She left no forwarding address."

"Is the apartment still vacant?"

"No such luck. It's a fancy high-rise with a view of the lake, and there was a waiting list. They cleaned and repainted it right away and new people moved in a couple of days later. There's no chance of lifting prints now."

Hugo Poole broke his silence. "It's not right."

Catherine Hobbes frowned. "What's not right, Mr. Poole?"

"I know you don't like me, but I'm trying to tell you something about my cousin."

"And I assume you don't like me, but I'm listening."

"The girl shouldn't be like that."

"Like what?"

"She's wrong for Denny. He was a forty-two-year-old computer geek. He had a stupid laugh, he was tall in the wrong way—kind of big-footed and narrow-shouldered. He didn't talk about anything women could stand to listen to."

Joe Pitt said, "That sounds like a million guys, most of them married. If she moved in, she was interested."

"Too good-looking," said Hugo Poole. "When I saw him with women, they were always on the same step of the food chain that he was on. She should be a nice fat girl with bad teeth."

Catherine Hobbes studied Hugo Poole. "What do you think was going on? Do you think she's a hooker?"

"I doubt it. She was with him for, like, three weeks," said Hugo. "He'd have died broke and still owed her money."

"That's what I thought," said Hobbes. "Besides, the Chicago police would probably have picked up that kind of information. She could have been some single woman willing to give a guy like Dennis a little slack. His spending a lot of money on her would be flattering. She was on vacation, so the rules and standards sometimes slip a little. Somebody she wouldn't go out with at home might do for an evening in a strange place."

"Okay," said Hugo. "Lightning strikes and guys like Dennis get lucky. But there's no way a woman like that would stay for more than one night unless something besides Dennis was the attraction."

"All right, you two have convinced me," said Pitt. "There was a hidden reason why she was with him. So what was it? If she moved out of her fancy apartment in Chicago and took off for Colorado, maybe she was hiding. Maybe Dennis got killed by somebody who was after her."

"You mean an old boyfriend or a jealous husband?" said Hugo. "Dennis Poole killed by a jealous husband?"

"It might explain what she was doing moving in with him," said Catherine Hobbes. "Living with somebody who's paying for everything makes a woman hard to spot. She could also have been the one who killed him."

Pitt said, "Do you know whether any of his money is gone?"

"Nothing so far," said Hobbes. "He had some charges from jewelry stores, and some women's clothing stores. We've found about twenty thousand dollars' worth."

"Are you sure he was the one who made all of the charges?" asked Pitt.

"He was alive on those dates," Hobbes said. "And he didn't report a lost credit card."

"Then I'll go with the odds," said Pitt.

"What are they?" asked Hugo.

Pitt said, "That when you have a murder scene and a woman is missing, it's not because she was the perpetrator. Usually when you find her, she's the second victim."

"Thanks for coming up to Portland and cooperating with us, Mr. Poole," said Catherine Hobbes as she turned off the tape and took the cassette out of the VCR. "I'm sure that Mr. Pitt will let you know the minute we find anything else." She walked out of the interrogation room.

A half hour later, Catherine Hobbes sat alone in the interrogation room in front of the monitor, watching the videotape

of herself, Hugo Poole, and Joe Pitt watching the hotel security tape. She studied the reactions of both men to everything
that was seen or said. Then she got to the part she had been
waiting for: the sight of herself walking out of the room.

She watched the tape of Hugo Poole as he stood up and
looked at Pitt. "What the hell did you do to *her?*"

Pitt went to the door ahead of him and reached for the
knob to open it. "I went to work for you."

"I was expecting her not to warm up to me. This was about
you. Whatever you're doing to her, you ought to either cut it
out or do it better."

On the monitor, Catherine Hobbes watched the two men
walk out the door. If either of them had anything enlighten-
ing to say about the murder of Dennis Poole, he had not been
foolish enough to say it inside the Portland Police Bureau.

8

Rachel Sturbridge emptied the
vacuum cleaner bag into the garbage dumpster outside her
rented house. She went inside, put on disposable rubber
gloves, and walked one last time through her house with a
bottle of Windex and a roll of paper towels. She stood at the
window that faced north. Between two apartment buildings
she could just see the taller office buildings along Market
Street. She stepped to the side, sprayed the glass, and wiped
it once more. It was important to be sure that she had not
missed any surface as smooth as a windowpane.

She sprayed and wiped all of the handles, knobs, and

latches, then took broad swipes over all of the flat surfaces where she might have rested her fingertips in the past few weeks. If David Larson had been lying about calling off his detectives, the least she could do was to deny them the gift of her fingerprints.

Rachel took a final look at the furniture that Mrs. Halloran, the landlady, had supplied with the house, trying to find any hairs that she might have left on a cushion. She wrote "Eve Halloran" on an envelope, slipped her house key into it, and left it on the mantel. Then she picked up her suitcase, went out the door, and pressed the lock button. Only after she was outside the house and in her car did she take off her thin rubber gloves.

She was out on Highway 101 by noon, driving south, away from the city. San Francisco had been a terrible disappointment to her, and she wanted to get away, but she had no destination in mind. Today it seemed to Rachel that the world was a cold and treacherous place, and the only act that was appealing was to keep moving.

For a few hours she drove and thought about her dissatisfaction with David Larson. He was a foolish man, one who had no idea what a wonderful future he had thrown away when he had betrayed Rachel Sturbridge's trust. He really deserved to die, and it bothered her that she had been forced to let him go. It didn't seem fair.

When she began to feel hungry, she looked at the clock on the dashboard and noticed that it was five o'clock. She stopped at a restaurant in Pismo Beach and stared out at the highway while she ate, wishing she could see the ocean.

She refilled the gas tank and drove all the way to the Los Angeles County line before she stopped again. She found a hotel off the Ventura Freeway in the west end of the San Fernando Valley and registered with her Rachel Sturbridge credit card. When she awoke in the morning, she showered, ate, and dressed, then settled her bill in cash. It was time to begin making herself safe from whatever problems David Larson might have caused.

She needed to be anonymous for a time while she rested and decided what she wanted to do next, and the nondescript neighborhood where she had stopped looked like a good place for that. All of Los Angeles seemed featureless to her, a vast sameness. A young, white middle-class woman could avoid notice for a very long time if she paid attention and didn't do anything stupid. She rented an apartment in Woodland Hills not far from the Topanga Canyon shopping mall by putting down money for the first month, last month, and security deposit in cash.

She went to a copying store, just as she had in San Francisco, rented a computer and printer, and took out the CD where she had stored the blank birth certificate. During the long drive from San Francisco she had been thinking of using the name Veronica, but the girl who waited on her was pretty and energetic, and she was wearing a badge that said, "Nancy Gonzales, Sales Associate." The name Nancy seemed cheerful, so that was the one she chose. She filled in the blank with the name Nancy Mills.

Next she bought a hair dye kit and lightened her hair again, then went to a salon to have it cut. She had worn it long and loose as Rachel Sturbridge, so now it had to be shorter. Long hair gave her an advantage with men, but she had decided it would be better if she didn't attract any more of them for a while. On the way home, she went to an optometrist's shop in a strip mall and bought some nonprescription contact lenses in different eye colors.

Two days later, when she went to the Department of Motor Vehicles to apply for a new driver's license, she wore the brown contacts, so in her license picture she had brown eyes and shoulder-length, light brown hair. She thought of the look as drab and ordinary, which was exactly what she wanted.

She sold Rachel Sturbridge's car through the *Pennysaver* to a woman she told she needed money to pay off a credit card debt. She could walk to restaurants, movie theaters, and even a grocery store from her apartment, so she decided that she could do without a car for the moment. Nancy Mills needed quiet and anonymity and solitude. She was disillusioned by her experience with David Larson, and had no desire to go anyplace where men might see her and talk to her, so she stayed away from health clubs, restaurants that had bars, and other spots where she had found men before.

After her first week in Los Angeles, Tanya Starling and Rachel Sturbridge had been erased. Nancy Mills was already nearly invisible. She would wait and watch and see if something troublesome had followed her from San Francisco.

9

Catherine Hobbes and Joe Pitt walked down the hall of the San Francisco police station, watching the numbers over the doors until they came to 219.

The door was open, so Catherine stepped inside. There were several desks in the room, where plainclothes officers gazed at computer screens or talked on telephones. She approached a group of three who were leaning over to look at a file opened on a desk, and said to them, "I'm looking for Detective Crowley."

"I'm Crowley. Welcome to San Francisco," said a tall, thin cop with a bald head. He straightened and held out his hand. "Are you Sergeant Hobbes?"

She flashed a smile and shook his hand. Crowley looked over her shoulder expectantly, and she remembered Joe Pitt. "This is Mr. Pitt, who is conducting an investigation for the victim's family. Do you mind talking to both of us?"

Detective Crowley shook his head, then reached past her, his arm almost touching her shoulder, and shook Pitt's hand enthusiastically. "Not at all. I've known Mr. Pitt for about a hundred years. How you been, Joe?"

Pitt said, "Can't complain, Doug. I hear you've got Tanya Starling's car."

"Well, we've found out where it is. We haven't impounded it. She sold it here about four days after you lost track of her in Portland. There was an ad in the *Chronicle*. The man who bought it is named"—he picked up a written report and scanned it—"Harold Willis. He bought it for fifteen thousand."

Pitt asked, "Was that a good deal?"

"It was close to the high blue book price, so it wasn't a steal or anything. She wasn't just unloading it fast."

"And did Harold Willis recognize the photographs of Tanya Starling I sent to you?" asked Catherine Hobbes.

"Yes. He said it was definitely her. She went on a test drive with him, took his check, made out a bill of sale, signed over the registration, and wished him luck. That took maybe two hours, so he had plenty of time to look."

"Where did the sale take place?" asked Hobbes. "Her place?"

"No. Her ad just had a phone number. She called Willis and brought the car to his house." He anticipated the next question. "She was alone with him all that time. She wasn't kidnapped or under duress. If she had been in trouble, she could have told him about it, or driven to any police station."

Pitt said, "How about the bank account where she deposited his check? Do you have anything on that yet?"

"It was a business account at Regal Bank." Crowley handed Pitt a piece of paper. "Here's the address of the branch where she deposited it, the account number, and her home address."

"Great," said Pitt. "Thanks."

Hobbes calmly reached over and took the piece of paper from Joe Pitt.

"Could be better," Crowley said. "We called on her and found that she's moved on again. She had signed a lease for a house with a roommate named Rachel Sturbridge. They paid three months' rent in advance, according to the owner, a Mrs. Eve Halloran. She says they moved out about a week ago. The date is vague, because they left without telling her."

"Did she have a job while she was here?" asked Hobbes.

"I'm not exactly sure," Crowley said. "The two of them had run a d/b/a announcement in the paper and took out a license for a business called Singular Aspects. It lists a newsletter, which I assume was a catalog. If it was a store, they didn't stay long enough to open."

"That's what you think it was—a store?"

"I don't know. That's my guess, from the sound of it. I defer to you, though, Sergeant Hobbes. Doesn't it sound like a women's clothing store? Anyway, less than a month later, the bank account was closed and they had both moved on."

"That's the part we need to know," said Hobbes. "Where did they move to?"

"We've got nothing on that yet," said Crowley. "Neither of them left a forwarding address at the post office or with their landlady. Before they left, they closed their account at Regal Bank, so there's nothing there, either. They might easily have found a good location somewhere nearby, like San Mateo or Richmond, and moved. By now they could also be in China."

"Either way, Tanya Starling doesn't seem to be in any danger, and she certainly isn't dead," said Hobbes. "But she's still our only potential witness on why Dennis Poole is."

Pitt said, "Did Tanya buy another car before she left?"

"No. Rachel Sturbridge has one, and maybe they drove off in that." He handed a piece of paper to Pitt. "Here's the DMV printout on it. A six-year-old Nissan Maxima, black. License plate and VIN are supplied. It's registered to the address they rented here. So until she gets wherever she's going and reregisters it with a good address, we won't know where she is. If she's in-state, she probably won't get around to it until next year."

"Keep us in mind, will you, Doug?"

"Sure," said Crowley. "When we get anything more, you'll have it."

Catherine Hobbes said, "Thank you very much, Detective Crowley. Here's my card. There are numbers for my direct line, the homicide office, my cell, and my home. It doesn't matter what time of day it comes in, I would appreciate it if you'd call."

"Of course," said Crowley.

She and Pitt walked out of the police station, and Pitt drove the rental car to the house where Tanya Starling and Rachel Sturbridge had lived. As soon as Pitt found a parking space at the foot of the long, inclining street, Catherine Hobbes got out and began to walk. Pitt locked the car and trotted to catch up. By the time he'd succeeded, he was winded.

"What's bothering you?" asked Pitt.

Catherine Hobbes walked along the street, her quick strides keeping her a half pace ahead of him so she wouldn't have to look at his fake concerned expression. "Nothing."

"Come on," he said. "You're going to give me a heart attack walking up this hill at this speed. Something's bothering you."

She stopped and looked at him. "We're not in some boy-and-girl relationship that requires your helping when something's bothering me. I'm a police officer working a homicide case. Your role is not to delve into my female sensitivities so you can talk me out of them. You're here with me only because my captain thought you might be able to contribute to the progress of the investigation. That was not an opinion I shared."

"It's Crowley, isn't it?"

"Do *not* tell me I'm imagining things."

"I won't. But—"

"I'm also not interested in being told it's not his fault because you knew each other twenty years ago, or because he's too old to get used to women in homicide, or because you two are from California and I'm not."

"Okay," he said. "It's just that it's a waste of time to get mad at me."

"I'm not."

"Or even at him."

"I'm not mad. I'm a woman cop. I'm used to being ignored, and to much, much worse. I'm looking for the house number."

"Okay," said Pitt. He followed her along the street for another half block, until they came to a narrow one-story house.

They walked up to the steps and Hobbes rang the bell, then listened for a moment to the door being unbolted and un-latched. It swung open to reveal a woman around sixty years old with dyed red hair wearing a pair of jeans with knee pads over them.

"Mrs. Halloran?"

"I've been waiting for you," the woman said. "I was just finishing up on the trim. Come on in, but don't touch any woodwork. Everything else is dry."

They went inside. The furniture in the small living room had been pushed together in the middle of the hardwood floor and covered with one large canvas tarpaulin. She pulled the canvas off on one side to uncover three chairs. "You must be Sergeant Hobbes."

"That's right," said Hobbes. "This is Mr. Pitt. He's a private investigator cooperating with us on this case."

It was not lost on Mrs. Halloran that Joe Pitt was hand-some, and closer to her age than to Hobbes's. She kept her eyes on Pitt as she said, "Here, this is the only place we can sit right now." Mrs. Halloran sat on one of the chairs. "You said 'case.' Tanya Starling is involved in a case?"

"We're looking for her so we can ask her a few questions. A man she knew in Portland was the victim of a crime."

"What's his name?"

"His name was Dennis Poole."

"Oh, my goodness," said Mrs. Halloran. "No wonder she left in such a hurry. You mean you think she killed him, or that she's in danger?"

Catherine Hobbes allowed some of her frustration to show. "We just want to talk to her. She knew him, and we would like to know anything she can tell us. She left Portland, so we haven't been able to talk to her." Hobbes reached into her folder and pulled out a photograph. "Can you identify the woman in this picture?"

Mrs. Halloran held the picture a distance from her face, then close up, then farther away. "Yes. That seems to be

Tanya. But you should try to get a better picture. It's so fuzzy."

"It's copied from a videotape. Did you talk to her much?"

"When I rented the house to her, we talked a bit. She said she was moving here from Chicago. Was that a lie?"

"No," said Hobbes. "Her last permanent address was in Chicago. We think she was only in Portland for a short visit."

"That makes sense. She had nothing much with her. Her roommate hadn't even arrived yet."

"What was the roommate's name?"

"Rachel Sturbridge."

"What was she like?"

"I never met her. She was going to arrive separately in a few days. I let Tanya sign the lease and add Rachel's name to it, but Tanya paid the rent and security deposit in advance with her money, and initialed the lease to agree to all of the provisions, so for the time being, she was my tenant. I assumed that later on, as a matter of course, I would meet the other one. But as a rule, when you rent to young people, you don't want to hang around all the time. You risk becoming a second mommy to them. And what you don't know won't hurt you."

"And you didn't see her when they moved, either?"

"No. They didn't tell me ahead of time, and if they had—I don't know—maybe I would have come to be sure they didn't leave the door unlocked or walk off with any of my furnishings, but they didn't anyway. They were perfectly nice. Later, when Tanya called and told me they had moved out, she said I could rent it to someone else right away. I asked if I could send her a refund at her new address, but she told me to keep the money for the trouble of renting it twice."

"Very thoughtful," said Catherine Hobbes. "Do you remember the date of the call?"

"Let's see," she said. "It must have been about a week ago."

"Did she say where she was calling from?"

"No, I don't think she did. She was in a hurry, and she said she was just taking the time to let me know about the vacancy, and had to go. I didn't want to keep her on the line."

Catherine Hobbes said, "Here's my card, Mrs. Halloran. We're very interested in talking with her, so if you hear from her again, or remember anything that might help us, please get in touch. You can call me collect. In fact, I'm going to add my home phone number so you can reach me anytime." She quickly wrote it on her card.

Mrs. Halloran took the card, glanced at it, and stuck it into the pocket of her jeans. "All right," she said.

"Thank you."

As soon as they had walked far enough from the house to avoid being overheard, Joe Pitt said, "Are you getting the same feeling I am?"

"Oh, yes. She knows somebody is looking for her, and she doesn't want to be found."

"This Rachel might be helping her lose the guy who killed Dennis Poole—if they use Rachel's car, and pay for things in Rachel's name, he'll have a hard time finding Tanya."

"But we won't," said Catherine Hobbes. "Now that we know about her it gives us two chances for a hit. When we find one, we'll have the other."

10

Nancy Mills found her walks through Topanga Plaza relaxing. There were gangs of old people who did power walks every morning before the stores opened, going the length of the mall, then clambering up the stalled escalator to the upper galleries and striding along beside the railings. Nancy was more subtle than they were, but she had begun to use the place for conditioning too, weaving through the crowds after the stores opened.

Nancy Mills didn't go on shopping binges the way Tanya Starling often had, and Rachel Sturbridge had once or twice. Nancy still owned all of their new clothes from Aspen, Portland, and San Francisco, and at the moment, her activities were too simple to require a big wardrobe. But she liked to look at clothes.

It was Thursday morning. The plaza was sometimes unpleasantly crowded on weekends, but Thursday was still perfect. She was in Bloomingdale's trying to decide which jar of bath salts had the right scent when she became aware that a man at the next counter was staring at her. He was in his early thirties, well groomed and nicely dressed. He wore a dark sport coat and shined Italian shoes. She assumed he must be a store floor manager or a salesman for one of the cosmetics lines, but she couldn't see from this angle whether he had a name tag without actually staring at him. Part of his job was to hang around being friendly to customers, so she dismissed him from her mind.

The saleswomen behind the counters were eager because Thursday mornings were slow, so one of them came right away to sell her the bath salts while another tried to raise the stakes by showing her the rest of that company's line of products. Nancy resisted the pitch and paid in cash, as she always did. As one of the women counted out her change and the other put her receipt in the bag, Nancy became aware that the man had not gone away.

She turned to look, their eyes met, and she had a horrible moment when she wondered if she knew him, then another when she had to endure his smile. It was at once shy and hopeful. There was even a trace of the conspiratorial, as though he and she shared a secret. He looked so familiar. Could she possibly know him?

She turned away, irritated. She wanted to say aloud, "I wasn't looking because I was interested. I just sensed that someone was staring." She took her bag, pivoted away from him, and walked back into the mall. She moved past the first couple of stores, then felt an uncomfortable sensation. She stopped and looked at the next store's window display, then quickly turned to walk to the other side of the mall.

She had been right. There he was again, a grown-up, smartly dressed man, following her around a mall like an awkward teenager. She supposed she should be flattered by the attention, but his behavior was very bad news: she had shortened her hair, dyed it a dull shade of brown, and worn clothes that weren't supposed to be eye-catching. All that seemed to have accomplished was to make her appealing to creepy, awkward men.

Nancy turned again, intending to leave him behind, but he was already at her shoulder, so when she turned she was nearly face-to-face with him. "Excuse me," she said, and stepped to the side.

"I'm sorry," he said. "I was almost sure I recognized you, and I wanted to check. I'm—"

"I don't think we know each other," she said, and took a step.

"Regal Bank? San Francisco?"

She froze. Now she remembered who he was.

"I was the man who helped you open your commercial account at the bank. Bill Thayer. I'm the branch manager."

"I do remember you," said Nancy. "What are you doing down here?"

"I have family here. I'm visiting. What about you? Are you expanding into the Los Angeles area? I still remember the name of your business—Singular Aspects. Right?"

He didn't seem to know that she had closed the account. She had to be extremely careful, because if he got curious, he could look things up when he got back to the office. "No, actually, we decided that San Francisco wasn't right for us, and we're thinking about starting the business here instead. Well, nice to see you." She stepped off.

"Miss Starling? Wait."

She stopped walking. This was awful. She had forgotten that to open the account in San Francisco she had called herself Tanya Starling so she could cash Tanya Starling's check from the old account in Chicago. This Bill Thayer didn't know it yet, but he already possessed enough information to destroy her. He had seen her in this mall in Woodland Hills, just a few blocks from where she lived.

He said, "I wondered if you would have dinner with me tonight."

"Gee, Bill," she said. "I can't tonight."

"I know it's kind of sudden, but I won't be here long, so I thought I'd better take a chance."

She was afraid: she was afraid to be with him, and afraid to let him walk away. She knew that dinner was impossible. He would go to his parents' house and say he was going to miss dinner tonight because he had a date. Unless they were comatose, one of them would say, "What's her name?" He would tell them who she was and where he had met her. She smiled. "I do have some time now, though, if you'd like to have coffee."

"That sounds good," said Thayer.

"Do you have a car?"

"You can't go anywhere in L.A. without one. I rented it at the airport."

"Then you can drive. There's a really great little place on Topanga just south of the freeway."

They walked out of the plaza to the parking lot. His rental car was parked about a hundred yards off, almost by itself. When she saw it she was surprised. It was a Cadillac that looked enormous to her. "Wow. Do you drive your mom and dad around when you visit?"

"Not much," said Thayer. "They think I've gotten rusty driving up north, so they don't trust me. The big car is for taking clients around. Whenever I come down I usually try to see a couple."

They drove down Topanga past the freeway, and she said, "Keep going. It's quite a bit farther, toward Malibu."

"Is it on the left or right?"

"The right. Oh, look. There's a nice little park up there. Can we stop for a minute?"

"I guess so," he said doubtfully. "Sure." Thayer drove off the road and stopped on the shoulder beside a grove of trees with picnic tables in it.

Nancy got out of the car with her purse over her shoulder.

"I've been looking for a good place to have a small party. I wonder if I could do it as a picnic, right here."

Thayer didn't seem to know what to do. He got out of the car slowly, and scrutinized the ground before he took each step, as though he were afraid of getting his shoes dirty.

"Come on," she said. "Let's get a better look." She took his hand playfully and began to walk among the trees.

Thayer looked a bit doubtful, but he began to stroll with her in the deserted grove, past picnic tables and trash cans. Nancy let go of his hand and moved off a few feet to disapprovingly rock a picnic table that was set on uneven ground. He strolled on, and got a few steps ahead of her.

She looked at her watch. It was nearly ten-thirty. It wasn't surprising that people weren't here in the morning, but someone could arrive before long to set up a picnic lunch. She looked back at the road. There were no cars going past, and she couldn't hear any coming. There was nobody nearby yet. It would have to be now. She let him get a few more steps ahead of her as she reached deep in her purse.

He suddenly stopped and turned to look back at her. He said, "What are you looking for?"

She smiled brightly at him. "My camera. I want to take a couple of pictures so I can compare it to some other places."

He turned away and walked on.

Nancy Mills gripped the pistol and lifted it out, then held it tight against her thigh as she walked to catch up with him. She took one last look over her shoulder and listened for the sound of a car on the road. Then she raised the gun and fired through the back of Bill Thayer's skull.

His head bobbed forward in a sudden nod and his body followed it, toppling straight onto the ground. She squatted beside him to take his wallet out of his back pocket, then pushed him over on his back so she could reach his car keys in front.

She stood and walked calmly to the car, started it, and drove back the way she and Thayer had come, north on Topanga Canyon. She parked his car in the mall parking lot, wiped the steering wheel and door handles clean with one of the alcohol-soaked antibacterial wipes she carried in her purse, then picked up the bag containing her bath salts and walked away.

Nancy thought about the morning's events as she headed back toward her apartment. She had not wanted to harm Bill Thayer, but he had made it impossible not to. He'd had no right to keep pestering her. What could he possibly have been thinking?

Of course, she knew what he had been thinking. When he had seen the woman he thought of as Tanya Starling, it had probably made him feel excited. He already knew her slightly. She was a small business owner, and he was the manager of her bank. Not only could she be sure he was respectable, but he was powerful. He could raise her credit limit and get her loans approved. He could also get in her way, make things difficult for her. He was a shy, quiet man who had made so little impression on her the first time she'd met him that she had not recognized his face when it was three feet from hers this morning. But he had exercised his power over her, following her from the store, making her talk to him, keeping her from leaving, then making her agree to go somewhere with him. She'd had to get rid of him.

When Nancy reached home, she put on a pair of the rubber gloves she wore to do the dishes and sat at her kitchen table. She took Bill Thayer's wallet from her purse and examined it. The credit cards were too risky to keep, but he had also been carrying almost a thousand dollars in cash when she had killed him.

A lot of people carried extra cash when they were traveling, but this was better than she had expected. Nancy took the money, wrapped the wallet in a paper towel to disguise its shape, and put it in an opaque trash bag.

Somewhere in the back of her mind was a feeling, almost a physical sensation that had not yet developed into a coherent thought—something pleasant, even titillating.

Her need to end the fear had been like an ache. When she had at last been able to pull out the pistol and blow a round through Thayer's head, there had been a feeling of release. When she had left his rental car in the plaza parking lot and walked off with her Bloomingdale's bag, she had felt herself smiling.

Nancy had not allowed herself to acknowledge it yet, but she had been missing the excitement that she took from men. She had missed the anticipation of watching and waiting for the right one, and then the care and calculation of drawing him to her. She had missed the thrill of the next phase, the charged, anxious period of flirtation and speculation, and then the longer game of divulging and concealing, withholding and succumbing. She had especially missed the sweet, warm, lazy time after that, when she was secure in the man's love, soaking in the attention and the luxury.

Now she was beginning to notice the puzzling fact that she liked the bad parts too. When Dennis had begun to disappoint her, the resentment and anger had made her feel powerful and dangerous and clean—not like a victim, but like a judge and avenger. The building anger had made her feel energetic and purposeful. The single shot had been the best possible climax to the relationship.

She had liked the killing. The breakup with David Larson had shown her that perfectly. When David had betrayed her, she had enjoyed the process of getting angry and rejecting him and punishing him. Seeing his devastation had given her the chance to know how beautiful and desirable she could be. But it wasn't enough. What was missing was that she had not gotten to kill him.

She took the bag with the wallet out with her garbage late that night and stuck it in the bottom of the dumpster behind an apartment building three blocks from hers. Her gun stayed in her purse. It would be foolish to get rid of her gun just when she had started to enjoy it.

11

"Hello? Mrs. Halloran?"

Eve Halloran wasn't quite sure, but the young female voice made her think it just might be. "Yes?"

"This is Tanya Starling calling. I'm very sorry to bother you, but I wondered whether anyone had tried to get in touch with me since I left, or asked about me. There might have been a man named David?"

"No, dear," said Mrs. Halloran. She spoke with barely suppressed excitement. "I haven't heard from anyone like that. But a couple of days ago I did have a visit from a pair of police officers." She stopped, waiting for a reaction.

"Police? Why? What did they want?"

Eve Halloran relished the suspense, loved holding back and tantalizing, but she could hardly withhold this information. It was too dramatic, too delicious. "There were two of them, a man and a woman. They came all the way from Portland, Oregon. They said—I don't know how to break this to you—that a friend of yours has been the victim of a crime. It sounded as though he's been murdered."

"Who?"

"I think they said Dennis Poole."

"Oh, my God. Dennis Poole?"

"That's right." Now Eve was feeling better. That last exclamation had carried the sort of emotion that she had been hoping for. What could that man Dennis Poole have been except Tanya's lover? "I'm very, very sorry, honey. I hated to tell you this way, but there just wasn't any other way."

"I can't believe it. How could he have been murdered? He was such a sweet man. He had no enemies. Was it some kind of robbery?" There were tears in her voice. Eve Halloran could hear the tension in the throat, the higher voice.

"They didn't say, but I don't think that was it," said Eve Halloran. She allowed herself to give in to an ungenerous impulse. "That was what they wanted to talk with you about." She felt a tiny bit of guilt about holding back the next part of what they'd said, but she was still too curious. "They seemed to think you might know something about what happened. They said you had left town just about the time when he was killed."

"You mean they think I had something to do with Dennis's death?"

There. That was said just as Eve Halloran had imagined it. She didn't mind that she had to say the next part now. "Oh, no, dear. They said you were not a suspect. They definitely said that. I didn't mean to imply anything of the kind. Stupid me. I should have said that right away, first thing."

"I'm just overwhelmed. It never seems as though something like this can happen to anybody you know."

Eve Halloran said eagerly, "Were you very close?"

"I just can't believe it."

That answer was unsatisfactory. In fact, it had been an evasion. "Was he your boyfriend?"

"No."

Mrs. Halloran waited, but there was no more to the sentence. "Well, it's very sad. I'm sorry." Eve Halloran was growing tired of this conversation. She had built an expectation of a flood of intimate details, but she had been repeatedly disappointed.

Tanya said, "Did the police say how I was supposed to get in touch with them? Did they leave a number or anything?"

"I'll see if I can find it." Her voice was glum. This had been a disappointing conversation, and the fact that there was no further excuse to prolong it made her feel even more frustrated. She had taped the card to the wall right above the

phone, but she stood leaning against the kitchen sink with
her arms folded for thirty seconds. Let Tanya wait. She had
become awfully demanding for a former tenant, calling up at
night and expecting Eve to be her message board. After a
time she sauntered back to the telephone. "Tanya? Still there?"

"Yes."

"Have a pencil?"

"Yes."

"The name is Detective Sergeant Catherine Hobbes. She's
on the homicide squad." She added that part with a tinge of
malice. She read off the various telephone numbers and the
address of the police station, slowly and distinctly, to prolong
the time of feeling important while Tanya silently copied
down every word, probably with her hands shaking. When
she had read everything on the card she said, "Got all that?"

"Yes, thanks. I'll give her a call."

Eve said, "Have you thought about hiring a lawyer?"

"No. I just heard about this."

"Well, from what I hear, the time to think about lawyers
isn't after you've talked to the police, it's before." She was
spiteful now.

"I'll think about it."

"You do that."

"Thanks, Mrs. Halloran."

"You're welcome." She was about to add a little jab about
how she was going to tell the police that she had talked to
her, but she realized that the line was dead.

Nancy Mills stood beside the row of telephones in Topanga
Plaza, gazing at the food court. She looked down at the little
spiral notebook she had bought at the stationery store to prepare for this call, and reread the phone numbers of the cop
who was after her. The name disturbed her: she had never expected that it would be a woman.

12

Catherine Hobbes sat in the homicide office. She had finished a long list of telephone calls that had not made her happy. Tanya Starling was turning out to be difficult to find. There was nothing helpful in her past—no way to find her family or her history. The apartment she had occupied in Chicago seemed to be an insuperable barrier: nothing was visible on the far side of it. A man named Carl Nelson had rented the apartment in his own name nine years ago. Tanya Starling had not been mentioned in the lease. At some point during those years she had moved in, and at some point Nelson had moved out, leaving the place to her. His accountants had continued to pay the rent until April, when she had moved out.

But it was as though she had come into existence in that apartment. Running a criminal records check on her name yielded nothing at all. She'd had an Illinois driver's license, and it had given the apartment as her address. None of the Starlings that Catherine Hobbes had found listed in Illinois had ever heard of Tanya.

Hobbes looked up and saw Joe Pitt appear in the doorway. She stood up and said, "Come on, Joe. I'll buy you a cup of coffee."

"Really?" he said.

"Really."

"I'm flattered."

She brushed past him and walked to the break room, then

put a dollar in the machine and watched the paper cup rattle into place, and the stream of hot black liquid fill it. She handed it to him, then bought one for herself. She went across the hall to the conference room, looked inside, then held the door open. "Let's talk."

He went in after her. "You have something new?"

She sat on the table, sipped her coffee. "Yes. I wanted to tell you alone. It's been mostly a positive experience having you come up here to cooperate in the investigation. You've been very helpful, and I've tried to learn what I could from your experience."

"But?"

"But. It's time to cut you loose."

"It is?"

"Yes. You've helped me to clarify a whole part of this case in my mind, and saved me quite a bit of time. I'm now convinced that this didn't have anything to do with Hugo Poole. At the same time, having a person acting as Hugo Poole's representative in this investigation isn't going to help us when we have to go into court for a conviction. So you've got to go."

"I understand."

"You don't sound surprised."

"I'm not. Does Mike know about this yet?"

"Mike Farber? My captain?"

"Yes."

"I told him this morning that this was what I was going to do."

"And he agreed?"

"He agreed that it was my case, and that I had the right to make the decision. I made it, not Mike Farber."

"Then I guess I'll try to stop and say good-bye to him before I leave. I wish you the best of luck on the case, and after watching you work, I have confidence that you'll handle it." He held out his hand and she shook it. He smiled. "See you," he said, and he walked out the door and closed it.

Catherine remained perched on the table for a full minute, sipping her coffee and thinking. She knew that this decision had been inevitable and right, and she was relieved that it had gone so smoothly. She was also just a bit regretful, and she wasn't sure why.

She had to admit that was not exactly true. During the investigation she had begun to forget the imposition that Joe Pitt represented, and become used to having someone she could talk to about the case—not just some other cop who had a dozen cases of his own to think about, or a superior who had administrative details clogging his mind. When she had talked to Pitt she could talk in shorthand, and he knew exactly what she meant. She could test her ideas on him, and expect him to have ideas of his own.

Catherine tried to analyze her feelings. When Mike Farber had first called her in to tell her he had assigned her to work on a murder with Joe Pitt, she had felt insulted. If her captain thought she was so incompetent and inexperienced that she needed help from some out-of-town retiree, then she should get out of homicide. A moment later, when she had heard what a hotshot Joe Pitt was, she had wondered how it could be anything but an insult to her sex. Would Mike Farber have expected one of the men to serve as tour guide to a visiting potentate? No, it had to be the woman, the pretty face to please the visitor, and because the visitor was so great, all the hostess really needed to be was pretty. Joe Pitt would solve the case.

She had tested Joe Pitt—maybe tormented him a bit—and found that he wasn't so bad. She had come to feel comfortable with him. Why was she putting it like that? She had liked him, felt attracted to him. Maybe that was the worst thing about him. She couldn't afford to have him around any longer.

She jumped down, took her coffee to the break room, and poured it down the sink, then walked back to her desk in the homicide office.

Catherine's telephone rang. Maybe this was it. Maybe this was Tanya Starling. "Homicide. Hobbes."

"Hey, Hobbes. This is Doug Crowley in San Francisco. Has Tanya Starling called in yet?"

"Not yet." Hobbes had been near her desk almost the whole shift. "Mrs. Halloran said that Tanya promised she would call, but she doesn't seem to be in a hurry to do it."

"Well, I have something else that might be useful. The DMV has a hit on the roommate, Rachel Sturbridge."

"What is it?" asked Hobbes. She sat at the edge of her chair and pulled her yellow pad toward her.

"It's her car. She's sold her car."

"Her too? They both sold their cars? When and where did she sell it?"

"Los Angeles, about two weeks ago. The new owner just got around to registering it with the DMV. It was already registered in California, so she didn't think there was any hurry—she wouldn't get pulled over or anything. Her name is Wanda Achison, and she lives in a suburb called Westlake Village."

"Has anyone talked with her yet?"

"As soon as we got this information I gave her a call. She sounded a little upset, because she was afraid it was stolen and we were going to take it away from her. She calmed down after a minute, though."

"Did she buy it from Rachel personally? No intermediaries or dealers involved?"

"Yes. Rachel advertised it in a local swap sheet, Miss Achison called the number, and Rachel drove it to her house to let her check it out. Miss Achison said Rachel was in her late twenties, long dark hair, five-five, one fifteen to one twenty. Rachel told her she was selling the car to pay off a credit card debt."

"That wouldn't be too unusual among people trying to start a business. Did she still have her address and phone?"

"No, but the paper did. It was a motel, and they don't have a record of Rachel Sturbridge staying there. I figured Tanya might have been the one who had signed the register, but they didn't have her down either. There must be a third person."

"Maybe," said Catherine. "Can you give me Wanda Achison's address and phone number, please?"

He read the information, and she copied it. "Thanks, Detective Crowley."

"No problem." He sighed. "Are you and Joe going down there to do an interview?"

"Joe isn't involved in the investigation anymore."

"He isn't? May I ask why?"

"Yes. He's been very cooperative, provided some information that eliminated some dead ends for us. Obviously he doesn't need a testimonial from me. But I don't think a civilian belongs in a homicide investigation."

"I've always liked Joe, and I was glad to see him," he said. "But I don't either."

"Thanks for all of your help," she said.

"Don't mention it. And let me know if you need anything else from us in San Francisco."

"I will."

She hung up the telephone, then picked up the photograph of Tanya Starling that had been made from the surveillance tape. There she was, caught from the side, entering Dennis Poole's hotel room. Catherine Hobbes stared at the face. Tanya was just a small-boned woman who appeared to be in her late twenties, her expression untroubled. The blond hair that had obscured the features for most of the tape happened to have swung to the other side of the face for this instant, so all of the features were visible. The outlines were just vague enough to frustrate the viewer's eye as it tried to focus perfectly on an image that could never be any clearer. The bright, shiny hair drew the mind's attention more than the face did.

Catherine opened the file and scanned the lists of other agencies that had been cooperating in this case. She found the telephone number she wanted, then called the Illinois Department of Motor Vehicles to make her formal request for the driver's license photograph of Tanya Starling. She had waited long enough for Tanya to turn up or respond to her inquiries. It was time to go after her.

Catherine thought for a moment. Crowley had said that Rachel Sturbridge's car had been registered in California, so that meant the driver almost certainly was too. She dialed the number of the California DMV and requested the license photograph of Rachel Sturbridge.

13

Nancy Mills sat in her small apartment, staring out the window. It was eight-thirty, the time of each evening that made her want to open the door and go. She could see the sky through the west window. It was taking on that beautiful shading, the lower edge of it red, then above that a blue that began as only a little bit darker than the daylight sky, but as the eye looked higher, the sky darkened into an indigo canopy, with a few stars beginning to show.

She could almost hear her mother's voice calling. This was the time of evening when she always had to come in from play, and she used to come home dirty, the dust sometimes held to her little bare legs by dried sweat. She hated having to come home when the air was full of promise and expectation. Big, important things were about to happen. She knew that they were good things, marvels and pleasures that the grown-ups kept all to themselves.

She would usually let the sky get too dark before she made it home, so she would have to come up the street running. She remembered the sound and feel as, breathing hard, she made her sneaker pound on the bottom step of the front porch, and she pushed through the screen door into the living room.

Her mother and the latest boyfriend would already be in the bedroom getting ready. Her mother's skin would be pink and moist from the shower, the tight straps of her bra making depressions in the fat on her back. She would dance to tug the panty hose up over her hips. If the girl came in right at dark, her mother would be in a cheerful mood, the morning's hangover and remorse erased by the afternoon's nap, and her mind set on the adult evening that was coming.

The bathroom would be steamy. She remembered the boyfriend picking up the hand towel from the sink to wipe off the mirror so he could see to slide the razor along his bristly jowl, leaving a swath in the white shaving cream, pink and irritated but hairless, his mouth pursed and squeezed to one side to present a smooth, tight stretch of skin to the safety razor. She thought of it as a joke name for something that left small bright cuts on his chin so he had to stick bits of white toilet paper there, and let the red blood hold it in place.

It was a summer memory tonight because of the summer sky outside. The man in the memory changed, because there were so many of them. They were both a series and a progression, the nicer, younger ones all part of earlier memories, and the older ones coming later, when her mother's body began to thicken and her skin to loosen and wrinkle. Each man was the same in every way that mattered—the drinking and the yelling—but they differed in small ways, like how much hair they had or what color it was, or their names.

The boyfriend would get ready, and be standing around getting irritable before her mother would really begin. She would go to the other bedroom she had converted into a closet in her panty hose and bra, and then begin to try on each of her dresses in front of a big mirror with a frame that was supposed to hang on a wall, but was propped against a chair at an angle.

Each night the dressing would proceed all the way to its end several times. She would choose a dress, put it on, then go into the bathroom to apply her makeup and brush her hair, and suddenly discover some invisible flaw in the way the outfit made her look or feel, and take it off again. The earrings, necklace, and shoes were specific to the outfit, so they had to go too. Then she would put on another dress and the same thing would happen. Eventually, she would announce she was ready and would emerge, suddenly impatient to go, as though someone else had delayed her.

The little girl would look at her mother in amazement. Already it was clear that they were not going to look alike. Her mother was short, with big blue eyes and skin like cream. The girl was tall and bony, with pale skin and stringy hair. Her mother would look at her on her way out the door as a kind of afterthought.

"Lock the door after us," she would say. "Don't open it for anybody."

Her mother and the boyfriend would go out and stand on the porch until the mother heard the click, and then they would get into the car. Usually they would be gone until just before dawn. The girl would sit alone in the house, feeling the loss as the sky darkened and deepened.

Often she heard voices outside her house in the calm night air as people passed by. Sometimes they sounded as though they were young, even her age. She was forced to stay in, lying on her bed in the dark, listening, while they were out there doing things and knowing things that she could not.

She would sometimes get up and go into her mother's room to look at the pageant trophies she had won. Her mother kept them in her own room, where the girl wouldn't break them or touch them and make them corrode. She called them "my trophies," just as an owner of a show dog would.

Nancy Mills had been inside this apartment every night for weeks. She'd had one problem turn up from San Francisco, but it had just been one of those rare coincidences that Bill Thayer had been here visiting his parents and seen her. The fact that it had happened once would seem to prove that it couldn't happen a second time. It was just too unlikely. Besides, this was night. There were fewer people out, and the darkness would help protect her from being recognized. As she was pacing back and forth thinking about it, Nancy Mills had picked up her purse. She noticed it, gave herself permission, and walked to the door. She went out and closed the door behind her.

She didn't know where she was going, and it didn't matter. She had been staying out of sight since she had arrived, never going out after dark, going nowhere even in daylight but to the plaza, and she had not left this apartment for several days. She felt as though a rope had been tightened around her chest so she could barely breathe. As soon as she was on the street again, the rope seemed to loosen. The warm night air filled her lungs.

She walked to the plaza, used a pay phone to call a taxi, and waited for it outside Macy's. She said she wanted a ride to La Cienega Boulevard in Hollywood. When the dispatcher asked for the actual building number, she didn't know. When the dispatcher asked for the name of the nearest cross street, she didn't know that either, so she said Sunset. He said a yellow cab would arrive in about fifteen minutes. Nancy looked around her and began to feel bored and awkward standing alone in front of the store, so she reached into her purse and found the notebook where she had written the policewoman's phone numbers.

She carefully dialed the home number and waited, her eyes closed to help her concentrate.

"Hello?"

"Uh, hello," she said. "I'm looking for Catherine Hobbes?"

"This is Catherine Hobbes." The voice was high and feminine. It sounded like a teacher. Nancy wasn't sure what she had expected, but this wasn't it.

"Hi. My name is Tanya Starling. Mrs. Halloran told me that you had come by the apartment in San Francisco to speak to me, but Rachel and I had already moved away."

"Yes," said Hobbes. Her voice was tentative, almost preoccupied. Tanya knew that she was probably reaching to turn on a tape recorder or even pressing some button to tell somebody to trace the call. Nancy would have to do this quickly. Hobbes said, "I have been trying to reach you. We need to ask you some questions. Mrs. Halloran didn't have a forwarding address for you. Where are you living now?"

"I'm still on the road. I stopped for the night, checked into a motel, and started to clean out my purse. I found the piece of paper where I'd written your number, and realized I should call you."

"Then I need to have the exact location where you are right now."

"I'm in Southern California, off the freeway in a small motel. I don't know the exact address. I'm leaving for New York tomorrow, but I don't know where I'll be staying yet."

"Please listen carefully. I want you to go to the nearest police station. Give the officer in charge my number. I'll fly there to talk with you."

"You know, that's not possible tonight. Why don't you just ask me your questions right now? I mean, my memory isn't going to get any better staying up all night waiting for you."

"I'm trying to help you, Tanya. But you have to cooperate, and you have to tell me the truth."

"I called you, remember?"

"I know that you're afraid. It's not a bad thing to be right now. You had a relationship with Dennis Poole, and then he was murdered."

"Are you implying that I had something to do with that?"

"I don't know any such thing. Someone killed him, and they could be after you too. I want to hear your side of the story. I want to know anything you can tell me about Dennis Poole. I want to know why you decided to leave Portland right after it happened."

"This is stupid. I'm just trying to be polite, return your call, straighten this out, and get past it. Rachel and I had planned for a year to go to San Francisco and start a business together. I wasn't running. I didn't know anything had even happened to Dennis until I talked to Mrs. Halloran. She was the one who told me."

"I need to get through to you, Tanya. You and Rachel are both wanted for questioning in a murder investigation. You don't seem to be grasping the seriousness of that."

"Well, sure I am," said Tanya. "That's why I called, so you could cross my name off your list and go on to somebody who knows something."

"I don't think you're understanding me. Even if you are telling the truth and you're not withholding any information about the death of Dennis Poole, you could still be charged with fleeing to avoid prosecution, obstruction of justice, and about fifteen other things. They're all serious, and they all involve jail time. I can make sure that those things don't happen, if you will just do as I ask."

"I will, if you'll ask for something I can do. I'm a thousand miles away from you, heading in the other direction, with very little money. I can't just leave everything I own in my car and park it in a lot someplace while I sit in a police station."

"Listen carefully. Wherever you are, you're on a telephone. Just ask the operator to connect you with the local police. Tell the police you've spoken with me about going in for questioning in the Dennis Poole case. They can find where you are, bring you in, and keep your car and belongings safe. Give them the piece of paper with my number on it, and they'll call me. I'll handle everything from there. All right?"

"This isn't a reasonable thing to ask. You're trying to get me put in jail."

"I'm trying to get you into a police station to talk to you. If you're running because somebody else killed Dennis Poole and you're afraid, the police will protect you. I'll make sure they do. If you're running because you're afraid the police will hurt you, then you can stop worrying about that too. It's a lot less scary when you go in voluntarily. I'll ask them not to put you in a cell."

"I told you. I'm not running. I'm just moving, trying to get on with my life."

"This is a detour you're going to have to take sooner or later."

Nancy paused, unable to think of what to say. Finally, she said, "I . . . I really don't think I should do that without a lawyer."

"That's fine. If you'd like, you can have one before you answer any questions at all. They'll get you one. But you've got to do this, Tanya."

"Let me think about it."

"How long?"

"I don't know."

"Tanya, the police are looking for you, not just here but all over. Right now nobody knows why you're not making yourself available, so they have to assume that you're dangerous. If you come in on your own, no harm will come to you. If you don't, then it's hard to predict what might happen. Go find a lawyer, and ask him to come with you when you turn yourself in. Tanya?"

Tanya didn't answer.

"Tanya? Please."

Tanya thought about how much better it was to be Nancy Mills, out on a summer night in Southern California. She was too restless to stay on the line. She lifted the telephone to its cradle and pressed it down. The soft, warm breeze blew across the ear where she had held the telephone, soothing it. She was free, and she wasn't going to risk that. She saw the cab prowling along toward the front of the building, so she waved her hand and trotted to it.

She got in, rolled her window halfway down, and looked greedily out at the buildings and the people on the streets all the way to Sunset.

When the driver let her off on Sunset and La Cienega she began to walk. She passed the big faux-ramshackle structure of the House of Blues, then several restaurants. She wasn't in the mood to go into a formal restaurant and sit in the middle of a lot of tables with men and women on dates. What she needed was a hotel bar. She knew there were a couple of hotels along the Strip that had famous nightclubs, so she decided to find them.

She walked along the sidewalk beneath huge lighted billboards of the beautiful people in movies. Paintings of giant women covered the brick sides of tall office buildings.

The dry air was electrically charged, as though it would soon reach some peak voltage and emit sparks. The cars were nose-to-tail on Sunset, moving ahead in small surges. She could feel the eyes on her, not one man that she could see but many at once that she knew were there behind the glare of headlights or beyond dark tinted windows. She knew that when one of them looked, he was evaluating, trying to see if she was Someone, or even the one they had been searching for. The once-over lasted only for the time it took for her image to move from the windshield to the rearview mirror, but then the man in the next car was already looking at her.

Nancy's anticipation grew until she reached the Standard Hotel. It was low—only three stories. She stepped in the front entrance, trying to see everything but also trying to look as though she knew where she was going. She saw two security men—this was Sunset Boulevard, and what stepped in off the street could be literally anything—and smiled at them as she moved past the front desk. There was a girl with a pretty white face and gleaming straight black hair standing there to check people in, and behind her head was a greenish glass panel like a huge aquarium, where another girl who was naked napped on a clear inflated mattress, so that she appeared to be floating there.

This was the kind of place she had imagined. It was a sign of her magic that she had made it here. While she was still in her stuffy little apartment off Topanga Canyon she had only conceived a sense of how she wanted to feel, and what sort of place would make her feel that way, then moved toward it. She kept going until she found herself in the rooftop bar.

On the way to the ladies' room, Nancy studied the other women she could see standing near the long curved bar and sitting at the tables. They all seemed young, thin, and attractive. A few of them wore skirts or pantsuits, but most of them wore tight jeans and tank tops. Nancy felt reassured. At the moment when the urge had taken her she had been wearing a good pair of pants she had bought in Aspen and a Juicy Couture velour jacket over a little T-shirt she had picked up in San Francisco, so she was all right.

She studied her reflection in the mirror, brushed her hair, and wiped off her makeup. She had been wearing daytime shades, so she put on thicker eyeshadow, eyeliner, and mascara, darkened her lips as she listened to the chatter in the ladies' room. She could tell that these were not women staying at the hotel but local women who came here for the social scene. That was fine—so had she.

Nancy needed to set herself apart somehow, and be in a place where she didn't have to compete for attention with all of these women. She went to the bar and waited for a couple of orders to be filled so she could survey the room to evaluate the men and let them see her, then ordered her martini. When she had it, she took it outside, onto the big open stretch of blue Astroturf surrounding the pool.

She sat on one of the white lounge chairs and gazed down the slope at the city, the billions of tiny distinct lights shining upward from the streets and buildings to make the air above the city glow.

The first man to follow her out had long, skinny limbs covered in an off-white suit and a black T-shirt. He had glasses with thick black frames, and hair that had receded into a widow's peak. She glanced up at him and sipped her drink.

"Aren't you the girl from behind the front desk?"

"No," said Nancy. "She's still there. Go check."

"I mean the one who pretends to be asleep. The naked one."

"I know you do," said Nancy.

"The girl from last night looked just like you. She's beautiful, and so are you." He paused for a moment, studied her, and then said, "You and I aren't going to be friends, are we?"

"Nope. Thanks for the compliment, though."

"You're welcome. Good night," he said. He turned and walked back into the bar.

After ten more minutes, another man came out. He walked to the pool, bent over and touched his hand to the water to test the temperature, then straightened, turned, and seemed to notice her. He was dark-skinned, with wavy black hair, and she imagined him to be Brazilian. When he spoke, the impression was destroyed. "Oh," he said. "I didn't see you there." He had an accent from New York, maybe New Jersey. "Have you been in the pool yet?"

"No," she said. She made a quick decision. "I just came out here to be alone."

"Me too. Would you like to be alone together?"

"No, I like to do it the usual way."

"Oh," he said. "Well, see you."

He walked back into the bar. This wasn't very promising, she decided, so she went back into the bar too. She moved to the wall, scanned the men in the room, and decided to choose one. He was standing a few feet to her right, looking over at her, when their eyes met. He was about thirty, with hair that must have been blond when he was a child but had turned brown later as hers had, and now lightened only when he had spent time in the sun. "Hello," she said. "Do I have spinach stuck on my teeth?"

He came closer. "Sorry if I was staring. What's the attraction out there?"

"It's really clear tonight. It's L.A., and you expect some smog."

"Yeah," he said. "Otherwise you feel like you're not getting your money's worth."

"They might have flown you to Bakersfield, and just told you it was L.A."

"There's smog there too. And when it clears, you're still in Bakersfield."

"I'll have to take your word for it. Or somebody's."

He took a step closer and leaned against the wall beside her. "Are you here on business?"

"Me?" she said. "No. I'm here for a cold martini."

"I can see you got one," he said. He lifted his drink toward her, a faint gesture to simulate clinking glasses. "Here's to it." He took a sip. "What I was trying to say was, you're a gorgeous person, and are you busy for the next few days doing work-related tasks all the time, or are you interested in meeting someone like me, getting married, and bearing my children?"

She made a show of appraising him, looking from his toes to his face and down again. Then she shrugged. "It depends. Where would I have to live?"

"We could live anywhere you want. Right now, I'm based in Miami. But it's negotiable."

"Based? What are you? A navy?"

"No. I just sell sound-imaging machines to doctors and hospitals, and that's where the office is. I'm Brian Corey."

"Pleased to meet you. I'm Marsha."

"No last name?"

"Corey. I'm going to be Marsha Corey, right?"

"True," said Brian. "Will you join me at a table, or do we have to keep our distance until after the wedding?"

"Now that we're engaged, you're welcome to sit with me, if you'd like."

They stepped to a small empty table nearby. He moved a chair so he could sit beside her and look out over the city. "I hate to descend to this kind of question, but where are you from?"

"I live here now."

"At this hotel?"

"No, this is just where my martinis live. I recently moved to Los Angeles. I used to live in Chicago."

"Why did you move here?"

"Because I was cold. There are a lot of songs about Chicago. But is there one that says you'll freeze your ass off? No."

"Oh, I thought you might have come here to be an actress."

"You mean you think I might be stupid."

"I can only hope. But you are beautiful, and you did move to Los Angeles, so it was a possibility."

"Are you disappointed that I'm not an actress?"

"No. I don't think that kind of career would leave enough time for me and the children."

"Very smart of you to think ahead."

"Ah, yes. Thinking ahead. Have you got plans for dinner yet?"

"Gee, we're barely engaged, and already you want me to cook."

"No, I was going to take you to dinner, if you're willing."

"After the kids and moving to Miami, dinner seems pretty easy. I'm willing."

"We can drive out to La Parapluie, which is in Beverly Hills, where I happen to have a reservation for dinner in about a half hour. Or we can have another drink first, and take our chances that by the time we get there it will be so late that we won't need a reservation."

"A quandary. My drink is dead, but since you mentioned dinner, I'm beginning to get hungry."

"Let's try to have it all. We'll go down to La Parapluie, and order drinks at dinner."

"Whatever you say, dear."

Brian Corey had rented a car to make his sales calls, and the valet parking attendant brought it. He was an experienced driver who knew enough to get off Sunset right away, and they were in La Parapluie within ten minutes. It was a large, noisy room with lots of white walls and linen and some bright mediocre minimalist paintings, but the waiter brought Nancy a martini with a tiny iced carafe of vodka on the side, so she forgave the restaurant its decor.

While they were sipping their drinks, Brian said, "I've been thinking about this since I met you, so I've got to say it: you really are beautiful."

"Thank you. I was rather pleased when I got you into the light, myself. I guess it's a marriage made in heaven. What do you like on this menu?"

"I've only been here one time, but I had the swordfish, and it was good."

"I'll try it, then."

"Anything you'd like. For tonight, you're the queen of my expense account."

"I'll have to tell you up front I'm not going to buy an ultra-sound machine."

"Then I hope you're willing to pretend to choke on a fish bone, so all the doctors in the place will rush to help, and I can deliver my pitch."

"Of course. If we want the children to go to Harvard, I'll have to do that every time we go out."

They ate dinner, and talked happy nonsense all through it. Nancy Mills was filled with manic energy. She felt that she should never have talked herself into believing that she had to stay out of sight.

After dinner they tried to move into the bar, but it was nearly midnight now, and the crowds of people in the restaurant had swelled. The knot of drinkers ordering at the bar was just the beginning of a line that stretched outward and made it an evening's labor to get another drink. Brian leaned close to her and said, "I've got a minibar in my room, and a better view than this. It's on the eighth floor of the Beverly Hilton."

She looked at him closely. "All right. Let's go check out your bar."

They drove to the Beverly Hilton and took the elevator up to his room. It was not the huge suite she had been hoping for, but it was a pleasant single room, and it had a balcony that was directly above the patio and a little to the left of the pool. He made her another martini while she leaned over the railing for a different view of the city.

She took her martini and sipped it. "Thanks, Brian. Considering the primitive conditions, that is not a bad drink."

"Thanks," he said. "I've found that I'm about as good a maker of third martinis as anybody."

"I guess you're right," she said. "It probably tastes like lighter fluid, and I don't know the difference. I guess I shouldn't drink so much." She walked past him into the room and set her drink on the desk.

The whole evening's adventure had been leading to this, hadn't it? She had sleepwalked her way here. She was with the right kind of man: she had chosen him. She stepped into him, snaking her arms around his body. He held her and kissed her gently. She remembered how much she liked this feeling.

His arms were thick and strong, and she could detect the definition of the muscles, but she could also feel his hands making soft, slow swirls on her back that made her feel small and sleek, like a cat. The nerves of her spine and shoulder blades shivered, waiting their turn to be touched, and she found herself moving to make him touch her there.

The kisses and caresses grew in intensity, building quickly with her impatience. She was excited by the rightness of whatever she thought to do tonight. Her impulses all seemed to be gratified instantly. Later she lay on the bed with the blankets tumbled in a heap at the foot, feeling the fresh night

air blowing in over her body, cooling and soothing her. She
stared at the ceiling, feeling her breathing slowing down and
becoming even again.

Brian was out on the balcony, leaning on the rail and cran-
ing his neck to look down at something. He still had no shirt,
but he had put on his pants in order to go out there. She studied him, gauged the attitude of his body. He was leaning on
his elbows, a picture of relaxation and ease. Minutes passed.
It was time now for him to come back in and lie down beside
her and say nice things to her, or at least put his arm around
her again, but he didn't. He didn't even turn and look at her,
to see how beautiful she looked lying on the white sheets, her
hair spread around her head in a halo. She began to be a little disappointed in him.

She gave him a reprieve. Was it possible that while she was
lying here sending him a signal, she was missing the signals
that he had been sending her? Maybe he wanted her to get up
and come out on the balcony with him.

Nancy slipped into the bathroom and snatched the thick
white hotel bathrobe from its hook behind the door. She tied
the belt at her waist and came out behind him. He didn't
seem to hear her coming. She put her arms around him and
pressed herself against his back, rocking slightly from side
to side. "That was really nice," she whispered.

He took a deep breath and let it out in a sigh. "Yes."

She felt her muscles tighten. "That's all? You don't want to
say something sweet to me?"

He turned, and that disengaged her arms from him. He
placed his hands on her shoulders and held her there while
he looked into her eyes, then kissed her forehead. "I loved
this evening. I think you're a really special person, and I feel
lucky to have met you."

"But?"

"I should have told you before. I have a girlfriend back in
Miami. She and I have been together for over two years."

Nancy shrugged, knowing it made her look good and that
the top of the bathrobe would open a bit wider. "I'm really
not that naive, Brian. I knew when I saw you that I wasn't the

first girl you'd ever met, and it's not like I thought that other girls wouldn't be interested in you."

"I really haven't been honest with you, or with her. I loved tonight, but I didn't really have the right to be with you. I was standing here thinking how unfair I've been."

She embraced him tightly. "I understand. This was just a onetime thing. It was only for tonight, and when it's over, that's it. But why ruin it? What if this turned out to be the last night of your life?"

"That's a funny way to look at it."

She smiled up at him, and she knew she was alluring. "It's the only way to look at it. If it was the end of your life, how would you want to have spent it—alone or with me, the way you are?"

"With you."

"Are you sure?"

"Yes. Absolutely."

"Then smile."

He gave her the smile she had asked for, and took her in his arms. They moved off the balcony and into the room. It was a moment before the bathrobe dropped to the floor and they were together on the bed again. This time there was something better than the eagerness and haste of the first. She imagined them to be a pair of lovers who had become old friends, and somehow had learned to enjoy each other without all the pain and hurt feelings and failed attempts to connect that people had when they were actively in love. She moved into a cycle of pure selfish wanting and receiving and appreciating and wanting. Then she lay motionless on the bed again.

Nancy waited until Brian got up and went out to the balcony again. Then she crawled to the side of the bed and swung her legs to put her feet on the floor near her pile of clothes. She dressed silently and efficiently.

She moved closer to the balcony, and she could see past him to the city below. It was the darkest, quietest time. The lightbulbs that were ever going to be switched off were off now. The fog had slid in from the Pacific, and dimmed even the streetlamps and traffic signals.

She took her first step on the concrete surface of the balcony, then the second, each quicker. If he heard her, he expected her to come up from behind and put her arms around him, just as she had done before. He did not move. He was still leaning forward, his arms crossed and his elbows on the railing.

Nancy went low, clamped her arms tightly around his knees, her legs already straightening to lift him up over the railing. Brian's head and upper torso had already been past the railing and leaning before she'd arrived, and he began toppling over the edge before he had any notion of what was happening. His arms started flailing now that there was nothing but air for him to grasp, and he half-twisted to try to face her, but his sudden movement only helped to propel him over. In an instant he was free of restraint, falling. As he went he said something that sounded like "Unh?" Nancy stopped herself against the railing and watched him accelerating toward the earth.

It took a long time for him to fall eight floors. She watched until he hit the concrete walkway beside the building, bounced upward a foot or two, and then lay still. She could already see that there was a splash of blood where he lay, but she had no more time to look. She snatched his wallet, then wiped a towel over the glass she had used and the doorknobs and faucet handles, and quietly closed the door behind her.

Nancy knew without having to think about it that it would be best not to be in an elevator, so she stepped into the nearest stairwell. She took the stairs all the way down to the bottom, moving as quickly as she could. The door was locked where it met the parking garage, so she had to go up one flight, come out on the lobby level, and go outside. She avoided the parking attendant, hurried around the building to the entrance to the lot, went down and found Brian's rental car with the key under the visor. She got in, started it, and drove up the ramp onto the street.

She turned to the east and then north, and drove as far as a public parking lot on Hollywood Way near the Burbank airport. She parked the car, then walked to the airport. She waited two hours until the first flights of the morning arrived at seven, stepped out of the terminal in the middle of a group of arriving passengers, and waited her turn for a taxi.

14

Catherine Hobbes placed the two photographs together on her desk, and looked from one to the other. Then she picked up the telephone and dialed the captain's office. "Mike, this is Hobbes. I've got something I think you should see."

She released the telephone and walked down the hall to the last office. She opened the door, then walked to the big desk where Captain Mike Farber, chief of homicide, waited for her. She reached across the desk and set the driver's license photograph of the young blond woman in front of him. "This is the Illinois DMV's latest license picture of Tanya Starling. It was taken less than a year ago." She set the second photograph directly below it. "This is the picture the California DMV sent us from the driver's license issued to Rachel Sturbridge. It was taken a month ago."

Mike Farber was a big, broad man about fifty-five years old, with bristly gray hair. He leaned down for a moment to study the photographs, then looked up at Catherine Hobbes. "Looks like you're not looking for an innocent witness anymore. What do you want to do about her?"

"I think it's time to get a new notice made up and sent out to other agencies," she said.

"We'll want to get the D.A.'s office in on this right away.

I'll handle that. We can get a warrant on the false ID at least, and possibly intent to flee. That way we can get her held wherever she turns up."

"She has turned up, in a way," said Catherine. "She wouldn't tell me where she was calling from, just Southern California. The phone company says it was a pay telephone somewhere in the 818 area code. That's the northwest part of Los Angeles. It's where Rachel Sturbridge's car was sold. I'd like to go down there to see if I can pick up her trail."

He studied her for a moment, then nodded. "Hand off the cases you have and go get her, Cath."

It took Catherine Hobbes two hours to clear her desk of the cases she had been working on by giving them to the other detectives, and to prepare to make another trip out of Portland. The first plane to Los Angeles she could get left early that evening.

On the plane she kept working her way through the telephone conversation she'd had with Tanya Starling. She had sounded very young, and maybe a little bit slow. Catherine had spent much of the time trying to persuade her that being wanted for questioning in a murder case was a serious matter, not something that she could ignore. She had worried about Tanya, because it might take a certain amount of common sense for a person like her—a potential suspect who appeared to have fled—even to get arrested safely.

But as soon as Catherine had looked at the two photographs on the two driver's licenses, she had begun to get a different feeling about Tanya. Innocent bystanders and slow learners with nothing to hide didn't turn up with two driver's licenses in different names.

As the plane came closer to Los Angeles, Catherine couldn't help remembering that Los Angeles was where Hugo Poole and Joe Pitt lived. She kept catching herself constructing scenes in which she would call Joe Pitt to let him know what was happening. He would offer to help her get around the unfamiliar city, and maybe to help her get the best cooperation from the local police. Every time she caught herself thinking about calling him, she shook her head and cut the vision short. She knew that she had only been imag-

ining these things because she had somehow allowed herself
to think about him in a romantic way. She could recognize
the idea of calling him for what it was—not a rational plan of
action but the foundation for a fantasy.

Joe Pitt had everything wrong with him. He was too old
for her, and he was a gambler. He was in his forties but had
never been married, and he talked to every woman as though
he had already been to bed with her. He was also a drinker.
He was a jovial companion, the sort of guy everybody loved
to have a couple of drinks with after work. When he had offered, she had always said no.

It made her feel a hot wave of humiliation to think of it
now. She had managed to convince him that she was too
prissy and rigid to have a drink with him. What Joe Pitt knew
was the warm, easy face of alcohol, the evening gatherings
with friendly people when he ordered a round and everybody
went home feeling relaxed and happy. But Catherine Hobbes
had a special knowledge about drinking.

When Catherine had been in college in California, she
had known the pleasant side of drinking too. She'd always
worked hard all week on her studies, and on weekends she
had gone out with her friends to parties where for a pretty
girl the price of a drink was holding out her hand to accept it.
She had been funnier and more fluent when she talked, sex-
ier and more uninhibited when she danced. She had felt that
way, at least. But near the end of her junior year, she had noticed things that had scared her. She had awakened some
mornings and spent an hour lying in bed waiting for the sick
headache to fade and trying to remember what she had done
the night before. She could retrace the stages of her night,
but more and more often there were periods that were simply
blank.

The problem had gone away. She had not been cured, only
distracted. One night, just after she'd accepted her first drink
at a party, Kevin Dalton appeared and began to talk to her.
She did not have another drink that evening, and beginning
the day after that, she and Kevin became inseparable. During
her senior year she didn't have any free weekends to go to
bars or parties with her girlfriends because she was with

Kevin. They were married the summer after graduation and bought a condominium in Palo Alto. She did not make a decision about drinking. She simply forgot to drink.

Five years later, after the marriage had detonated and blown apart, she remembered to drink. The hard side of drinking came on her gradually. She began to go out after work with some of the other young brokers each evening. They all worked long days that began at five A.M., when the New York markets opened. They all lived in the same atmosphere of controlled panic, each of them paid on commission and all of them doomed to be fired the first time their sales figures fell enough to get the managers' attention. They drank and joked together for a few hours, then went home feeling a little better.

On most evenings, she was one of three women in a group that was overwhelmingly male. She somehow found herself more comfortable talking with the men than the women, and soon she was drinking with them glass for glass, listening to their jokes and their complaints, and making a few of her own. Early in the evening the other two women would go home, and then the party would be only Catherine and the men. Often, after she was home alone in the empty silence of the condominium where she and Kevin had once lived together, she would pour herself one last drink of whiskey to put herself to sleep.

One night she stayed late until the group dwindled down to Catherine and a friend named Nick. She let him take her home, and then she slept with him. Catherine fended off feeling ashamed by telling herself that the whole event had been good-natured—something that had happened between close friends—but they both felt awkward seeing each other at work after that, and the friendship diminished to a tacit agreement not to mention the incident again.

A couple of weeks later, it happened with another one of the men in the group. This one was Derek, a tall, thin British broker with a sallow complexion and an overbite. This time she had not even thought about being with Derek. He had simply paid the last tab, conducted her out of the bar, and kissed her. Derek drove her to his apartment, and they slept together.

In the morning she called her supervisor, said she was sick, and spent some time wondering why she had slept with Derek. All she could do was shrug and tell herself that she'd just had too much to drink—it wasn't her fault. But it wasn't the first time, and it was her fault. She brought back every moment of the night and analyzed it. She had not especially wanted to be with Derek, who wasn't a close friend like Nick, and wasn't even attractive. The alcohol had made her feel a lazy acquiescence: she had lost control of her will in exactly the way she had lost control of her arms and legs. It had just seemed like too much effort to exert them.

Later that day she quit her job, poured her supply of liquor out in the sink, and packed her belongings into her car for the drive home to Oregon. Driving back to Oregon was a desperate retreat. During every mile of the drive, she was afraid. She had failed to keep her husband, and she had run away from her career as a broker. She had developed such a taste for the forgetfulness and indifference that alcohol gave her that she had kept drinking even after she had done things that made her ashamed. She had slept with the two men who had asked, but it could just as easily have been five, or ten, or none. Things had just stopped mattering. The landscape behind her—the past, the people, the places where she had lived—was as dead and comfortless as a pile of bones.

She had no business considering a relationship with a man like Joe Pitt. She couldn't take the risks, and he shouldn't have to tolerate the rules she had made for herself. He didn't have any incentive to be constricted by her vulnerabilities and her past. She couldn't bear even to tell him about them. By the time the plane landed in Los Angeles, she was ashamed of herself for even considering speaking to him.

A few minutes later she was in Los Angeles International Airport, pulling her rolling suitcase along the concourse toward the escalator down to the car rental counters. She walked past the gift shops, looking in as she went. On the back wall were always racks of paperback books and magazines. There was the jumble of stuffed animals, hats, and T-shirts, all purporting to be from Hollywood or Beverly Hills. And in front of the store were racks with newspapers.

The New York Times and *Los Angeles Times* were in stacks, but the *Daily News* had one paper propped up where she could see the big color picture above the fold. The picture was a blurred security-camera shot, and that might have been what made her notice the resemblance immediately. The young woman seemed too much like Tanya to be anyone else. This time she had somewhat shorter, brownish hair, and she was wearing pants and a little sweater with a hood.

Catherine Hobbes read the caption above the picture: WOMAN SOUGHT IN SUSPICIOUS DEATH AT HOTEL. Beneath the picture was "If you recognize this woman, please call the Tip Number . . ."

Hobbes started toward the cash register, then, on second thought, came back for another copy. She bought them, took them to a seat in a waiting area off the concourse and looked at the picture once again, then scanned the article.

The woman had been seen at a hotel with a young man named Brian Corey, who had later jumped, fallen, or been pushed from the balcony of his eighth-floor room. The detective who had spoken with the reporter was listed as James Spengler of the Hollywood Division.

Hobbes held the paper on her lap, got her cell phone out of her purse, and realized that her hand was shaking. She took a deep breath, then asked the information operator for the number of the Hollywood Division. When she reached the station she was transferred twice.

Finally, she heard a male voice say, "Homicide. Spengler."

She took another deep breath and tried to speak calmly and distinctly. "This is Detective Sergeant Catherine Hobbes of the Portland, Oregon, Police Bureau. I just arrived in Los Angeles a minute ago and saw the front-page picture in the *Daily News.*"

"That was fast," he said. "What you've seen is tomorrow morning's edition. You don't, by any chance, know the woman in the picture?"

"Yes, I do."

"Do you have a name and address for her?"

"I've got several."

15

Nancy Mills had been awakened by the sun, which had somehow found a way through the blinds and made her pillow glow with painful brightness. She had dressed quickly and gone out, eager to be moving again. The killing of Brian stayed on her mind, even though he had been dead over a day now. She walked for a time, ate breakfast at the Red Robin in the plaza, then walked to the Promenade Mall and back. She spent most of the day wandering, finding anything she could to keep from staying in one place.

She tried to think clearly about killing. She remembered that she had felt a kind of emotional satisfaction after she had killed Dennis Poole: the act of shooting him had served to purge a great tangle of complicated feelings that she'd had about him. Then she had felt frustrated, interrupted, when she had not been permitted to end the relationship with David Larson the right way. The chance meeting with Bill Thayer had been pure adventure—a strong dose of fear, some quick thinking, and then it was over. But it had left her with a peculiar tingling, a pleasant excitement. The night with Brian Corey was different from all of the others. It had been wilder, riskier, and more exciting.

She loved being with men and feeling the strength of her

ability to attract them. She liked the way they looked at her. She liked having sex with some of them. But afterward, she always detected in herself a surprising resentment for what they had taken from her. Even though she had gone out hoping that she would have the chance to make this happen, and had then struggled to get their attention, she didn't exactly wish them well—she just needed them to want her. With some of them, she suspected that they felt superior because they had cajoled and flattered her into bed. Even when she was with the best of them, the physical act made her feel that they were controlling her, making her feel one sensation, then another, always at their discretion. After she had put all the effort into seducing them, she felt as though she had been coerced.

She had felt that with Brian from the beginning. There had been a joy in attracting him, and in spending the beautiful warm night with him, but there had been another kind of pleasure in knowing that all along she was fooling him, manipulating him, spending the whole time patiently moving him toward that balcony.

It was getting to be dinnertime again when she walked back to the apartment. She still felt the energy that wouldn't let her rest, but she knew that she must be as close to invisible as she could manage. She went up the steps and opened the door, walked through the little lobby, past the mailboxes, and had entered her hallway when the door across the hall opened. "Nancy?"

It was Nancy's nearest neighbor. A woman of about sixty, she always looked worn, haggard, and upset, as though she were engaged in some great task in her apartment when the door was closed. What was her name? The label on her door of the big mailbox in the lobby said M. Tilson. They had met down there several times. What was it—May, Mandy, Marcie, Marilyn? No. Just Mary. "Hi, Mary."

Mary Tilson pulled her door open wide and touched her short brown hair nervously. "Do you have a second?"

Nancy stepped inside. Mary seemed anxious, a bit more upset than usual. Nancy had never been inside her apartment before. She could see that the layout was exactly the same as hers, only on the other side of the building, reversed like a mirror image. There was a lingering smell of chlorine, as though Mary had recently scrubbed her sinks with cleanser. Nancy imagined her as one of those women who were always scrubbing and cleaning things, and a glance around the apartment confirmed it. The light beige carpet looked new, and the shelves filled beyond capacity with horrible china dogs were free of dust.

Mary hurried to the well-waxed dining room table, snatched up a newspaper, and hurried back. Nancy could see it was the *Daily News,* the smaller Los Angeles morning paper. "Honey," said Mary. "I'm glad I heard you come in." It seemed an odd way for a woman who didn't know her very well to talk. "I just came in myself. I was out at the grocery store, and I picked up both papers, because I like to see the early edition."

"Oh?" said Nancy. "What a smart idea." It didn't seem to her to be a smart idea. It seemed sad. She sensed that Mary was going to be a neighbor who bothered her with bulletins about tiny aspects of her daily life. Soon it would be recipes and coupons for the supermarket. She made a resolution to avoid being cornered like this again.

"Yes," said Mary. "I started doing it with the Sunday papers, because they came out on Saturday afternoon, and there was so much extra stuff in them." She seemed to struggle to get past these topics that made her comfortable, and into something that was making her uncomfortable. "I don't know how to tell you this, but I think I have to." She handed the newspaper to Nancy. "Is this picture you?"

Nancy held the newspaper in both hands and stared at the picture on the front page. She realized that she was in a state of amazement that was making it hard for her to think past the brute fact of the photograph. How had anyone taken a picture of her in the hotel? How could they have it in the newspaper? The picture was a random blow to her, like a runaway car suddenly veering off the street to run her down. She knew she had to force herself to react, to talk. "That's something, isn't it?" she said.

"Is it you?"

"Of course not," said Nancy. "I guess there are a lot of girls who look like me, or sort of like me. What's the story about?" As she chattered, she was trying to scan the two columns of print below the picture, but she was too agitated to keep her eyes on the print and too impatient to decipher it. She knew what it had to be about. She had instantly recognized the lobby of the Beverly Hilton hotel, recognized Brian, recognized herself, recognized the clothes she had been wearing.

"It's . . . it says that the man this woman was with the other night fell out of a hotel window." She seemed alarmed by the way she had said it, then gave a nervous laugh. "I'm glad it wasn't you. That would have been really awful. The man who fell, or jumped, would have been somebody you knew."

Nancy handed the newspaper back to her. "Well, thanks for checking. If it had been me, I guess I'd want to know."

"No trouble at all. When I saw it in the store, I just couldn't believe it. I said to myself, 'It can't be.' And I was right. It wasn't. What a relief."

Nancy started toward the door. She had been so edgy and full of restless energy when Mary had stopped her that she had barely been able to force herself to enter, and now the smells and the impression of clutter from the unnecessary furniture and the china dogs and clusters of framed pictures made her want to run.

"Wait."

Nancy's mind was racing. She stopped because she knew she had to. But she needed to get out and think, and her mind kept jumping from one thought to another, never settling on one. She fixed an inquisitive, friendly expression on her face, and turned to look at Mary. "What's wrong?"

"I was thinking. That picture looks so much like you. I wonder if you ought to call the police and tell them it's not you."

"What?"

"It looks just exactly like you. There will be other people who see it. What if everybody in the building calls them, and the people at the supermarket and everywhere else you go call them and say that the picture is you?"

"I could hardly blame them," said Nancy.

"Well, then would it be better to call the police and say, 'I know you're going to get calls saying that's me,' so they know they can eliminate you ahead of time? That way, they're not going to come looking for you. It could save you a whole lot of trouble and unpleasantness."

"What kind of trouble?"

"The paper said they want to talk to you about that man's death, which they said is suspicious. You know what that means. If they come, they might arrest you."

"I doubt it. I'm a pretty harmless person."

"I saw this show on TV not too long ago about this young black guy who got arrested because he looked like this other young black guy who had robbed a liquor store and shot people. He was really a teacher, and he was just driving home from coaching the debating team, and they ended up convicting him of murder. When the real killer confessed, he didn't even look all that much like the innocent guy. Not nearly as much as you look like that picture."

Nancy shrugged. "If I have time tomorrow, I'll give them a call. I might end up saving them a trip. Thanks."

"Would you mind if I called them for you in the meantime?"

"Why would you do that?"

"Because tomorrow morning, when this picture is on doorsteps all over the city, it's going to be too late. We could have a SWAT team here kicking down the door."

The restless energy that Nancy had felt since the moment when she had pushed Brian off the balcony was beginning to overwhelm her again. She could feel her neck and shoulders tensing, and she clenched her hands like claws to keep them still. "I wish you wouldn't do anything like that."

"I'm giving you the chance to do it yourself."

In the next instant, Nancy's distraction and nervousness died away. She saw the events of the past two days and the next two days at once. She knew now that she should never have gone out and found Brian Corey. It had been a horrible lapse of judgment.

She knew that Mary was right about the picture in the

paper. At seven tomorrow morning there would be copies on thousands of doorsteps. People would remember seeing her at stores and restaurants in the plaza, in the apartment building, on the nearby streets. Tomorrow morning might be optimistic. It was a sensational story, the kind that might turn up tonight on the local television news. She had to get out of Los Angeles as quickly as she could. It would take only a few minutes to pack her clothes and her money. But that wasn't good enough. There was no time to get a car, and no time to build a new identity.

She looked at Mary. "You're right." She knew that what she was considering was a form of perfection. It would fend off all of the people who wanted to do her harm, and it would give her a way to supply all of her immediate needs. It was so right that it began to happen without her choosing to do it. She didn't plan. She simply started.

"You're absolutely right. I wasn't really thinking clearly. In fact, I'd be doing them a favor too. Eliminating the need to investigate calls from fifty people is probably as good as a tip."

"At least it helps. And if they've already been called about you, it might be important."

Nancy gave an apologetic smile, and a shiver. "I'm actually a little nervous. I don't know why."

"Then let's do it together. Here. Let's have some iced tea. That'll help us cool off and calm down. Then we can make the call."

Mary walked to the small kitchen and Nancy followed closely. Nancy's eyes and ears had been so sensitized by the excitement and agitation that they almost hurt. She saw Mary reach for the refrigerator's door, and she saw the black grips of the kitchen knives sticking out of the slits in the butcher-block holder on the counter. She snatched a big one out and had it in motion before Mary's hand could close on the door handle.

She stabbed it into Mary's back in the spot below the left shoulder blade that she judged must be the heart, but it hit a rib and she had to push it upward and over before it would go in.

Mary's arms flew out from her sides, she tried to turn, and she cried loudly, "Oh! Oh! Oh!"

Nancy had to silence her. She tugged out the knife, clutched Mary's hair, wrapping it around her fingers, and jerked the head back. She drew the knife blade across Mary's throat under the jaw. She had heard someone use the term "ear to ear," so she did it that way, trying to make the slice as deep as she could.

Mary's hands came up to her throat. There was a hissing, gurgling noise, and spurts of blood spattered the white metal surface of the refrigerator door like carnations, then streaked down to the floor.

It was horrible. Why wasn't she dead? Nancy held her there, her hand still caught in Mary's hair. She hooked her right arm around Mary from behind and plunged the knife into Mary's torso just below the center of the rib cage. She knew she had missed the heart again, so she pushed down on the handle to lever the blade upward, then grabbed the handle with both hands and drew it toward herself.

Mary's knees buckled and she collapsed to the floor. Nancy released her hair and stepped backward, leaving the knife in her. Nancy looked down and saw that her arms were covered with blood from the elbows to the fingertips, dripping into the pools that were merging into each other beside Mary.

Nancy turned and stepped to the sink. She ran the water to wash the blood off her arms, twisting every few seconds to see whether Mary had moved. Was she finally dead? Maybe she was, but it seemed that as long as the pool of blood kept growing, the heart must still be pumping it out onto the floor.

Nancy knew that her jeans and her top probably had droplets of blood on them somewhere, but she couldn't see them and she was clean enough to accomplish the next tasks. She took the rubber gloves that Mary had left on the sink beside the cleanser and put them on.

Mary's purse was easy to find. She had left it in plain sight on the counter near the telephone. Nancy opened it and examined the contents. There were Mary's keys. The apartment key was exactly like Nancy's. The car key had a black plastic sleeve stamped with an *H* for Honda. There was a small wallet with Mary's credit cards and identification, but no cash. Nancy unzipped each of the handbag's inner pockets until she found one with a zippered change purse. Inside was folded currency, and on top were some fifty-dollar bills.

Nancy stood in the kitchen and looked through the doorway at the rest of the apartment. Here was the grotesquely crowded living room, one bedroom, and a bath, all laid out facing hers across the hall. She knew she should spend very little time searching the place, but she knew she wouldn't need much. If something of value wasn't in the bedroom, it had to be hidden in the kitchen—in the freezer, or inside the pots and pans, or high on a shelf in a sugar bowl.

Being near Mary made her feel uneasy. She wasn't really sure that Mary was dead yet, and she had the feeling that Mary was lying there awake, looking at her and listening to her as she went about her business. She had a curiosity about how Mary's bedroom would look, so she chose to begin her search there.

Nancy hurried to the hall and stopped in the bedroom doorway. It was just as she had expected. The furniture was pseudo-Victorian, heavy and dark, with scrollwork all over it. The bed had six ruffled pillows propped on a flowered duvet. There were corner shelves with china and glass objects, and thick brocade curtains in an ugly green smothered the windows.

Nancy switched on the light. She knelt and looked under the bed, but found it was where Mary stored out-of-season coats and boots in see-through plastic boxes. She searched the closet, then moved to the dresser. She was disappointed to find that there were only clothes in the drawers, and the jewelry box on top contained nothing that was worth stealing.

When she moved to the nightstand beside the bed and opened the top drawer, she felt herself flush with excitement. In the drawer, where it would be ready and within reach while she was sleeping, was a small, short-barreled revolver. Nancy picked it up cautiously and examined it. The gun was silver-toned, with white plastic handgrips. She aimed it at an imaginary target and saw the brass bullet casings at the back of the cylinder. Mary had stored it loaded.

It occurred to Nancy that she was lucky she had chosen to kill Mary right away and in the kitchen. If Mary had been in here, or even in the hallway or the closer parts of the living room, Nancy might have been the one who was lying on the floor bleeding. The thought of it made her heart beat harder again. She had never imagined that someone like Mary would own a gun. She had been ambushed and lured into this apartment by a woman who had a gun hidden ten feet from the door. Nancy had narrowly saved herself.

Why would Mary even own a gun? But then Nancy remembered that in one of their first encounters at the mailbox, Mary had warned her that rapists sometimes waited in the dark parking lots behind big apartment buildings. It had sounded as though rapists were a regular part of the landscape, swarming around like hornets. In other conversations she had seemed obsessed with some horrible crime she'd seen reenacted on television that had happened to some unwary single woman. It was probably inevitable that she would have a gun.

Nancy looked deeper in the drawer. There was a box of ammunition, so she took it. There was also a key that looked as though it belonged to a safe-deposit box, but she couldn't think of a way to use it. She found a canvas tote bag in the closet that had an ugly picture of a rose on it. She put the gun and the box of bullets inside, then moved to the kitchen and took the wallet, keys, and change purse.

She found a plastic bag in a drawer, took off the rubber gloves, put them in the bag, and dropped them into her tote. She moved close to Mary, careful to keep from stepping in the blood, and touched her bare leg. It felt cold. She had to be dead. Looking down at her now, Nancy realized that she must have been hysterical to have imagined that Mary was not dead before.

Nancy took one moment more to take two paper towels from the roll on the counter. With one she wiped off the handle of the knife that was stuck in Mary's chest. As she passed the table she picked up the copy of the newspaper with her picture in it. She used her other paper towel to keep her hands from leaving prints when she turned the doorknob. She locked the door and went to her own apartment.

Nancy's nervous energy was not an infirmity now. It was the power that might save her. She quickly packed her clothes and personal effects in her two suitcases, closed them, and took them to the door. She went to the sink and ran water over a dish towel. She began in the kitchen and wiped every surface with the towel, using the wetness to tell which surfaces she had wiped and which she had missed. She even cleaned the undersides of appliances, then put the few cups, dishes, pans, and silverware she'd bought in the dishwasher and ran it on the pots and pans setting.

She moved into the rest of the little apartment and wiped every window, every handle, all of the smooth surfaces of every piece of furniture. It was a quicker, more efficient process now than before, because now she was used to doing it. She never hesitated, never needed to stop or decide. Her manic restlessness kept her working. When she had finished, she made one last stop. She went to the mailboxes in the lobby, opened hers, wiped it off inside and outside, then re-locked it.

She returned to her apartment, slipped her suitcases into a plastic trash bag so anyone who saw her would think she was taking out the garbage, locked the door, and hurried down the back stairs to the parking garage below the building. She had to search for a minute to find the Honda. Mary's car was hidden by two elephantine sport-utility vehicles that couldn't fit into their own spaces and overlapped Mary's.

Nancy put her bag in the trunk of the car, started it, and listened to the engine for a minute while she located the various controls and adjusted the seat and mirrors to fit her taller body. The engine sounded good, and the gas tank was full.

Nancy backed up to get out of the space, and drove up the ramp onto the street. She turned right onto Topanga Canyon and headed for the freeway. She took the southbound entrance because heading into the city would bring her to the tangle of interchanges onto other freeways. She brought her

new Honda's speed up to merge into the moving river of cars,
then glanced down at the tote bag beside her that held her
new wallet, her change purse full of money, and her new gun.

16

Catherine Hobbes sat in the
unmarked blue police car beside Detective James Spengler,
watching the streets of the San Fernando Valley slide past her
window. It was early morning but it was already hot, and the
traffic coming eastward toward them was virtually stopped.
The sun reflected off the windshields, so that she kept seeing
flashes and then a lingering green glow on her retina. When
she thought of the West Coast, she thought of her part of it—
Portland, Washington, California as far south as San Francisco. Los Angeles was hard to get used to.

"You seem pretty calm about this," said Spengler.

"It's an act I developed to keep male cops from thinking
I'm emotional."

"Right."

"I promise I'll get excited when this woman is in custody
and I know for sure she's Tanya Starling," she said. "You'll
think you've won a football game. I'll be running around
high-fiving you guys and slapping you on the butt."

"You spotted the picture as soon as you got off the plane.
She sure looks like the same one."

"Your picture of a girl looks like my pictures of a girl. But
we don't know if the apartment where we're going belongs
to her. And whenever you put out a picture to the public, it

strikes a lot of people as the spitting image of somebody who doesn't look that way at all."

"Three calls tipping you on the same person don't usually turn out to be nothing."

"That's why I'm nervous," she said. "I've been gritting my teeth for an hour hoping this is Tanya. But I've learned not to be too quick to assume anything about her. When we began this investigation, we all thought she was probably a kidnap victim. I'm still not sure whether some guy killed Dennis Poole because he was jealous over her and she's still running from him, or she's running because she killed him herself."

"You want a prediction?"

"Sure."

"Your first version is right."

"Which one is that? I forgot."

"The killing will turn out to be about her, but she didn't kill the guy. After you get her, you'll find out she was a drug mule who took off with somebody's shipment. Or she's a hooker who had a particularly possessive pimp, who wasn't about to let her go off with a client."

"One of those was *my* first version?"

"I'm just going with the odds. You said before that they met at a hotel in Aspen and she came to visit, but nobody at home ever saw them together. That sounds like there·was something about her that kept him from showing her off. And women don't usually do a gunshot murder on a guy unless they're married to him."

"If you want to kill somebody bigger than you are, and you've got a gun, you use it—no matter who you are."

"Maybe. But then there's the death of Brian Corey in the Hilton. They met in a bar, had dinner in Beverly Hills, and went up to his room and had sex. Afterward, she leaves alone, and so do his wallet and his rental car. What does that sound like?"

"It sounds like a hooker."

"Right. And there was no gun, so she couldn't have done the murder. The girl I saw in the picture didn't throw a full-grown man off a balcony. It had to be a man, or maybe two men—somebody like the pimp. In fact, it would have to be a really uneven match, somebody who could completely over-power and silence him. There were no signs of a struggle in the room, and nobody on the floor heard a fight."

"You can push an elephant off a balcony if he's off balance and you give him a shove at the right time."

"Joe Pitt agrees with me."

It took an effort to hide her surprise. "Joe Pitt? When did you talk to him?"

"He gave me a call when he saw the picture in the paper. He told me he had been working on this with you, and the girl looked like the one on your tapes. He also asked us to give you our best cooperation."

"He did?"

"Yeah. He's very complimentary about you. But when we were talking about the Brian Corey thing, he figured there was no way she could have done it herself."

"Let's concentrate on getting her into custody," she said. "Then we'll find out." Catherine looked away. She had been thinking hard about Tanya Starling, but the mention of Joe Pitt was distracting her now. She wasn't sure what to think. She'd had a pleasant sensation when she had heard that he had complimented her, but then there was a suspicion that maybe the compliment had not been about her police work. He and Spengler were men, and they talked like men. And after all, he had told Spengler he disagreed with her theory. She was irritated at Pitt for calling Spengler and talking about her at all. What business did he have interfering with her investigation? No, that wasn't fair either: he had recog-nized Tanya's picture in the newspaper, and it was his duty to call the cops. But why hadn't he called her?

"Here's the street. The apartment is coming right up." They glided up the street and a moment later the other two un-marked cars turned off Topanga Canyon after them. Spengler pulled the car into a parking space near the front steps, the next car drove around the back of the building, and the third pulled in beside Spengler.

"Well, let's see if we can scoop her up quick," he said. "Then, while she's telling us who killed those two men, you'll have plenty of time to congratulate me on being right."

"Just don't assume she's not dangerous until she's hand-cuffed," said Hobbes.

Spengler got out and conferred for a moment with the two officers in the car beside them, then joined Hobbes on the front steps.

The two officers stationed themselves at the building exits while Spengler and Hobbes stepped into the lobby. Hobbes stopped to check the names on the mailboxes. "Mills" with no first name was on box 5. They went up two steps into the hallway on the right, and knocked on the door to apartment 5. They waited a few seconds, listening. Then Spengler knocked again, harder. After a minute, he knocked a third time. There was no answering call, no sound of movement in the apartment.

"Let's try across the hall," said Hobbes. She knocked on the door across the hall, waited, then knocked again. "Nobody's home in number four, either."

Spengler said, "Let's hunt down the manager."

"Apartment one. I checked the mailboxes."

They walked back to the lobby and into the opposite hallway, and knocked on the door. There was a small sign taped to it that said R. NORRIS, MANAGER. R. Norris was an unshaven man about forty years old who seemed to have been awakened by the knock.

Catherine Hobbes stood back and waited while Spengler said, "Mr. Norris, I'm Detective Spengler, Los Angeles Police." He held his identification up so that Norris could compare the photograph with his face. "I'm very sorry we have to bother you this morning, but I have a warrant for one of your tenants. It's Miss Nancy Mills, in apartment five. She doesn't seem to be answering her door, so I'd like you to open it up for us."

"She goes out most days. She walks a lot."

Hobbes took a step closer. "You mean for fitness?"

"In the morning she goes out and jogs. Then around ten or so, she goes out again. She doesn't have a car."

Hobbes looked at Spengler. He reached into the inner pocket of his sport coat and produced some papers. "Sir, here's a copy of the warrant. I'd appreciate it if you could open the apartment for us. It will save us all some trouble if we don't have to break the door down."

Norris stared at the warrant, uncomprehending. After a moment he either found the part that permitted a search of Nancy Mills's domicile or he simply gave up. "Hold on a minute. Let me get the key."

A moment later, he returned with a set of master keys. He led the way down the hall to the apartment, unlocked it, and stepped back.

Spengler said, "Thank you, Mr. Norris." When he swung the door open, he looked in and said, "She's certainly neat, isn't she?"

"That's not it. She's gone," said Hobbes. "She's moved out." She slipped past him into the kitchen and examined the cleaning supplies on the counter.

"Are you sure?"

"It's a furnished apartment. There's nothing here that's personal." She stepped carefully along the edge of the living room to the hallway, her eyes on the floor to keep from disturbing any evidence. She continued into the bedroom and looked into the open closet.

She turned and saw Spengler standing behind her, his eyes on the empty hangers on the pole in the closet. He took the radio off his belt. "Don't hold your breath, guys. She's out of here. She must have seen her picture in the paper."

Hobbes heard a couple of tinny voices on the radio. "Roger." "Got it."

Hobbes said, "Can you please call for a forensic team? I'd like to be sure it's the same girl I've been looking for."

"Dave, call this in to the station," he said into the radio. "Let them know we'll need a forensic team. Everybody else come on in and help us canvass the rest of the tenants, and see if anybody knows where she went."

Catherine Hobbes had tried to stay two steps behind Jim Spengler. Even though she carried a badge and a gun, she was only a guest in Los Angeles, and this was officially the investigation of the death of Brian Corey at a Los Angeles hotel. But it became evident almost immediately that she was a less intimidating interviewer than Spengler, so she began to take the lead.

The man in apartment 8 was not able to recall ever having seen the woman in the picture, nor could the couple in apartment 9. The others seemed to know very little about her. The person who lived across the hall from Nancy Mills was the one Catherine wanted most to talk to. She went back to knock on the door again, but the neighbor still wasn't at home.

After about twenty minutes, the forensic team arrived and set to work in Nancy Mills's apartment.

Catherine Hobbes had conducted enough interviews to persuade her that the woman who had called herself Nancy Mills had kept to herself and revealed very little. Catherine left the other detectives and returned to apartment 5, where two men and a woman were crawling on the living room carpet with rubber gloves, plastic bags, magnifiers, and tweezers, searching for physical evidence. The woman technician looked up from the carpet, and Catherine said, "Catherine Hobbes, Portland Police."

"Hi," said the woman. "I'm Toni."

"Have you noticed the streaks yet?" asked Catherine.

"Streaks?"

"Yes," said Catherine. "Look at this coffee table, and you can see what I mean. You can see it best if you look at it from the side." Catherine knelt beside the coffee table, and Toni joined her. They sighted along the top, then along the side. It was marked with a striated pattern. "See the streaks?"

"They're from washing it," said Toni. "It's been washed with a rag that was soaking wet. If you use furniture polish or wax, it forms a coating. This was just wet."

"Any fingerprints on it?"

"Not yet. And we're finding this everyplace. It's on all the furniture, the windows, the counters, even the walls. Every surface has streaks on it, because it's been washed down with a rag or cloth. You can see white cotton fibers in some spots. There were a couple of places that were still wet, so this wasn't done long ago. Maybe last night."

"No prints at all?"

"Not yet," she said. "It's pretty hard to keep prints off

everything, so we undoubtedly will find some. But she sure didn't want us to. Right now we're collecting hairs. So far all of them are ten to twelve inches, light brown." Toni leaned over and picked up some hairs with a pair of tweezers. "Oh-oh."

"What?"

"More hairs. But these didn't fall out. They were pulled out."

"You mean violently?"

"Yes. See, even without magnifying them, you can spot little bits of tissue. That's the root. Judging from the length, it's probably a woman's hair, but it's a different woman. This is thicker and wavier, like a perm, and it has a gray root, so the brown is almost certainly a dye job."

Catherine Hobbes said, "Excuse me, Toni." She went to the doorway and looked down the hall. She could see Jim Spengler talking to the manager in the lobby. She walked up to them.

She said, "Mr. Norris, can you tell me about the tenant who lives across the hall in apartment four?"

"Her name is Mary Tilson. She's almost always there this time of day. I'm surprised she isn't now. She usually doesn't go out until the afternoon."

"How old is she?"

"Maybe sixty or so."

"Can you describe her hair?"

"Her hair?"

"Yes. Is it long and straight, short, blond or brunette?"

"It's brown. It's not straight. Kind of wavy, maybe almost to her chin."

"Thanks. Can you excuse us for a second?" She took Spengler's arm and pulled him a few feet off. "The forensic tech just found some hairs that had been pulled out of a woman's head, like in a fight. They're six to eight inches long, brown and wavy, with a gray root."

"You mean you think they belong to the woman who lives across the hall?"

"It wouldn't hurt to take a quick look in her apartment. If she's not there and everything looks normal, fine. But somebody got some of her hair pulled out, and Toni says they don't belong to Nancy Mills."

Spengler said, "Mr. Norris, can you come with us, please?"

They reached the door of apartment 4, and the manager unlocked it. Spengler pushed the door open a few inches, and his eyes focused on something. He said, "Thank you, Mr. Norris. We'll take it from here."

He turned to Catherine as Norris was moving off. "It's not good." He stepped into the apartment, and Catherine followed. She could see the woman lying on the kitchen floor in a pool of blood. Spengler was already hurrying to the woman, but Catherine had noticed that the outer edges of the big pool of blood were dark and dry, which meant she had been there a long time. Spengler touched her carotid artery. "She's been dead awhile. Her throat was cut. And a knife— looks like a regular butcher knife—is still in her."

"I'll call the forensic people over from the other apartment."

"Yeah, thanks. We'll get them going on this."

Catherine stepped across the hall and said, "Toni, we've got a deceased victim in apartment four."

"Oh, man." Toni began to put her equipment back into the tackle box on the floor. "I had a feeling about this," she said. "Too many hairs. Come on, guys. Let's see if we can get anything fresh over there."

Jim Spengler was gathering the other detectives in the hall to tell them what had been discovered in apartment 4. Catherine approached.

She said, "The manager says Nancy Mills didn't have a car."

Spengler said, "That's right. Ron, get a description of Mary Tilson's car, check the parking spaces downstairs, and see if her car is gone. If it is, run her name and get the license and description on the air. Dave, get on the radio and let them know what we've got here."

He saw the forensic team move to the doorway and peer inside before stepping in. "Toni, you want us to call for reinforcements?"

"Thanks, Jim, but I'll call them myself as soon as I've taken a look."

"Fine." He turned back to the other police officers. "Al, see if anything is missing in the apartment, especially credit cards or ATM cards. If they are, get started on finding out if they've been used yet."

The detectives moved off, and Catherine went down the hall to Mr. Norris. She said, "I'd like to take a look at Nancy Mills's rental agreement."

They entered Mr. Norris's apartment, and he produced a file from a desk drawer. Inside were five-page lease agreements for all of the tenants. Catherine leafed through them carefully until she found the one that said Nancy Mills. Norris said, "You can take that one if you want. I've got a Xerox copy in the file, and the rental company has a duplicate original."

"Thank you," she said. "Do you have a spare file folder or an envelope?"

"Sure." He handed her a manila envelope.

"Thanks very much," she said. She slipped the agreement inside, and walked out of the room. She went down the hall and found Toni in the kitchen of apartment 4.

She said, "Toni, this is the rental agreement for Nancy Mills. I'd appreciate it if you could take it to the lab and examine it for latent prints."

Toni took it. "Sure thing. I'll try dipping it in ninhydrin to bring up the amino acids, and give you a call." She put it into a cardboard carton with her growing collection of plastic evidence bags.

Catherine turned to Spengler, who was staring down at the body of Mary Tilson. He said, "I guess this just about finishes the idea that the girl is the one doing this stuff. I can't see her cutting a woman like that and leaving her to bleed out on the floor."

Catherine walked out of the room, down the hall, and outside, where she leaned against the car and took a few breaths of air. Her mind had been fully occupied since the moment she had arrived, but now it was still racing, and there was little for her to do until either the crime-scene technicians or the officers searching for the girl gave her something new to interpret.

Her mind kept returning to Joe Pitt. She was tempted to call him and tell him what she thought of him for interfering with the relations between her and the Los Angeles police. But this was his town, where he had been the D.A.'s investigator. She had no right to tell him what to say to the L.A. police, and any homicide detective here would know him personally. He had seen the photograph in the paper and recognized Tanya, and he'd had to report it. But why had he called the L.A. homicide people, and not her? She could think of two answers, without even asking him: the newspaper had said to call Spengler, so he had. And she had essentially told him not to bother her again, and so he hadn't.

17

As the girl drove along Interstate 15, the brightly lighted hotels appeared against the sky in the distance, and minutes later the town rose up around her. She was afraid to stop, but she was too tired not to. She had been up since sunrise, spent the day on her feet, and then been forced to defend herself from Mary's ugly demands and clean up afterward. The hours of driving since then had drained the last of her nervous energy.

She saw the exit for the Mandalay Bay hotel, and then she was on it, and then in the thick traffic on the strip. The first place where she was able to make a right turn was the entrance to the MGM Grand, so she gave her car to the parking attendant there and watched him drive it into the parking structure.

She wanted to check into a hotel and sleep, but she didn't dare. If the police were searching for her, one of the things they would do right away was get in touch with the Las Vegas hotels. She was hungry, so she went inside to the long promenade where the restaurants were and looked into a few. The customers had all moved into the drinking phase of the evening, so she kept going.

She found a coffee shop farther on the promenade, bought a piece of lemon cake she saw in the glass case, and ate it. She rested her eyes and cradled her head in her arms for a moment. When she awoke, there was a tall man in a dark blue suit standing over her. As he leaned closer, she could hear low-volume radio chatter coming from his coat pocket. He said, "Miss? Are you all right?"

"Huh? Oh my gosh," she said. "I must have dozed off."

His sympathetic concern vanished. This was not a medical emergency. "You can't sleep here." It was as though he had already heard and penetrated the lie she had not told yet.

She stood, took her purse, and strode off. She had the feeling that he was behind her, talking into the radio about her. She never decreased her speed until she was out of the building.

For the next few hours she was one of the thousands of people walking from casino to casino. She had stopped in Las Vegas to rest, but there seemed to be no way for her to do it. When she was too tired to keep walking she would sit at a table in a bar and order a soft drink. She caught another cat-nap at six A.M. on the couch in a ladies' room in Caesars, but the attendant politely woke her as soon as she had entered deep sleep. Later in the morning she ate brunch at the Aladdin. When big groups of people began to check out of the hotels at ten-thirty, she joined the line at the entrance to the MGM and had the valet retrieve her car.

She drove out the Boulder Highway toward Henderson, and stopped at a shopping mall. She left her car inside the parking structure, where it would be less visible, and walked to the mall's cinema complex. She bought a ticket to the first movie that was showing. It was an awful film about two evil children, and there were few other people in the theater to watch it, so she found a seat in the middle of a row and fell asleep. She spent the whole afternoon and evening in the complex, going from one small theater to the next, each time sleeping for an hour or two and waking when the lights came up and people shuffled out.

When she felt that she was able to drive again, she ate dinner in a Denny's in Henderson. It was eleven-thirty when she drove into the desert to the east. She had wasted a whole day in Las Vegas, and she was nearly as tired as she had been when she had arrived.

Her troubles were building up. She had done a rash, unconsidered thing, but it had not really been her fault. She had not set out to kill Mary Tilson. She just had not been able to think of a way to avoid it. Mary Tilson wouldn't shut up, and she wouldn't leave her alone, and she couldn't be dissuaded from calling the police.

She was just a regular person who had always wanted what everybody else wanted—to be happy. She had been smart in school and had been accepted to the University of Illinois. She remembered that the letter had arrived in April, and she had taped it to the wall of her bedroom so she could look at it every morning when she woke up, and every night when she went to bed. The habit had lasted until June. It was a Sunday when everything changed.

She remembered waking up and seeing the letter that morning: "Dear Charlene Buckner: It is my pleasure to inform you . . ." She had used a single small piece of tape on the top so she could take it down in September and bring it with her in case she needed to prove that she had been accepted.

As she always did, she lay in her bed, looked at the tone of the light, and touched the wall beside her bed to see if it was warm or cool, because that side was the outer wall of the house. She could feel that it was warm. In those few seconds she sensed that something was wrong. The house was more than quiet. It was a vacuum, because something big had moved on, and nothing had yet filled the space. She knew what it was.

She got up and stepped to the door of her mother's bedroom. The drawers of the dresser were still open, a little askew and out of their tracks because her mother had been in a hurry to empty them.

Charlene walked through the little house, moving from room to room and looking. She was not exactly searching for her mother, just looking at her world to see what it looked like without her. There was a note on the kitchen table, a glass placed on it to hold it down, as though a wind might blow through and take it. Charlene picked up the glass and smelled the strong, turpentine scent of whiskey, so she set it in the sink with the other dirty dishes.

She picked up the note. "Dear Char, I had an unexpected opportunity, and I had to take it. If you need to reach me, write to me care of my sister Rose. I'll check with her later. Don't forget to ask the college for scholarship money. Bye for now. Mommy." The *o* had a smiling face drawn in it. Charlene put the note in the garbage bag and began to clean up.

She rinsed the dishes and put them in the sink with very hot water and detergent to soak a bit while she went outside to pick up the Sunday newspaper from the sidewalk. She had always done that to keep the neighbors from noticing that her mother stayed out late and slept for the first half of the day. It was a warm, sunny morning, and there were flowers blooming in the neighbors' yards. She went back inside, closed the door, and locked it.

She was halfway through the dishes before she really felt what had happened to her. She was as alone as a person in a raft in the middle of the ocean. She spent a few minutes thinking about how it must have happened.

Her mother had been in one of her depressions lately, because of her most recent boyfriend, Ray. About two months ago, Ray had hit her and then left. The next day she had pretended that she had gotten tired of Ray and made him leave, then bumped into a kitchen cupboard in the dark because she'd been trying to get a glass of water in the middle of the night without waking Charlene. But Charlene had awakened and heard her sobbing, pleading with Ray not to leave: "Ray, I wasn't even interested in him that way. It just happened. It didn't mean anything. Please don't leave. I'll never do it again." Her mother's voice had been the shrill kind that carried, but Ray was a mutterer, with a deep voice, so Charlene couldn't make out anything he was saying. She hadn't needed to.

Charlene's mother had hated being alone. It wasn't clear to Charlene from the contradictory stories she told when she had ever been alone, but the experience must have been terrible, because she was willing to do anything to keep from being alone again. Some of the time when a boyfriend moved out, she had heard her mother saying, "I'll do anything," and known that she meant it. Charlene was sure she knew what the opportunity in the note had been. Somebody had offered her a chance not to be alone.

It struck Charlene at first that since her mother was so scared of being alone, it was odd that she would abandon Charlene. But she always had been that way. If the weather was hot, then she was hotter than other people. If there was only one piece of meat left, then she was hungrier than anyone else. Charlene should have seen this coming, from the moment when she had received her letter from the college. Her mother had read the letter on the wall too, and to her it had meant that Charlene was going away.

Charlene didn't like her mother very much, but she missed her in some deep, awful way. After another day, however, she realized she still had to get herself through the rest of June and graduate, then find a way to survive July and August on her own and get to college. The remark about a scholarship in her mother's letter had been her only mention of money. That had been her way of saying that she had not left Charlene any.

That morning, as soon as Charlene was showered and dressed, she went to the only place she could think of in Wheatfield to find work. It was the Dairy Princess on Highway 19. It looked almost exactly like a Dairy Queen place, but it actually wasn't. It was a transparent counterfeit, relying on the notion that people would see what it was imitating and then pull over, exactly as though it were a Dairy Queen. They would realize that it wasn't, but they would forgive the small imposture.

The summer manager was a boy named Tim she remembered from high school; he was two years older than she was, and was already off for the summer. There was a line at the order window, so she waited until it was her turn. She said she wanted to see Tim.

When he came to the window, he said, "Hi, Charlene. What can I get you?"

"I need a job, thanks. Do you have one that's open?"

Tim looked at her for a long time. She could see him trying to calculate, and he actually looked worried, as though he couldn't figure out the answer. "If you're willing to work hard, there's one left."

"Okay," she said.

She started right away. At first she worked only on weekends, because that was when most people wanted ice cream and hamburgers. When graduation came and summer began, she worked six days a week, from twelve until nine. She got minimum wage, which wasn't much, but she ate something during her break each night that served as dinner, and once in a while some man would give her a tip.

She took her mother's advice and wrote a letter to the admissions office at the university, informing them that she was going to need a scholarship. She told them that the reason she had not applied before was that her mother had never managed to fill out the Parents' Confidential Statement about her finances, but that her mother's finances no longer mattered because her mother had moved on. Two weeks into the summer she received a gently worded letter that said it was too late for this year, and included some application forms for federal loans.

Charlene remembered sitting in her empty house at the kitchen table reading the forms and feeling absolutely bereft. The next two nights she came home tired and worked on the forms. The third night, she finished at midnight and walked to the letter box outside the post office to mail them.

Charlene made a friend at the Dairy Princess named Alice.

She was a woman of about twenty-nine who had a little boy but lived with her parents not far from where Charlene lived. At seven each night they went outside, away from the heat and the smells, and while Alice smoked, they talked. She had seen Charlene staring at Tim when he wasn't looking.

Charlene had not let her thoughts about Tim get beyond the speculation stage, where she felt a small tingle when he was near her in the narrow, hot kitchen and they accidentally brushed against each other as she was carrying food to the pickup window. She didn't have any room in her life for another person. But Alice had caught her looking at him, and from that day she spoke to Charlene about her crush on Tim.

One night when Charlene left at her usual time, Alice offered to close the store so Tim could go too. Charlene noticed him walking along the street twenty feet behind her, so she slowed and gradually they began to walk together.

He said, "Alice told me you're having a hard time saving the money you need to start at college."

She was alarmed, humiliated. She had not formed close relationships with other girls in high school, because they always seemed to turn any confidence into gossip. Alice was so much older that Charlene had assumed she wouldn't behave that way or betray her. She fought the panic and answered, "I guess it's true. I've got to pay my own living expenses, because my mother is away right now."

"I heard that too. It must be hard."

"I don't miss the company. I'm out most of the time anyway. It's just that I got used to having her pay for things."

They walked along the dark streets toward her house. They talked about the day's customers who had looked strange, or acted superior, and about the pressure Tim felt to keep the receipts at the Princess high so the owner, Mr. Kallen, wouldn't give him a bad recommendation when he left in the fall. He knew he wouldn't be fired in the middle of the summer, and his parents had enough money to pay his tuition at Purdue whether he worked or not, but he was convinced that a bad recommendation in his first supervisory job would ruin his future.

Charlene walked along beside him, most comfortable while

he was talking but feeling something like stage fright whenever a topic had been exhausted and another hadn't replaced it. She became ashamed of the fact that the items that occupied her mind weren't theories or ideas, only the personal obsessions and problems that consumed her—the fact that she wasn't paying the rent on the house or the utility bills, just trying to ignore the increasingly ominous late notices and not answering the telephone in the hope that she wouldn't be evicted before September, the fear that people would know she was alone in the house and too young to have any rights—and she didn't want him to know any of them.

When they reached her house they stood for a moment in silence on the porch in the dark, and he kissed her. It was a shock for her, a soft, sweet moment in a life that had turned into an emergency. She had come to expect days full of sweat and the smell of burning grease and overflowing, fly-swarmed garbage cans. As he held her, she seemed to be floating, her eyes closed. When he released her, she stood motionless for a few seconds.

He said, "I've been thinking about you a lot. I watch you in the Princess."

"You do?"

"Yeah. You're the best-looking girl in Wheatfield."

"Of course, Wheatfield is so huge. There must be twelve girls. And I'm not, anyway."

"I'm serious. Everybody knows it. I remember when you came into high school. I was a junior. Everybody was blown away."

She looked down, afraid that she might be blushing and that he could see it, even though they were under the porch roof, so the moonlight didn't reach them. She couldn't think of anything to say, so she said, "Thank you."

They kissed again, and she began to feel her nervousness being replaced by a relaxed, lazy sensation that she sensed might be a sign of danger. If she didn't stop, she was going to let him go too far. She broke off the kiss. "I'd better go in now. Thanks for walking me home." Then she grinned. "And everything."

She found her key chain in her purse and turned to unlock the door. He said, "Can I come in?"

She said, "I'm sorry. I can't tonight. See you tomorrow." She slipped inside and locked the door.

The next day Alice watched her and watched Tim during the day. At three, when they were outside for their break, she said, "Tell me exactly what happened." After some hesitation, Charlene did tell Alice.

Alice said, "That's it? That was all?" She seemed disappointed.

Charlene was slightly offended, but she realized that a woman twelve years older than she was, with a child, was probably used to more than that. She was tempted to embellish the story, but she didn't know what to say that would be satisfactory, so she decided to wait and see whether anything else happened.

That Saturday, Charlene stayed late to help Tim lock up, so that he would walk her home again.

This time when they reached the porch, she said, "Would you like to come in for a minute?" He came in. She felt the heat of shame as he looked around him. She had always been aware that the house was smaller and less fancy than other people's houses, and her mother's boyfriends had been a problem, because she didn't want to introduce them and then have to explain who they were and what they were doing here. Now they were gone, and she had spent hours over the past few days cleaning the house, washing curtains, arranging furniture, and putting fresh flowers from the front yard in jars.

She reminded herself that it was different now. She was only seventeen and this was her own place, where she could do anything she wanted. Tim still lived with his parents, and he was two years older. She had bought a six-pack of cola, so she offered him a drink, and brought it in one of the glasses her mother had only used for adults. Then she sat on the couch with him.

He kissed her, but it wasn't the same as it had been the first night. He seemed more eager, but not more affectionate. He was insistent, implacable, barely letting her take a breath. She still liked him, but tonight she was a little bit afraid. She let him unbutton her uniform shirt, but then he took it all the way off, and her bra too. Once he had done that, it didn't matter when she put her hands on his and tried to keep him from taking her other things off too. He just did it. She whispered, "At least turn the lights off," but he said, "No. I like to see you this way."

Pretty soon he picked her up, carried her into her bedroom, and set her on her bed. She said, "Tim, I don't think we should do this. I don't want to. I'm still a virgin," and "Stop. Don't." Finally he hesitated, and she thought he had realized it wasn't a good idea, but he had only paused to slip on a condom. And then he took her.

When it was over, she wrapped herself in the covers and lay there, quietly crying. He put on his clothes right away and tried stroking her hair and her bare shoulder, saying softly, "Please don't cry. I'm sorry. I really like you, and I couldn't help it. I thought you liked me too."

Charlene hated him, and she loved him, and she hurt. She wanted him to go away, and to die, and to stay forever, being nice to her now that he'd had what he wanted. Then, without expecting to, she stopped crying. It was like a fever that abruptly broke. "Go home now," she said. She heard his heavy steps on the floor as he walked out of the room, then heard her front door open and close.

The next day she didn't go to work. The day after that, she went in at the usual time, started working, and wouldn't look at Tim or answer him when he spoke. She didn't go and sit outside with Alice during the three o'clock break, because she couldn't bear to answer her questions.

At quitting time she left without a word. He left too, and walked beside her. As soon as they were on a dark street and alone, he said quietly, "I really care about you, Charlene. I want you to know I couldn't sleep for the last two nights. I didn't mean to make you hate me or anything." They walked on for a dozen steps. "Charlene?"

"What?"

"Aren't you going to say anything?"

"Okay." She walked in silence for another few seconds. "You raped me."

"No, I didn't. It was just—"

"You did. I said no, and you did it anyway."

"I thought you were just saying that, like 'no, no, no-oh,' and then you stopped saying it. I thought that meant you really wanted to."

"I was crying, Tim. You didn't even notice."

"I'm sorry. I'm really, really sorry," he said. "I didn't think I was doing anything you didn't want me to. If I'd thought I was, I would have stopped."

They were at her house now. She climbed the porch steps and turned to face him, but he stayed down in the shadows by the railing. She took her keys out of her purse and unlocked the door. "Come in."

"That's okay," he said.

"No. It's not okay. You're coming inside. Now."

She held it open, and the light from the lamp she had left on so she wouldn't have to come in alone in the dark was shining on his face. He looked down, but he came up the steps and followed her into the house.

Charlene shut the door and locked it. She didn't turn on any more lights or offer him a drink. She said, "You were horrible. I liked you so much, but you hurt me and treated me like you didn't care what I felt. You were like an animal or something, and you made me feel like one too. You were a pig."

"I feel terrible. I don't know how to make it up to you."

"You've done it. You can't undo it. But you're not going to leave me feeling like this."

"I can't go back to two days ago. What am I supposed to do now?"

"You're going to do it one more time. People say the first time is awful for everybody, but once you're past that, it's nice. You have to be sweet to me. Do it the right way this time, not mean."

All these years later, she remembered the look on Tim's face—shock, then something like relief. He treated her gently, as though she were made of porcelain, like the dolls in the window of the antique store. He was very slow and cautious, very patient. This time it was the way she had always imagined it would be, and she almost liked him. He stayed until three-thirty, then hurried home so he would be asleep before his parents woke.

For the rest of the summer, she allowed him to think of her as his girlfriend. At the Dairy Princess he did all of the heavy lifting that was involved in her job, then did the cleanup and walked her to the local hangout, where his friends were already drinking and talking with older girls.

Alice began to resent Charlene. She made a remark about how nice it must be having somebody to do her share of the work. Once when Charlene yawned, Alice told her she should sleep alone sometimes, then turned and went to the order window, leaving her alone. Charlene felt as though she had been slapped. She thought about it for a while, and then decided that Alice didn't matter. Charlene just had to endure a few weeks, and summer would be over.

By mid-August, Charlene's unpaid bills had all been turned over to collection agencies, and their attempts to get the money from her became more aggressive. She had to unplug the telephone to keep from being called all the time, but then when she plugged it in to make a call, it wouldn't work.

The customers of the Dairy Princess had moved into the strange frenzy that seemed to hit people just before each summer ended, and made them frantic and selfish. She knew they were trying to get the last few days of pleasure before things turned dark and cold and wet again, so they lined up at the Princess in surly, sweating queues, crowding the lot in front of the store on the way home from some activity that had left them discontented. The sweet residue of ice cream and sugary drinks they spilled made the wasps drunk and vicious.

Charlene waited one night until she and Tim were alone and cleaning up before she said, "Tim, I'm pregnant."

His mouth was open and he seemed to reel, as though he didn't have enough air. She waited a few seconds, then said more loudly, "I'm pregnant."

"I heard you," he said, the slightest tinge of irritation slipping into his voice. She waited for him to say it, and he said it, exactly as she had imagined he would: "What are you going to do?"

"I don't know, exactly," she said. "What are you going to do?"

"What do you mean?"

"You're the only one I was with," she said. "Ever. It's yours too."

"I know that." This time the irritation had shaded off into sadness. "Of course I'll do what I can. What do you want me to do?"

His suffering resignation inspired her to torment him. "I guess we could get married. I'll be eighteen in a few months."

She could see that behind his widened eyes a film was running at great speed. It was about the things he wanted desperately—education, good jobs, prosperity, a beautiful young wife who would come into his life in about ten years—moving beyond his reach forever. He looked faint. "I don't know. I want to marry you," he lied. "But that's—I don't know. You're not even eighteen, and I'm only twenty. We don't even have a job after the first of the month."

"Wouldn't your parents help us? They must have some money."

"I don't know. My father will be pissed. My mother—God, I can't tell her this."

"It's their grandchild. I'm pregnant, and I can't even afford vitamins." She was very proud of that one.

"Oh, God," he said. "We always used protection. How did this happen?"

She looked at him with distaste. "Obviously, once it didn't work. It leaked or something."

He said, "We've got to think this through. How pregnant are you?"

"My period was supposed to start eight days ago, and I'm never more than a day or two late. I bought a test, and I took it yesterday. I bought another today, and used it. I wanted to be sure, and now I'm sure. I called the doctor because he doesn't charge to talk on the phone, and he said the accuracy of the test is almost a hundred percent." She gave a sad little smile that she had practiced for this moment. "He told me congratulations." Then she made herself cry.

Tim held her and rocked her back and forth, but she didn't stop, so he released her and finished closing the store. They walked to her house, but when she asked him to come in, he said he needed to be alone to think.

For two days, they exchanged looks of worry in the kitchen, where Alice and the customers couldn't see them. Three days after that, when she arrived at the Dairy Princess he was waiting for her outside the back door, and they walked to the park. He was so nervous that she could see the sweat on his forehead. They sat on a park bench and he said, "I've thought about this. I have something for you." It was a plain white business envelope. Inside were some green bills. He said, "It's twelve hundred. Most of what I saved this summer."

"You're trying to buy me off?" Tears came to her eyes. "For twelve hundred dollars?"

"No," he said. "It's not to buy you off."

"Keep it." She tossed the envelope on his lap. "I can't live on it if I have the baby, and I'm not getting an abortion." She stood up. "I thought by now you would have talked to your father. You can't keep him from knowing this."

Tim was horrified. His eyes were swimming, but he wasn't crying. It looked like the way a person's eyes watered when he was hit in the nose. "You're not going to go to him. He'll kill me. He'll disown me. Really."

"We'll see." She got up and started to walk.

"Wait. You're right." When she heard him running to catch up with her, she kept going. "Please," he said. "Give me one more day."

The next morning when she was almost dressed for work there was a loud knock on the door. She could see from the shadows on the curtain that it was two men. She was afraid it might be the sheriff's deputy with an eviction order, but when she pushed the curtain aside a quarter inch, she saw it was Tim and an older man wearing a business suit, who didn't look happy. She smiled into the mirror, fixed her hair, then went to the door.

When she opened it, Tim surged forward. "Can we come in?"

The older man held Tim's arm in his hand and pulled him back, then stepped in ahead of him. "I'm Tim's father. I know who you are."

"I'm Charlene."

"Tim tells me he knocked you up."

"That's right."

"You've both been very foolish. Neither of you had the right to do that. I'm here to try to settle this right now, while we still can."

"How?"

"Tim tells me he offered you some money, and you told him it wasn't enough." He reached into the inner pocket of his suit coat, took out an envelope, and held it out. Charlene could see it had come from the same box of envelopes as Tim's had.

"How much is in it?"

"Enough to see you through the pregnancy, or to get you an abortion. Three thousand dollars. In return, you sign this paper, saying he's not responsible."

Charlene said, "I appreciate your coming here to help me. But I haven't decided what to do yet."

"What do you mean?"

"The first time it happened, Tim forced me."

Tim's father's head spun to face the boy, his eyes protruding. He looked like a bull. Tim's eyes stayed straight ahead, staring at her as though he had been punched. "Charlene . . ."

Charlene said, "He was my boss at the Dairy Princess. I was afraid to tell, and afraid to say he couldn't do it again. It was the only job I could get in town. I needed to work to pay for college, and I'm only seventeen, so I couldn't work in a regular restaurant where there's a bar. I'm thinking about talking to somebody about it—maybe a lawyer."

Tim's father's eyes blinked as though he had a pain in his stomach. She could tell he had a suspicion about her, but he did not dare voice it without knowing the truth. He had to assume that this meeting was his only chance to settle her complaint quietly. She knew he was considering letting Tim take his chances, but the risk was enormous—greater than Tim knew. If she really was seventeen and pregnant, and told that story in court, Tim could end up in prison.

He said carefully, "Charlene, I'm sorry. I didn't really understand the situation until now. I want to pay for your medical care and your first year at the university—tuition, room, and board. I make that about—" He looked up at the ceiling. "Three thousand medical. Fifteen thousand for the university is eighteen thousand."

"Is that how much it costs?"

"Yes. I'll be honest with you, that doesn't include a lot of frills. But it should cover things."

"All right, then."

He said, "Here's the paper." He handed it to her, then held out a pen.

She took the paper but ignored the pen. "By the time you get back here with the money, I'll have had a chance to read it."

Late that afternoon, she packed and stripped the house of the few items she cared about that fit in her two suitcases, and counted the money Tim's father had given her. The next morning she was on the early bus to Chicago.

Tonight, as she drove along the dark highway in Mary Tilson's car, she remembered how much she had enjoyed the day when she had left Wheatfield on the bus. Lying about the pregnancy had given her some satisfaction—planning it all summer, then springing it on Tim's father like that, right in front of Tim, when she hadn't left him a way to even deny any of it—but what she had enjoyed most was the money. She remembered sitting on the bus staring out the window at the long line of telephone poles going by, and thinking about the beautiful things all that money would buy.

18

Catherine Hobbes sat at a stainless steel table in the crime lab and watched Toni Baldesar pouring epoxy into a small dish. Toni carefully placed the kitchen knife in the vapor chamber, then lifted the dish of epoxy onto the hot plate, closed the door, and began to heat it. She turned to Catherine. "All we can do is wait and see if the epoxy vapor makes some latent prints show up. If they match the ones I got from the rental agreement, we'll have her."

"I don't think there will be any," said Catherine. "She's not careless. She's got an obsession with cleaning things and wiping off surfaces to be sure she doesn't leave anything. I don't see her leaving prints on a murder weapon."

"I know, but you'd be surprised at how often I get lucky with things like that. They get emotional, and then everything is such a mess, and they have so many things to think about at once. Sometimes I think that a person's brain just skips over the things that it doesn't want to think about—especially things that involve getting blood on them or going back to touch the body."

"Maybe," said Catherine. She had a blown-up copy of the driver's license photograph of Tanya Starling on the table in front of her, and while she waited she was using a pencil to fill in the background to make the hair shorter. "And it's just possible that my theory about her is wrong. Some man may have come looking for her and killed Mary Tilson because she saw his face."

"I'd rule that out," said Toni.

"Based on what evidence?"

"Based on no evidence—no evidence that a man has been in that apartment since the day the plumbing was installed," said Toni. "No prints, no hairs, no shoe marks, nothing."

"That's what I've been telling people," said Catherine. "So far I've got two of us convinced."

Toni was staring through the small window in the front of the vapor box at the butcher knife. The epoxy vapor had filled the small chamber. She flipped a switch and an exhaust fan cleared the vapor. She opened the door and examined the knife with a flashlight, then turned it over. "Score one for the pessimists. She wiped the handle clean."

"What have we got left?" asked Catherine.

Toni looked up at the clock on the wall. "It's nearly eleven. What I've got is a load of laundry and a sink full of dishes waiting at home."

"I'm sorry," said Catherine. "I know I kept you here half the night."

"No," said Toni. "You didn't. When we've got one that fresh, I always try to squeeze all the information I can out of the trace evidence the first day. Sometimes you find something that helps catch the killer that day, and not just convict him two years later."

"I know. That's why I've been hanging around."

Toni carefully poured the warm epoxy back into its jar. "How long have you been a cop?"

"Seven years. Four in homicide."

"You went through the ranks fast." She began to sponge off the counters where she had been working.

Catherine shrugged. "It's a small department and I'm good at taking tests."

Toni looked at her for a moment. "I'll bet you are."

"How long for you?"

"Fifteen years this June. For me, it's a little different. I see some horrible things, but I don't have to chase anybody down and drag him off to jail. There's less stress." She took off her lab coat and hung it on a hook. "And no fear."

"Well, thanks for staying late tonight," said Catherine.

"I'm sorry we didn't get everything we wanted, but we'll keep working on it."

"Thanks to you, we know for certain Nancy Mills is Tanya Starling, and we can place her in the victim's apartment. That's plenty for one day." Catherine folded her picture of Tanya Starling as they walked toward the door.

"Do you need a ride to your hotel?"

"No, thanks," said Catherine. "I have a rental car." She stepped out in the hallway and Toni locked the door of the lab. "Good night."

She went to her car in the police lot and drove through the dark streets toward her hotel. Talking with Toni had made her think back on her first days as a police officer. She had not grown up planning to join the police bureau. She had decided to apply to the academy during the long drive home, away from the wreckage of her life in California. It had been an act of desperation, just grasping for something in her life that made sense and didn't need an excuse or an explanation. The months in the academy that followed, the grueling physical training and the Spartan discipline that bothered other recruits so much, had been her salvation. At times she thought it had saved her life.

She remembered the first day after she had graduated from the police academy. She reported for work at the police bureau more than an hour early, all dressed in her uniform with her shoes shined and her heavy gear creaking against her leather belt. She had been assigned to the precinct station on the northeast side of the city.

When she walked in the front entrance and approached the desk, a big man with a military haircut and a neck that seemed to overflow from his starched collar stepped in from the side and said, "Hobbes?"

"Yes."

"I'm Lieutenant Morton. Come with me."

She followed, watching his broad back swaying from side to side with his rolling gait. He went into his office and closed the door, then glared at her with bloodshot eyes. His face seemed to have some kind of pink, irritated rash on it that she later came to believe was a reaction to contained anger. He said, "Catherine Hobbes."

"Yes, sir" was all she could think of to say.

"Your father is Lieutenant Frank Hobbes, and your grandfather was the first Frank Hobbes. Is that right?"

She smiled. "Yes." She felt a moment of pride, and maybe some relief.

"I hate dynasties." He paused, then narrowed his eyes. "A police force is a government operation, which means that nobody in this town owns any more of it than anybody else. It doesn't matter whose daughter or granddaughter you are. You are the greenest of green rookies, and you will be treated like all of the others in every respect. You got that?"

"Yes, sir," she said. "I never wanted any special privileges." Her stomach began to sink, and she knew her face was beginning to turn red.

"You are also a woman," he continued. "I'm very suspicious of that."

"Of what—that I'm a woman?"

"Being a woman and wanting to be a cop. In this precinct we deal with a lot of street crime. Every day a cop has to go out and drag somebody back here in handcuffs or push somebody around. You coming here and exercising your constitutional right to wear that uniform has grave implications for the rest of the people I put out there. You coming here means to me that you must be assuming that some male cop is going to be willing and able to do his share of the physical stuff and yours too."

She knew that her face was bright red, but there was nothing she could do about it, and she was not going to retreat. "I'm not—"

"Being Frank Hobbes's daughter, you cannot pretend that you didn't know what a cop does. You can't possibly imagine you're going to take down some crystal meth monster who's six feet six and two eighty."

"No, sir," she said. "Most of the men in my academy class aren't up to that either. But any one of us will do our best to help subdue a person like that if the occasion comes up, and to use our brains to be sure it doesn't come up often."

He glared at her for two seconds, then smiled, and said, "You are Frank's girl. Welcome to my shop. Now get to roll call and go to work."

19

Nancy Mills drove deeper into Arizona in the night. She had hoped to be better off than this by now. When she had seen Carl for the last time in Chicago, she had said she would have more money than he had within one year. It had been most of a year already, and what did she have so far? Forty thousand? No, less. She probably had thirty thousand left, and she was driving a dead woman's car along a highway that had signs telling her to watch out for elk. Carl would have laughed at that if he could have known.

Carl had hated nature. He had told her that golf courses were about the wildest places he ever wanted to be. He said that people who went on hikes in the wilderness or liked animals were stupid. Now that she could look back, she knew he had thought that most of the people he knew were stupid. Compared to Carl, they probably were.

She had met Carl in a restaurant in Chicago. She had just finished her final exams for the fall semester, and she had taken herself out to dinner to celebrate.

The celebration felt due, because the semester had been a difficult time for her. Charlene had come to Chicago on the bus four days early. She had slept in the bus station the first night, then rented the only lodging she could afford, a room in a dirty motel not far from the campus. She had walked past her dormitory each day to see if it was open yet, and then sneaked in on the fourth day at seven A.M., when the last of the janitorial crews were cleaning up after the painters who had given the hive of cubical cinder-block rooms a fresh coat of bile green.

She had dreaded the way the first day at the dormitory would be. She had seen simulations of that day in movies and television shows—the happy, eager students, the resigned, tearful mothers, the proud, worried fathers all haunting the dormitories—and had known there was no place for her in that event. For her it could only be an unmasking. Everyone would see that nobody cared about her, and that she was nothing.

She put her clothes into one of the two dressers in her room, left a note to claim one of the beds, and went out until evening, after the other girls were settled and their families gone. She told the girls on her floor that her parents were living in Europe, and couldn't come with her.

College began badly and became an ordeal. She had hoped college would change her life, but the girls snubbed her, the city was gray and filthy, and the work was demanding and monotonous. The world was pretty much the same everywhere, and her status in it was fixed at the lowest slot. Nothing Charlene Buckner ever did was going to make more than a minor change that would probably be temporary and might not even be an improvement.

Near the end of the semester, Charlene began to make her first visits to another life, one that existed because she chose it. She bought two good outfits at Marshall Field's. One was a black cocktail dress that was on deep discount because there was a tiny tear in the hem that she could fix in a minute. The other was a sleek black skirt and three different tops to go with it.

She found a good pair of black shoes on sale because they had heels too high for most women to bear. Her mother had trained her from the age of four to dance in high heels for the beauty pageants, so she loved them. There was also a pair of black flats that she could wear in less formal places, and a small, elegant black purse. The coat she bought was intended as a raincoat, too light for a Chicago January, but she knew it looked right, so she tolerated the cold. She began to dress and go out alone at night.

Charlene would call for her reservations in various names that she made up while she was standing at the dormitory pay phone, like Nicole Davis or Kimberly De Jong. She would go into the bar after dinner, and when men asked her name, she would give them the latest one. During the long weeks of classes she was Charlene, but once or twice a week, there would be a night when she became Nicole or Kimberly or Tiffany.

She discovered that she could attract men. Occasionally she would go out on a Friday night, meet a man, and then not return to the dormitory until Saturday, or even Sunday. If anyone asked where she had been, she would say she had gone to visit an old school friend in Boston, or met her parents for dinner in New York. But the other girls had so little interest in her that they seldom asked.

She loved the nights when she was someone else. The only disappointment was the men. They excited her at first because they were a few years older than she was, but they were all so involved with their careers as stockbrokers or sales representatives or junior executives that they were unable to convey anything to her about their lives that she understood, except that they worked very long hours.

On one of those Friday evenings, at a restaurant called Luther's, she met Carl. She'd walked in from the dining room and stepped toward the bar when she became aware that someone was close behind her. There was a tap on the shoulder, and she turned to see Carl. He smiled and said, "Please join me at my table."

Carl was older than the men she had been meeting: he looked about forty-five. He wasn't exactly handsome, but he was trim and had good posture, and his dark suit was beautiful. For a second when she had first turned around she'd thought he might be a hotel employee who was going to check the forged identification she'd bought outside the stu-

dent union. But she looked at his expression and saw his eye-
brows raised in an offer rather than knitted in anger, so she
assumed a look of self-assurance she had been practicing,
and went with him.

He introduced himself as Carl Nelson, and said he had noticed her at dinner and had not been able to let her leave
without meeting her. He spoke without any embarrassment
or uncertainty, a feat that she could not imagine any of the
younger men performing. Everything he said seemed effort-
less. He told her she was a young woman who deserved to be
congratulated on her beauty and told her that seeing her gave
him pleasure.

She was so pleased that she invented a name for the occasion. She said she was Tanya Starling. It came to her because
Tanya had always seemed to her to be foreign, and therefore
frankly sensual. Starling was the corrective, a word that
made her sound tiny and vulnerable, a way of protecting herself from the Tanya part.

Carl liked her name, and he liked her. When the waiter
arrived, Carl didn't ask her what she wanted. He simply ordered two vodka martinis, up, with an olive. When they arrived, cold and clear, she recognized them. As a child she had
always imagined her mother in an elegant place like this with
a man like Carl, drinking something from a stemmed glass
that moved back and forth to throw off reflected light when
she lifted it.

Carl was a lawyer. Unlike the younger men, he didn't say
much about his work, but it was clear he had made money.
Tanya didn't exactly lie about what she was doing, but she
made getting a bachelor's degree into "studying the arts at
the university," so it would sound like a whim of an older
woman.

When she went back to the dormitory she had to tell her
roommates that she would take any calls for her friend
Tanya. Two days later, Carl called her and took her to another
good restaurant. After that he took her out every couple of
days, and called her whenever he happened to be thinking of
her. He sent her flowers because they reminded him of her.
He began to buy her other things—a set of sapphire earrings

that would set off her blue eyes, a dress that would make her proud of her tiny waist.

He called one day at the end of February, when the ground was covered with dirty snow that had partially thawed and then frozen into ice, and the wind was punishing. He said, "Honey, I'm going to Florida for a few days on business. I thought you might like a little break, and I'd like some company."

"Florida?" was all she could say.

"I've got to meet with a client in Palm Beach. That part won't take long, but I'm staying until Friday. Can you spare the time for me?"

She packed her two suitcases with the few good clothes she owned, said good-bye to her roommates early in the morning, and told them she'd be back in a week for midterms.

That day she learned what life with Carl Nelson would be. When they arrived in Florida a limousine waited to take them to the hotel and then to the country club for lunch with the client. The client was about sixty years old with impossibly white capped teeth, a pair of red-tinted glasses, and a suntan of a depth that had not been stylish during Charlene's lifetime.

Carl introduced them by saying, "Tanya, this is Richard Fellowes. Richard, this is the most beautiful girl in the state of Illinois, and her name is Tanya."

After only a moment she realized that Carl had brought her there to be decorative, so she imitated the haughty, bored look of the fashion models of her childhood and kept all of her movements graceful, while showing no awareness that the men were having a conversation. She answered direct questions and smiled politely at Richard Fellowes when it seemed necessary, but smiled much more warmly at Carl.

The lunch told her a bit about Carl. Fellowes had owned a chain of dry-cleaning plants in the Midwest. Carl had helped him sell his controlling interest in the business at a large profit and move to Palm Beach a few years ago. Fellowes had remained on the board of directors, but now that the new owners were considering selling it, they wanted to buy his remaining shares.

Carl went over the papers with Fellowes while Tanya Starling gazed out over the shady veranda at the deep green lawns and the first hole of the golf course, a tree-bordered straight stretch of grass that looked to her about the length of an airport runway, with, at the end of it, a tiny flag. The only sight beyond the flag was the blue of the ocean she had never seen before.

Carl's voice was deep and calm and reassuring. She could tell he was smart, that he had instantly seen what he had needed to in the contract and knew exactly how much of it to explain to his client. At the end, he handed Fellowes an onyx fountain pen and had him sign. When Fellowes said, "What's this?" he answered, "You're just initialing there to show that you know I'm also getting a fee from the company." Tanya let her face reveal nothing. Carl was being paid by both sides.

On the way back to the hotel, Tanya wanted to say something to Carl about the opulence of the country club, but she didn't. She wanted him to believe that she was sophisticated from birth, a creature of natural taste who belonged in luxury because she was unimpressed by it.

When the week in Florida was over, they flew back to Chicago at night. There was no discussion about Tanya going back to the dormitory. Carl simply had the driver go directly to his apartment in a high-rise building overlooking the lake. The driver carried their bags to the lobby, and the doorman put them into the elevator and transported them to the apartment on the top floor. Carl put her two suitcases in the guest bedroom and said, "You can have the closets and bathroom in here to yourself. When you're undressed, come into our bedroom."

After two weeks Tanya thought to make a telephone call to the office of the dean of students and let them know she wanted a leave of absence. The next day she went to the university in a taxi, found the boy outside the student union who had sold her the fake driver's license she'd used to get served in bars, and ordered identification in the name Tanya Starling.

She wanted to be the perfect mistress, but it took her some time to realize what Carl expected her to be and to do. She went about it with the discipline she had been taught in the beauty pageant competitions when she was a child, and the determination that had gotten her to college. She used the pocket money Carl gave her to buy custom-mixed makeup, and had the store's experts teach her the latest looks and application techniques. As soon as Carl left each morning, she entered the home gym he had installed in the apartment, and exercised. She studied the articles in women's magazines about how she should look and what she should wear, and what men liked in female behavior but didn't necessarily know they liked, and how to improve her skin, hair, nails, body, and small talk.

In the evenings when she went to parties and dinners with Carl, she closely observed the other women. Some were attorneys or clients, but most of them were wives or girlfriends of very successful men. They were all a few years older than Tanya, and very elegant and poised. She studied manners and personality traits that she envied, and took them for herself.

From the beginning, some of the men Carl knew would find ways to be alone with her for a moment and try to interest her in meeting them somewhere without Carl. She was extremely careful to be unremittingly loyal to Carl, but never derisive or threatening to the suitors. She understood instinctively that making enemies of Carl's friends and colleagues could only lead to trouble for her. As she got better at her new vocation, she gained knowledge of what men were really thinking and feeling. She saw that they might have complex minds full of information she was not capable of understanding, but in their dealings with women, they were no more able to think beyond the mere prospect of sex than Tim had been.

Carl dressed her expensively, took her to wonderful places, and treated her as his protégée. His conversation taught her things—which paintings in a gallery were the best, which wines were the right ones to serve, which writers were the ones to read, which orchestras were the ones to hear.

Carl was a recreational talker, a man whose own voice enchanted him so much that for him speech was like singing. As soon as he was home each evening, drinking the martini she had mixed for him, he told her anecdotes about what he had done all day and what he had thought, and shrewdly analyzed the people he had seen. They were all minor players in his personal story, which was essentially comic, because he always triumphed.

He taught her how much to tip various people who provided services, and to remember that it was wise to tip the most when the service was still in doubt, not afterward, in gratitude for something she already had. Once, when Carl needed to leave her alone for a few days, he opened a drawer in the bedroom and showed her where the gun was.

He picked it up, then said, "It's loaded, see?" He moved the cylinder to the side to show her the bullets in the holes, then flipped it back. "It's smart to consider all of them loaded, but this one always is. If somebody knows I'm gone and thinks that makes it a good time to break in, you hold it like this, arms extended in front of you, and pull the trigger. Fire three or four times. It's a .357 magnum, so I guarantee it will stop him. It's got a bit of a kick, so hold on."

"You mean it's legal to kill someone because he's trying to break in?"

"It's not murder if he breaks into your apartment and tries to harm you. If he's still outside in the hall when you shoot him, drag the body inside before you call the cops." Then he added, "And if he's not dead, shoot him again, in the head. If they live, they sue."

For nearly nine years, she lived with Carl Nelson and learned from him. In return, she was even-tempered and companionable. She was aware that his attraction to her was sexual, so she cultivated the attraction. His manner in bed was much like his conversation. He was affable and he wanted to charm her and be the one directing the proceedings, teaching her things he thought she would like. All she really had to do to please him was to be available and submissive, willing to be impressed.

Just before Tanya's twenty-eighth birthday, Carl Nelson came home from his office early. He didn't sit where he usually did, on the couch where she had been waiting for him. He sat instead in the chair across from her. He said, "I'm finished with the Zoellner case. I'm going to Europe for a while."

She said, "Wonderful. Should I call to make arrangements with the travel agent?"

"No, thank you. They've already handled that at the office."

She understood then, from the way he said it. He was going. She was not. She controlled herself as well as she could. "You deserve a break. When will you be back?"

"In about a year. I'm taking a sabbatical. I'll be doing some work while I'm over there, handling some things for regular clients."

"You're taking a secretary, aren't you?"

He nodded. "Mia is going with me."

She had seen Mia at his office. Mia was nineteen years old and already a failed model. She was taller than Tanya—taller even than Carl—and she had striking green eyes. She was Tanya Starling's replacement.

Tanya stood up and said, "Excuse me, Carl. This is hard for me." She went into their bedroom, crawled onto the bed, and cried. She stayed there for a long time. Then she heard noises. It was Carl in the big walk-in closet. There were sounds of hangers scraping sideways along the pole, and drawers opening and closing.

Tanya went into the bathroom, spent a few minutes fixing her hair and makeup, then stepped into Carl's closet. She said, "Packing? You're leaving that soon?"

"My flight is at ten tomorrow."

She could feel herself beginning to lose control. Tears were coming, and her knees felt weak. She said, "I'll have my stuff out of the apartment as soon as I can. I think the doorman will let me leave a few things with him while I find a place."

"There's no reason to do anything like that, Tanya. In fact, I've been counting on you to stay here while I'm gone."

"For the whole year?" Maybe he was going to have the secretary for a while and then come back to her. Men loved variety. That was okay. Her mind was already accommodating itself to the idea. Maybe he would even send for her.

"Sure. It will give you the time to figure out what you would like to do with your life, and get a start on it. You're smart, beautiful, and you should be doing something. Maybe real estate, or decorating. Take some time and think it over. And your staying here gives me somebody I know I can trust to care for the place and keep an eye on it. I'll have the office pay the bills and send you an allowance."

"Sure." The word *allowance* was a deliberate reminder of her dependency, but he would have had to maintain the lease anyway, and pay someone to occupy the apartment and care for his tropical fish, his paintings and antiques.

She considered taking Carl's pistol out of its drawer and shooting him. She considered simply slipping the loaded gun into his suitcase, so he would be arrested at Heathrow or De Gaulle or wherever he was flying to. But then she detected a contradictory impulse. She stopped being angry because she wanted him to stay. She began to be impatient for him to leave.

She spent some minutes exploring feelings she had not acknowledged before. She was humiliated, hurt, shocked, but now she realized that her situation was not so simple. She had been exploited, certainly, for her sexual attractiveness and her docility. In return, she had been educated, entertained, and pampered for nine years. The part that she was astounded and ashamed about was that she had not anticipated this moment or prepared herself for it.

Carl's ability to appreciate women was limited to girls of about eighteen. He found them interesting only during this phase of their lives. His was an entirely sexual addiction, but it wasn't because they were at their best. The exercised, massaged, and rested Tanya Starling looked much better, even younger, than the lonely, sad, frightened Charlene Buckner had, and she was more adventurous. And Tanya had seen

Mia, who was going to take her place. Mia was pretty, but not prettier than Tanya. The attraction was that she was the right age: Tanya no longer was.

Tanya couldn't be taught which clothes to wear or which wines to serve, how to behave at a cocktail party or how to please a man in bed, because by now she knew. She couldn't be taken to a great hotel and stare in awe at the paintings on the domed ceiling, because she had already seen others as good. She had heard Carl's stories, and he could never tell them to her for the first time again. She was no longer a protégée, just a sycophant massaging his ego, more desperate each day to keep him fooled, so she would not lose her increasingly unpleasant job.

He had betrayed her, certainly, but he had also set her free. He had supported her so lavishly that she would never have been able to translate her vague feelings of dissatisfaction into the irrevocable act of walking out the door. Now he was sending her away. It didn't feel good, but it felt overdue, like a task she had been putting off.

Tanya went to bed in the spare bedroom, but when, a couple of hours later, Carl finished his preparations for his trip and climbed into the bed with her, she didn't object to having sex with him. He seemed to believe he had one more night due him, and she didn't feel like fighting. It gave her a chance to observe the extent to which she had only been going through the motions, and to try to think back to the time when sex with him had still been exciting. She realized that tonight, when she had no feeling except impatience for his departure, was not much different from the last fifty nights.

The next morning, Carl was up at five. He wrote her a big check and placed it on the antique table in the entry. "Cash this," his note said. "It's just in case you need anything. Call the office any time you need more." At the door, he turned and noticed that she had stepped into the room to watch him. He set down his suitcases and embraced her. "I know you're a little scared, but you'll be fine. I know you're going to be a very successful woman someday."

She remembered her answer: "In a year, I'll have more money than you do." She had looked through the window to the street far below and watched the cab moving off, the tailpipe spewing steamy white exhaust into the cold morning air.

Tanya spent the next few months looking for work in the daytime and looking for a man in the evening. The evening hunting was better, but she didn't find the sort of man she needed. Rich men were nearly all married, and they were all aware that the most expensive catastrophe likely to befall them was a divorce. They were willing to spend lots of money on her, but they weren't willing to stay the night.

She went through a period in which she stopped looking for work and applied for readmission to the university, then spent her days trying to devise a course of study that would help prepare her for a career in law. Her observation of Carl had taught her that his clients paid him lots of money for very little work, as long as he kept them afraid.

She had begun to feel optimistic when she received a telephone call. She thought she recognized the voice on the other end as Arthur Hinman, one of the other partners in Carl Nelson's firm. He said, "May I speak to Miss Starling, please?"

She wasn't absolutely positive it was Arthur, so she said, "This is Miss Starling."

"This is Arthur Hinman, one of Carl Nelson's partners at Colefein, Park and Kayslander. I'm calling to let you know that Mr. Nelson has died."

"Oh, my God. How? Where?"

"I believe he had a heart attack, but I'm not sure yet. He was in Spain." He paused a full breath, which was his mourning period for Carl Nelson. Then he said, "We're handling his estate, and the lease for his apartment is being terminated. We'll be closing it up to inventory his effects. That means your services won't be needed anymore."

"Arthur," she said. "Don't act as though you don't know me. You've been here dozens of times. You know I'm not the maid or something."

"I'm sorry. I know it's inconvenient. But please be out of there by noon tomorrow. You can leave the key with the doorman downstairs."

She hung up the phone and went to work, taking everything from the apartment that she was sure Carl would have missed but the law firm would not. The art and antiques, the huge record collection, the old books were probably all insured. The cash Carl kept in the toe of a shoe on his upper closet shelf, and his cuff links, tie clasps, and tuxedo studs were all small enough to take. His watches were probably insured too, but nobody would be able to prove he hadn't lost one in Europe, so she took his Rolex. Then, as an afterthought, while she was tossing things into her suitcase, she opened the drawer that contained Carl's gun, and slipped it into her purse.

20

Catherine Hobbes sat in the homicide office of the North Hollywood station. She had borrowed a table beneath the whiteboard where someone had drawn a crude diagram of Mary Tilson's apartment, with a body that looked like a gingerbread man. She shut the sounds of ringing telephones and the voices of the detectives out of her mind, opened the file, and looked at each of the crime scene photographs again, and then at the list of fingerprints from the two apartments that had been identified so far. There was the copy of the print that belonged to Nancy Mills. Staring at it gave Catherine a strange feeling: this was more than something that the woman had touched. It was more intimate, the touch itself.

Catherine had spent a career listening to the confident voices of experts who assured her that there were no mysteries, and that the physical evidence always told the story. This was a physical world, every cubic centimeter crammed with molecules. Any motion created a disturbance that left a trail, and anything the killer touched stuck to him. They were right about Tanya: she was leaving a growing collection of trace evidence behind her. But where the hell was she?

Jim Spengler came into the room. "I brought you some coffee." He set a white foam cup on the table, then sat in the folding chair beside her.

"Thanks. I'll bet when you do interrogations, you're always the good cop."

"I would have brought it sooner, but I've been checking to see if there have been any other homicides since she got here that might have something to do with her." He looked at the photographs in front of her. "I heard you were in the lab half the night. Anything new?"

"No. I think Mary Tilson let her in, and they went together into the kitchen. I think Miss Tilson was turned to the left, maybe getting something out of the cupboard or refrigerator. When she turned away, I think Nancy Mills took the butcher knife out of the holder and stabbed her."

"You don't think a man did that?"

"I'm looking at the list of prints Toni's people found. I don't see any male prints anywhere in the apartment, identified or not. I don't see a forced entry."

"So she let him in."

"A sixty-year-old single woman like Mary Tilson is going to be nervous about letting a man into the apartment if she's alone."

"So Nancy Mills was with him. She let them both in."

"Even if the man is with Nancy Mills, he doesn't go into the kitchen with Mary Tilson and wait until she turns her back."

"Why not?"

"Because she won't let him, and if he comes, she won't

turn her back. If a single woman comes over to see another single woman, they both might go into the kitchen while they talk. The guest at least offers help while the hostess gets refreshments. If it's a stranger, a man, he doesn't go in the kitchen, he stays in the living room. If it's a man with Nancy Mills, the one who goes into the kitchen is still Nancy, not the man."

"Why not both?"

"Because. It's just the way it is. I've been a single woman for long enough so I know all the moves." She shrugged. "And there's no evidence that there was a man."

"You're also assuming that the stab in the back came first, not the throat."

"That's right. If you cut the throat first, the victim is as good as dead. If you stab her first, maybe she's still up to making some noise, even fighting. That's when you have to cut her throat—to keep her from yelling. We know the stab in the lower chest was last, because that's where the knife ended up." She glared at him. "I know what you're going to say next: No woman would do that."

"I was still back on the part about single-woman etiquette. You said you've been single for a long time, as though you weren't always. Have you ever been married?"

She frowned. She had been careless, because she hadn't been thinking about herself, or about him: she had been thinking about the sequence of events at the crime scene. "Yeah," she said. "I was." She avoided his eyes. Could he possibly not know that bringing up a woman's failed marriage would cause her pain?

"When were you married?"

"None of your business." She still didn't look at him.

"Come on. What am I going to do, gossip? Nobody knows you down here, and all I asked was when. That's a public record. I could look it up."

She turned to him, feigning boredom with the topic. "A long time ago. We were young, just out of college. It was a classic starter marriage. After a couple of years we both started to realize that we'd made a mistake."

"What was your reason?"

All right, she thought. Evasion would just prolong the badgering. "He had a problem with the 'forsaking all others' part."

"So you got a divorce. And that's how you got to be an expert on women living alone."

"Correct. Divorce is a costly way to find out how to choreograph murders of single women, but it works."

"Okay," he said. "For the moment, we don't have any sign it was a man. But my gut is telling me there is one." He looked over the lab reports.

From across the room Al Ramirez, one of the officers who had been at the apartment building, called out, "Detective Hobbes? There's a call for you from your department. Captain Farber."

She stood. "That's my boss. Where can I take it?"

"That phone on the desk in the corner. I transferred it."

"Thanks." She stepped over and picked it up. "Mike?"

She noticed that Jim Spengler had found something to do that kept him nearby, in earshot. The captain said, "Hi, Cath. What's up?"

"Tanya Starling was here in Los Angeles, using the name Nancy Mills. She seems to have pushed a man off an eighth-floor balcony at the Hilton hotel in Beverly Hills the night before last."

"How do you know it was her?"

"She got herself on another hotel security camera."

"Pushing him?"

"No. Picking him up in a bar earlier that night. The LAPD released a picture of her with him. She seems to have seen it and panicked. She packed up, cleaned her apartment, killed the woman in the apartment across the hall from hers, and went off in the victim's car."

"You really think she's doing all of this herself?"

"You sound just like Jim Spengler, the homicide detective in charge of the case." She looked at Spengler, who shrugged. "Who also sounds like Joe Pitt, and everybody else. I can place her in Dennis Poole's hotel room in Aspen with a picture and witnesses, and her hair places her in his house. I have pictures that can put her in a room in the Hilton hotel with the second victim, Brian Corey, and a fingerprint that places her in the apartment where Mary Tilson was murdered. What I can't do is find a single bit of evidence that there was an unknown man with her, or after her."

"I've seen a few pros who could come looking for her, kill witnesses, and take the evidence with them. I'm just saying, don't rule out the man just yet. I assume the LAPD has the car's description and plates out to every department."

"Yes. I think we're about twelve hours behind her. I think she'll get as far as she can in a day or two, and then dump it."

"So what do the L.A. cops need you for?"

"I suppose they don't. I'd like to stay at least another day in case the car is found and she's still in it."

"All right. You've got a day. And I know how I want you to spend it. We still don't know for sure that Dennis Poole's murder wasn't some kind of reprisal against his cousin Hugo—whether the girl did it, or someone helped her, or someone came for Dennis and she became an inconvenient witness."

"How can I eliminate a reprisal against Hugo Poole?"

"Find out if Hugo Poole is fighting back."

Catherine Hobbes parked her rental car on Sheldrake Avenue and dialed the number of the homicide office on her cell phone.

"Spengler."

"It's me. I'm on Sheldrake and I can see the theater."

"I hear you."

"All right. Here goes." She put the cell phone into the compartment on the side of her purse without ending the call, got out of the car, and walked toward the old movie theater. Long experience made her dislike being on foot and alone in this kind of neighborhood: there was nobody else walking, and there seemed to be no place to take a defensive position, only big brick office buildings with bars across their doorways. She considered the possibility that Hugo Poole cast such a big shadow that it kept minor predators away from his door.

When she reached the front of the theater, a tall, muscular man about thirty-five years old was waiting on the other side of the glass with a set of keys. He unlocked the door and held it open for her, then scanned up and down the street before he closed and locked it again.

"I'm Sergeant Hobbes, Portland Police."

"I know."

"And you are—?"

"We're not in Portland."

The man turned, and she followed him into a big, ornate old lobby with an empty glass candy counter and faded art deco murals on the walls. He climbed a carpeted staircase to the upper hallway. On both ends of the hallway were loges, but in the middle there was a wall of dark polished hardwood. It took her a moment to see that there were two doors cut into the wood. One had worn gold letters that said PROJECTION, and the other was unmarked. The man knocked on that one, and a muffled voice said, "Come in."

The man held the door open for Catherine Hobbes. "Thanks, Otto," said the voice inside, and Catherine entered.

Hugo Poole stood behind a big old desk that must have been part of the theater's original furnishings. He came around it, smiling. "Hello, Catherine. Or is it Cathy?"

"It's Sergeant."

"Oh. Should I be asking to see a warrant?"

"I'm just here to chat. When I called, I figured you would have Joe Pitt with you. Is he on his way?"

"No. I paid him off, and he went back to gambling full time." Hugo Poole looked at her suspiciously, and for a moment she wondered if he had sensed that her question had a personal interest behind it. But he said, "I don't know if you're wearing a wire or not. I often have Otto frisk visitors who might mean us harm. With you that policy seemed fraught with difficulties."

"Yes," she said. "Fraught."

"So I'll have to assume you are wired."

"Suit yourself."

"Are you here to tell me you've finally caught Tanya Starling?"

"No, I'm here because a disturbing suggestion keeps coming up as we search for her."

"What's that?"

"She seems to be doing things that some of my colleagues believe she couldn't, or wouldn't, do—at least alone. They think that your cousin Dennis was killed by some man who was trying to hurt you, and she was either a witness or an accomplice."

Hugo Poole stared at her unhappily, but said nothing.

She said, "Two days ago, another man she had been with in a hotel fell off an eighth-floor balcony. There are pictures of her on the hotel security tapes, just as there were with your cousin Dennis. The day after that, the woman who lived across the hall from her was stabbed to death with a butcher knife. LAPD is saying that it seems as though a dangerous, angry man is looking for her, and killing anyone who tries to protect her."

"I've heard that theory."

"What do you think of it?"

"Not much." He stared into her eyes. "But I don't know much about these things."

"No?"

"No. You're the cop. I'm just a small businessman. But it seems to me that all of these theories are based on the idea that women don't kill people."

"True."

"It seems to me your colleagues aren't willing to see anything that isn't statistically likely, because they're afraid of looking stupid."

"You could be right. But it's hard to prove that somebody isn't after her. And the only person anybody can think of who has a motive to hunt for her, and might have found it necessary to kill anyone near her, is you."

"I haven't been out of town since I was in Portland with you."

"The last two were in Los Angeles. The hotel was right up there on Wilshire."

"I haven't been in any hotels lately. You said there are pictures of her on the security tapes. Did you see any pictures of me?"

"No. But I didn't see any pictures of anyone else, either."

"Then she did it herself."

Catherine hesitated. "I'll be honest with you, Hugo, but I need you to be honest with me too. I think she's the only one. But if there's anything going on down here that would have made someone kill your cousin, I need to know about it. Now."

Hugo Poole shook his head and held out his hands. "I don't have any active enemies that I know about. I haven't heard a word from anybody taking credit for Dennis and threatening me. And I didn't kill any of these people or pay anybody to do it."

"I noticed that you didn't say that you've never killed anyone."

"And I noticed that the cops haven't been able to find one young girl in all this time, even though she's been leaving bodies all over the place."

"She'll be found. Be sure of that."

"Is there anything else I can do for you?"

She looked at him closely. "No. I just had to check and see if you knew anything I didn't."

He walked to the door and held it open for her. "Then you'd better be going. The traffic gets bad in this part of town right about this time of the afternoon."

"Well, thanks for your time, Hugo. Take care."

She walked past him into the carpeted upper level of the theater and let Otto conduct her to the front door. When Hobbes was outside and walking toward her car, she took her cell phone out of her purse and pretended to dial it. Then she said in a voice too low to be audible beyond a few feet, "Did you get all that?"

Jim Spengler's voice said, "Sure. I haven't heard the recording, of course, but it should be fine."

"Thanks for doing it," she said. "Not that it got us anything."

"Do you think he was lying?"

"No," she said. "I didn't see any sign that he was lying, and I'm good at spotting it. I think he was actually glad to see me at first, because he thought I'd come to tell him we had Tanya Starling." She reached her car. "Well, I'm at my car. I'll be there in a half hour or so."

"Wait," said Spengler. "I've got news."

"What is it?"

"Remember that I was checking other homicides that happened since she came to town? Well, after you left, the detective who was working on another case came to talk to me. He was investigating the murder of a young man a couple of weeks ago. The victim was a bank branch manager from San Francisco named William Thayer. He was here to visit his family. He was found shot in the head in a picnic area in the hills above Malibu. His car was found in the parking lot of the Topanga Plaza, about a mile from the apartment building where Nancy Mills lived. It seems the dead guy was the manager of the bank branch where Tanya Starling and Rachel Sturbridge had a joint account."

"Shit."

"What?"

"Nothing. I'll be there soon."

Inside the lobby of the Empire Theater, Otto locked the front door again. He watched Detective Hobbes get into her car and drive away, then turned to see Hugo Poole standing behind him, watching too. Hugo asked, "Did she say anything to you on her way out?"

"No. Anything I need to know?"

Hugo Poole nodded. "Yeah. All this time has gone by, and they're no closer to finding the woman who killed my cousin than they were two months ago."

"They're not?"

"No. She was back here to see if I did it. She's starting over."

"Is there something you want done to speed this up?"

"See if you can reach Calvin Dunn. Tell him I want him."

21

It was three-thirty A.M. and Nancy Mills seemed to be getting used up. She had been driving for hours and she was on the outskirts of Flagstaff, Arizona. At night like this, the city looked like an outpost on another planet. She found a street on the southwest side of the city where there were a few run-down apartments, parked Mary Tilson's car by the curb in front of an empty lot, and opened the trunk. She needed to cut down on what she was carrying.

She put her money and the drabbest, plainest clothes she had into one suitcase. She put the Colt Python pistol that had been Carl's into the zippered pocket on the outside of her suitcase, checked to be sure the smaller pistol she had taken from Mary Tilson's bedroom was loaded, and slipped it into her purse. She closed the trunk, then drove until she came to a shopping center, and cruised along the back of a row of stores until she found a dumpster. She placed the unwanted second suitcase into it, and drove off again.

She was lost in a way that felt hopeless, because there wasn't any place she was looking for, or any reason to believe that anywhere she stopped was going to be safe. She knew that she had to find a way to get some sleep. When she turned onto the next street, she saw that there were cars parked all along the curb, below some apartment buildings. She let the car coast to a stop and looked around her. Maybe if her car was parked with so many others, she could sleep in the back seat and nobody would notice her until morning.

But she couldn't let herself be here in the morning. The sun would come up, the new day would already be under way, and she would be caught in the light in the open.

She had to think hard, but she was so tired that getting her brain to do more than keep the car on the road was too much effort. She drove on for another mile of flat pavement, each side lined by one-story bungalows on plots of land that had ornamental stones or desert brush instead of grass.

She realized that it was the car that was making her vulnerable. The police would be searching for it, and without it she would look just like anyone else—just an anonymous girl. That gave her an idea, and she drove on, following the signs toward the airport. She parked the car in the long-term lot, wiped off the steering wheel, door handles, and trunk lid, took her suitcase, and caught the shuttle bus to the terminal.

She went inside the baggage area to the row of courtesy telephones for local hotels, picked the ones near the airport, and began trying to find a vacancy. When she found a room at one called the Sky Inn, the man at the desk asked for her name. She hesitated. The police were looking for Rachel Sturbridge and Tanya Starling, and probably Nancy Mills by now, so she said, "Nicole Davis." It was one of the names she had used in college when she had gone out alone. She stepped outside and into the first taxi at the curb.

When she arrived at the Sky Inn, she saw that the clerk who had talked to her was in his twenties but had taken on the mannerisms of middle age. He never smiled, and the only thing that seemed to give him pleasure was his own efficiency. He spoke in a monotone, as though he were reading, held the registration card so that it faced her, and used his pen to point to the room rate, the check-out time, and the place for her signature. As she signed, he said, "And I'll need a major credit card."

She stared at him, and her mind was blank for a second. She had become so exhausted she hadn't thought this through. She reached into her purse and pulled out a stack of bills. The rate was a hundred and sixty-five dollars a night, so she placed two hundred-dollar bills on the counter. "I'll pay in cash. I don't use credit cards."

He looked at her closely for the first time, but she sensed that it was only because she was a curiosity—a person who had gotten herself into trouble because she didn't know when to stop charging things. He took her money, went to the back room, and returned with her change. He handed her a small envelope with her key in it. "Up the elevator behind you to the second floor, then turn right." As Nicole Davis left, the young man busied himself clicking the keys of his computer terminal.

She entered her room, locked both of the locks and set the chain, put her purse where she could reach the gun, took a hot shower, and collapsed on the bed.

Several hours later she awoke and sat up, then reminded herself of what this room was, and that she was Nicole Davis. She stood and opened the curtain on the window just an inch, and the light blasted in to illuminate the whole room. She squinted out at the parking lot. The sun splashed off the roofs and windshields of the cars and into her eyes. She retreated.

The idea of stopping here to sleep had seemed brilliant last night. She had been on the edge of collapse, driving a car that belonged to a dead woman. She had felt she needed to be rid of Mary Tilson's car, and she was at least four hundred miles from Los Angeles. But now she was stranded.

She was in a hotel in a place where she had never been before, and she had no easy way out of here. How long had she slept? She looked at the clock by the bed, then picked up the watch she had left on the nightstand. It was nearly noon, check-out time. She remembered that geek downstairs saying it in his monotone voice. She stepped to the bed and picked up the telephone, then pressed the button for the front desk. "This is Miss Davis in—what is it—room 256. I'd like to stay another day. Is that all right?"

"Let me see." This time it was a girl's voice. A child's voice. "Um . . . you paid cash in advance for one night. What credit card did you give us?"

"I didn't. I don't carry credit cards, but I can come down there in a few minutes and pay for another day in cash."

"Well, there's a problem. I'm afraid your room, the one you're in right now, is rented for tonight. We might be able to move you to a new one, but check-in time isn't until four."

"All right. I'll just wait. Give me a call when the new room is ready."

"I'm so sorry. The thing is, we need the room you're in, and it's check-out time now. The staff has to clean it and change the sheets and so on before the new people arrive. They can't wait until four to do that. See?"

"So I have to check out now, and then check back in at four?"

"I'm afraid that's the only way we can accommodate you."

Nicole Davis had to be very, very careful. She closed her eyes to keep the frustration from turning into a red, blinding rage. "I can do that. I'll be right down."

She dressed quickly, then went through her suitcase. She removed all of the cash she had been carrying there, and the jewelry that David Larson had given Rachel Sturbridge, and put it into her purse. She closed her suitcase, and then opened it again. She couldn't leave the two-pound .357 magnum Colt Python with its four-inch barrel in the outer pocket the way it was. Somebody might brush against it or read its shape in the bulge it made. She slipped it inside the suitcase among her clothes and locked the suitcase.

She took the elevator to the lobby. At the front desk she found the female clerk she had spoken to, and she was glad she had kept her temper. The clerk was a small blond girl who seemed to be about seventeen. She smiled and tried to be helpful, but she didn't have enough authority to accomplish much.

Nicole Davis made a formal reservation for the first room that became available, and managed to force the girl to take the money for it in advance. Then she said, "Can I leave my suitcase with you and go out for a while?"

That was something the girl knew how to do, so she came around the desk with a label, wrote "N. Davis" on it and attached it to the suitcase, then wheeled it around the desk into a back office.

Nicole Davis found that it wasn't as hot outside as she had

feared. The sun was bright and the sky cloudless, but the altitude in Flagstaff was much higher than she was used to along the coast.

Nicole was uneasy. The police were looking for her, and Flagstaff wasn't big enough to hide her for long. She needed to get out of town, but how she did it made a difference. She couldn't get on an airplane or rent a car without identification, and the police were waiting for her to use ID that said Tanya Starling or Rachel Sturbridge. When she thought about the police hunting her, she always pictured the woman cop from Portland. That Catherine Hobbes had followed her to San Francisco, and she was still thinking about her every day, waiting for her to make some tiny mistake.

Nicole needed a car. She couldn't buy one at a car lot, because they would ask to see a driver's license. She needed to find a car on the street that had a For Sale sign on it. She would give the owner a few grand in cash and drive away with it. She began to examine every car parked along her way for a sign, but she couldn't find one. Then she turned a corner and saw something better—a bus station.

Nobody who was looking for Tanya Starling would imagine her getting on a bus. Everything they knew about her habits would lead them to look in the most expensive hotels or expect her to turn up at the luxury car lots. They knew Tanya Starling. But what they knew was a person she had invented. They didn't know that she had ever been anything but rich and spoiled. They didn't know that she knew how to be poor and alone.

She walked into the bus station, stepped to the counter, and picked up a copy of the printed bus schedule. She could see that business was slow today. There were a couple of men who looked like drunks slouching in and out of sleep in the waiting area, a couple of old people she decided were Indians, and a middle-aged woman with two children who looked the right ages to belong to her daughter. The bored man behind the window seemed to have nothing to look at but her, so she left with her schedule.

* * *

Thirty feet away, Tyler Gilman let his small blue Mazda coast to a stop at the traffic light on South Milton near the bus station. He looked at the clock on his dashboard. It was twelve forty-nine, and he still had to park and carry the five lunch orders to the women in the insurance agency on the next block by one.

He let his eyes drift to the sidewalk and saw the girl step out into the bright sunshine, looking down at a bus schedule she held open in her hands. Tyler's lazy glance settled on her and he didn't want to look away. She had straight brown hair that she had tied up in a neat bun like a dancer's, because it was so hot on the street. The sunlight caught the wisps of hair at the back of her delicate white neck. As though she sensed someone was staring, she abruptly looked up, then, not seeing Tyler behind his tinted side window, looked down at the schedule again.

He had seen her wrong at first. She was older than he was—not a girl of sixteen or seventeen but a young woman, at least twenty-five. Tyler felt a sadness that he knew was irrational. He knew he would have had little chance of attracting a female like her at any age, but her extra years moved her entirely out of his reach. Looking at her, he regretted it profoundly. He studied her rounded hips and breasts, feeling cheated. Wanting her wasn't his fault: she was a creature who had been deliberately designed to arouse his sexual longing. In his peripheral vision he caught the red light going out and the green coming on. He stepped on the gas.

Tyler drove to the next block, stopped in front of the insurance office, and turned off the engine. As he got out of the car, he looked back along South Milton, but he couldn't see the woman anymore. He leaned into the back seat to pick up the box of bagged orders from El Taco Rancho and thought about his reaction to her. He knew it was another odd thing about him he could thank his parents for. When he had started to be curious about sex at the age of nine, they had insisted on sitting down together to explain it to him. They were both religious people, so everything that existed was God's plan to accomplish something else. God wanted people to be fruitful and multiply, so he made women in a shape that you could barely keep your hands from touching, and that you kept thinking about and couldn't get out of your mind, even while you were asleep and dreaming.

Tyler kicked the car door shut, hurried across the sidewalk, and leaned his back against the door of the insurance agency to ease his way in with his box.

"Tyler! Where have you been?" It was Mrs. Campbell. She was a big, broad-faced blond woman who sat at the desk closest to the door. She went to the same church his family went to, and she seemed to think it gave her a special right to criticize.

He said, "I had to put your orders together, then drive over here from the restaurant."

"At Domino's, if your order doesn't arrive in twenty minutes, it's free."

"At El Taco Rancho they don't have that," said Tyler. "I'd have to pay for it myself."

"Maybe if you had to, you'd be faster." She was up from her chair, blocking his way and opening each of the five bags, looking inside them at the food.

Tyler began to sidestep. "Where can I put this down?"

Mrs. Campbell glared at him, but she pointed at a long table nearby, where there were a couple of coffee cups. He set the box down and stepped back while she continued to paw through the bags.

The four other women had heard her voice. They came out of the back offices and pulled chairs to the table where Tyler had set the food. Two of them were old, nearly retirement age, but the other two were young, and one was pregnant. The other young one gave him a smile as she passed close to him, and he watched her as she went to the table to identify her lunch. Tyler had written on the bags with a marker what was inside, so she took only a second.

The pregnant one said, "Whose turn is it to pay for lunch?"

"Julie's," said one of the older women. Nobody disputed her.

Julie was Mrs. Campbell. "How much is it?" she asked.

"Thirty-four eleven," said Tyler. He held out the cash register slip. He was sure that she had been the one he had told on the phone when he had taken the order. None of the others sounded anything like her.

"I'll get a credit card," she said. She took her purse from her desk and reached in.

"We don't take them," he said. "I mean, we do at the restaurant, but I can't do that here. I asked on the phone if it was cash or charge."

Mrs. Campbell took out her wallet. "All I have is a hundred-dollar bill." She held it out, sensing a victory.

"I don't have that much change."

Mrs. Campbell looked triumphant. "Then you'll have to come back for the money tomorrow."

"But I'll have to pay when I go back. The managers count the receipts against the orders every night, and everything has to add up."

Mrs. Campbell took a breath, but the pregnant woman said, "Don't worry. I'll get it this time, and Julie can take my turn tomorrow." She walked over to a desk, opened a drawer, and took out a purse. Tyler waited, avoiding Mrs. Campbell's eyes while the pregnant woman counted out the money, hesitated, then added three dollar bills. "And that's for you."

"Thanks." The amount of money didn't matter now. She had saved him.

Mrs. Campbell snapped, "I wouldn't tip him. He didn't bring extra salsa or extra hot sauce, or even enough extra napkins."

Tyler clenched his jaw and turned toward the door. He could feel his cheeks burning in anger and humiliation. He wanted to kill her. He wanted to go to the trunk of his Mazda, take out the tire iron, come back in, and swing it through her skull. But he couldn't. He couldn't even say anything back to her. She was in his parents' church.

As he reached the door, she called, "I'll be talking to your parents about the way you do your job, and the way you treat your elders."

As he opened the door and stepped out, he heard a voice say, "Oh, Julie." He closed the door behind him, walked quickly to his car, got inside, and started it. In the car it was quiet, and a stream of cool, breathable air surrounded him.

The car was a place of sanctuary. He put the transmission into drive and moved ahead a few feet, but he saw Mrs. Campbell come out the door and step toward him. He quickly pulled out into traffic and moved up the street away from her.

Tyler drove around the first corner, then came along the back of the bus station, turned right again and looked at the front entrance. The pretty young woman he had seen was gone. He wasn't sure why he had felt he needed to look at her again, and then he knew. At that moment he had felt reckless enough to offer her a ride. It was probably a good thing that he had missed her, instead of suffering the embarrassment of having her look at him with contempt.

Tyler charged that loss against Mrs. Campbell too. She had held him up until the pretty woman had disappeared, as though Mrs. Campbell was acting on behalf of the church. He knew the young woman was nearby, probably waiting inside the station out of the sun, but he had no more time. Already he was going to have to apologize to the other people who worked at El Taco Rancho for taking such a long time. The worst part was that what he really hated was not Mrs. Campbell. It was the way his parents had put him in the power of all of the people like Mrs. Campbell.

He knew that she really would corner his parents after church next Sunday and tell them that he was lazy and slow and disrespectful, and hint at causes for it that were worse. She would tell other people too, and he would see them looking at him with suspicion. His father and mother wouldn't defend him. They never did, and never had. They would believe Mrs. Campbell. Even if all four other women in that office said he was a good person and a responsible worker, it would make no difference, because Mrs. Campbell was saved, and the others weren't. They were members of false churches.

Tyler was sixteen years old and working full-time by himself while his parents went on vacation. He always got good grades at school and had competed all winter on the wrestling team and started all spring at second base, but they would believe that rotten old bitch instead of him. They would punish him, take something away from him. It would probably be his car, because they knew he loved his car. It had been his mother's for several years, but now it was his on the condition that he worked all summer for it.

Maybe they would even have a conference with Pastor Edmonds. Then he would have a chance to add on new punishments for Tyler too. They had done it when he had gone with Diane O'Hara to that party, because she was a Catholic. And then they had searched his room and found that magazine. Tyler's parents were gullible and weak and more worried about what a lot of people in the church thought than they were about their son. They had never protected him from anything—unfair teachers, the older guys who beat him up after school, people who said things about him.

He wished he could kill Mrs. Campbell and get away with it, but he knew he was being foolish to think about it. He was only concentrating on her because he didn't quite want to face the fact that the ones who most deserved to die were his parents. They had done what Joseph's brothers had done to him in the Bible—delivered him into the hands of his enemies—only they had done it over and over again all his life. He wished he could kill all of them, all of the tormentors and the betrayers who told him what to do and never left him alone.

Tyler made it back to El Taco Rancho, swung into his space near the dumpster, and trotted inside. It was already one-thirty, and the lunch rush was over. Nobody seemed to care that he was late. Danny and Stewart were busy scraping the griddle clean, and the girls were all refilling salt shakers and napkin dispensers in the space beneath the television set on the wall. Maria stepped up on a chair to change the channel to a station where a woman dressed up as a judge shouted at people who wanted a divorce.

Tyler started wiping down the tables and chairs with a dirty rag. A few customers straggled in while he worked, but most of them only wanted cold drinks, so one of the girls would leave the television set to draw the drinks and take the money. After a while, when Tyler was mopping, the sound of the television changed. Instead of voices there was urgent music. He looked up and saw the words "Breaking News" in red on an orange background. He stopped and watched.

There were two pictures of the pretty woman he had seen at the bus station. One had long blond hair, and the other much darker brown than she had now, but it was definitely the same woman. The newsman was calling her a fugitive, armed and dangerous. Tyler's chest expanded with excitement. He had seen her. He knew where she was. He looked at the clock on the wall. It was two fifty-three, almost time for the three o'clock break, when half the staff took off for a half hour. The others would go at three-thirty and be back at four to prepare for the dinner rush.

Tyler thought about the woman, and he felt that she was his, in a way. If he wanted to be a good citizen, he simply had to take out his cell phone and call the police. If he wanted to be a hero, he could drive there and make a citizen's arrest. He had seen her, and he knew that she wasn't really dangerous. Knowing about her was power, and having power was a new feeling for Tyler. He had to guard it. He pretended that he had not noticed the television. He moved off, mopping the floor near the front window, where he could not see the television screen, and thought about the pretty young woman and what he should do with her.

At three o'clock, Tyler took the mop and bucket he was using into the back of the kitchen, leaned the mop handle against the wall, and continued out the back door. He got into his car and drove it toward the bus station.

Nicole Davis had stopped for a quiet lunch in a small Mexican restaurant a block away from the bus station, and looked at her bus schedule. There was a bus leaving for Santa Fe, New Mexico, tomorrow at ten in the morning, so she had returned to the station and bought a ticket. She would get another night's sleep, then take the bus to Santa Fe.

She knew she was probably too early to get into her new room, but she seemed to have accomplished what she could for the moment, so she began to make her way back. She headed in the right direction, but after a time she did not see any buildings she remembered. She had somehow gone past the street where she should have turned. At each intersection she stared up the street and down, until she recognized the sign above a store on the corner two blocks to her left.

She considered correcting her course, but the street she was on had a long row of two-story buildings that threw shade across the sidewalk, and the shops had window displays of jewelry with turquoise and coral set in silver, weavings that might be Indian, and pretty clothes.

As she walked she could see that she was going to approach the hotel from the back, and that seemed fine to her. But as she came closer, she saw something else. There were four cars parked near the loading dock, all of them big American-made sedans that had short antennas sticking up on their trunks, identical but in assorted colors: navy blue, white, black. There were two men inside one of them. One seemed to be talking on a radio, and the other had his head bent down as though he was writing something.

Nicole stopped and retreated a few steps, until she was out of sight of the cars. She wanted to run, but she had to control herself, and fight the panic. She told herself there was no good reason to assume they were here for her. She walked back the way she had come for two blocks, then turned, making a wide circle around the building, trying to see more of it without being seen.

From the front, the hotel looked exactly the same. There were no police cars, no big men standing around. When she came to the parking lot side, she picked out the window of the room where she had spent last night. It was on the second floor, three windows from the elevator shaft. The curtain was open, and she saw a man walk past the window and disappear.

She walked quickly back toward the bus station. As she walked, she took out her bus schedule and scanned it. There was a bus leaving for Phoenix in thirty minutes. When she arrived, she bought a ticket for that bus, then sat in the dismal waiting room to stay out of the sun. But after a few minutes she began to be aware that somebody was staring at her.

A teenaged boy must have come in the side entrance while she was buying her ticket, and now he stood near the wall watching her. He was tall and thin with sandy blond hair, and when she looked at him, his blue eyes would turn away, toward other people in the station, then look out the windows at the street, and then return to her again, staying on her unblinking until the next time she caught him at it.

She went outside and waited near the pay phone until she saw her bus arrive and discharge the passengers from its last leg. When their luggage had been unloaded and the driver was standing by the door taking tickets from the line of new passengers, Nicole stepped to the telephone and dialed the front desk of the hotel. She heard the young girl answer, "Sky Inn. May I help you?"

Nicole Davis said, "This is police dispatch. Are any of the officers who are waiting for the female suspect close to you now?"

The girl said, "Yes. Would you like to speak with one of them?"

Nicole Davis said, "Cancel that. We've just reached the one we wanted by radio. Thank you." She hung up and walked toward the line of passengers waiting to board the bus.

Suddenly the teenaged boy who had been staring at her came out of the side door of the bus station, stopped a few feet ahead of her, and said, "Come with me. Hurry." His expression was anxious and scared, and even though he was as tall as a man it made him look young, like a boy.

She said, "What?"

"I know you," he said with quiet urgency. "I saw you on TV. I can get you out of here. I've got a car."

She looked at him for a moment, then at the bus. She put her ticket into her purse and walked toward him. She followed him from the station at a distance of about ten feet all the way down the block. He went to a small, dark blue Mazda with dark tinted windows that was parked beside the curb. He opened the door for her and she got in.

When he sat down behind the wheel, she was staring at him. "How old are you?"

His blue eyes clouded, and his soft, unlined face seemed to flatten with disappointment. "I'm sixteen. Now you don't want my help, right?"

"Yes. I want your help. Please."

He glanced into his mirrors, then cautiously pulled away from the curb. The sound of sirens reached their ears. He looked at her furtively as he drove down the street away from the bus station. "The cops are coming from the other direction, where their station is."

"And where are we going?"

"My place."

22

It was Catherine Hobbes's last night in Los Angeles. Mary Tilson's car had not turned up, and Catherine had a reservation for a morning flight to Portland. She sat at the desk in her hotel room making an inventory of the duplicate case files from the murders of Brian Corey, William Thayer, and Mary Tilson before packing them. As she leafed through the collections of photographs, lab reports, interview notes, and drawings, she began to feel a sensation of dread. All of this had happened in a period of just a few weeks since Tanya had arrived in Los Angeles.

Catherine had seen videotapes of Tanya and spoken to her on the telephone. Tanya had seemed very young and harmless, maybe even a little empty-headed, someone Catherine had needed to explain things to. But what had been behind Tanya's pretty face and her soft, feminine voice had been this—the capacity and intention to cause the horrors in these files.

A knock on the door of her hotel room startled her. She left the files on the desk, flopped on the bed to reach into her purse, came up with her service pistol, then stepped to the door and looked through the small fish-eye lens into the hallway.

She held the gun behind her right thigh and opened the door. Joe Pitt stood in the doorway wearing a sport coat and a shirt that seemed better than the ones she had seen him in before. "You?" she said. "I thought I'd already given you the brush-off."

"You did," he said. "I've never been so thoroughly dismissed in my life."

"I just wanted to get that straight. So what are you doing here?"

"I'm not making any money on this visit, but it's business related. I'd have to say it's not going to make you happy."

"As long as it doesn't involve my making you happy, you can come in." She stepped away from the door, and he could see she had been holding her gun in her right hand. She slipped it back into her purse.

He advanced past her into the area near the window, where there was an armchair. "Kill any bellhops?"

"Not when they were on duty." She closed her files and piled them on the desk, then sat down on the bed. "Go ahead. Make me miserable."

"I heard something tonight that you need to know."

"Hugo Poole sent you to tell me he didn't kill anybody. I already knew that."

"I don't work for Hugo anymore. He paid my fee and we parted company."

"That was a great job. You didn't even have to show up."

"During the twenty years I was the D.A.'s investigator, I never had an easy one," he said. "Not once. Now that there's money involved, it seems to happen a lot. Funny, isn't it?"

"Not to me. What did you want to tell me?"

"That Hugo Poole has hired Calvin Dunn."

"Who's Calvin Dunn?"

"He's sort of a well-known figure in this part of the world. If you don't know anything about him, you should have Jim Spengler run his record for you. Dunn does investigations. I don't know if he's still got a license or not, but it doesn't matter."

She shrugged. "So Hugo replaced you. I wouldn't work with you, and I won't work with him, either."

He shook his head. "Calvin Dunn doesn't want to work with you."

"What do you mean?"

"He works for people who would never go to the police for any reason. If a criminal has a relative kidnapped or a shipment hijacked, he wants to find out who did it. Calvin Dunn will find out. He's not one of us. He's one of them. He goes down the rabbit hole, and when he comes back he's got blood on his teeth, and there's no rabbit problem anymore."

"When did Hugo hire him?"

"Today, I think. It could have been yesterday."

She stared at the wall for a moment. "Why did you decide to tell me this?"

"Because Calvin Dunn is dangerous. He isn't going to be out collecting evidence or something. He's not interested in seeing the girl go to trial. Even if you see him go through two sets of metal detectors, you should assume that he's armed and doesn't mind if you're the one he needs to hurt to get to her."

"Thanks. I appreciate the warning. I probably won't be the one to run into him, though."

"Why not?"

"I've got to leave for Portland in the morning. My captain let me stay this long only because we thought the California police might stop her on the road. But there are other cases in Portland, so he wants me back."

Joe Pitt shrugged. "I suppose he's right. She could turn up anywhere at this point, and L.A. probably isn't the most likely place now that she's been here." He brightened. "You know, since you're just going to spend tomorrow in airports, you could come downstairs and have a drink with me."

"I don't drink."

"Then come and have a soda with me."

She gazed at him for a moment, wavering. She detected in herself a kind of affection toward him, maybe just because she had worked with him and then expected not to see him again. She had been feeling very alone, and maybe even depressed tonight. "All right. Just for a little while. Then I have to get to sleep." She took her purse, went to the door, and opened it for him.

As she walked beside him to the elevator, she sensed an odd feeling of familiarity, and then realized it was walking beside a man in a hotel corridor. It reminded her of being with Kevin.

She dismissed it, irritated at her own stupidity. Joe Pitt was very different from Kevin. The two had absolutely no shared qualities except that they were both about the same height and weight. That had been all that was necessary, she supposed. The voice came from about the same distance above her ear, the sound of his shoes on the hotel carpet was the same, and so it had set off the feeling of loss again.

It was ridiculous, because it wasn't Kevin that she missed. She missed having another presence, the other person who was seeing things at the same time and reacting, so that her thoughts were not just voices inside her own skull.

She had been surrounded by male colleagues most of the time since the academy, but she had never allowed her relationships with them to become close, let alone romantic. She had exerted her will to ignore any inconvenient feelings. It was like forcing herself to tune out a particular sound so she wouldn't hear it, and listen instead to the other sounds that competed with it. Any approaches from other cops that she could not ignore she had brushed aside with humor. But now and then she would be surprised by a feeling, a memory, a sound.

She analyzed her vulnerability. Joe Pitt was very male and he was smart, and the fact that he seemed to like her had surprised her, so that forbidden part of her mind had been switched on when she had not been guarding it. All she had to do now was switch it off again.

"I'm only going to stay for ten or fifteen minutes. I've still got packing to do, and when I get home I'll have to try to catch up with what's been piling up on my desk."

He pressed the elevator button and the elevator took them downstairs to the lobby. She was surprised when he stopped at the bar, ordered two colas, and carried them to a small table for two. She took hers and said, "I thought you were a drinker."

He shook his head. "Been known to, but tonight I'm driving."

So maybe he wasn't a problem drinker. She found that she was losing one of the barriers that had kept her distant from him. She had to build others, distract herself, keep everything impersonal. "What do you think of the fact that she's killed a woman this time? They were always men before."

"Don't you ever think about anything besides the case you're on?"

"I'm still learning. You've seen more killing sprees than I have. I've seen solitary men, or pairs of men doing strings of killings. I've seen one where there was a man taking his girlfriend along for the ride. Have you ever worked a case where a woman traveled around alone killing people?"

"Is learning the only interest you have in men, or is it just me?"

"I don't think I know what you mean."

"You're interviewing me. I feel as though there's a tape recorder in your purse. Why not let yourself relax? Your subconscious will still be working on the case, I promise."

"I'm just making conversation," she said. "The case is what you and I have in common."

"We have lots of things in common. We just don't know each other well enough to know what they are. We need to tell our life stories."

"No, we don't."

"I'll start. I was raised in Grand Island, Nebraska. I dropped out of college, spent four years in the air force, and then became a state trooper. Then I was a police officer in Los Angeles, and finally became a district attorney's investigator. I retired from that a couple of years ago, and now I'm a private investigator."

"Okay," she said. "I was raised in Portland a few blocks from where I live now. I graduated from college, got married instead of going to law school, dropped out of the marriage, and then went to the police academy. I'm still in the first law enforcement job I ever had."

"See? Our lives are exactly alike."

She laughed. "Uncanny resemblance."

"If I fly up to Portland tomorrow, will you have dinner with me?"

"No."

"Why not?"

"I don't date people from work."

"Wait a minute. You've made it very clear that you and I are not working together, and that we aren't going to be working together. We don't live in the same city, or even the same state. There's no way I can be considered to be 'from work.' "

"I guess that's probably true," she said. "But people up there know who you are. They know we were on the same case, traveling and sharing information. If you turn up when I do and take me out, it will put me in an uncomfortable position."

"Why?"

"People will think that we're sleeping together."

"Do you always behave like this—all these rules?"

"Yes."

"Then they won't think that."

She laughed again and shook her head. "I'll go out with you. I *am* out with you. It's nine o'clock, and I haven't had dinner. How about you? Are you hungry?"

"Starving."

"Then let's go across the lobby to the coffee shop and see if we can get a booth."

"No," he said. "I want to take you to a place I like. My car's outside."

"That's too hard. I'd have to change, and then it would be too late."

"You look beautiful, and I'm past fixing. The place is not far, and the food is better than the coffee shop. Come on." He was already standing, and he took her arm so that in a moment they were out of the bar and on their way.

He drove her to the Biltmore Hotel, let the valet parking attendant take his car, and led her into the ornate lobby, to Bernard's. "This is really formal," she said. "You implied that this was going to be some kind of interesting dive."

"I don't think I implied it was a dive," he said. "I distracted you by reminding you that you were beautiful."

The restaurant was large and dimly lighted. She could see that in her business suit she was dressed as well as most of the women, so she began to feel more comfortable.

When the waiter came, Pitt said to Catherine, "Would you like a drink before dinner?"

"No thanks," she said. "You can have one if you like."

But he looked at the waiter and shook his head. When the waiter was gone, he said, "So tell me about your family, your pets and hobbies. All women have them."

"I don't have any pets right now, and not much time for hobbies except reading and exercising, which are just two aspects of the same futile, late-onset urge to improve myself. I do have parents, though—one of each. My father is a retired cop. How about you?"

"My parents are still in Nebraska wondering where they went wrong."

"Where did they?"

"Nowhere, actually. They're terrific people. Everything I've done to myself is my own fault."

"What have you done to yourself?"

"Oh, I don't know. I guess what I've done is spend too many years doing nothing but thinking about murder cases. When I came into your hotel room before and saw you with three case files open on the desk, it reminded me of myself. I used to lay them out everywhere in hotel rooms—on the bed, usually. Then, one day, I noticed that about twenty years had passed. I had cleared a lot of cases. I'd made a succession of

D.A.s who were elected because they had good hair look smart. But I hadn't gotten married or had kids. I didn't even own a house."

"How sad." She smiled. "I'll bet you lived just like a monk."

He laughed. "I didn't say that. And since I retired, I've bought a house. It's pretty nice."

In spite of her misgivings, she liked him. He was realistic about life, and yet he had a cheerful, optimistic temperament that seemed to have come through the sad and ugly things that he had seen in his career. She kept asking questions to listen to him talk.

Catherine ordered too much food and ate all of it because she didn't want the dinner to end. She knew that as soon as it did, she would have to get back to packing and preparing herself to return to her town, her house, her job.

Finally, he asked the waiter for the check. On the way back to her hotel she was quiet, thinking hard about the way she had been conducting her life. She had been reasonably contented for the past few years, because thinking about nothing but her job had been better than being in a marriage with a man who had seemed more and more often to hate her. The life she had constructed for herself was good, but this evening with Joe Pitt was better. She wondered how much of her pleasure was just a sense of release after years of discipline and solitude.

He pulled the car up at her hotel and started to get out to let the valet take it. She said, "Uh-uh. Don't get out. I really do have to get packed and go to sleep now."

He got out and opened the door for her, but waved the parking attendant off. "Then have a good flight home."

"Thanks for dinner, Joe." She stood beside the car for a second, uncertain. The evening had been something that could only have happened unexpectedly, something she had tried to avoid and thought about at the same time. What was she hiding from? At this moment, what she wanted most was to make him want to see her again. She leaned into him, put her arms around his neck, and gave him a soft kiss on the lips, then stepped back. "If you do come up to Portland sometime, I will go out with you." Then she turned and strode into the hotel lobby and was gone.

23

Except when he was desperate to get somewhere quickly, Calvin Dunn liked to travel by car. Today he was driving a new one, a customized coal black Lincoln Town Car. It had steel plates fitted into the door panels and a front end that had been reinforced with steel bars. The rear seat sat on a false floor so that he could carry a few extra pieces of equipment without subjecting them to public scrutiny.

The extra space permitted him more ways of administering rewards and punishments. At the moment it contained fifty thousand dollars in cash, eight pairs of plastic restraints, a set of night-vision goggles, three pistols, a short-barreled shotgun, and a 7.62-millimeter rifle with a four-power scope.

His customary attire included a black sport coat with thirty hundred-dollar bills zipped into an inner pocket and a ten-millimeter Smith & Wesson pistol in his shoulder holster.

He was in a good humor today. He was in the business of doing things nobody else would do, so usually his ego didn't get much involved, but Hugo Poole had given him the sort of compliment that meant something to him: a great deal of money and the promise of more.

It was a pleasure for Calvin Dunn to work for a man like

Hugo Poole. He didn't have to explain the things that every adult male ought to know. Dunn had not needed to say, "You will pay what you owe me on time and in cash, or I'll have to come take it and leave your body in the desert for the coyotes." Hugo Poole had not needed to say, "If you rat me out, I'll find you in prison and drive a sharpened toothbrush through your temple." They both knew how business was done.

Hugo had given him the names the girl had used so far, and this morning Calvin Dunn had driven to the police station in the Kern County town of Paston, where he lived, and obtained a photocopy of the police circular. The circular had good photographs taken from driver's licenses and her accurate height and weight. There was some confusion about eye color, but if he got close enough to see that, the job was as good as done.

Outside the police station he studied the printed information on the circular, then started his engine. He knew where to begin the hunt. He drove to Los Angeles County and found the address in the San Fernando Valley near Topanga where the girl had lived under the name Nancy Mills. He parked his car where he could easily see it from the windows at the front of the apartment building, then went inside and knocked on the door of the building manager's apartment.

The man who opened the door had a short beard that looked like a permanent three-day growth. Calvin Dunn held up a small leather case with an identification card in it that had his picture in an official-looking format and an embossed gold badge under it that had no insignia and didn't say he was anything in particular. But Calvin Dunn was tall and had muscular arms, so he looked like a cop.

"My name is Calvin Dunn, and you are—?"

"Rob Norris."

"Pleased to meet you. I'd like to ask you a few questions about a tenant, the young lady who called herself Nancy Mills."

Calvin Dunn's stare transfixed the manager. Dunn's pale gray eyes appeared to be focused on a point two inches deeper than the manager's forehead, inside the manager's skull. It was an uncomfortable feeling for him, and he felt an urge to close the door.

"Can I come in?"

The manager had no desire to let him in but no confidence in his power to stop him, so he said, "Okay." He stepped back just in time to prevent Calvin Dunn from colliding with him. When Calvin Dunn arrived, violence was not a remote possibility but something already present in the room with him. The manager sensed that his task was to keep it from becoming overt.

The manager watched Dunn standing in his small living room, his hands clasped behind him as though to emphasize the difference it might make if they weren't clasped, and rocking toe to heel on his shoes. "I'm afraid I'll have to ask you some of the questions you already answered," said Dunn.

"Okay."

"Tell me about Nancy Mills. Why did she decide to live here? Did she know anybody here?"

"No. She just called up and said she liked living near the mall."

"How did she pay the rent? Did she have a credit card?"

"She gave me cash. It was a lot of money, when you add up first, last, and security deposit. Over three thousand bucks. I had to deliver it to the company that owns the place that day, because I didn't want to keep that much around."

"Just like that? Didn't you do a background check to see if she was a problem tenant?"

"What do you mean?"

Dunn was patient. "A deadbeat, who skipped on her last landlord. Or a drug dealer, or a prostitute. That's the kind of person who has lots of cash."

"I don't do that kind of checking. I think that the company does sometimes. On the application they ask for a lot of information. They want the last three addresses and phone numbers. They ask for references too, including an employer they can call."

"Do you have her application here?"

"No," said the manager. "The company gets it as soon as the place is rented."

"I'd like you to see if you remember anything at all about her that might help me find her. Does she like to wear particular colors or a special style of clothes, for instance?"

"She has a nice little body, so she tends to wear pants and tops that are sort of snug. Not tight, exactly. Fitted. I never saw what she wore when she went out at night, but the picture from the hotel camera looked like the kind of thing I always saw on her. It was pants and a yellow top, and a matching yellow jacket thing over it, with something written on it."

"You mean like a brand?"

"You know, there's always some smart-ass thing written on it, like to tease you. Maybe the brand is mentioned, maybe not."

"Oh. Any friends, anybody she talked to a lot?"

"I don't think so. I guess she must have talked to Mary Tilson, the woman across the hall from her."

"Nobody else? No guys?"

"None that I ever saw. If you're an apartment manager, you have to kind of watch for that too. You get a sweet-faced little babe into an apartment, and then all of a sudden there's a boyfriend living there and his drinking buddies are in and out all the time, making noise and pissing off the other tenants."

"What did she do all day? Did she work?"

"I don't know. She used to go out for a run in the morning, then come back. After that, I guess she would go for the day. Now and then she'd come home with bags from stores."

"Interesting. I'd like it if you'd let me into her place now, so I can have a look around."

"I'm not really supposed to do that. The police won't let me rent it out or anything yet."

Dunn said quietly, "If you help me, I'll pay for your cooperation. If you don't, I'll still get what I want, but you won't."

The manager noticed again the strange way that Calvin Dunn looked at him, his eyes appearing to focus on a point inside the manager's forehead. "All right."

They went to the apartment, and Dunn waited while the manager unlocked the door, then ducked under the yellow police tape across the doorway and into the room. Dunn looked at everything closely, and sighted along the woodwork where the police had dusted for prints. There didn't seem to be any spots where they had put tape down and lifted a print. Then he examined the furnishings. "Did she pick out this stuff, or did it come with the place?"

"It's furnished. The company buys it in lots, I think. It all looks the same. They have a lot of other buildings."

Calvin Dunn spent a few more minutes looking for anything that Nancy Mills might have left, carefully opening and closing cabinets and drawers with the edge of his hand, but looking only experimentally, to be sure the police had already searched. Then he said, "Let's go back to your place."

When they were in the manager's apartment again, Calvin Dunn reached into his inner coat pocket and handed the manager three hundred-dollar bills. "This is for your cooperation."

"Thank you," said the manager.

"You're welcome. Now get me the application."

"I already told you—"

Calvin Dunn held up his hand to interrupt. "I want you to think about it. You just saw that I'm a truthful man. No harm came to the apartment and you got a reward. Look at me. Do you want me to be your friend, or do you want me to be your enemy?"

The manager said, "I can't give you that."

Dunn lunged forward, his right arm across the manager's chest, and flipped him backward over his hip so that he landed facedown on the floor. Dunn held the manager's wrist with both hands and placed his foot against the manager's back. "You keep a copy of the application. Where is it?"

Norris gasped. "In the desk. Over there."

"Thank you," said Calvin Dunn. He released the manager, walked to the desk, pulled open the deep file drawer, and found the applications filed alphabetically. He took the photocopy of the one that Nancy Mills had filled out, and examined it closely. Then he set it on the desk. "That will do it for me. Don't worry, your arm will be okay in a day or two." He stepped to the door. "You look too smart to say anything to anybody about my visit. Are you?"

The manager looked up from the floor. "Yes." And then Calvin Dunn was out the door and gone.

24

The boy drove Nicole Davis to a long, one-story suburban ranch house with a low rail fence at the sidewalk and a small rustic wooden sign on the lawn that said THE GILMANS. The boy used an automatic garage-door opener, drove all the way in, and closed the door behind them before he got out of the car.

Nicole Davis looked around her at the garage in the dim light. It was big, made for three cars, and the little Mazda seemed lonely in the center of it. When the boy went to the wall and switched on the overhead light, she could see a workbench along the back wall with a vise, and a pegboard with outlines of hand tools traced on it, most of the tools in their places. She got out of the car. "The Gilmans. Is that you? Are you a Gilman?"

"I'm a Gilman. I'm Ty. That's for Tyler."

"Where are your parents?"

"Don't worry about them. They're at Lake Havasu right now. They won't be back for almost a week. On the way home they're going to swing by my grandmother's house in Scottsdale."

He went to the side of the garage, unlocked it, and let her into the kitchen. She took in everything quickly. It was small and a bit worn. There were dishes in the sink and the floor was dirty. He wasn't coming in with her. She looked back to see him going to the car. He noticed her watching. "I've got to get back to work now. I'll be home around eight. Make yourself comfortable, but don't let anybody see you. Okay?"

"Okay." She closed the kitchen door, then listened while he opened the garage door, started the car engine, backed out, and closed the garage again. She went through the kitchen to the living room, knelt on a chair, and moved the curtain aside a quarter inch to watch him drive off.

She looked around her and had a feeling of unreality. Being here was strange and sudden. She had been rushing to get on the bus, and now she was here, alone in this quiet suburban house. He had said he'd seen her on television, so she went to search for a television set. The living room was the kind that she suspected the family seldom used. The furniture had awful patterns on it that looked defiantly fresh and clear, and there wasn't a book, magazine, or anything else on the coffee tables.

As she explored the house she wondered about the boy. She felt sympathy for his awkwardness. He looked to her as though his hands and feet had grown too fast and the rest of him had not caught up yet. His sandy blond hair had been cut short and tousled with his hands instead of combed, which unintentionally accentuated his baby face and thin neck. She could almost see his ribs through his shirt, and his pants seemed to be barely held up on his hips. He had earnest, open eyes, and his chin and cheeks were still smooth and looked soft, because his beard had not been shaved enough times to make it bristly and rough.

He had saved her life a few minutes ago. That horrible girl at the hotel had undoubtedly told the cops about her call, because it had taken them practically no time to head for the bus station. They had probably stopped the bus and dragged the people off it looking for her.

What had Ty seen on television that had induced him to get in the way of that? She kept looking for the television set. Had she missed a small one in the kitchen? No. There was a cookie jar that looked like a fat puppy on the counter. The clock in the wall was supposed to look like a sunflower, so the dark part in the center had hands on it. It said five o'clock. She went to a door past the pantry and found a kind of den, a room with only one window high on the wall, a couch, an easy chair, and a big television set.

Nicole located the remote control and turned it on, then worked her way through the channels until she found a local news show. The newswoman assumed a fake-sorry face and said something below hearing. As she was replaced by another young woman, this one dark-haired, standing in front of the Sky Inn, Nicole turned up the sound.

". . . a murder suspect who police say was on the run from California. She apparently arrived in the Flagstaff area last evening and was scheduled to stay a second night at the hotel, but became suspicious at some point and fled, leaving her suitcase. Police have made photographs of her available."

The scene was replaced by two pictures that Nicole recognized. One was the Illinois driver's license she had gotten years ago in the name Tanya Starling, when she had been given her first car. The other was the California license of Rachel Sturbridge. The excited voice of the young woman said, "She is five feet five inches tall, approximately a hundred and twenty pounds. When last seen she had brown hair and blue eyes, but she has been known to wear colored contact lenses and dye her hair to alter her appearance. If you see her, call the police immediately. The number is at the bottom of your screen. Do not try to apprehend her yourself."

Nicole switched the remote control to move from channel to channel. "The manhunt continues for —" There was her picture again. ". . . is considered to be armed and—" This time it was a pudgy middle-aged man in a police uniform standing at a podium outside a building she didn't recognize. ". . . will be cooperating with law enforcement authorities in California, Oregon—"

She turned off the television set and realized she was hearing an unfamiliar sound, then recognized it as her own breathing, coming in shallow huffs, amplified by the intense silence in the house. She had to think. She had to make a plan, invent a way to get herself out of here.

She couldn't collect her thoughts, and she knew that the plan had to be based on knowing what the police were doing, so she turned the television set back on. The pudgy cop was saying, ". . . are now completing a building-to-building search of the blocks around the bus station where she was seen. We ask that people take alternate routes to avoid that area until we've given the all clear. We know that she purchased bus tickets to both Phoenix and Santa Fe, so authorities in both cities have been notified."

He looked attentive while he listened to a question from a reporter, then said, "She may have just been getting some sleep so she could go on to the next place."

Nicole said, "Then why are you chasing me, you fat asshole?"

She turned off the television again. All it was doing was making her so agitated that she couldn't think. Things were bad out there, but she wasn't out there anymore. She was in here, thanks to Ty.

She spent the next half hour examining the house to learn about him. What she saw confirmed her first impression. There was a mother. She had more sweatpants than a track star, and about four or five outfits for going out, besides whatever she had taken with her. She was at least three inches taller than Nicole, but thin, like Tyler.

The father seemed to have a job that involved more physical labor than paperwork. He had three pairs of brown ankle-high boots with steel toes, and several pairs of dark blue pants that looked like the work pants that janitors and mechanics sometimes wear—almost a uniform, but not quite.

Ty's bedroom was at the far end of the house. It contained relics of his childhood—his baseball glove and bat, trophies for various sports, a row of three-inch robots on a shelf. But he was growing up. She saw a DVD player with headphones, a computer, huge posters of female rappers striking provocative poses as they danced and shouted openmouthed into wireless microphones. Ty had quite a few more expensive gadgets than Charlene had owned, but things had not changed too much.

She wandered the house to satisfy herself that everything

conformed to what she had seen so far. When she reached the kitchen again, she drew the curtain on the window over the sink, just in case some neighbor had a view across the backyard. Then she washed the dirty dishes.

She could tell that they had accumulated over a couple of days, at least. There was sour-milk residue in the bottoms of half a dozen glasses, and egg yolk hardened on two plates. She decided she liked Ty's laziness and disorganization. He was still a kid and would wait until his parents were practically pulling into the driveway before he washed a dish. After a time she began to regret waiting so long to start the housework, because the sunlight was getting dimmer, and she did not dare turn on a light.

She found a bucket and mop in the laundry room off the kitchen and mopped the kitchen floor. She took a sponge and got down on her hands and knees to wash the most neglected and dirty areas near the sink and the cooktop. When she had finished the floor, she looked at the sunflower clock again and saw that she still had an hour before Ty would return.

She knew it was not a good idea to turn on the television again before his car was in the driveway, because the screen would throw light that the neighbors could see. It didn't matter. She had driven for a day without stopping, had had a partial night's sleep, had walked all over town, and had been afraid for so many hours that she was too tired to be afraid anymore. She lay on the couch in the television room, listening to the unrelieved silence in the empty house. Then she was asleep.

She awoke, startled. The light was in her eyes, and a big male shape was standing over her. She quickly rose to a crouch, and heard his voice. "It's only me."

"Oh," she said. "I guess I fell asleep."

"Yeah, I guess you did."

She rubbed her eyes and smoothed her hair with both hands to be sure it wasn't horrible. She made herself smile. "How did everything go, Ty? Your job and everything."

"No problem. When I went to find you I was on my three o'clock lunch break. I made it back and nobody paid much attention."

"Where do you work?"

"At the Taco Rancho restaurant, up by the interstate. That was where I saw you on TV. They have the TV on all day. A lot of people think it makes the day go faster, but usually it's on some crappy thing like those fake courtrooms where people sue each other and a fake judge bitches at them."

She smiled. "I hate that too."

"Well, they cut right into it today—one of those breaking-news alerts. At first everybody thought your picture was up because somebody had kidnapped you." He shrugged. "I could tell you were wanted, because they showed two pictures of you with different hair."

She made her eyes wide and innocent, and kept them on his. "I didn't do it."

"Do what?"

"What they said I did. I want you to know I'm innocent."

He looked down at his feet thoughtfully, then nodded. "I brought some food. You hungry?"

"I guess I am," she said. "You didn't have to do that, though. I would have cooked us something."

"It's okay. Every night I bring stuff home from the restaurant."

"I hope you didn't buy too much more than you usually do. Somebody could notice things like that."

"No," he said. "I fill my own order, pay for it, and get my own change. I got us two El Pollo Grandes and a bean burrito. We can split it."

"Sounds great." She reached for her purse. "I'd like to pay you back."

"Don't," he said. "We can talk about that stuff later. Come on."

She followed him to the kitchen, where he looked around. "Oh. You washed the dishes, huh?"

"Yes. The floor, too. It appeared as though you hadn't had time lately."

He looked at her as though he had not liked the gentle chiding, then turned and opened the cupboard and pulled out two glasses, set them on the table, and got two plates. They sat at the kitchen table and he divided the items from his El Taco Rancho bag with scrupulous care.

"I watched TV after you left," she said. "They seem to be looking for me everywhere. Did you hear anything while you were at work? Do you think I'll be able to leave tonight?"

He finished chewing, then said, "I saw a bunch of cops. They're eyeballing people in cars, and stopping some of them, mostly women driving alone." He shrugged. "They haven't given up."

"Then would it be all right with you if I stay longer?"

"I think you have to. If they catch you, then I'm in trouble too."

"Why did you help me?"

He stared at her for a few seconds, then looked away. "I saw your picture. I thought you were nice looking. I wanted to do you a favor."

"You could go to jail for it."

"I know that."

After dinner, they sat in the den on one of the couches and watched the television again, but there were no more special bulletins. At eleven, the local news shows repeated the whole story, with the same reporters standing in front of the hotel again, even though there was nothing to see. But one of them also showed a roadblock at an entrance to Interstate 40, where police officers shone flashlights on the faces of women in the cars, then waved them on.

Nicole felt her pulse rate increase again. She stood up and said, "I'd like to take a shower. Is that okay?"

Ty said, "I guess so." Then he said, "Can I watch you?"

She was paralyzed for a second. "What?"

"Can I come and watch?"

"Why?"

He shrugged. "I want to see you naked."

She tried to laugh, but it came out hollow and false. "Of course not. That isn't what you really want."

"Yes. It is what I want," he said. "I've been thinking about it since I first saw you."

"I'm so much older than you are. I'm twenty-eight, twelve years older. It would seem weird. I'd be embarrassed."

"It's not much to ask. If I hadn't come, you'd be in jail now. Or maybe dead."

"I'm grateful for what you're doing. I want us to be friends. That's just not the way."

His face was darker and grimmer. He was feeling resentful, more and more unappreciated and ill-used, and she could see anger growing behind his eyes. She said, "Haven't you ever seen a woman before?"

"No. Just movies. Pictures."

She was desperate, miserable. She couldn't afford to make him angry and resentful. "Look, Ty. You don't have to feel rejected, or that I'm just too selfish to give you what you want. I like you. I really do. And I know that what you're thinking about seems like something you really want, but this isn't the right time. I'm not the one."

His eyes were fixed on the wall ahead of him. "It's not that big a thing to you. You take off your clothes in front of doctors, people like that, people who haven't done anything for you."

She said, "Please, Ty."

"Please yourself. Please."

She sighed. "All right then, I suppose."

"Now?"

"If I have to."

25

As soon as Catherine Hobbes had learned that Tanya had been sighted in Flagstaff, she had taken a plane to Arizona. Now, as she sat in the passenger seat of the police car, staring out the window while Officer Gutierrez drove, she wondered if she had missed her again. At night Flagstaff didn't seem big enough to hide Tanya Starling. There didn't seem to be enough places for strangers to sleep, enough people on the streets to keep her from being seen. There didn't seem to be enough men.

Gutierrez was about forty years old and the sort of officer that Hobbes would have appointed to guide a visitor if she had been the one to pick. He was proper and experienced and pulled together like a military man, in a fresh uniform with razor creases and spit-shined shoes. All the steel on him shone in the dim light of the dashboard.

He drove past the hotel and around to the parking lot, then kept the car idling. "See the window up here with the blinds drawn and the bright lights?"

"Second floor, third from the end?"

"Right. That was her room."

Catherine Hobbes looked around to determine the lines of sight from the nearest street. "Think she saw somebody waiting for her in her room?"

"I don't know," he said. "I know there were a few unmarked cars parked back here, so she might have seen them. Or maybe she's just getting into the habit of calling places to see if there are cops before she shows up. Whatever it was, she picked up the signs." He pulled into a space. "Ready to go in?"

"Can you show me the bus station first?"

"Sure. It's just up on South Malpais Lane." He pulled across the lot and back out onto South Milton, drove a couple of blocks, then turned left. "It's up ahead, there. It's been about eight hours since she's been here, though."

"I'd like to take a look anyway," she said. "I'm trying to get to know her, and I'd like to see what she saw."

Officer Gutierrez drove a few yards past the station entrance and stopped the car at the curb, then got out with Catherine Hobbes. Catherine could see the pay telephone attached to the stucco wall at the front of the building. It could have been the one Tanya had used to call the hotel, but there were probably others inside or around the back in the boarding area. It was too late to take prints from any of them now.

She pushed through the glass doors, into the station. It was late evening, but she could see that the station had the forlorn, always-two-A.M. look that bus stations had, the fluorescent lights just bright enough to make a person who was stuck here feel defeated. She walked over to the counter and picked up one of the small folded bus schedules.

While she was examining it, Gutierrez said, "The first ticket she bought was to Santa Fe for ten o'clock tomorrow morning. She bought the one to Phoenix just before it was due to leave at five after three. That was the next bus out."

Hobbes went to the front door, stepped out, and looked at the city. "The hotel is about four long blocks in that direction, right?"

"Right," said Gutierrez. "Maybe a half mile."

Catherine stepped back inside, then walked to the door on the opposite side of the waiting area, underneath the sign that said BOARDING—TO BUSES. She went outside again and stood under the overhanging roof. A bus came up South Malpais and made the wide turn, shouldering up the slight rise onto the blacktop, then emitting a hiss as it came to rest. The lights came on and the doors opened. The sign above the windshield that said FLAGSTAFF changed to HOLBROOK.

As Catherine watched, an assortment of people slowly made their way, one by one, down the bus's narrow steps to the pavement. They were the people Catherine had become accustomed to seeing on sweeps through the bus stations in Portland: old men and women who stared down at their feet as they walked, or very young, solitary men with faces that were pinched with watchfulness, or teenage girls in twos or threes, talking and laughing as though the rest of the world could not hear them.

The driver and a ticket agent opened the luggage compartment on the side of the bus, hauled suitcases out, and set them in a row, where passengers came to claim them. Then Catherine saw the people she had been waiting for, the first of the riders for the next leg of the bus's journey, forming a line. They were like the last group, people too young or too old to drive, people who had no money for a car. Catherine got into the line behind a lady carrying a large carpetbag, looked around her, then moved close to the bus.

She said to the ticket taker, "Do city buses stop here? I don't see a bus stop."

"They don't stop at the station. The nearest stop is on the corner at South Milton."

"Thank you."

Gutierrez stepped up to Catherine, curious. She said, "I think somebody picked her up."

"What do you mean—like she had someone waiting for her?"

"No. She came in here and bought the ticket to Phoenix just before the bus was going to leave. She walked to the front door, made the call to the hotel, then got into this line to board the bus."

"Right. That's what the witnesses said."

"But when the state police stopped the bus she wasn't on it."

"I'm with you."

"Well, something happened while she was standing here, right where I am, waiting to board. Something changed her mind, diverted her from the bus. But from this spot, you can't see any alternatives. There aren't any taxicabs, or rental cars, or anything else. If she had just turned and started walking, she would have been spotted. The police units arrived within a minute or two after she called the hotel, and they searched for blocks around the station, questioning everybody who might have noticed her. The only possibility is that she met somebody, and he or she gave her a ride out of the area in a private car."

"You think she could do that? She works that fast?"

"You saw her picture. She looks young and sweet and vulnerable." Catherine looked around her at the entrance to the station. "The only thing I'm wondering about is who it could be. The reason people are in a bus station is that they don't have cars."

"Whoever it is, he's going to get a big surprise."

As Catherine stepped away from the line with Gutierrez and they walked along the street toward his police car, Calvin Dunn took a step backward behind the idling bus to keep the headlights of a passing car from shining on his face. When he had seen the two of them behind the bus station, the woman standing in line and then going with the cop, he had experienced a moment of interest. She was about the right age, size, and shape. But apparently she was just another damned cop.

26

Nicole Davis lay on the bed, her eyes open wide, staring into the darkness. She tried closing, then opening her eyes, but the darkness looked the same.

She wanted not to be here, not to be who she was. She turned and listened to Tyler asleep beside her, snoring a little in his dream. She knew what he was dreaming about.

She had foreseen exactly what would happen as soon as he had gotten his wish. She had known what his next wish would be, and that there would be no way for him to resist, and no way for her to stop him. Of course she had known, because for the first time in her life she was the one who had lived enough to know what he would feel before he felt it. So now she had become the knowing seducer and the unwilling victim, both at the same time. Ty had been all eagerness and joy at what was happening, while Nicole tried to be patient and instill patience, to teach.

She felt that time had fractured and slipped, two sides meeting in the wrong place, like a break in a fault line. She should have been with him when she was sixteen too, and they would have been a match. They would have groped their way into the same experience at the same time. She would have been the way he was now—amazed. After that, she would have been so happy with a boyfriend just like Ty all those years ago, on the other side of the chasm. It would have made everything different, every moment of her life after that.

She felt a pair of wet tears spill from her eye sockets and streak down both sides of her face to her ears. She had come a very long way from sixteen, and none of it had been the way she had imagined it.

Events seemed to be coming faster and faster now. She was being forced to make choices without warning, without having the time to consider the consequences. Whenever she made a move, the reaction to it seemed to come instantly. If she took a step, the police sirens were wailing before she could take the second step.

It was that woman cop she had talked to on the telephone: Detective Catherine Hobbes. She was probably still all the way back in Portland, but what was happening here in Flagstaff was her fault. In fact, everything that had happened since Dennis Poole had been because of Catherine Hobbes.

She was the reason why there were all of these cops blocking the roads tonight.

Dennis Poole's death had been the end of a private dispute, a contest between equals. Dennis had been getting ready to accuse Tanya of taking his money. He could have gotten her sent to prison, and that would have been the end of her. She had shot him in self-defense. All that Catherine Hobbes had needed to do then was report it as a homicide, fill out her stupid police forms, hand them in, and go home. But instead she had decided to use poor Tanya Starling to transform herself into a hero. It was disgusting.

If it had not been for Catherine Hobbes, there would have been no reason for her to protect herself from people like Bill Thayer or Mary Tilson. There would have been no reason to give in to the sexual fantasies of a sixteen-year-old boy in Arizona. She lay in the dark and closed her eyes until she fell asleep.

At daybreak she awoke and looked at the sleeping face of Tyler Gilman on the pillow. It was untroubled, almost blank. He was in absolute repose, his mouth closed and his eyes unmoving.

She slid off the bed and walked to the bathroom where she had left her clothes. They were still hanging from the hook behind the door, where she had hung them as she took them off. She carried her clothes to the living room before she quietly put them on, because she wasn't ready to be with Tyler yet. As she sat alone, hugging her knees, her bare feet on the couch, she concluded that she had done the only thing she could possibly have done. If she had refused, he would not have done anything else for her. She needed for him to do much more, or she was going to be caught. It was that simple.

Now she needed to decide what she wanted him to do for her. She wanted to get out of Flagstaff. That required waiting several days, until the police had searched everywhere in town that they could search, and then having Ty drive her to another city. It should be outside Arizona.

Eventually she would need her own car, and she would

need a suitcase full of clothes that didn't look much like the ones she had left in the hotel. She would have to think of a way for Ty to acquire those things without drawing attention to himself. As she considered her situation, she realized that it probably wasn't too bad. All she had to do was control Tyler Gilman.

She heard him stirring. There was a thump as he bounced off the bed to the floor. She heard him pad up the hallway toward the living room, then felt the vibration as he walked across the room to her.

He was standing in front of her, a blanket wrapped around him. "I woke up, and I was afraid that you were gone—that you had left while I was sleeping."

She slowly lifted her head to face him. "I'm not gone. It's just that you made me do a serious, important thing last night, when I didn't want to. That's why your mind did that to you."

"I'm sorry," he said. "I mean, I'm not sorry I did it. I'm just sorry for you, that you feel bad."

"I understand. I told you last night that I understood why you wanted that. It's the way men are." She stood and walked toward the kitchen. "I'll make your breakfast. You like eggs, don't you?"

"Are you mad at me?"

She looked at him pensively. "It's too late for that now. You did something big and risky for me, and then in return you wanted something big from me, that's all. So now it's another day. What kind of eggs do you like?"

"Will you ever let me again?"

She cocked her head. "I don't know. After we've had breakfast and a shower and brushed our teeth, I might think about it. Now go sit down at the table."

He walked toward the kitchen. As he passed close to her, she noticed that he lowered his eyes. He would be fine.

27

Calvin Dunn sat in a winged armchair in the farthest corner of the Sky Inn lobby, so that his back was against the wall in the corner next to the stone fireplace. There was no fire tonight, because the temperature had been in the nineties today, and the heat lingered in the brick walls of the building. Calvin Dunn read the newspaper.

It seemed to him that the story of the female serial killer had already begun to get overripe in Flagstaff. It was not on the front page anymore. There were enough car accidents and killings of local people by their friends and neighbors to keep the cops busy and provide the reporters with copy. Nobody seemed excited anymore by the girl's visit to town. She was like a cloud that had passed overhead without getting anybody wet.

He lifted his eyes over the newspaper and watched the young man at the front desk. It was after two A.M. and the last guest had come into the lobby an hour ago, but the clerk was always busy looking busy, trying to keep himself in line for a promotion to—what? Head night clerk? He was the only night clerk. This time of night he was running low on things to do, so he polished his counter with a can of Pledge and a hotel washcloth. He was aware of Calvin Dunn's presence, and looked up at him occasionally.

Calvin Dunn folded his newspaper under his arm, stood up, and walked to the desk.

The clerk said, "Can I help you, sir?"

"Do you happen to be the one who checked in that girl I've been reading about in the newspapers?"

"Yes, sir. That was me."

Calvin Dunn looked interested. "That must have been something. What was she like?"

It was a momentous question, one the young man had probably been asked many times at first, but that people had stopped asking since the girl had disappeared. "She was really nice looking. That was the first thing I noticed, the first thing anybody would notice. But then, when I asked her for a credit card, she said she didn't use them. She didn't look like the kind of person who doesn't use them. She didn't look poor, or political, or anything."

"She's a criminal," said Calvin Dunn. "I would have expected a criminal would be eager to use a credit card—somebody else's, of course."

"I wouldn't really know," said the clerk. "But she had a purse full of cash. I could see it when she paid for her room. I thought for a minute that maybe she was, like, a movie star who didn't want to be recognized."

"Happen to see a gun?"

"No. I'm sure she probably had one, but she didn't let me see it."

"You know, you might have been killed."

"I know," said the young man. He seemed pleased that at last somebody had realized it.

"The thing is, you were brave to turn her in."

"Not really," he said. "I was at home, and I happened to see her picture on television. I called the police from my apartment."

"That's what I mean. You were the only one who recognized her, and turned her in." He paused. "The only one."

"I was?"

"Yeah," said Calvin Dunn. "She's probably given a lot of thought to you during the past couple of days. Of course, there were other people later who said they remembered her going by one place or stopping in another. You and I know that it's mostly because people hate it when anything big happens right in front of their noses and they don't see it. So they convince themselves that they did see it. The point is, you were the only one who really did notice and got the police after her."

The young man seemed uncomfortable. "Are you a police officer?"

"No," said Calvin Dunn. "I work for the family of one of the victims."

"I wondered why you were sitting by the fireplace reading the newspaper so late at night, so I thought you were the police, watching me."

"You're not far off."

The young man looked into his eyes and understood. "You've been waiting for *her*, haven't you? You think she's going to come back here and try to kill me."

Calvin Dunn said, "The thought had crossed my mind."

"Oh, man."

"It's just a precaution. The police are watching the bus station and the car rental places and the airport and even the highway entrance ramps. They've got all the rational places covered. They know what she looks like, and if she shows up where they are, they'll probably get her."

"You sound as though you don't think she will."

"She's got another side besides the rational one, and that makes all the difference. She looks as though she wouldn't say boo to a goose, but once in a while, she pulls out a big old pistol and shoots a guy through the head. That shows that she doesn't necessarily do what other people would do."

"But she wouldn't get anything from killing me."

"It's hard to say what she got from killing those other people either. Some killers get a thrill out of it, and some are just pissed off." He shrugged. "I'm a little surprised that the police haven't considered the same thing. They're acting as though they think she's already a thousand miles from here."

"You don't think she is?"

"I don't know, and neither do they."

"Are you planning to stay here until my shift ends?"

"If you don't mind."

"Not at all," said the young man. "Make yourself comfortable." He held out his hand. "My name is Donald Holman."

Calvin Dunn shook his hand. "I know that. Calvin Dunn."

"You know, the light up here in the lobby is better for reading. Hardly anybody sits by the fireplace in the summer."

"I noticed that. But it's the only place where someone outside can't see me through the windows."

"Oh. Yeah. Well, if you need anything while I'm on duty, just let me know."

"You know, there is just one thing. Do you, by any chance, have a woman staying here named Catherine Hobbes?"

Donald looked troubled. "I'm really not supposed to talk about any of the people staying here."

"I didn't ask for her room number or anything. I could go over to the house phone over there and ask the operator to connect me with her room."

"I know," said Donald. "It's a silly rule. She is staying here. She flew in from Portland to interview me a few hours after I reported Tanya. After that Detective Hobbes checked in, and one of the local cops told me she wanted to be in this hotel because she likes to see everything that Tanya Starling sees."

"Maybe that works for her. What it does for me is put you both in one place, and that makes this the place to be."

Donald frowned. "You think she's in danger too?"

Calvin Dunn shrugged. "She's a detective hunting for a serial killer, she's in a strange town where the serial killer is— or was—and the killer knows her name. The thing that keeps cops alive isn't that they're especially smart, which most of them aren't, or tough, which a few of them are. It's that they come in bunches, an inexhaustible supply, like ants. But she's here alone."

"I guess you're right. She's probably as much of a target as I am."

Calvin Dunn was leaning on his elbows at the counter with his arms folded. He straightened, and his right hand opened his coat to reach into his inner pocket. Donald saw the knurled handgrips of the big pistol in its shoulder holster, but the coat closed again and Calvin Dunn held a thin stack of hundred-dollar bills. "Tonight I expect to be in sight of you until your shift ends, but maybe I won't be tomorrow. This is five hundred, and here's my card. I would like you to call my cell phone number any time Detective Hobbes goes out or has a visitor. If you happen to overhear anything, I can promise you a lot more."

"Gee, I don't know . . ."

"Please take it. She's a dear friend of mine, and she's just too proud and stubborn to let me protect her." Then he had Donald's wrist in a grip that wasn't hard, but it was so strong that Donald was afraid to let any of his muscles contract for fear the grip would tighten and break his wrist. Dunn put the money into his hand, then released him.

"I shouldn't be taking this money, or spying on a police-woman."

"It's for her own good, and yours. This way I can keep an eye on both of you at once."

"But I don't feel right about taking the money."

"I'm going outside to look around the parking lot now," said Calvin Dunn. "And don't worry about my money. The only reason to have money is to help your friends."

28

It was Thursday morning, and Nicole sat at Tyler Gilman's computer in his bedroom. The scanner he had beside his printer had given her an idea. She scanned the pattern from the back of an honor roll certificate that had been posted on Ty's wall onto a blank sheet of paper. She did it on four sheets, then turned over the paper and did it on the reverse side. "Ty," she called. "Help me think of a new name."

He lay on the bed, staring up at the ceiling. "How about Tara?"

"Too unusual."

"You are unusual."

"No. I want something that sounds like everybody else's name. I want to fade, Ty. I want to be invisible for, like, two years, and have a life."

"Victoria? Veronica? Melissa?"

"Too long. Maybe I'll be an Anne. Let me see. Foster, no, Forster. Anne Forster."

"That's good," said Ty. "That's really good."

She reached into her purse, took out the disk she carried, and put it into the computer. She opened the file containing the blank birth certificate. She selected the type font that fit the rest of the document and filled in the blanks to make Anne Forster a woman born twenty-two years ago, on the nineteenth of July. She put one of her sheets of paper with the filigree patterns on it into the printer and printed the certificate. Ty reached for it, but she said, "Don't touch it. The ink will smudge."

He stopped himself, and held his head at an angle to see the certificate in the tray. "It's just like the real thing. What should my name be?"

"Your name?"

"Yeah," he said. "It should sound real too. How about Joshua? Josh Forster."

"Uh . . . not quite right." She managed to conceal her surprise, but her mind was not moving quickly enough. "Who are you?"

"What do you mean?"

"Why do you and I have the same last name? What are you trying to be?"

"Your husband."

She smiled indulgently, but she shook her head. "That's so sweet. But Ty, you're twelve years younger than I am. That difference is three-quarters of your life. Nobody would believe we were married. More likely, they'd think I was one of those teachers who run off with one of their students. They'd call the police."

She saw his eyes begin to cloud, and he lay back on the bed and stared at the ceiling. She had said too much, and she had to fix things instantly or she was in trouble. "How about my brother? You could easily be my brother. That way, if we traveled together, people wouldn't think anything of it."

"I don't want to be your brother."

"Ty, please. Don't insist on taking extra risks. Our lives could depend on this. We can't be lazy-minded and draw attention to ourselves."

"I don't even look like your brother."

She thought about what she had seen of his parents' room. "Does your mother dye her hair to get rid of the gray?"

"Yeah."

She got up and went into the master bathroom off Ty's parents' bedroom. When Ty caught up with her she was opening cabinets and drawers. She knelt at an open cabinet under the sink, and took out a hair dye box with a picture of a beautiful woman on the front. She stood and pulled Ty to the mirror, then held the box up beside his hair. "Look. Her hair color is exactly the same as yours."

"You're going to dye your hair the color of mine?"

"Yes."

"Our eyes are different."

"My eyes are a paler blue than yours," she said, "but I have blue contacts. And brown and green. But I'll wear the blue. We'll look amazing."

He said nothing, just stared unhappily into the mirror at her. She looked at him from the corner of her eye. "Brothers and sisters can stay in the same hotel room at night. They do it all the time to save money."

He smiled.

"Come on. Help me."

"Now?"

"Yes, now. Ty, we've only got about three days left before your parents show up. Anything we need to do to prepare has to be done well before then. And some little thing might be what saves us." She tore open the top of the box.

"What if she notices it's missing?"

"I don't know," she said. "She probably won't notice, at least right away. She's got three boxes. I do know that if she can't find a box of hair dye, what she does about it isn't going to be calling the police. That's all I care about." She started to take small bottles and plastic gloves out of the box and set them on the sink.

"This looks really messy."

"It is."

"Then let's do it in my bathroom."

"But that's smaller and darker."

"If they come back and we're gone, you don't want them to figure out what happened right away. If there's a stain on the counter or something, they'll know the exact color you dyed your hair."

She stared at him. He kept surprising her. She followed him into his bathroom and set up her kit on his sink. She pulled her top off over her head, and heard the intake of breath from Ty. "Don't," she said. "Not now. I just can't take a chance that I'll stain my clothes. I don't have any except these."

He said, "I . . . I'm sorry. I should have thought about that. I have, like, three hours before I have to go to work. I can go out and buy you some now. I'll bring them when I get back from work."

"Where were you thinking of going?"

"I don't know. The mall?"

"Go someplace big, where nobody pays any attention to you and you put stuff in a shopping cart. Is there a Wal-Mart or a Target or something?"

"Yeah. Both."

"Then I'll give you a list of what I need, with my sizes. Buy some stuff for yourself, too, and mix it all together, like it's for your family. Okay?"

"Sure."

She stepped into his room, took a blank sheet of paper from the printer, and wrote out her list. She picked up her purse and took out some money. "This is six hundred dollars.

If you spend all of it in one place, they'll notice you." She handed him the list, and watched him read it. "Can you handle all of that?"

He shrugged uncomfortably. "I can do it. I've bought things for my mom."

"Just do your best, Ty. Be careful." She leaned close and kissed him slowly, passionately, then held him at arm's length. "The thing I care about most is that you keep yourself safe. If anything in or around the store doesn't seem right, then avoid the place. Don't go in."

"Okay," he said.

"Then go. Get the exact sizes I said. Try to stick with dark colors and earth tones. Don't worry about the lengths of the pants. I'll shorten them if they're too long. And try to find me a small, cheap suitcase with wheels, about the size to hold the clothes."

She kissed him again, and he looked a bit dazed. He didn't want to go. His arms lingered around her, until she grasped his wrists and removed them. She spun him around and pushed him toward the door. "Get going!" She snatched a pillow from the bed and hurled it in his direction. He sidestepped it easily and was out the door.

She listened to his footsteps going out, then the sound of the car. She went into the bathroom, took off the rest of her clothes, and opened the bottles. The strong, acrid odor of the chemicals filled the room. Some people hated that smell, but for her it brought back very early memories. The first time she had smelled that smell she had been five. Charlene and her mother had arrived in the downtown hotel the night before the Tiny Miss Milwaukee pageant, and she and her mother had gone down to the ballroom to watch the other contestants being brought in by their mothers for registration. As they watched the other little girls, her mother had looked increasingly worried. Finally she had locked Charlene in their room, gone to a drugstore down the street, and come back with two hair-dyeing kits. The next morning at the opening of the pageant, Charlene and Sharon Buckner had appeared with the same fresh golden hair and the same carefully applied makeup. They had looked almost alike, the pretty daughter like a miniature of the pretty mother.

As she worked, she reflected that it was a relief that Ty was gone. The dyeing wasn't difficult to do, but it did require that she pay attention to the time, and he was always trying to distract her.

She finished, and she could tell even while it was still wet that she had done a very good job. She went to her purse, found the little plastic case with her colored contacts in it, selected the blue ones, and put them in. She stood in front of the mirror. "I'm a Gilman."

29

Catherine Hobbes waited until Officer Gutierrez had pulled into the long-term parking lot at the airport and come to a complete stop. "This is probably about as close as we ought to get," he said.

They both got out of the patrol car and Catherine walked toward Mary Tilson's small gray Honda. She could see uniformed officers outside the perimeter of yellow tape that had been set up around the car. They were stringing more tape to force cars coming into the lot to go up another aisle, one that led away from the technicians who were working around the Honda.

Catherine reached the tape, and a police officer in a pair of suit pants and a white shirt with a lieutenant's badge clipped on the pocket stepped up to meet her.

When he talked she could see him making decisions. Even

though he must have seen her get out of Gutierrez's patrol car, he had to verify that she was Hobbes. "Hello. Are you Sergeant Hobbes?"

"Yes," she said.

Next he had to tell her that he was in charge. "I'm Lieutenant Hartnell."

She held out her hand so he could shake it. "Pleased to meet you."

She saw him decide that he wanted to have her think he was informal and spontaneous, not the sort of man who made decisions every time he spoke, so he said, "Steve Hartnell" as he shook her hand.

"My name is Catherine." She had her small notebook in her hand, and she compared the California license number on the plate of the Honda with the number in her notebook, then put the notebook away.

Hartnell said, "We've got it roped off so we can screen the area around the car for footprints, dropped items, and so on. The flatbed will be here in a few minutes to bring it in so we can have the trace evidence people give it a closer look."

"Do you know the time when it was left here?"

"The ticket is on the floor on the passenger side, as though she tossed it there after she took it and the automatic stile went up. It says three forty-eight A.M., two nights ago. In a way, it's a relief. It means she went to the terminal and took a taxi right to the Sky Inn. She didn't have time to stop off and kill a family of six."

Catherine ignored the last sentence because she was thinking about Tanya. "She must have been exhausted."

Hartnell looked at her as though he wondered about her sanity.

Catherine saw his expression. "She killed a woman in Los Angeles early in the evening, cleaned her whole apartment, packed up, and drove off in the victim's car. She must have stopped somewhere for a day and traveled after dark, but it took her until three A.M. on the second night to get here. I think she must have been worn out."

"I'm not exactly moved to sympathy," said Hartnell.

"I'm just ruling a few things out in my own mind," Catherine said. "I don't think she had somebody here that she was trying to reach—somebody who would take her in or help her get away. At four A.M. the person would almost certainly have been home, and she would have gone there. Instead, she ditched the car here and went to the Sky Inn. I think she probably stopped here because she was falling asleep at the wheel."

"But somebody picked her up within a minute after she called the hotel from the bus station the next day," said Hartnell. "She could have made an arrangement for that during the daytime. Maybe the accomplice worked nights or wasn't home until then."

"I don't think so," said Catherine. "She seems to be an expert at getting people to help her, to take an interest in her. Usually it's a man, but it doesn't have to be. I think that's what got Mary Tilson killed. She befriended the young woman who lived across the hall in her apartment building. She had invited her into her kitchen and started to get her something to eat or drink when she got stabbed."

"Do you have any way to use that?" asked Hartnell.

"I think we've got to concentrate on the person who picked Tanya up. If he drove her someplace, we need to know where he let her off. If he's still with her, we need to persuade him to turn her in."

Hartnell seemed to be making one of his decisions. He said carefully, "I'll talk to the chief about having a press conference."

"Great," said Catherine. "I also think we ought to check with your missing persons section to find out if there's anybody with a car who hasn't been seen in the past two days."

"Good idea," he said. "See you later." As he walked to his unmarked car, Catherine knew that she had gone too far, trying to tell a lieutenant in another state how he ought to organize his investigation. She had alienated him. She watched him start his car and drive out of the parking lot.

She turned to look at the car again, and thought about Tanya. She had been stuck in Los Angeles, on the verge of being discovered because of the photograph on the front page of the *Daily News*. She must have reacted desperately to get herself out—gone across the hall and stabbed her sixty-year-old neighbor to death just to steal her car. She had driven the car just about as long as she could without getting spotted: she had probably known that she had to get rid of it before daylight. When she had run out of time, she had ditched the car here. She had picked a place where she could leave it with a collection of other cars, and not have anyone wonder about it for a few days. She had been trying to buy time. She was pressed. She was running hard, and she was feeling vulnerable and scared.

Officer Gutierrez appeared at Catherine's shoulder. "Looks as though she didn't leave any footprints or anything. The tow truck is here."

"We may as well go," Catherine said. "Can you drop me at the station?"

"Sure."

Gutierrez drove her to the station and let her out at the front entrance. "What are you going to do now?" he asked.

"I'm going to try to persuade Lieutenant Hartnell to get me a chance to talk to Tanya."

30

Driver's licenses were difficult, and they were the form of identification that counted. She judged that the Rachel Sturbridge driver's license from California was the best one to scan. It had been issued most recently, and it had the greatest number and variety of devices on it to deter counterfeiters. There was a large color picture of her on the left side, a smaller one on the right, and lots of overlapping silver hologram state seals with the letters DMV. But once she was out of California, the address and numbers had no meaning to anyone.

She scanned the Rachel Sturbridge license onto a CD, typed in the name Anne Margaret Forster, her new eye color, hair color, and birth date, printed and cropped it, then inserted it into the plastic sleeve in her wallet. With the slight clouding, the license looked perfect.

She scanned Ty's high school group picture, and began to play with the images. In a few minutes she had separated Ty's face from the others and superimposed it on the image of the California license. Then she typed in the name James Russell Forster. She put in a new eight-digit number in red and changed the birth date. Then she printed it and cut it to size.

She took off her clothes and washed them with Ty's. While the clothes were in the dryer she took a hot bath. Before it got dark she found Ty's mother's nail kit and did her nails. In the last of the natural light she did her makeup and brushed her hair.

When she heard Ty's car come up the driveway, she moved to the kitchen to wait for him. She heard the garage door open and the car glide in. Ty closed the garage door, then came to the kitchen door, opened it, and turned on the light. He was carrying a bag of food from El Taco Rancho.

"Welcome home, Ty."

At first he was startled, but he recovered quickly. He stepped closer to her, looked at her hair, stared into her eyes. "Unbelievable."

"Do you like it?"

"It's awesome. You look like my aunt."

"Now I'm your aunt?"

"I didn't mean that," he said. "You just look a little bit like her. Not like she looks now. It's my aunt Darlene, my mother's sister. You're a lot younger, but I bet that's what she looked like when she was young. She was supposed to be hot. My father says she was a piece of ass, but now she's just a pain in the ass." He walked around her in a circle. "I can't get over this. You look so different. Your eyes and everything."

"So it looks all right?"

"Yeah, it does. It's a turn-on."

"You're a sixteen-year-old boy. Everything is a turn-on to you."

"Everything about you is." He set the bag of food on the counter and put his arms around her, so she had to kiss him. When his hands began to move from her waist, she grasped them and held on.

"I've got some other things to show you. Come on." She pulled him to his bedroom, where she had the new birth certificate and driver's license for James Russell Forster.

He picked them up and looked from one to the other. "Man, I can hardly believe this. It's . . . like, perfect. Can you make me one that says I'm twenty-one?"

She laughed. "You mean so you can get into bars?"

"Yeah."

"I want you to use this one when we're traveling." She grinned. "But later I'll do my best."

"That's all I ask." He went to his closet, opened the door, and took off his uniform shirt. As he pulled out a clean shirt, she saw something.

"Is that a gun?"

He reached into the corner of the closet and grasped it by the walnut foregrip and pulled it out. "Yeah. See? It was my father's old one, the first one he ever had, when he was my age. It's a thirty-ought-six."

She touched the smooth wooden stock, the bolt, and the scope. "Have you ever fired it?"

"Hell, yes. A million times. I'm a great shot."

"What have you shot at?"

"Deer, elk."

"You kill deer?"

"We didn't last year. My dad had to work weekends for practically the whole season, and I had football practice."

"But you've used it?"

"Yeah. Now you're going to tell me you hate me because I iced Bambi's mom, aren't you?"

She realized she must have had a lapse of concentration and let him see her disenchantment with hunting. She touched his arm. "There's nothing about you I don't like, Ty. You're a special person."

He put the rifle back in the closet, turned back to her, and said, "Shit. I forgot to bring in all the stuff I bought. It's still in the trunk." He hurried out of the room, then came back a few minutes later with three large shopping bags.

He reached into his pocket. "I had about sixty bucks left from buying that stuff."

"Hold on to it. I need to give you more, so you can get some supplies tomorrow for the trip."

He studied her. "Is that when we're leaving?"

She shrugged. "The longer we wait, the safer it is. But I'd like to be out of here at least two days before your parents show up." She frowned. "Why don't they ever call you?"

"They do. They called me about five times while they were in Lake Havasu. I think they were feeling guilty. Or maybe they just wanted to be sure I was going to work. Since then I called them twice on my cell phone."

She grinned. "You don't want me to hear what you're saying, huh? Do you call them 'Mommy' and 'Daddy'?"

"No," he said. "I just don't want any trouble. If they heard you talking or I sounded like somebody was with me, we'd be screwed." He asked, "Where are we going? We haven't talked about it at all."

"I don't know."

"Where were you going before?"

"I didn't know then, either. We need to get out of Flagstaff, out of this part of the country, where people expect to spot me. Beyond that, it doesn't matter. Every place has something nice about it."

"But we have to be heading somewhere."

"I have an idea. After dinner, why don't you go on the Internet and see if you can work out a route heading east, with maps and everything?"

"Okay," he said. "I'll map out a couple of ways, in case the first one is too dangerous."

"Good idea." Then she added, "Jim."

"Thanks, Anne."

After dinner she cleared the table and went into the living

room to examine the clothes he had bought. She looked into the first bag with trepidation, but in it she found two pairs of pants—one black, which was perfect, and one brown, which was ugly—a pair of blue jeans, and a pair of Nike running shoes. The tags told her he had bought the sizes she had given him. She was relieved.

In another bag were six pairs of socks, six pairs of panties, and three bras, supposedly obtained for the price of two. She thought of Ty going into that section of the store to buy those things and it made her smile. He had bought himself a jacket, as though to assuage his embarrassment.

The third bag had a couple of T-shirts, one of which had a picture of a cat and said "Cat-fight Boxing"; the other said "Hotel Juicy." The sweatshirt with them mercifully said nothing. There were three other tops, one a hideous pink, one sky blue, and the other the sort of green that people wore on St. Patrick's Day. All of the tops were completely wrong for her, but with the exception of the green top, none of them stood out, and all seemed to be the right size. She had never been seen wearing anything like them before. The more she considered the clothes, the happier she was.

She noticed that Ty was standing in the doorway, looking at her anxiously, so she said, "Ty, this is just fabulous. You did a wonderful job, much better than I ever expected." She put her arms around his neck and hugged him.

"Did I get the right sizes?"

"I haven't tried them on yet, but the tags say you got what I asked for."

"How about the suitcase?"

She took it out of the bag, unzipped it, and said, "It's perfect. Thank you so much." She busied herself removing all of the tags and pins, and throwing them in the trash with the plastic bags. Then she went into Ty's parents' bathroom to try on the clothes. She went through the process quickly, and found that everything would serve its purpose. Since she had been trying to hide, she had found little in the refrigerator, and nothing Ty had brought home from El Taco Rancho was more than marginally edible, so she had lost weight. She put on the black pants and the sky blue top, and went back to Ty's bedroom.

She opened his closet and studied herself in the full-length mirror that was attached to the closet door. Today she had made some good progress. She studied her eyes, her hair, her clothes. She looked like a new person again, and felt strong. She heard the sound of the ink-jet printer taking in a sheet of paper, and raised her eyes slightly to look into the mirror at the part of the room behind her.

Ty was printing his maps and directions, but he wasn't looking at the printer. He was staring at her now, looking at her longingly, hoping that the lightning was going to strike again.

She looked into the mirror at herself. "They fit," she said. She locked her eyes on his. She had to keep him happy, just a little bit longer. She began slowly, deliberately, to take off her new clothes.

Two hours later she lay on the couch in Tyler's bathrobe with her head on his lap. As he held the remote control and flicked from channel to channel, she said, "Stop." The policeman with the potbelly that hung out over his silver belt buckle was behind the podium again.

Behind the chief were four severe-looking men in suits and a woman in a navy blue pantsuit with the cuffs and collar of a white silk blouse showing. She liked the look of it, she decided. She would probably look good in navy, now that her hair was light again.

"Nicole?"

"Anne. Learn to call me Anne. Get used to it, Jimmy, because we leave in a day. We're Anne and James Forster."

"Do you think—"

"Hush," she said. "I want to hear this." She took the remote control out of his hand and turned up the volume.

The chief said, ". . . and now I would like to let Detective Sergeant Catherine Hobbes of the Portland, Oregon, Police Bureau have the microphone."

"Oh, my God," Anne whispered. "It's her."

"It's who?"

Someone off camera shouted, "Sergeant!"

"I'll be around to take questions after the conference," said Catherine Hobbes. "I just wanted to speak for a moment to Tanya Starling. Tanya, we've spoken on the telephone, so you probably recognize my voice."

"You bet I do, bitch."

"If you're anyplace where you're able to hear me, I want to appeal to you to turn yourself in now. If you can't get to a police station, just dial nine-one-one, and officers will come to pick you up and take you there. At this moment police organizations in at least fifteen states are watching for you, and it's only a matter of time until you're found."

In the pause, Anne said, "Fuck you."

"I know you're frightened," said Catherine Hobbes. "But everything I told you on the telephone still holds. I can guarantee your safety if you will come in voluntarily."

"You see?" said Anne. "She's threatening me, trying to scare me and get her face on television at the same time."

Tyler Gilman gaped at her. He had never seen her when she wasn't in control of her emotions. She seemed to be irrationally angry.

"She's hounding me. She won't leave me alone until she runs me down and gets her cops to kill me."

"She doesn't seem like that," said Tyler.

Catherine Hobbes left the podium, and the chief took her place. He said, "We believe that someone picked up Tanya Starling and gave her a ride away from the Flagstaff bus station in a private car. I urge and appeal to this person to call the police immediately. We need to know where you took her, what name she is using, and anything else that might hasten her apprehension. I caution you that her appearance is deceptive. We believe she is armed and extremely dangerous. If you are with her now, you are in peril. Get as far as possible from her right now and dial nine-one-one. You need not fear prosecution. We believe that you merely intended to help a stranger in need."

"Liar!" said Anne Forster. "He's lying."

"Him too?"

"They all are. She's just the worst, because she's decided I'm going to be the one that makes her into a success."

"It'll be okay."

"No, it won't. People think the devil is a cartoon character, all red with horns, but that's not what it is. It's a person like that, all self-righteous and sure that anything they do to you is right because you have to be punished. She keeps trying to tempt me. She says, 'Come in,' like she was asking me to come to the doctor's for a checkup. But as soon as I let them know where I am, the cops will come and nobody will ever see me again. They'll take me out into the desert and shoot me."

"You really think they'd do that?"

"Do you believe her instead of me? Did she come to your house because you said to, and have sex with you to prove that she was a sincere person?"

"Obviously not, but—"

"But what?"

"Don't worry about her," Tyler said. "She can't do anything."

"You look at her, and I know you only see that she's pretty, and she's talking with a soft voice, so you think she must be telling the truth. She's not. Take a look. See her standing there? That's what death looks like."

The press conference vanished from the screen, and the television stayed on, but neither of them was watching or listening to it, so after a half hour, they turned it off, went into Tyler's room, and collapsed on the bed.

She awoke early the next morning and started to make her preparations for departure. She packed her suitcase, then went to Ty's closet and dresser to pack a suitcase for him too. When they spoke they practiced calling each other Anne and Jim.

Later that morning she sent him out to run errands. The first was to fill the Mazda's tank with gas. "Jimmy, when you're trying to get away from a place, you don't take a single risk that isn't necessary, and you prepare. Stopping for gas anywhere near here later with me in the car is foolish, so we won't do it. You do it alone ahead of time, when it's safe."

"Sure," he said.

"And go to the grocery store. I made a short list, and here's the money. Buy at least twelve bottles of water, some nuts—peanuts, cashews, almonds—a few candy bars, some apples, and pears."

"What's all that stuff for?"

"The drive. We don't know how long we'll be on the road. In this heat we'll need water, and the nuts have fat and protein, so they prevent you from being hungry, and they keep. And by the way, Jimmy. Don't just buy gas. Check the oil, water, tire pressure, and whatever too. We get one chance at this."

"I guess I'll get started," he said. "What time do you want to leave?"

"Tonight. Right after you finish work."

"Why then?"

"Because your going to work gives us extra time before anybody notices that anything else is wrong. Just before you leave, tell your boss you want to take tomorrow night and the next night off. Your parents have car trouble in Lake Havasu and you have to go get them and leave the other car there to be fixed."

"I don't think he's going to be okay with that."

"You say, 'Gee, I'm sorry, but I don't have any choice. If you have to fire me for it, then you do.' "

He looked at her with admiration. "That's really good."

"Either way, it keeps anybody from noticing you're gone until your parents get home, which gives us two full days. Now get going."

He went out, and she listened to his car going up the street. She selected the clothes she wanted to wear for the trip and laid them out on the bed: the black pants and the blue top, with the sweatshirt out where she could reach it if she got cold during the night drive. She took out some clothes of Tyler's too.

Now that she was used to Tyler's computer and scanner and could make birth certificates and driver's licenses, she made sets in the names Barbara Harvey, Robin Hayes, Michelle Taylor, Laura Kelly, and Judith Nathan. She spent hours diligently performing the kind of cleaning that she had done before in the other places where she had lived. She managed to finish wiping down the surfaces in the master bedroom and bathroom, the den, and the living room before Tyler returned with the supplies.

She cooked a steak and baked potato for Tyler's lunch, and served it on plates from the best set she could find in the cupboards, with crystal stemware for his milk. "This is the way you deserve to be cared for, Jimmy. I want you to know what it's going to be like when we get settled somewhere."

Before noon he left to go to work. She made such a big event of his departure that she was afraid for a moment that she had done too much and he would refuse to leave her for his final night of work. While he was gone she cleaned the rest of the house of all traces of her presence, did the rest of the packing, showered and washed her hair, then searched the shower stall for any hairs of hers that might have fallen. She knew that her hair was exactly the color of Tyler's mother's, but she did it anyway.

She dressed and then prepared herself, sitting alone in the house that had now fallen into darkness. When Tyler came in the kitchen door he had to walk through the house, looking for her. He found her in his bedroom, sitting on the bed, looking grave. Beside her on the bed lay his rifle and two boxes of .30-06 ammunition.

"What is it, Anne? What's wrong?"

"You know," she said. "You saw last night."

"What do you mean?"

"All day I kept telling myself what I always do—that next time it will be better, next time things will be different. But it won't. There's really only one thing we can do."

"What do you mean?"

"We've got to get rid of her."

31

Catherine Hobbes had been in the Flagstaff police headquarters for eighteen hours, and she was tired. She had helped to work the leads that developed every time Tanya made a move—the abandoned car, the witnesses at the hotel and in the stores between the hotel and the bus station. As the time of the press conference had approached, she had been gripped by nervous energy that had lasted until she finished speaking in front of the cameras and then left her feeling drained and anxious. Finally she had spent hours sorting through the dozens of calls from tipsters, all the time waiting for a call from Tanya, hoping that something she had said would persuade her to pick up the phone.

There was no way of knowing whether Tanya was hiding in a place where there was no television, or had managed to escape beyond the range of the television broadcast, or had heard Catherine's plea and ignored her.

Everything Tanya Starling did made Catherine Hobbes uncomfortable. Serial killers usually had patterns and compulsions that made them perform a series of killings in the same way, often with elaborate planning and victims who were similar. Tanya didn't seem to do anything the same way twice in succession. Maybe she killed people out of fear.

It was confusing, because she didn't act as though she was afraid. She didn't hide from potential victims; she seemed to seek them out. She went to resorts and hotels and restaurants to find them. Tanya appeared to form relationships with strangers effortlessly. She cultivated them, made them trust her. She convinced them that she was smart and attractive and personable, and they didn't seem to notice that she was missing something. She was like a machine that didn't have some crucial part. The motor whirred and the wheels turned, but it didn't work right.

Hobbes had wanted to try to talk to her one more time. Tanya seemed to be susceptible to self-interest, and that implied that if she were approached in exactly the right way, she might be persuaded to come in quietly. Hobbes had now made two attempts, and both had failed.

Around eleven-thirty, after the press conference had been repeated on the eleven o'clock news, the telephone calls had increased for a while, then gradually stopped, and the police officers in the station had begun to look at her with curiosity, obviously wondering when she was going to give up.

She stood up, stretched, stepped out of the station, and got into her rental car. She drove along Route 66, then turned down South Milton Street toward the hotel. It was going to be another night when she arrived at the hotel long after the kitchen had closed, and it was too late for dinner.

She supposed that it wasn't so bad. There was something awkward and depressing about sitting in a restaurant alone late at night. People at that hour in restaurants were in groups or couples, and they always seemed to her to be looking at her strangely. Men were either considering offering her their company or forming theories as to why she was alone. Women seemed to think either that she was to be pitied or was up to something, possibly attracting the attention of their husbands.

She knew it was the aloneness that made her think about Joe Pitt again. He had begun to make more frequent appearances in her consciousness over the past few days. She was still not sure whether their relationship was going anywhere, but she missed him. He had called her in Portland the day after their impromptu dinner, and they had stayed on the phone for half an hour, talking like teenagers. But when she had received the news that Tanya had been sighted in Flagstaff, she had left Portland without letting him know. She wasn't used to calling men, but maybe she should.

Catherine gave a silent huff of air as she drove, a laugh at herself and her firm rules and requirements. She had a big foolish crush on him. As soon as she reached her hotel room, she would be forward and give him a call. He would undoubtedly be out at this hour, doing everything that she didn't like to imagine him doing. He might not be, though. If he answered, she would ask him for an opinion of what she had been thinking about Tanya's motives. Having something sensible to talk about would help preserve a little bit of her dignity. She saw the hotel's sign and turned into the entrance to the parking lot.

A blow like a hammer strike hit the car, the force of it making the frame shiver slightly; she could feel it in her back and feet. Catherine was so startled that her hands jerked the wheel sharply, and the car wobbled as she corrected it. Then she hit the gas pedal.

It had to have been a rock. Somebody had thrown a rock at her car, and all she had to do was get out of range and see who it was. She stared into her rearview mirror, but could not see either the rock or the thrower. He was undoubtedly some jerk who had decided to scare some defenseless young woman from out of town who was staying at the hotel.

She decided to do what she would have done if this had happened in Portland. She kept the car going about a hundred feet to get out of effective range, hit the brake, and spun around in the parking lot to swing her car's front end toward the rock thrower, then hit her high-beam lights.

Her car swayed a bit from the spin and settled, a smell of burned rubber from her tires pervading the air. She saw no human shape, and there was no hiding place, only neatly trimmed grass on either side of the driveway. She turned in her seat and craned her neck to see if she had missed him. Her eye passed across the metal strut just ahead of the rear window. There was a clean, round bullet hole just above it at the edge of the roof.

Catherine saw the side window behind her explode into the interior, bits of glass like little cubes of light spattering the back seat, stinging her right cheek and temple with a pain that seemed to intensify into a burn during the first second. The window on the opposite side of the car was gone, blown outward by the bullet, so she knew the approximate direction of fire.

She guessed that it was probably a hunting rifle, because the time between shots was too long for a semiautomatic assault rifle. It felt to her like the time it took to cycle a bolt, and it was due again . . . now.

Bam! The next shot punched through the door behind her. She swung the car to the right and accelerated again, slouching to bring her head and body down as low as she could and still see out the windshield to drive.

She knew that the shooter was lining up the next shot at the back window of her car as she drove away from him. That made her almost as easy to hit as she would have been standing still, so just as she felt it was time for another shot, she jerked the wheel abruptly to the left.

She heard the distant report of the rifle—a miss—and swung the car to the right, up an aisle between two rows of parked cars. She turned at the end of the aisle and put two more rows of cars between her and the shooter, then pulled into an empty space.

She killed the engine, switched off the dome lights, opened her door, and slid out to the pavement. Catherine held her sidearm with her right hand and dialed her cell phone with her left. After a half ring, the operator answered, "Emergency."

"This is Detective Sergeant Catherine Hobbes of the Portland Police. I'm under fire from a person with a rifle in the parking lot of the Sky Inn on South Milton Street in Flagstaff. The sniper is on the west side of the hotel, firing from a distance."

There was another loud bang as a shot punched into her car's trunk, and then the report of the rifle. She said, "I would say from the sound that he's about two hundred yards west of the hotel. He's probably up high."

"We're dispatching units to your location now. Have you been hit?"

"No. I'm staying low in the parking lot, and I'm about to move to a spot where I don't think he'll be able to see me. Remind the officers not to overlook the possibility that the shooter might be a woman." She closed her cell phone and put it into her pocket, then dashed across the open aisle. There was the sound of a bullet burying itself in the asphalt behind her, and then the report as she reached a tall truck in the next row of vehicles. She ran around to the front of it, where the height of the cab would hide her from sight.

Calvin Dunn's black car accelerated out of the delivery entrance of the parking lot on the other side of the hotel, sped two blocks up South Milton, and pulled to the curb. In a heartbeat Calvin Dunn was out and running. He ducked between two buildings and trotted up the alley behind the row of stores. He wasn't sure exactly where the shooter was, because the shots had come from a distance and the reports had echoed among the buildings, but he had seen Catherine Hobbes's car, and he could make an educated guess. He just had to make it to the right spot without tripping over the sniper.

As he trotted, he kept his body in the deepest shadows close to the back walls of the buildings, where the light from cars and streetlamps could not reach him. When Calvin Dunn approached the end of a large store with a loading dock, he judged that he must be near the shooter. The buildings along here were the right height, and the ones on the next block didn't have a clear line of sight to the hotel. He slowed to a walk and began to hunt with his ears.

He kept moving steadily in the shadows toward the area where he knew the shooter would be, keeping his head up and his eyes scanning for human silhouettes or movements. He knew that this time he might be looking for the much smaller, slimmer shape of a girl. Beyond that, the size and sex didn't matter. A person with a gun was mostly gun.

There: he had seen a change in the borders of a shadow high on the fire escape of a four-story building directly ahead. What had looked like a part of the black iron railing moved, and the bigger shadow behind it shifted. There was

the sharp bang of the rifle's report, and in the muzzle flash a
man with a rifle appeared and disappeared again.

Calvin Dunn advanced another twelve feet closer while
the man was staring through the scope to see if he had hit his
target, and another ten while he was flipping the bolt up and
pulling it back to eject the spent brass, pushing it forward to
seat the next round, and down to lock it again.

By the time the hot brass casing flew from the rifle and went
spinning down to the pavement thirty feet below, Calvin
Dunn was close enough to have reached out and caught it.
He stared upward to find the ladder suspended below the fire
escape. It was on a weighted cable that made it rise above the
reach of a burglar when nobody was on it, but Calvin Dunn
could see how the shooter had gotten up.

Dunn took off his sport coat, wrapped his gun in it, and set
the bundle in a doorway. Then he climbed to the top of a
dumpster, took the bar that was meant to slide across the lid
of the dumpster to lock it, stuck it between the bottom two
rungs of the ladder, waited for the next shot, and pulled it
down. He began to climb carefully and silently toward the
man.

Calvin Dunn could see him on the third-floor landing of
the fire escape, staring through his telescopic sight at the distant hotel parking lot. As Dunn climbed, the man fired again.
Dunn knew from experience that the noise of the rifle would
cause a ringing that would deafen the shooter for a second or
two while he was fighting the barrel down after the kick, and
then he would make noise working the bolt. Dunn used the
time to climb closer.

The shooter prepared himself again, holding one of the
vertical supports of the railing with his left hand to form a
solid rest for the rifle's foregrip. Calvin Dunn was almost
there. He climbed slowly and steadily, watched the man take
careful aim. He heard him blow the air out of his lungs, then
squeeze off a round. The shooter cycled the bolt and ejected
the brass, but Dunn could tell from the sound that the gun
must be out of ammunition. The shooter fiddled with the
magazine release, removed it from the underside of the rifle,

reached into his jacket for more ammunition, and heard Calvin Dunn's feet on the steel steps of the fire escape.

The shooter was seated with his legs in front of him and his knees bent, so getting up in time was impossible. He pushed a couple of rounds into the magazine and clicked it into place, then twisted his torso to bring the long gun around, but Calvin Dunn was already there. Dunn gave a quick tug on the barrel to stimulate the man's reflex to yank it back toward himself, and then pushed it up violently so the butt plate pounded into the man's face.

The voice that grunted "Uh!" sounded young. It was a kid, and his left hand went to his injured face. Dunn snatched the rifle out of the boy's right hand, swung it around, and worked the bolt to bring the first round into the chamber.

Dunn stood with his back against the wall of the building as he stared down at the young face, now streaked with blood from the nose and mouth. "Listen carefully. I'm going to give you one opportunity to tell me exactly where Tanya Starling is at this moment. Do not waste your one chance."

The reply was surprising, even to Calvin Dunn. The boy opened his bloody mouth, revealing that a couple of front teeth were gone. He took a deep breath, and let out a bellow. "Tanya!" The yell was a louder sound than he would have thought the boy could make, a howl like an animal. "I'm caught! Get away!"

Dunn pulled the trigger, the rifle kicked, and the bullet tore through the boy's chest. Dunn leaned over the boy and noted the location of the hole. He was dead.

Dunn left the rifle on the fire escape beside the body and climbed down the fire escape stairs until he came to the ladder. He stopped there to wait for the police car he could see at the entrance of the alley to drive all the way to the end.

32

Catherine Hobbes sat on an uncomfortable wooden chair at the side of the interrogation room while Lieutenant Hartnell sat down at the table to question Calvin Dunn. As she looked at Calvin Dunn, she understood why Joe Pitt had warned her. The face below his graying hair was smooth and almost unlined, devoid of emotion. The pale eyes revealed no concern, or even much indication of an interior life. They were merely watchful.

As soon as she had heard the name of the man who had killed the sniper, she had asked to be in the room while he was interrogated. Lieutenant Hartnell had said, "You're welcome to watch the video monitor, or even have a copy of the tape afterward." But she had said, "I want him to see me." Then she had told Hartnell what Joe Pitt had told her about Calvin Dunn.

While Hartnell prepared to begin, Catherine watched Calvin Dunn. He took note of each of the people in the room and looked up at the video camera suspended from the ceiling, but nothing he saw surprised him. He turned his attention to Hartnell, and Catherine could see that it made Hartnell uncomfortable.

Hartnell said, "Your name, please."

"Calvin Dunn."

"I'm Lieutenant Hartnell, Flagstaff Police Department. I would like to ask you a few questions about what happened tonight. I want you to know that you have the right to refuse to answer them. What you say could be used against you in court. You also have the right to have an attorney present while we talk to you. If you cannot afford an attorney, we will get you one before we proceed. Do you understand your rights?"

Calvin Dunn never took his eyes from Hartnell as he listened to the recitation. "Yes," said Calvin Dunn. "I think that for the moment I won't need an attorney, thank you."

Hartnell did not like the exaggerated politeness. "I assume that you're saying that because you think that you won't be charged with anything?"

"I can't control what somebody might accuse me of. But I won't be convicted of anything. That's not a possibility."

"What makes you so certain?"

"Because there was only one gun up on that fire escape, and the dead man brought it with him. I climbed up there carrying no weapons. While I was struggling to take his rifle away from him to prevent him from using it on me and others, it went off."

"Mr. Dunn, your identification says you live in Los Angeles. What are you doing in Flagstaff?"

"I'm a licensed private investigator. I'm searching for Tanya Starling."

"Why were you at the Sky Inn tonight? Are you registered at the hotel?"

"No. I was watching for Tanya Starling."

"Why? She hasn't been seen at the hotel for several days."

"Hasn't been seen. Right," Calvin Dunn said. "That doesn't mean she hasn't been there, or wasn't nearby, just out of sight, doing the seeing."

"All right. You know she hasn't been seen at the hotel, but you were waiting for her to show up anyway. Why would she do that?"

"Because of that lady right there." His right forefinger pointed directly at Catherine's heart. It made her want to flinch, but she controlled the impulse. "I went there at first because that was where Tanya Starling had been spotted last, but then I developed a hunch, and verified that Miss Hobbes was staying there. And that made it a good place for me to be."

"Explain."

Calvin Dunn looked directly at Catherine. His pale eyes made her uncomfortable, but she met his gaze. "You can't just follow a killer around and hope you'll catch up with them. You have to think about what makes them want to do it."

"Can you elaborate on that?"

"Sure. There are some people who kill once because they lose their temper or they're drunk and don't think it through. Others do it because they get a charge out of it, like sex. Tanya Starling isn't either kind. She solves problems that way."

"Solves problems? What kind of problems?"

"Whatever comes her way. She goes along doing what she wants until somebody becomes a problem. She solves it by killing them."

"And how in the world did that theory lead you to sit in the parking lot of the Sky Inn tonight?"

"The place you want to be isn't where the last victim was. It's where the next one is going to be."

"You thought that Tanya Starling was going to the hotel to harm Detective Hobbes?"

"It seemed likely."

"How long would you have stayed?"

Calvin Dunn turned to Catherine Hobbes. "How long would we have stayed?"

The others sat in silence, and Catherine realized she had to answer. "I can't say."

Calvin Dunn turned to Hartnell. "We can't say."

"Why would she think killing Detective Hobbes would solve her problems?"

"Miss Hobbes was the one who investigated Tanya's first killing and has been after her ever since. If it wasn't for her, nobody would care about Tanya Starling. Cops don't get much appreciation from the general public. But you can bet there's one person who knows exactly who you are and exactly what you did in each case. I figured Tanya has to know who's after her."

Hartnell sat still with his lips pursed. "It must have been kind of a disappointment to you that the shooter turned out not to be Tanya after all."

"It *was* her," said Dunn. "That kid up on the fire escape was doing it for her."

"I'm sorry to cast doubt on your theories, but we have people killed around here that have nothing to do with Tanya Starling."

"Did he fire at anybody besides Miss Hobbes? Are there any bullet holes in any of the hundred other cars in the hotel parking lot or the two hundred that went up the street past him while he was waiting for her?"

Hartnell's eyes shot to Catherine, and she could tell he wanted to throw her out of the room. But Hartnell's voice remained calm and deliberate. "Mr. Dunn, I think you need to remember that it's my job to ask the questions."

"I'm just pointing out that the kid was doing it for Tanya."

"I caught that," said Hartnell. "Let's concentrate on you. Had you ever seen the sniper before you saw him on the fire escape?"

"I think I probably did. It's probable he was one of the people who drove by the hotel parking lot a bit earlier tonight. I was mostly looking for women, but I did take a look at everybody I saw."

"What do you suppose he was doing?"

"I don't know."

"Come on, Mr. Dunn. You have a theory on everything. Was he looking for Detective Hobbes?"

"More likely, her car."

"How did he know what her car looked like? How could he possibly know?"

"I would guess he might have seen that press conference in front of the police station on television, then driven by the station parking lot and looked for a rental car. I don't imagine there were a lot of them out there."

Hartnell knew Dunn was right, and that made him more frustrated. "All right. You were in the parking lot of the Sky

Inn at around eleven-thirty, when the first shots were fired. Is that right?"

"Almost. I think it was around eleven-forty."

"Take us through the rest of this. What did you do then?"

"Well, I saw the car with Miss Hobbes in it come up the road and signal for the lot entrance, so I started looking at the cars behind it to see if Tanya was following her. The first shot looked like it drilled the rear strut, just in front of the rear window. Miss Hobbes jammed the gas pedal, hit the brakes, and spun around. Then a second shot hit the side window and went through the car, so she drove off across the lot as fast as she could. But because the bullet had hit both windows I could tell which direction the shot came from."

"Did you try to help her?"

"Help her do what?"

"Get to safety."

"She was already doing what I would have done, which was to drive like hell to get behind something to block the shooter's view. She was weaving around a bit to give him a harder shot."

"Did you call the police?"

"No. I knew she would do that."

"So what did you do?"

"I drove around the hotel building to get out on a side street, then drove toward the place where I thought the shooter was."

"And you thought the shooter was Tanya Starling."

"I didn't have any other candidates in mind at the time, but I didn't know who it was."

"But your theory that told you to be there suggested that that was who it was. So you didn't call the police or try to help the potential victim to safety or warn the innocent by-standers who might drive into the lot. What did you do?"

"I went after the shooter."

"And where did you find him?"

"Perched on the fire escape of one of the taller buildings, about two blocks west of the hotel."

"What was he doing when you found him?"

"Shooting."

"He wasn't trying to get away?"

"No. From up there he had a pretty good view. He probably figured he would see any police cars in plenty of time to get away."

"What do you think? Was he right?"

"If he was wrong, he would still have been up on that balcony with a thirty-ought-six and a couple of boxes of ammo when the first cop cars came up that alley. Then you would have had a couple of those bagpipe funerals."

Hartnell was clenching and unclenching his teeth. Catherine could see his jaw muscles tightening and relaxing. "So when you got there, he was still shooting."

"Yes. Otherwise, he probably would have noticed me, but he had his eye in the scope."

"Why didn't you shoot him? We found your gun in your coat."

"I've been deputized by the sheriff of Delacruz County, California, as an auxiliary officer, and if you found the gun you found the concealed-carry permit with it. Arizona and California have a reciprocal agreement."

"Answer my question. Why didn't you shoot him?"

"Because I wanted to try to get him alive."

"Why?"

"So he would tell me where she was."

"So we're back to Tanya Starling again?"

"We've never been anywhere else."

"Who hired you to find her?"

"A victim's family."

"What's the client's name?"

"It's the Poole family."

"Hugo Poole hired you to kill her, didn't he?"

"He hired me to find her."

"You thought the boy on the fire escape was Tanya Starling, so you climbed up there intending to kill her. It must have been an incredible disappointment when you saw it wasn't even a woman. It was a boy."

Dunn said, "I can see the friendly part of our talk is over. Now you can get me a lawyer at your expense, and I'll be ready to continue."

Hartnell turned to the uniformed officer beside Catherine and said, "Put him in a holding cell for now."

Calvin Dunn stood up and faced Catherine while the police officer handcuffed his wrists behind his back. "Be careful for the next couple of days, darling. It looks like I won't be around to watch your back."

33

Anne Forster heard the news on the radio at seven in the morning, when she had already driven halfway into New Mexico. She had the radio tuned to the strongest signal she could find, the Albuquerque morning drive-time program.

The woman who served as sidekick to the funny morning man read the story. "There's a bizarre twist to the hunt for Tanya Starling, the woman wanted for questioning in multiple murders in several states. Last night in Flagstaff, Arizona, a sniper opened fire on a police detective from Portland, Oregon, who has been pursuing the case. Police say the sniper shot at Detective Sergeant Catherine Hobbes in the parking lot of her hotel. The sniper, in turn, was killed in an attempt to apprehend him, and remains unidentified. There is no word on the whereabouts of Tanya Starling."

"I'm sorry, Ty," she said quietly. The words sounded really good to her, with just a small break in her voice. She said it again, and it was even better. That bad-little-girl voice would have made Tyler's knees buckle. The thought made her miss him for a moment.

She was irritated that the woman on the radio was trying to make everything sound like her fault. Was she supposed to feel guilty now that this Catherine Hobbes had killed a sixteen-year-old? Anne's eyes passed across the items that Ty had left in the car when he had gone off with the rifle. He had left his baseball cap, some pocket change he'd been afraid would jingle, his jacket. She reached into the jacket with her right hand and found his cell phone.

She set it down and reached into her purse. She found the little notebook where she had written the phone numbers of Catherine Hobbes in Portland, Oregon. She dialed the home number and listened to the recorded invitation to leave a message.

"Hello, Catherine," she said. "It's me again. I'm thinking about you." She was pleased with that. She had not practiced or even planned it, but it had sounded scary. "I just heard on the radio that you killed the boy. He saw the press conference where you and the fat cop said nothing would happen to him. I told him to trust you. But you killed him. That was a disgusting thing to do. Good-bye, Catherine. I'll be thinking about you."

She turned off the telephone and smiled: pretty good. If she had made the call any spookier, it would have seemed intentional. She left the telephone open and dropped it out the window, onto the pavement. This route—Interstate 40—was one of the busiest east-west roads in the country. In a few seconds one of the big fourteen-wheelers she had been passing for hours would come along and crush Ty's phone to powder.

She put on Tyler's baseball cap so the brim would help shade her eyes as she drove east, toward the rising sun. She glanced in the mirror on the back of the sun visor. She looked cute. Maybe she should wear hats more often.

When she reached Albuquerque, she watched the signs and took the turn at one that said I-25 North. She wasn't sure where she was heading, but soon she began to see signs that listed cities, as though they were items on a menu: Santa Fe, Colorado Springs, Denver, Cheyenne. She would have to

start avoiding little places, where people remembered everyone they had seen in their whole boring lives.

"She called me again." Catherine Hobbes stood in Lieutenant Hartnell's office, still holding her cell phone in her
hand.

Hartnell lifted his eyes from the file on his desk. "Tanya?"

"Yes. She called my house in Portland and left a message
about a half hour ago."

"Can I hear it?"

She lifted her cell phone, tapped the keys to replay her
message, and handed it to him. He listened to it, then took a
small tape recorder out of his desk drawer, turned it on, and
hit the 1 key on Catherine's phone to replay the message beside the microphone. Then he pressed the 2 to save it, and
handed it back to her. "She seems to think that you ambushed
him."

"She seems to," said Catherine. "The phone company says
the call came from a cell phone, and the origin was Albuquerque. Here's the number." She handed it to him on a sheet
from a desk message pad. "They say it belongs to Tyler Gilman, of Darling, Arizona."

"That's just down the road, outside of town," he said. He
stood up and went to the door, then beckoned to someone.
When one of the detectives came in, he said, "I need you to
find out what you can about a Tyler Gilman. The address is in
Darling. I think he's either another victim or he's our sniper."
Hartnell turned and came back to his desk.

"Well," said Catherine, "thanks for letting me in on the investigation. I'd better be going now."

"Going?"

"The call came from Albuquerque. I've got to see if I can
get on a plane."

"You know she definitely talked that boy into trying to kill
you?"

"Think of it. She can talk somebody into that, and I can
barely get my dates to open a door for me."

He didn't laugh. "If you know, then you ought to take
some precautions."

"I spend all my time with other cops."

"Think about tomorrow or the next day," said Hartnell. "She could do it again. Some man you never saw before could walk up and put a bullet in your head, just to win points with her."

"Absolutely true," said Catherine Hobbes. "It's always been a crummy job." She stepped to his desk, leaned across it to hold out her right hand. "Thanks for everything."

34

Anne Forster was exhausted from driving, but she was excited. Denver was big and busy and had lots of traffic. There were crowds of pedestrians on the downtown streets who walked past one another without really looking, just as they did in Chicago or Los Angeles. Their memories must be so overloaded with faces that ones they saw on the street left only an impression that blurred and faded within seconds.

As she came into the central part of the city on I-25, she saw a sign for something called City Park, so she took the exit. When she got to the park entrance, she pulled into a lot and turned off the engine. There were hundreds of people in the range of her vision, and they were all sorts—most looking relaxed and happy, walking or sitting, throwing Frisbees, chasing children. She got out of the car to hide her purse in the trunk, but on the way she glanced in at the back seat. She had brought along a blanket from Tyler's bedroom in case she wanted to nap while Tyler drove. She hid the small pistol she'd taken from Mary Tilson in the pocket of her jacket, locked the trunk, took the blanket with her to the shade of a big tree on the vast lawn, and arranged herself on it.

She rolled the jacket up and used it as a pillow. She knew that since she didn't look either poor or crazy, nobody would object to her dozing off under a tree in the park in the daytime. All she really had to worry about was the very slim chance that somebody who had seen her picture on television would come by and recognize her despite her dyed hair and new clothes, or that a patrol car would pick out Tyler's car among the hundred parked in the lot. She listened to the sounds of the people and gradually slipped into sleep.

She slept peacefully until seven, when a car drove along the edge of the parking lot with a booming bass beat on its stereo, and she sat up quickly with her hand on the jacket and looked around. The young mothers and their toddlers, the old men and women had all gone home now. They were being replaced by teenagers, mostly slow-strolling couples or gangs of boys patrolling the park for girls. She decided it was time to go.

She stood up, put on Tyler's jacket carefully so the gun would remain unseen in the pocket, and folded up the blanket. She stared up at the big trees and decided that she liked Denver. It was going to be the place where she would make herself safe again. She walked to the car, put her blanket in the trunk and got her purse, then went into the public restroom to wash her face and brush her hair.

She drove until she found the right kind of restaurant, a diner with vinyl booths. She ordered a big dinner, and while she ate she thought about the steps she needed to take, each in its place in the logical order of things.

The way to survive was to find someone to be. She had read somewhere that the best place to find the sort of information she was going to need was in people's trash, and she decided that the best kind of name would belong to a middle-class home owner. She drove through nice neighborhoods until she found streets where there were garbage containers rolled out to the curb to await the morning collection, but she did not stop. Instead, she kept driving until she knew the boundaries of the next day's pickup area.

She chose neighborhoods as though she were buying a house. She wanted houses that were recently painted, solid buildings with good landscaping and no signs of neglect or disrepair. She stayed away from the homes of the very rich, because she had a suspicion that the richest people must have security patrols watching their neighborhoods late at night.

At one A.M., after she had selected the right block, she parked and walked to a set of cans. She began to open the lids, lifting and touching the trash bags. The ones that felt heavy and solid or gooey she put back. The ones that felt as though they contained paper, she took with her. She went on for an hour, collecting bags of garbage and putting them in her car trunk. When she had collected all the car would hold, she drove to a shopping mall and parked away from the lights near a dumpster.

She used the flashlight from Ty's trunk and began to go through the garbage bags, working quickly. She set aside all of the pieces of paper that looked like bills or receipts. She dropped the bags in the dumpster and went out to get more. She kept working in the same way for four more trips. By dawn she had a big pile of other people's discarded papers in the back seat.

When daylight came she parked in the shade of a tall, windowless self-storage building and went through the bills and papers. After an hour she had gone through all of the papers but had not found any of the information she needed.

At seven she drove to a part of the city park where she had not been before, found a parking place, and lay on her blanket under a tree to sleep. At three o'clock, the sun had moved far enough so she was lying in the sun. She awoke with a terrible glare in her eyes, and reached up to feel her face. It was hot but not tender, so she had hope that she had avoided a sunburn. She had to be careful, because people who lived on the street all seemed to have faces damaged by the sun. She had to look middle-class as long as she could.

She went to the nearest public restroom and examined her appearance as she washed and brushed her teeth. She was still okay, still clean looking and undamaged. But the fear had been planted, so she went to a drugstore and bought sun-block, shampoo, conditioner, and moisturizer, then drove back into the park to a restroom near the zoo. She washed her hair, gave herself a sponge bath, and rubbed her skin with lotion, then put on fresh clothes.

She went to the telephone beside the restroom and used the phone directory to find the addresses of three hospitals. Tonight was going to be a hard one for her, but she judged that it had a better chance of bringing her success than last night had.

She drove to the first of the hospitals, a sprawling newly expanded place with several wings and several driveways. She picked one and drove the perimeter of the hospital. There were dumpsters all around the building, but all of them had their tops locked down. When she reached the driveway where she had entered, she left. She had not been thinking clearly. Probably the hospital had to lock the dumpsters, because otherwise addicts would be there looking for half-used bottles of painkillers and narcotics.

She widened her search to the surrounding neighborhood. There were always medical office buildings within a block or two of major hospitals. The hospital might have strict security procedures, but all of the clerks who worked in all of those doctors' offices couldn't possibly be that careful. People just didn't care that much.

She spent the evening finding and searching the dumpsters outside the office buildings surrounding the three big hospitals. At four A.M. she found something that looked right: a carbon copy of a physician's office-visit checklist. On it the doctor had checked off the exams he had performed and the tests he had ordered for a patient. The patient's name, birth-date, and social security number were on the sheet. It was not going to help her in the way she had hoped, because the patient's name was Charles Woodward, and his age was seventy-one. But she put the sheet in her pocket and kept working.

At seven she went back to the park to sleep. When she woke for dinner at four, she was already breathing hard—

panting, almost. She had a panicky certainty that she had been letting time go by without doing the right things, or doing them assiduously enough. She decided she was already running out of time. She had left Flagstaff on Friday, and it had taken all night and most of the next day to drive here. That made it Saturday afternoon when she had arrived in Denver, so now it was Monday. She had to get moving.

She drove to a mailbox-rental store, paid in cash to rent a mailbox in the name Solara Estates, and took a couple of business cards so she would remember the address. After it was dark, she went to a big Kmart and bought an adjustable wrench, a screwdriver, and pliers.

She drove to a street where there were auto repair shops, muffler shops, tire stores. One of the cars that had been left outside a mechanic's shop caught her eye. It had a cover over it, and she looked beneath it to see that the hood had been removed and so had the engine. She stole the license plates, drove to a dark alley down the street, and used them to replace the Arizona license plates on Tyler's car.

She drove to the Aurora Mall, went to the ladies' room near the food court, washed, and did her hair and makeup. She went to Nordstrom's, bought a purse, a pair of black pants, shoes, and a top like the ones she had always worn by preference, and changed into them. As she studied herself in the mirror she judged that she had held up surprisingly well. Sleeping in the park during the day had not been something she would have chosen, but she had actually gotten more undisturbed sleep than she'd had since she'd left Chicago. The work of wandering the city and hauling trash bags around by night—or maybe the one meal a day that she had eaten—had kept her trim. She looked good, even healthy.

When she returned to her car she opened her suitcase and put on some medium-good diamond earrings that Dennis Poole had bought her and a matching tennis bracelet. She put her Anne Forster driver's license into the little ID wallet that came with her new black purse, then stuck a hundred dollars in with it. She locked everything else in the trunk, and kept the keys in her pocket.

She found a singles bar near Larimer Square early in the evening. There was a line outside, and it gave her a chance to see the kinds of people who thought the bouncers and door-men should admit them. It was too early in the evening to see the staff make any difficult decisions. They turned away only a couple of young men, who seemed to have done something the night before: "Sorry, man. If the boss sees you two in there after last night, I'm going to be looking for a job." They didn't turn any women away, which was a good sign.

When she reached the head of the line, she held her home-made license inside the wallet, but the bouncer barely glanced at it before he waved her in. Inside, the light was dim and the recorded music was loud. There was a D.J. in a booth high above the dance floor choosing cuts and operating the col-ored lights that strafed the crowd. The line at the bar was al-ready three deep, and the five bartenders were lip-reading and pouring drinks methodically.

She had to have a drink to hold in her hand, so she ordered a 7UP with a lime twist, which looked enough like a gin and tonic in the changing light. As soon as she was away from the bar, men started asking her to dance with them, so she did. She had an extremely clear vision of what she had to accom-plish tonight, so she used the dancing, making turns to watch the way the crowds were forming and reconfiguring.

As she danced, she could see groups of single girls sitting at the tables in the corner of the room just off the dance floor and farthest from the front door. Men lingered near that spot or walked by, surveying the selection while pretending not to, and the women made their own evaluations and decisions while pretending not to.

When she had danced enough to be sure that the young women at the tables had become used to her, she bought an-other 7UP and went to the women's area to sit on the uphol-stered bench that ran the length of the wall beyond the tables. She began to make overtures to the women around her. "This is a great place," she said to one of them. The woman ap-peared not to be able to hear her over the noise of the music. She tried the one on her other side, a thin blonde who seemed to be there alone. "Wow. I absolutely love those shoes. Would you mind telling me where you got them?"

"Zero Gravity."

"Can you tell me where that is? I'm new here. I just moved here from Florida." She laughed. "I don't know anything."

"It's on Colfax, not far from the capitol building. It's really a great place."

"Thanks so much. Do you know a good place to get a jacket? The fall stuff is out already, and I thought I might pick up a jacket now. With the altitude here and everything, I'm freezing half the time."

"Zero Gravity would be a good place to start for that too. Or, you know, there's a mall in Aurora that has just about everything." The woman's eyes left hers and rose to focus on someone standing over them.

"Would you like to dance?" asked the man. He was looking at Anne.

She said to the blond woman, "Would you mind watching my purse for a minute?"

The woman said unenthusiastically, "Okay. Sure."

She got up and danced with the man. He was tall, skinny, and young—so young that she wondered if he had used a false ID to get into the bar. She smiled at him, wondering if the blond woman she had chosen was right. If she had chosen wrong, the woman would be gone and so would her purse, fake driver's license, and hundred in cash.

When the song was over, the young man said, "Want to dance again?"

"I shouldn't. I left my purse with that girl."

She went back and found the blonde still there. She said to her, "Thanks for watching my purse."

She worked to shape the evening and make it conform to her vision. She talked with the woman and made observations, tried to make her laugh. They moved to a table when its occupants left. They became more and more comfortable with each other, and their smiles and laughter attracted another man. The blonde got up to dance with him, and she said, "Your turn to watch my purse, okay?"

"Sure."

She waited until the girl had disappeared into the surging crowd of dancers, took out her little notebook and pen, and reached into the purse. She kept the purse beneath the table, her head up and her eyes on the dancers, so even if the lights had suddenly come on it would have been difficult to say she had been searching the purse. She looked down only when her fingers had identified something.

The driver's license gave the blonde's name as Laura Murray, her address as 5619 LaRoche Avenue in Alameda, and her date of birth as August 19, 1983. She copied quickly, then found the health insurance card, which gave an identification number that started with XDX and ended in a social security number. She looked into the wallet to see the issuers of the credit cards. Then she closed the purse and put away the notebook and pen. The whole process had taken barely sixty seconds.

The young woman came back after ten minutes to find her slightly bored and tired. They talked for a few minutes longer, and both went to the ladies' room. As soon as they returned, the young man who had danced with the blonde before asked her to dance again. At that moment, Anne caught the blonde's eye, pointed at her watch, and waved. The blonde smiled and waved back.

She stepped outside into the cool night air and breezed past the doormen, feeling eager. It was going to work. She knew it was going to work. She walked back to her parked car, retrieved her real purse with the gun and money in it, and drove to a 7-Eleven store that had a pay telephone on the wall outside. She searched the directory for an all-night copy service that rented computers, then drove there.

When she reached the copy center, she was pleased. This seemed to be a business that served people from the university. The customers were all her age or younger, and there were at least two dozen of them, even though it was after midnight. There were a dozen using the self-service copying machines, paper cutters, and laminating machines. There were another dozen people using the computers. She claimed one and went to work.

She went to bank Web sites and found one that would allow her to apply for a Visa card online. She brought up the application and checked her notes to be sure it wasn't one of the banks that had already given Laura Murray credit. She entered Laura's name, address, birth date, social security number, and driver's license number. She said Laura was an executive trainee, effective a month ago in case the credit check revealed some other job, and that she made approximately fifty-one thousand dollars a year. Then came the question "Have you moved within the past two years?" She said yes, typed in "Solara Estates," the mailbox number, and the street address of the mailbox-rental store. She put the effective date as today, and clicked that address as the current one.

She had noticed that the application form she had filled out had asked, "Would you like to apply for a second card for another person on this account?" It gave her an idea. She applied for two cards in the name of Charles Woodward, the elderly man whose medical record she had stolen. After filling in his name, social security number, and birthday, she said he was retired. His annual income was eighty-seven thousand dollars. Yes, he did want a second card on his account. It was for one of the names she had made up for herself, Judith Nathan. She said her full name was Judith Woodward Nathan, and that they both lived at Solara Estates.

She checked to see that the copy center was still safe, then used the scanned images of her Illinois, California, and Arizona driver's licenses to make the paper fronts of licenses for Judith Nathan and Laura Murray, and signed off. She used a copier to copy the backs of her licenses, used a laminating machine to join them to the front sides, and a precision paper cutter to trim them to size. They still were not good enough to fool a policeman in their home states, but if she put one of them into the plastic holder in her wallet, it looked real.

When morning came, she bought a *Denver Post* and searched for furnished apartments. The place she found was an old motel that had become less and less desirable to travelers and was living an afterlife offering rooms by the week at cut-rate prices. After a few days of sleeping during daylight in a park, she was not critical of the place's faults. She was delighted to have a shower and a door with a lock on it, and there was even a television set.

She drove to a hardware store and bought four sliding bolts. Late on the first night she installed two of her sliding bolts at the top and bottom of the door, and one bolt on each of the two windows. When she had done that, she slept with Mary Tilson's gun under the spare pillow beside her head.

She slept ten hours a day, exercised, took long showers, gave herself facials, treated her skin with moisturizer, and did her nails. She watched television, thought, and planned. She went out only to buy food and newspapers and check her Solara Estates mailbox.

On the tenth day, she found her first credit card, in the name Laura Murray, in her mailbox, and on the thirteenth, the one for Judith Nathan. By the twenty-first day, she was ready to drive again. Judith Nathan packed her suitcase and began the long drive toward Portland, Oregon.

35

It was five-thirty in the morning. Catherine Hobbes stood at the big window of her dining room, sipped her coffee, and stared down at the city of Portland. Each morning since she had returned from Albuquerque, she had gone to work at five-thirty so she could spend an hour or two before her shift trying to follow cold leads to Tanya. It had been a month since Tanya had made the call to this house from Albuquerque and then disappeared again, and Catherine had begun to let a new possibility enter her mind.

Not all serial killers got caught. Catherine had thought Tanya would turn up in Albuquerque, but there was no guarantee she would ever be recognized again anywhere. At some point people would say, "Maybe she died." Or, "Maybe she's in a prison somewhere for something else." But she wouldn't be, and from time to time, when the urge came on her again, she would kill someone else.

Catherine put her coffee cup in the sink and went to find the lightweight hooded raincoat she kept for unpredicted rains. She slung it over her forearm, checked her watch, and appraised herself in the mirror near the stairs. The gray suit looked good, so she ran an inventory of the gear by touch: the belt with her gold badge clipped to the right of the buckle, the handcuffs at the hip, the pistol on her belt to the right side of her spine under the tailored coat.

She went downstairs and out to the garage, got into her teal blue Acura, and conceded that she was letting her mood weaken her. She had even failed to keep herself from thinking about what day this was. The divorce had happened long enough ago so the day shouldn't matter anymore. It was the twenty-first of August—Kevin's birthday. He would be—what? Thirty-five—today.

Each year had made her feel it less and less, and after eight years, Kevin was no longer real. He existed only as a part of her mind now, an altered point in her brain. What would the doctors call it? A lesion. Everything in medicine was a lesion, from a mild scratch to a fatal tumor.

The part that was hard to believe now was that Kevin had been the other half of the conversation for so long. She had been with him for years and talked without any dissembling, and eventually without filtering or even reserve. When, at any time during those years, she had said something funny or profound, he was the one who had heard it, and probably the only one. For years after the divorce there had been times when she would catch herself in a forgetful impulse to describe something, and then remember that he wasn't there anymore. There were other times when she would be talking to someone else—a friend, a colleague—and realize that the point she was making was something that she had heard Kevin say.

The birthday was not a good memory. It had been on his twenty-seventh birthday that the quiet explosion had occurred. She had taken a half day off from her job at the brokerage. At just before noon she had rushed out, bought a birthday cake, and gone to his office to surprise him. She remembered that when she had grasped the doorknob of the office on the fifth floor, she had sensed that something was different. She had felt odd, almost dizzy, and she had attributed it to the elevator ride, but it didn't feel that way. It had felt as though she were holding on while a subtle tottering of the universe occurred, a tremor.

She opened the outer door of the office and walked into silence. The sales center wasn't the sort of place where customers simply walked in, because the company worked on enormous construction projects. Usually somebody stayed to watch the office during lunch, but the desks were empty. It occurred to her that maybe the whole office had shut down and taken Kevin out to lunch to celebrate. It was a young, social group, and Kevin was a popular manager. She should have called ahead instead of surprising him, she thought, and then she could have gone too. He would have loved that.

The thought gave her an idea. Maybe there was a notation somewhere, a scrawl that would tell her where they had gone. Paula, the receptionist, would be the one likely to have made the reservation, so Catherine looked first at the notepad on her desk, then the Rolodex, to see if the card that was showing was a restaurant. It wasn't.

Catherine went past the empty desks in the outer office, through the bay past deserted cubicles, to the hallway that led to the offices of the sales executives. She knocked on Kevin's door, then opened it.

He wasn't there. She went to his desk to see if there was anything on his calendar. There were a few scribbled lines—

his morning appointments, a meeting at four. She put the cake on his desk, then sat in his chair and typed on his computer, "Happy birthday, Kev. I just stopped by for a minute to tell you I love you. See you later, Catherine." She highlighted it, made the type twenty-eight point and red, and left it on his screen.

She was pleased with that, because it implied that she had just breezed through in a rush, and not that she had blown half a day of work for nothing. He would feel happy instead of disappointed or guilty. She stood up, stepped out of the office, and heard something down the hall. It seemed to be a muffled female voice, as though one of the salespeople had stayed and was on the telephone. There was the voice again. It was definitely a woman's. Maybe she would know where Kevin was.

She followed the sound to a door down the hall. She put her ear to the door. She knew. There was no way to introduce doubt, no way for Catherine to save herself. Catherine had no right to open the door, but she did.

It was Diana Kessler's office, obviously. Diana was bent forward over her desk, her skirt up over her back, and Kevin was behind her. They didn't hear Catherine open the door. She stood there, paralyzed and speechless, for two or three seconds before she took a step back and closed the door again. Catherine remembered the cold, empty feeling in her chest, the tightness in her throat. She had simply stood there, listening to their alarmed voices, the rapid, hurried rustling, and the quick footsteps.

When Kevin flung the door open and saw her, his eyes widened with what looked like fright. He tried to cover, forcing a smile. "Honey! Are you here to surprise me? I'm so glad to—"

"I saw," she interrupted. "I opened the door while you were with her." She turned and began to walk back along the hall toward the outer office.

"Wait. Please. Let me talk to you."

"I don't want to talk."

His voice became jocular, but it was unconvincing. "Come

back. I don't know what you think you saw, but you misinterpreted it. You're wrong."

She stopped walking and turned to glare at him. "Kevin. You don't seem to have heard. I saw. I am not 'wrong.' "

His brows were knitted in worry and unhappiness. He put his hands on her arms, as he had a thousand times, and looked into her eyes. "Diana can tell you. It's a misunderstanding. Let's talk. The three of us."

He seemed to have lost his mind. "I don't want to talk to Diana, and Diana doesn't want to talk to me. Now let me out of here." She shook his hands off her arms, spun, and walked out of the office. That had been the explosion, and it had propelled her away from his presence, his life.

When she thought about it, she usually summarized the story as though she had caught him one day and never seen him again. It wasn't that simple. There had followed months of surreal scenes with him. There were meetings with him to sign off on the property settlement, two meetings that were supposedly by chance when he was clearing out, and others she couldn't quite bring to mind now. But she had been forced to hear his denials, then his excuses, then his anger.

During those months all of their mutual acquaintances seemed to discover the need to unburden themselves of their knowledge about some girl who had slept with him. Two had even admitted to having done it themselves. They felt that they, too, belonged to a larger category of women mistreated by Kevin. It had all ended eight years ago, and every one of those people had vanished from her life.

36

She drove through the city, toward the bureau. Portland was not huge, so if she was up early enough she never had much trouble getting across the river and into the homicide office in fifteen minutes.

She was there before six, and went to work immediately on the next phase of the search. Today she was sending copies of the photographs of Tanya Starling to Department of Motor Vehicles offices in major cities all over the country, warning them that Tanya Starling would probably soon be applying for a new driver's license somewhere.

Catherine was nearly finished with the flyers for the motor vehicles departments when she looked up and saw Captain Farber approaching her desk. "Catherine, I need to assign you to help Tony Cerino this morning." Cerino specialized in missing persons complaints. She could see him standing beyond Mike Farber's shoulder in the entrance to the homicide office, so she didn't protest. Instead she turned to Cerino. "What can I do, Tony?"

He stepped closer. "I've got a three-day missing person. It's pretty straightforward on the surface, but when Ronny Moore did the interviews, he thought there was something hinky about the whole thing. I want to bring a homicide officer with me to the second interview."

She shrugged. "It feels that wrong?"

"Well, the husband says she's only been gone for three

days. The parents say that she usually calls every day, but she hasn't in a week. They filed the report."

She put her circulars into a file folder and stuck it into a desk drawer. "Let's go."

The house was a low bungalow painted green with a roofed porch in front. It seemed identical to most of the others on the street, but this one had a chain-link fence along the sidewalk. Catherine had been a police officer long enough to open the gate cautiously and wait to see what sort of dog responded, but Cerino said, "The dog belonged to the previous owner."

Cerino knocked on the front door, and a man came to open it. He was small but muscular, with sandy hair combed to the side over his balding head and the sort of expression that Catherine classified as habitually dissatisfied. He was wearing blue jeans and a short-sleeved pullover that seemed tight over his biceps. She manufactured a smile. "Are you Mr. Olson?"

"Yes," he said. He was somber, but she noticed that he looked relaxed and well rested.

"My name is Sergeant Hobbes, and this is Sergeant Cerino. We wondered if we could come in and talk to you."

He opened the door and let them in, then went to sit in a worn wing chair in the living room. The gesture made Catherine almost feel reassured about him, because it was so human: he was in a nightmare, and he instinctively went to the chair for comfort. But there was something about his movements that made her uneasy. His limbs seemed to be rigid, mechanically stiff. "Have a seat," he said.

Cerino sat on the couch to the left, and Catherine moved to the chair directly in front of Olson. She kept her back straight and both feet on the floor.

"You found her body, didn't you?" said Olson.

Catherine looked into his eyes and she knew. She had no evidence yet that this call concerned anything more than a woman who had taken three days off from a lousy marriage. The missing woman's parents had told Ronny Moore, the first officer on the case, that she had gotten into arguments with her husband and left him before, so this could easily be just another spat. But Catherine knew it wasn't.

She shifted almost imperceptibly in her chair to keep the back of her coat from impeding her reach for her gun. "No," she said. "We're just conducting a preliminary inquiry. We're hoping that she hasn't come to any harm. Usually if somebody's missing for only two or three days, they come back on their own." She paused. "Do you know if there is any reason to believe she might not have left of her own free will?"

His face assumed an expression of frustration, as though he were trying to make himself understood by people who barely spoke the language. "She left here on her own. She went grocery shopping. She should have been home two hours later at the most, but it's been three days. What I think happened is that there was a guy in the parking lot waiting for somebody like her. She went to put her bags in the trunk or something, not paying attention to what was going on around her, and there he was behind her with a gun."

Catherine kept her face attentive and sympathetic, and recognized that she had just heard the story he was going to be pushing. She knew too that when his wife's body was found, it would have bullet holes. "I certainly hope that's not what happened," she said. "Please excuse this, but we have to ask some personal questions. It's part of the procedure. Has she ever left you like this before?"

"No," he said. "She hasn't left me now. She's missing."

"I mean, has she ever gone away without explaining where she was going, and possibly stayed away overnight?"

"I just answered that. She hasn't ever done that. Three days ago she said she was going to the supermarket, and never came home."

"Which one?"

"The Safeway, on Fremont Street. At least that's where she usually goes."

She turned to Cerino. He answered, "We've checked the lot and all of the parking areas nearby."

She turned back to Olson. "Did you have any kind of disagreement during the day or two before she went shopping?"

"No. We didn't. We always got along just fine."

"You never had arguments?"

"Once in a while. But never anything that mattered much, and nothing that day," he said. "Look, if I had any reason to believe that she had just gotten pissed and run off, I wouldn't call the police and embarrass myself, would I?"

"*Did* you call the police?"

"Well, no. I guess her parents called first, but I would have today."

"But you had thought she would be back in an hour or two. After a day passed, weren't you scared? Afraid for her?"

"Yes. But I always heard the police don't consider anybody missing unless they've been gone for at least three days."

"So you didn't call us. What *did* you do?"

"I called some other people. I drove around to the store to see if her car was there. Things like that."

"Whom did you call?"

"Let's see. Some people she worked with. The neighbors across the street."

"Did you call her parents?"

"Yes. No. I think they called me first."

She handed him a pen and a piece of her notebook paper. "Can you write down for me the names of all of the people you called?"

"Gee."

"And if you can remember their phone numbers, that would help too."

He frowned and began to write, then crossed something out, then wrote some more. "This isn't as easy as it looks. I was in a real panic, and I'm probably forgetting some." He glared at her. "What's this for, anyway?"

She took the paper. There were only three names, one of them crossed out. "If you think of anyone else, you can add the name later."

He shrugged. "Why aren't you out looking for her?"

"There are other people doing that," she said. "They'll be interviewing lots of people, asking questions and comparing notes."

"Oh, I get it. I'm going to be the suspect, right? Whenever somebody gets killed, it's the husband."

"I certainly hope not," she said. "Most of the time when we receive a missing person call, it has a happy ending. People get depressed. They get upset or overwhelmed by something in their lives. They go off by themselves for a while to think. Those are possibilities we always have to look into."

"All right. I understand. I'm just worried about her, that's all."

Cerino took his turn. "Was your wife on any medication? Insulin, lithium, antidepressants, anything she had to have regularly?"

"No."

"No recreational drug use? Alcohol wasn't a big factor?"

"No."

"You said your marriage is in good shape," Cerino said, looking down at his notebook as though he were checking off items on a list. "Does that include all aspects? Neither of you had a sexual relationship outside the marriage that you know of?"

"Absolutely not."

Catherine caught Cerino's eye. "I'd like to look around a bit."

Cerino turned to Olson. "With your permission, we'd like to examine the house to see if there's anything that will point us in a new direction."

Catherine watched Olson. His shirt was tight across his chest, and she saw his breathing stop for a moment, then start again. She nodded to Cerino.

Cerino said, "Do we have your permission?"

"What do you want to search here for? I told you she left to go shopping, and she hasn't come back."

Catherine said, "It's just one of a few dozen steps we have to take in a case like this. It's part of the checklist."

"I can't think of one reason for you to search my house."

"I can think of a lot of reasons. A wife who has been secretly planning to leave her husband might very well leave signs of it somewhere—correspondence from another man, brochures about some destination. A suicidal person might leave a note or a secret journal."

Olson's forehead was moist now, his jaw muscles working. He looked as though the room temperature had suddenly risen twenty degrees. "My wife could be less than a mile from here right now, pleading for her life."

Catherine knew she was hearing small hints of what had really happened, his mind simply throwing out the first thing it stumbled on. The wife really was less than a mile from here. Maybe she had begged him to spare her life. Catherine said, "All you have to do is say yes, and we'll be able to get started. Your quick cooperation might make all the difference."

"It's not logical," he said. "You're not trying to find her."

Catherine looked at Cerino. She had found a weakness, so she increased the pressure. "Sergeant, would you mind calling in our request for a forensic team on the radio? If you go to the captain, I'll bet we can have them here in fifteen minutes."

Cerino wasn't sure he understood what she really wanted. He stared at her as he slowly got to his feet, reluctant to leave her alone with Olson.

Olson said, "I just told you, I don't want you people in here tearing up my house."

Catherine said, "They won't tear up your house. They don't have to."

"What are you talking about?"

"They can eliminate certain things quickly. They can spray luminol on a surface, and it will show if there's ever been any blood on it. The spot glows in black light. It doesn't matter how thoroughly it's been washed. It will still glow."

The more she spoke, the more his face went limp and blank, like the face of a poker player. She knew she had hit another of the vulnerabilities. Whatever had happened, it had been here. There had been blood somewhere in the house. She said, "Go ahead, Sergeant. I guess we'll need a warrant."

Cerino walked out the front door.

Olson's anger was more apparent now that he was alone

with Catherine. "You don't seem to be hearing me. You can't do this."

"Mr. Olson," said Catherine. "I'm sorry you haven't decided to cooperate, but this isn't a violation of your rights. There's the suspicion of a crime, and my partner is requesting a search warrant. As soon as it's granted, we'll be—"

Olson's lunge came so quickly that she was barely able to react. She ducked sideways and down, and his fist caught her forehead instead of her nose and mouth. She dodged off the chair to the floor before his spring brought him into it. He went over her, hitting the chair back and taking it with him to the floor. He pushed himself away from it and stood, then turned and took a step to begin his run toward the back of the house.

Catherine swept out her leg, caught the tip of his right foot, and tripped him just as he was bringing it forward for the second step, and he went down. As he sprawled on the hardwood floor, Catherine heard Cerino fling open the front door.

Catherine flopped across Olson's legs and clung to them while he tried to kick free, and Cerino dashed to straddle Olson's back. The three struggled in silence for a few seconds. Catherine snatched her handcuffs off her belt and handed them to Cerino, who closed one on Olson's left wrist, then dragged the right behind his back to force it into the other cuff.

Catherine recited the Miranda warning, then said, "Do you understand these rights?" She poked his leg hard with her knuckle. "Do you?"

"Yes."

Cerino twisted his body to look at Catherine. "You okay? Looks like you got hit in the head."

"I'll live. Give me your handcuffs."

"Here," said Cerino.

She took them and closed them on Olson's ankles. "That ought to do it. Watch him for a minute, okay?" She got up and took a few steps away from them, and when Olson didn't move or try to struggle, she trotted out to the police car and made the call. "This is One-Zebra-Fifteen. We need a unit to transport a prisoner and we need a forensic team. The address is 59422 Vancouver."

She went back into the house and entered the kitchen. She didn't touch anything at first, simply looked. The kitchen was extremely clean and tidy. Everything seemed to be in its place, freshly washed and put away. She opened the refrigerator without touching the handle. The shelves were packed with closely arranged items—jars that still had the plastic around the tops because they had not been opened, fresh fruits and vegetables. She looked through the transparent side of the meat drawer at the packages on top. There were a steak and lamb chops dated September 19. That was two days ago.

Catherine kept going. She went up the stairs to the bedrooms. There was a guest room that was neat and empty, with a well-made bed, the sheets pulled tight and tucked with hospital corners beneath the bedspread. She moved to the master bedroom. The room had been cleaned. There were two dressers, but only the tall one without the mirror—the male one—had anything on its surface. She looked into the closet. There were clothes for Olson and his wife on hangers, with an empty space between them.

She moved to the bathroom. There were items that had to belong to the missing wife, but they had all been moved to a small space at the far end of the long tile counter.

She was sure that he had wanted to get rid of his wife's things, but doing so would have been evidence that he knew she wasn't coming back. As soon as her body was found, he would have been able to do it. But Catherine had another intuition about Olson. He had been calm and controlled until the final moment when he had been sure he had lost the argument and she was going to order a search of the house. Then he had panicked. The reason he had decided to run was that there was something here that he knew would convict him. It was something big and obvious that a search could not miss. She had an idea of what it might be.

Catherine went downstairs and then into the garage. There were two vehicles in it, and an empty space for the Toyota Camry Myra Olson had supposedly taken to the supermarket. Catherine looked at the floor, and she could see the faint images of stains on the concrete that had been cleaned. They didn't seem to be blood, but she could not be sure. She turned her attention to the two vehicles. One was a Lexus sedan, and the other a big Cadillac Escalade.

She walked toward the Escalade. Catherine had worked homicides for four years, and she knew exactly what she was looking for. In the back of the SUV near the tailgate, there would be a plastic tarp or a rug, and it would be rounded, probably tied. Maybe there would be a shovel. She opened the driver's door so that the light went on, flicked the switch to unlock the rest of the doors, and looked. The back was empty, except for a neatly folded blanket on the floor of the rear cargo area. She slammed the car door.

She heard something. It was a low whining sound. It seemed far away, but it couldn't be. She stood still and listened. Then there was a faint knocking sound.

Catherine followed it. She walked slowly, listening, her heart beating fast. The sound stopped, and she stopped too. She put her hand on the trunk of the Lexus. This time when there was a rap, she felt it from the heel of her hand and up her arm like an electric shock. "I hear you," she shouted. "Hold on." She patted the surface, then turned and ran into the house.

Cerino had lifted John Olson so he could sit on the couch, but his wrists and ankles were still cuffed so he couldn't attack Cerino. Catherine said to Cerino, "Did you find any car keys on him?"

"No," said Cerino. "There weren't any keys. No wallet either."

"Where are your car keys, Mr. Olson?"

"I don't know." His face looked angry, spiteful.

She marveled at it. He was caught, trussed up and about to be exposed, and yet he was taking some last bit of sadistic pleasure out of frustrating her. Catherine remembered the direction he had been running after he had hit her, and extended his trajectory.

She entered the kitchen, checking the counters and opening drawers. As she searched, she took out her cell phone and called the emergency number. "This is Detective Sergeant Catherine Hobbes. I need an ambulance at 59422 Vancouver. We have an injured victim here. Thank you." She kept going to the back door. There were some jackets hanging on pegs beside it. She patted the pockets of a jacket, then felt the hard shape of the wallet and heard the clinking. She reached in and pulled out the key ring.

She dashed out to the garage. First she tried the wrong key, and then found the right one. The springs of the lid made it pop up a few inches, and instantly the smell of fear—urine and sweat—came to Catherine in a wave. She raised the lid the rest of the way.

The woman rose to the light like a drowned body rising from the depths to break a calm surface. She had streaks of dark dried blood that had run from her nose and lips, and from a cut at her hairline. All of them had run in stripes on both sides of her face as she lay there in the dark. The bleeding seemed to have stopped a long time ago, so the blood was cracked like old paint. She was naked, and Catherine could see purple bruises on her arms, ribs, hips. Her wrists had been tied behind her. A separate strand of cord had been tied to keep her elbows back and make it harder for her to move. Catherine helped her sit up, and untied the cords. "Are you Myra?"

The woman nodded and her chin began to tremble.

"I'm Sergeant Hobbes. It's over now, and you're going to be all right."

"Did he kill my parents? He said he had already killed them. He had insurance on all of us."

"No. They're fine. They're the ones who called us."

"He said he had already killed them, and that he was going to kill me today." She began to sob.

"Don't worry, Myra. They're just fine, and you'll see them later. Don't worry. He can't hurt anybody again. You don't have to worry about anything. Let's get you out of there." She helped Myra ease one foot out of the trunk to the floor of the garage, then the other. She opened the Escalade, snatched the blanket, and wrapped it around her.

"You're safe," she said. "It's all over now." She held her in a gentle embrace and rocked her back and forth. In the distance there was a siren.

37

When Catherine got home and picked up her telephone, there was a message tone. She dialed her code and listened. "Catherine, this is Joe Pitt. You said you would go out with me if I came up to Portland. Well, I'm here. Meaning Portland. I'd like to see you tonight, and I'm making reservations for every half hour from eight until ten at different restaurants. Give me a call whenever you come in. I'm at the Westin hotel." He recited the telephone number, but Catherine was not ready to write it down.

She replayed the message, wrote down the telephone number, and then dialed it. When Pitt answered, she said, "Hi. You're pretty sure of yourself, aren't you?"

"No. As far as I can tell, there's nothing in our history together that would give me the least bit of confidence," he said. "I just haven't been able to pin you down on when I could come, so I figured I would come now and wait until you have time to go to dinner with me."

"What a speech. I'd have to be a fool not to go. What should I wear and how much time have I got?"

"Dress up—really fancy. You have five minutes."

"I might be able to make it to your hotel at eight, so keep the eight-thirty reservation."

"See you then."

When she arrived at the hotel, Joe Pitt was standing inside the entrance in a dark suit. Catherine was glad that she had taken him seriously and worn her only recently purchased fancy outfit, a black cocktail dress. She had also put on her white-gold necklace that had been her grandmother's. Pitt walked outside as soon as he saw her, and told the valet, "Take her car, please, and bring mine." He handed him a ticket.

She got out and watched her car disappear down the ramp to the garage, and said, "What—you don't want to be seen in a working woman's unpretentious Acura?"

"No. I just like driving when I'm on a date, so I rented a car."

The valet returned with a Cadillac, and she smirked at Joe Pitt. "You can't impress me with that. I used to pull those things over all the time with a crummy Crown Victoria Interceptor."

"Me too," he said. "But I always wished I had one."

They drove to the restaurant, and the maître d' conducted them to a table. They ordered their dinners, and ate while they talked about Catherine's near miss in catching up to Tanya in Flagstaff, and then her failure to head her off in Albuquerque. Joe Pitt said, "I'm sort of surprised you haven't told me about your day."

She frowned. "You know about that?"

"Yes," he said. "But I'd be delighted to listen to the story again if you'd like to tell it."

"How?" she said. "How do you know already?"

"I called your office at around noon, trying to reach you. I talked to Mike Farber, and he told me about it."

She looked crestfallen. "That's why you came? Because you heard about the Olson thing and felt sorry for me?"

"Sorry for you?" he said. "I came because I thought you'd be in a good mood and let me celebrate with you. You're a hero," said Joe Pitt. "In the next couple of days the wire services will pick up the newspaper stories, and the networks will pick up the television news." He sat back to let the waiter clear their plates.

"I hope they run my picture," said Catherine. "I'll be able

to cash a check at my bank branch without having to show my ID anymore."

"Probably not. But next time the promotions get handed out, there might be something in the goody bag. They need people like you, and they know it."

"Why say 'like you'? I'm me, other people are other people, and we're not alike."

" 'Like you' means cops who actually got to a murder victim before the guy killed her. When the brass see a young, beautiful homicide detective who saves an abused victim—probably by minutes—they want to throw a party. You're the proof that what they're doing makes sense. With that bandage on your forehead that you're bravely trying to hide under your hair, you're a photo op they couldn't buy for anything."

"It's a Band-Aid, and I put it on myself." She smiled. "Want one?"

"No, thanks."

"You certainly do bring a better brand of malarkey than you used to."

"Malarkey? I don't think I've heard that word in about thirty years."

"Ladies don't say 'horseshit.' "

"Oh?"

"At least not to somebody who flies a long way and takes them to a nice restaurant."

"If compliments embarrass you, I'll stop talking about it." He lifted his wineglass. "I'll just drink to your courage and sagacity."

She lifted her glass of water. "And I to your discerning taste."

They sipped, and put down their glasses. Pitt looked at her closely. "You never drink. Did you ever?"

"Sure," she said. "When I was young. Not for a few years, though."

"Are you an alcoholic?"

She was taken aback. "What?"

"A lot of friends of mine who will never touch a drink are alcoholics. A lot of them are cops. I wondered if you were."

She felt defensive and angry for a second, but as she looked at him, she detected nothing but honest sympathy. "I don't know," she said. "Let's just say that alcohol does things to me that I don't particularly want done, so I stopped drinking."

"Good for you," he said. "But bad for me. I'll just have to try to seduce you with my wit and charm alone."

She smiled. "I guess your strategy doesn't include surprise. I did like the flattery, though."

"It was admiration," he said. "And I really meant it."

"Now that I know your intentions, I'll have to be a bit skeptical."

He looked at her with a serious, contemplative expression. "My intentions have been on the surface since the beginning. I'm not here just to confer with an esteemed colleague. I asked you out on a date."

"Asking for a date is kind of ambiguous," she said.

"Maybe to you."

"To everybody. To the world."

"It isn't to me, and only I can say what I meant. When somebody asks you out on a date, you can accept or not, and your acceptance means whatever you want it to mean."

"And what does your asking mean?"

"It means that I've already watched and listened to you and thought about you enough to have made my decision about you. I'm not window-shopping."

She picked up her glass of water and took a deep swallow. Then she put it down and said, "That's what it meant when I accepted."

He looked into her eyes for a few seconds before the smile reappeared on his face. His eyes focused on the waiter and he nodded, and the waiter approached. "Check, please?"

Hours later, Joe Pitt rolled onto his side, leaned on his elbow, and looked down at her on the pillow beside him. "What made you change your mind about me?"

"I haven't changed my mind about you. You're exactly the way I always thought you were."

"You always acted as though you didn't approve of me, but here you are."

"Yep. Here I am. I'm lying naked in a hotel bed with a man on a first date. I guess that means I'm pathetic."

"If you're fishing for compliments, I can give you a few thousand new ones now. I've been holding back."

"Spare me."

"You can't really feel bad about this."

"No, I'm glad we're here. I was just afraid you'd want to talk about it."

"You don't believe in talking about sex?"

"No, I don't. There's nothing anybody can say about it that isn't embarrassing and stupid. Yes, it was as good for me as it was for you. Yes, you're the best ever. As if you didn't know. If I didn't say that, you'd kill yourself, after all those years of practice."

"I just want you to be happy—about tonight, about me, about you. No regrets."

"There is one part I regret. It's that the minute I let you look at the Poole crime scene, all the old boys were thinking, 'Hmmm. She's not bad. I wonder how long it'll take good old Joe to get her in the sack.' And here I am. They were right, and I hate that."

"What old boys?"

"Jim Spengler and the homicide guys in Los Angeles, your buddy Doug Crowley in San Francisco. My own friends up here."

"Do you think it's possible to be too conscious about what other people might or might not be thinking?"

"No."

"Oh. So I take it you don't do this kind of thing often."

"Practically never."

"I hope that will change."

"If you want it to, it will."

"Really?"

"Yes. I make big decisions carefully, and with both eyes open. I wouldn't have done this once if I didn't think I might be interested in something more lasting."

"Would you consider having an exclusive relationship
with me?"

"That's pretty quick," she said.

"I make big decisions with both eyes open too. Will you?"

"Only if you're willing to do it sincerely," said Catherine.
"If it isn't working out, we'll see it right away."

"Then what?"

"Catch and release."

"Sounds humane."

"Practical too. Neither of us has to bury a corpse."

"Deal," he said. "As of some hours ago—I don't have my
watch on—you and I have been seeing each other exclu-
sively, with serious intent." He lay there for a time, staring at
the ceiling. "You've always insisted on being professional, so
we don't really know anything about each other. We'll have
to start talking about personal things from the start. How
many children were you thinking of?"

She pushed him over quickly, rolled onto his chest, and
kissed him. "Oh, boy. I've got to take you to meet my parents
before you come to your senses and get away."

38

It was shocking. Judith Nathan
could hardly believe what she saw in front of her on the television screen. She stood up and stepped closer to the cabinet
where the hotel had secured the television set and squinted to
be sure that it wasn't just someone who looked similar. No, it
was Catherine Hobbes, absolutely. She was getting out of an

unmarked police car with a tall male cop. Now she came around the front of the car and they both pulled another man out of the back seat. He was a shorter man wearing a short-sleeved pullover shirt that looked tight. He seemed to be a bodybuilder.

The picture cut to Hobbes and the other cop, standing outside a police station, and it must have been later. Hobbes was saying, "During our visit Mr. Olson became agitated and tried to run. We searched the house and found Mrs. Olson bound and locked in the trunk of Mr. Olson's car. The hospital says she's in stable condition and will recover from her injuries." She listened to a reporter's virtually inaudible question, then touched a spot on her forehead where there seemed to be a bruise and a scratch. "This? Yes." She smiled. "It was a lucky punch." She turned away from the reporters and went inside.

"Bitch," said Judith Nathan. "You horrible bitch." Catherine Hobbes was becoming a celebrity, practically. She was placing herself in front of the television cameras all the time now. Was anybody supposed to believe that it had been just little Catherine Hobbes fighting with that man? What had that big male cop been doing while that was going on? The man they had in handcuffs didn't even look like a bad person, just some ordinary man the cops had scooped up to use as a fall guy. He would be destroyed to give Catherine Hobbes one more moment of glory. Disgusting.

Everything had turned into a disaster. She had not been given time to start living. Every time she began to get settled, Catherine Hobbes would start in again, telling lies about her, circulating her picture everywhere she tried to live. Every time she went anywhere, Catherine Hobbes seemed to show up a day later. Maybe Judith should have taken Catherine Hobbes more seriously. She had thought that coming back to Portland was a clever idea, because it was the last place anyone would expect to see her. But the price was that she had to live in the same city as Catherine Hobbes.

That night she lay in bed, unable to sleep. Staying free could not be that hard. There seemed to be lots of people who had done things but never got found. It all seemed to depend on who was looking. The main one who was looking for her, the one who kept traveling around and convincing everyone that they had to drop everything and search for small, solitary Tanya Starling, was Catherine Hobbes.

The video clip of Catherine Hobbes on television kept repeating in her memory. It was like one of those dreams she sometimes had that reminded her there was something important that she had forgotten. There was something she was supposed to do that she had not done.

In the morning Judith Nathan left her hotel room, bought a newspaper in the lobby, and went out to begin searching for an apartment. She found one early, and gave Solara Estates in Denver as her last address. Because she had just arrived in town and had no local bank account yet, the landlady didn't mind taking her rent and deposit in cash.

Judith Nathan drove Tyler's Mazda to see a garage that was for rent about a mile from her new apartment building. The entrance was in an alley, and the rent was cheap, so Judith Nathan paid the owner in cash for six months' rent in advance. Judith stopped at a hardware store and bought a good combination padlock for the bolt on the garage door.

Over the next few days Judith Nathan drove to stores where she could buy the things she needed to furnish her apartment—unassembled furniture, a few lamps, and a television set. The apartment had a refrigerator and stove, so she bought groceries.

She was comfortable now, so she filled Tyler's Mazda with gas, drove it to her rented garage, parked it inside, and locked the garage door. As she walked home, she began to make her next set of plans. It was time to find out what Catherine was doing.

39

Hugo Poole sat in his office beside the projection room of the Empire Theater. He was thinking seriously about going out to a club tonight, just for the sake of being seen. Since Dennis had been killed he had virtually shut himself away, and that was not good for business. Just as he stood up, the telephone rang. He picked it up, and said, "Yeah?"

"Hugo Poole?"

"You got me."

"This is Calvin Dunn."

"What's happening?"

"I called to find out what Joe Pitt is doing in Portland."

"Joe Pitt? I don't know."

"You don't?" said Calvin Dunn. "It's a relief to me that you don't know. I would really hate it if you were trying to set up a competition."

"A competition? Why? So I could take bets on who bags her?"

"Sometimes people who are smarter than anybody else think too much. They figure out ways to get themselves twisted around and meet themselves coming back."

"Not me, Calvin. I paid him off and thanked him for his efforts before I ever called you. Where did you see him?"

"He's at the same hotel where I'm staying," said Dunn. "If you didn't send him, then he's just part of the mix. I'll change hotels. This girl has popped about four people now, so it's possible somebody else hired him to find her. I'll let you know when it's done."

Hugo Poole put his telephone down and stared at the office wall. It was clear that he had just managed to duck while Calvin Dunn's resentment had whistled past him. Dunn was said to be very good at what he did, but he was too temperamental. Hugo didn't like having to be tolerant of jealousies and fits of egotism.

The call made him wonder what Pitt was doing. It could be the little policewoman, Catherine Hobbes. She was single and a very nice little handful. The whole thing could be completely harmless—Pitt going up to Portland to spend time with Catherine Hobbes. Hugo reached for his telephone, but held his hand. It was not a good idea to call back. Calvin Dunn had seen her in Flagstaff, and he was smart enough to figure the rest out. If Hugo was right, he gained nothing, and if he was wrong, he would weaken his position with Calvin Dunn.

Calvin Dunn was not somebody he had ever wanted on his payroll. Hugo had resisted the idea for a long time. He had tried waiting for the Portland police to handle things, and then tried hiring Joe Pitt—a reputable detective who had some appreciation of the complexities of Los Angeles life that might have caused a killing way up there in Portland. What more could anybody expect? Hugo had been as patient as he could be, but he'd had a limited period of time.

He had needed to be sure that unfriendlies in L.A. didn't get the idea that Hugo Poole would permit someone to kill a member of his family without paying for it. He had to be sure that the friendlies didn't get the same idea and conclude that they had to make common cause with the unfriendlies. He had to be sure that the people who worked for him weren't put in danger by the rumor that he couldn't protect or avenge them. He had been in this life for so long that he had seen all of the moves in advance. He had given the authorities all the time that he could. Then he had hired Calvin Dunn.

He had also owed it to his aunt Ellen to do something. She was his aunt because she had been briefly married to his father's brother. She had barely known Hugo's mother, who had never even lived with his father, let alone married him. Hugo had been conceived on a late-night pickup in a bar. After Hugo's mother died, Ellen had come to the funeral and then driven him back to the apartment to pack and come with her.

She had put him into a bedroom to share with her son, Dennis, and explained that they were cousins. Then she had treated them exactly the same. Everything she had bought for Dennis, she had bought two of and given one to Hugo. Anytime she'd gone out, she'd carried three pictures in her wallet—her ex-husband, Dennis, and Hugo.

When he was seventeen, Hugo had left Ohio and come to California. He had not talked to Aunt Ellen again for four years, then called her on the telephone and asked her how she was. She had cried so much that he had barely understood anything except that she had been worried about him. He had told her that he was sending her a present, and he had mailed her a check for fifty thousand dollars.

He had kept calling her and sending her checks. Half of every conversation had been about Dennis—some degree he had earned, some job he had gotten, some promotion he'd won. When Dennis had started his own computer business, Aunt Ellen had put up half the money. It had come from Hugo's checks.

A few days after Hugo had heard about the new business, Dennis had called him. "Is this Hugo?"

"Yeah?"

"This is Dennis."

"Hey, Dennis. I hear from your mother that you're doing great, starting your own business and everything. I'm proud of you."

"Thanks, Hugo," said Dennis. "That's really why I called after all this time. I wanted to tell you about it. The place is a computer sales business. I'm good at the technical part of it, but I'm finding that I need help. I wondered if you want a job. You could be vice president, and help me handle the people."

Hugo had been paralyzed for a moment: Aunt Ellen had not told Dennis where the money had come from. Dennis had simply decided that because he'd had some luck he would share it with his cousin Hugo. Hugo had needed to answer "Dennis. I want you to know that I'm honored. It makes me happy that you would do this. But I can't accept."

"Why not?"

"Here are three reasons. I've got a good job here, and I'm happy in L.A., and I don't know a thing about computers. I really appreciate it, though, Dennis."

He remembered hearing his own voice and being shocked. People always said that they regressed when they talked to their parents, became themselves as children. Hugo didn't have any parents. What he did that day when he talked to Dennis was go all the way back to the fork in the road—the day he had left Ohio—and take the other choice. He sounded like the Hugo who would have existed if he had stayed in Ohio.

Hugo might be a failure and an embarrassment to people like his aunt Ellen and his cousin Dennis, but he was considered an enormous success in this part of the world. It was a place where things were for sale. If a man had a name for his wish, or if he could only describe it, somebody could be paid to make it happen. At least Hugo could do this. He could get the one who had killed the poor, ignorant sucker Dennis.

40

As soon as her telephone service was working, Judith bought a laptop computer and printer and signed up for Internet service. She entered the online telephone directory and typed in Catherine Hobbes's telephone number to find her address. When she had it, she began to get restless.

The night was coming again, and Judith was always restless in the early evening. It was the time when other women were putting on their most attractive clothes and makeup. She had always loved dressing to go out at night. Even when she was a little girl on the pageant circuit, she had pretended she was getting ready to go out dancing instead of just out past the flat pieces of scenery and the electrical circuit board and onto the stage. The beginning of an evening out was the best that a person ever looked, the best that she could be—the most beautiful, the most excited, and the most eager.

Judith Nathan could not dress that way tonight. She slipped on the black pants and sneakers, the blue sweater and the jacket Tyler had left her, then put on Tyler's baseball cap and went out to walk. Night in Portland was much cooler and wetter than she liked, but she knew that she could get used to it if Catherine had. She walked toward the Adair Hill neighborhood, overlooking the west side of the river south of the downtown section, because that was where Catherine lived. It was a long walk, but she amused herself by watching the few stragglers driving home from work, while others were coming out of their houses in nice clothes, getting into their cars to go to restaurants and bars.

People didn't really see her as she walked by, her hair under Tyler's baseball cap and her hands in the pockets of the jacket. In the dark she was just a shape that was merely human, and even when the headlights from a turning car swept over her and she became female, she was just another young woman who walked after business hours to keep in shape.

She found the right street at around ten. She stared up the block cautiously, getting a feel for it before she dared go farther. It seemed fitting that Catherine would live up a hill, where she could look down on the city but not be touched by it, or even seen.

Judith studied the neighborhood, but saw nothing that looked threatening. It seemed to be the kind of residential area where people walked, but there was nobody out now to see her. East of the Willamette River and to the northwest of it, Portland was laid out on a north-south, east-west grid. It was only here, below West Burnside Street, that streets angled off a bit, and Catherine's street wound and cut back to get up the hill.

Judith liked it, because the curves in the road kept headlights from settling on her for more than a second or two. Before a car came around a bend she would see the cones of the headlights shining on the trees, and then the pair of lights would appear like eyes opening for only a second, and they would go past.

Catherine probably walked along this street fairly regularly, Judith decided. Maybe she even ran. Judith had not been going for her morning runs since she had needed to leave Los Angeles, and she could feel this climb exercising her calves and thighs.

Because she was on foot, Judith could watch the house numbers closely, and she became aware of each house that she passed. The core of the neighborhood was old houses built in the 1920s and '30s, and the details and proportions were different from the few brand-new houses. The old ones had narrow, arched doorways and steep, pointed gables that held small windows divided into many panes. The trees and shrubbery had been given whole lifetimes to grow and thicken around the walls, so some of the houses looked as though they were from the illustrations of children's books.

As the road climbed, the trees thinned and the yards were less heavily planted and impenetrable. At the top, the land leveled to become a rounded bluff, and there was a whole row of small, nearly uniform houses that seemed to have burrowed into the cliff. Each had two stories, with a garage on the lower level. There was a set of steps on the left side of each house leading up the hill to a back door.

There it was, number 4767. It was white with a bright yellow door. The lights were off except for a couple of automatic outdoor floods that had sensors to switch them on at dusk. Judith stood across the street where the lights did not reach her, studied the house for a long time, and then moved on.

Three nights later, Judith began to wonder what was going on in Catherine Hobbes's life. There seemed to be something going on, because every evening when Judith walked by Catherine's house on Adair Hill the windows were dark. Judith kept taking her walks later and later, and still Catherine was out. Judith began to be afraid that Catherine Hobbes was out of town scouring some other city for signs of Tanya Starling. She didn't want her doing that. Catherine Hobbes had to be home. She had to be in her bed up on the upper floor, in a deep, peaceful sleep.

On the fourth evening, she arrived on Catherine Hobbes's block at one-thirty A.M., just as the garage door below Catherine's living room opened and a small car pulled into the garage. Judith Nathan sidestepped onto the grass strip in front of the nearest house and knelt behind a fragrant, flowering bush to watch. Judith could see the car was a new Acura, teal blue. She wasn't sure how she knew, but she knew Catherine had chosen the model and color so it wouldn't be anything like the unmarked cop cars that Catherine drove at work. She saw Catherine get out of the car in the lighted garage, then walk to the side of the garage and press a switch on the wall. As the door rolled down, Catherine's head, then shoulders, then torso, legs, and feet disappeared.

The lights on Catherine's main floor came on. Judith walked past, looking at the other houses in the row. Judith could see that all of the houses must have been built by one contractor from a single set of blueprints. All of them had balconies facing the river except Catherine's; she had a set of greenhouse windows in place of the balcony.

Judith could see identical bowl-shaped light fixtures in the center of the ceilings of two of the houses, and the rest seemed to have replacement fixtures in the same spot. The garage doors were wide enough for two cars. The straight, plain staircases to the upper floor were all on the left sides of the houses. As Judith walked home, her body seemed weightless, her step was light, and it seemed to her that a day was beginning instead of ending. Things were starting to seem clear to her. That was really all that Judith asked, that she be able to discern what she should do.

In the morning she got the *Tribune* and the *Oregonian* and began to look at the ads for Acuras. The dealers were really the only choice, because she wanted hers to be in exactly the right color, and no private owner who had one seemed to be trying to get rid of it. She needed to have exactly the right one. She decided to let the question simmer in her brain for a time while she concentrated on settling into the new city. Judith kept herself busy most of the time, and she found that it gave her a kind of contentment. She had missed the sense that everything she did contributed in some way to a practical goal, and now she had it again.

Judith decided two days later, as dusk came on, that it was time for her to go out for the evening. She had a special problem, because her photograph had been on television many times, and probably most often in Portland. The color and style of her hair were different now, but she would have to be careful.

In Portland there was seldom a reason not to be dressed for rain, so Judith Nathan could wear a black raincoat with a high collar that she could use to abbreviate the profile of her face, and carry a small umbrella. She tried on the outfit and the coat and studied her appearance in the mirror. Then she put on some flat black shoes and walked to the bar she had selected. It was called Underground, and it was decorated to look like a London tube station.

Judith Nathan walked comfortably in the dark. It was her time. She had Mary Tilson's revolver in her coat pocket and her right hand on the grips. It amused her as she walked to study the men who passed her on the street, imagining each one of them recognizing her from her picture. She would anticipate how each one would go about his offense—rushing toward her, or pointing at her and yelling—and then think through exactly how she would free the gun from her raincoat, aim, and fire. The pistol she was carrying wasn't like Carl's .357 magnum. She would have to fire five or six times to silence a full-grown male. She would place three in his torso to put him down, and then be sure to fire one into his head. She was sure she could do that.

She found the bar, and looked at it warily as she walked up. It was impossible to determine anything subtle from outside, but she could tell that it was crowded, and that the lighting came indirectly from some tiny spotlights behind the bar and some jars with candles in them on the tables. She could see that men wore coats and women wore dresses and business suits.

Judith Nathan slipped in the front door and used the bodies of a group of tall men to shield her from view while she verified her impressions. It was the sort of place where people went after work. Most of them bought their drinks at the bar and stood around talking rather than sitting at tables and waiting for the waitress. The one difficult part was that she had to come in, make her choice, and establish a relationship almost instantly. She glanced at the three men in front of her, and then sidestepped into one of them.

He was about six feet two and had a sculpted body that he showed off by taking off his sport coat just inside the door. His only imperfection was that he had a terrible complexion. His face was rough and pitted by acne scars. She smiled up at him and said, "I'm sorry. I was just trying to slip through to the bar. If I've hurt you, I'll buy you a drink."

He seemed to overcome years of shyness to say, "I've got a longer reach. I'll buy us both one."

She said, "Thanks so much. I'll have a vodka martini." Then she looked around her and said, "I'm right in the doorway. Can you find me if I go to a table?"

"Sure."

That gave her a chance to pick a dark corner of the room and claim it while she waited. She sat down at a table and blew out the candle.

The arrangement she had made held its own dangers for her. She knew nothing about this man, but she had grown up in a world that included date-rape drugs like GHB and Rohypnol, so watching her drink was a reflex. She saw the bartender ice a martini glass, pour vodka and vermouth in the silver shaker, fill the glass. She kept her eye on both of her new man's hands as he held the two drinks level and made his way through the crowd to her.

When he sat down at the small table she had chosen, she gave him another expert smile before she accepted her drink and took a sip. She felt the bright, icy liquid travel down her throat, and then a sudden glow as it reached her stomach. She had always imagined that reaction as small magic, a sudden warmth that exploded under her heart and spread outward to her toes and fingertips.

She looked over the rim of the glass at the crowd around her. This was the first time she had dared come out to a nightspot since she had been in Portland. There was always a chance that somebody in a bar would have seen a picture of her on television and be able to spot her even with her new light hair and different makeup. But this was a very dark bar, she was in the darkest corner, and the rest of the people here were fully engaged in trying to pick one another up. "Thank you very much," she said.

"You're welcome. I'm Greg. And what's your name?"

"Judy," she said. "This is a really good martini."

It was enough to trigger his prepared sequence of small talk. He said, "I haven't seen you here. Have you been here before? Were you brought up in Portland? I was. What do you do? I design software. Where did you go to college? Are you dating anybody?" with such relentless rapidity that it was like a series of combination punches he had practiced so there would never be a moment of awkward silence.

Judith Nathan needed to help him avoid the silences, so she answered each question, some of them as though she were blocking or diverting his blows, but others more carefully. She said, "I'm not working right now. I'm going to be an entrepreneur, but I haven't figured out the best business to be in right now. It's a tricky economy."

"What have you done before?" he asked.

"I've tried a couple of things, but I haven't hit the right one yet. I tried starting a magazine, and I wanted to do a gift-buying service for men but couldn't get funding. If you've got any surefire ideas you'd like to share, I'd be delighted to hear them."

She also answered the one about college. She said, "I went to school in the East, at Boston University. I was only there for about three years, and then I left."

"Why did you do that?"

"Fatal pragmatism."

"What's fatal pragmatism?"

"I was out alone like this. And I met a man."

"I'm sorry. I guess I was being nosy."

"Don't be sorry. There's nothing mysterious. He was older. He had some money. I just compared what I was doing—being snubbed by snotty girls in the dorm and writing term papers—with what he was doing. His life was better, so I decided to do what he was doing."

"What happened? Did you get married?"

"No. We broke up and I moved on."

She had him within the first two minutes. Because he was shy, she was saying enough to make it clear that having a relationship with a man she met like this had a precedent. But in order to build on her progress she had to help him win himself over. He had to feel that when he was with her he could be smart and attractive.

She said, "What is it like to be a software designer?"

"I like it a lot, but it's probably boring to other people."

"That's perfect job security," she said. "If it looked like fun, everybody would be doing it."

"I guess that's true," he said. She could see he was beginning to trust her enough to forget his fear of seeming dull and foolish. He said, "It's actually a lot more exciting than it looks. The code we write is moving to the edge, and changing a lot of things fast."

"You mean things in people's lives?"

"Sometimes. Okay. You've got all these machines already, with incredible capacity. Every two years the next chip doubles the speed of the machine, and the minute you have a new machine you can make a hundred million of them. The competition, the hard part, is that somebody has to think up the killer application and then write code to make a computer do it. It's like—" He paused. "I don't know, because the second I say it, somebody's already doing it. Say you want to control your house with your cell phone."

"Control my house? Why?"

"Just say you do. Set the temperature, lock and unlock doors, turn lights and appliances on and off, take a look to see what the dog is doing, set the alarm. There's not a bit of new technology involved. It's all a lot of simple operations using pieces of equipment we already have. But somebody has to design a new chip for the cell phone and program it both to send intelligible signals to a phone receiver in the house with a chip that would serve as a switcher, and to receive messages to tell it the status of each of the appliances. You can't change the thermostat if you don't know what the temperature is."

"That's what you do?"

"It's a dumb example, but that's the general idea. What we do is a lot more complicated than that. Most of it has to do with defense."

"But that's really exciting. That kind of thinking extends the range of things a person can do. It makes us stronger and smarter. Is that what you meant by being on the edge?"

"What I think of as the edge is the next step—moving into code that's computer generated."

"That's the next step?"

"For me it is. That's what I work on. The idea is that the computer gets designed and programmed to recognize the points in the world around it where there could be an application. It will say, 'You're doing this task this way. Why not do it a different way and save a step?' Or 'Can you combine this task and that task?' See? It's computers suggesting their own applications."

"What a great idea." She had him. He was absolutely hers now, a possession like a pair of shoes or a car.

He said, "Then once you have this machine analyzing your operations for things to do, you give it the capacity to write code. Computers do most operations faster than we can, and they have digital memories that are theoretically unlimited. We could have the computer see and analyze a task, go into its memory or online to find existing programming that can accomplish the task, customize it in a second or two, and do the task."

"That would put you out of business, wouldn't it?" she said.

Greg was delighted, intoxicated with the unfamiliar pleasure of having an attractive woman listen to what he was saying. "It will put us out of one part of the business—the dull part, where you're just writing derivative code, testing, finding bugs, and making patches—and into a hundred others."

"Wow," said Judith Nathan. "I envy you so much. You're working on such exciting things. You must jump out of bed in the morning and run to work."

He said, "I do run to work." He had finished his scotch, but he didn't notice it until he picked the glass up, put it to his mouth, and had the ice clink against his teeth. "I think we need another drink, don't you?"

She looked at her martini judiciously. "I don't usually have more than one of these, but I don't usually have anybody interesting to talk to. Okay."

She watched him bring two more drinks to the table. He drank his while they talked, but Judith Nathan simply brought hers up to wet her lips now and then.

She manufactured a special evening for Greg. What he said was brilliant, because she was impressed by it. When he tried to say something mildly witty, it was hilarious, because she laughed at it. He became physically attractive, because she focused her attention on the parts of himself he was proud of. When she laughed, she touched his biceps or leaned on his shoulder. When he spoke she stared directly into his eyes, never letting him remember that she must have noticed his rough, pitted skin.

She knew that he had, at some point in his teens, begun doing exercise to compensate for the attractions he lacked. He had studied to compensate for the fact that he wasn't clever or charming. He was a man who had learned one thing well—that patient, tireless effort would be his salvation—and he was slowly developing confidence.

When the bar began to lose some of its customers, she said, "Well, Greg, it's getting late. I'm glad I met you. I was beginning to think that there weren't any men left who were smart enough to talk about something that hadn't been on TV." She pushed her chair away from the table.

He said, "It's been a pleasure talking to you. I—uh—wonder, would you give me your number?"

"Sure," she said. "I thought you'd never ask." She took a pen out of her purse, wrote it on her cocktail napkin, and handed it to him. She stood up, and he stood up with her, but she didn't move. "I'm waiting to be sure you can read it. Can you?"

He held it up and scrutinized it in the dim light. "Yes. I can."

"Good. Then if you don't call me I'll know that wasn't it." She quickly turned and walked to the door. Just before she went out, she glanced back at him. He was leaning close to the table, transferring her number to his Palm Pilot. She kept moving, trying to keep from being face-to-face with any of the patrons lingering near the doorway.

The night air had turned cooler now, and after she had walked a few blocks it began to rain. She found that she was in the mood for walking, so she opened her umbrella and kept going. It took her forty-five minutes to get home, and it seemed to rain harder and harder as she went. When she arrived she was wet, so she slipped inside, locked the door, and undressed in the entry. She went into the bathroom and took a long, hot bath. She was winning again. It seemed to have been a long time since she had felt that way.

41

It was still raining in the morning when Greg called Judy Nathan. He spoke as though he had read some article that said women liked to be approached in surprising ways at surprising times, but she tolerated the call anyway. She accepted his offer to take her out to dinner, then said, "Wait a minute. You know, I have an idea. The weatherpeople say it's going to be raining all day and all night, and maybe we don't need to get all dressed up to tromp around in the rain. Why don't we just have dinner at my place? It'll be really simple, I promise. I have this tiny apartment and I don't have the equipment here to cook anything elaborate anyway. Come on. It'll be nice."

He protested feebly, but she seemed not to have heard. She said, "Good. I can't wait. Be here at seven, and don't get dressed up."

"Be where?"

She told him the address and was ready to hang up when he said, "There was one other thing I wanted to talk about."

"What's that?"

"Do you want a job?"

"What?"

"A job. Our company, Prolix Software Design, has an opening. It's not a huge salary, but it's okay, and it would put you in a better position to start your business."

"It would?"

"Well, you can save money, or at least stop living off your capital, and you'll learn more about the city and the business climate and all that."

"Let me think about it later," she said. "Right now I'm busy planning dinner."

She heard a smile in his voice. "Okay. Just keep it in mind."

"Sure. See you at seven."

The clock above Judy Nathan's stove said exactly seven when she heard the door intercom ring. She said, "I assume it's you?" and heard Greg's voice say, "I hope I'm not late." She said, "Think I'd eat without you?" and buzzed him in. She opened the door and waited in the hallway for him to appear.

He came up the stairs carrying a bouquet of flowers that had the distinctive paper wrap of Fleuriste, and a paper shopping bag from a gourmet shop that held two bottles of wine, one red and the other white. She stood on tiptoes to kiss his cheek. "Somebody raised you right."

"Thanks," he said. "I'll call my mom and tell her." He was looking around him anxiously.

She took the flowers and the bottles. "These aren't wet. Did the rain stop?"

"No. I kept them under my raincoat."

He took off his raincoat and she saw that he had followed her orders to the extent of not wearing a coat and tie, but he had on tailored pants, a cashmere sweater, and a pair of shoes that were too good to wear out in the rain. "What beautiful shoes."

"Huh? Oh, thanks. I got them on sale about a year ago."

"You did not," she said. "They're new. Somebody told you that women are impressed by nice shoes. Take them off, and your wet socks. I'll get you something to wear."

He waited while she took his coat to her bedroom and hung it up, then snatched a pair of wool socks from a drawer.

He held them in his hand and looked at them. They were just about his size. "Why do you have these?"

"One time I didn't notice somebody had put some men's socks on the women's rack, and I bought a few pairs in a hurry." She had bought the socks this morning while she was out preparing for the evening.

He put the dry socks on and followed her toward the kitchen area. The open kitchen was separated from the living room only by a high counter with two high stools. She had moved the dining table and chairs out of the kitchen, to the other side of the counter. She arranged the flowers in a vase she had bought this morning, and placed them on the dinner table.

"I have some scotch if you'd like that before dinner," she said. "I noticed that was your drink."

"Thank you," he said.

She poured him a scotch and water that was a good facsimile of the drink he'd ordered last night. Then she brought canapés and caviar to the coffee table, and sat on the couch with him.

He said, "I thought this wasn't going to be fancy."

"I said it was going to be simple. You don't cook caviar. You just open a jar. So how was your day?"

"It went kind of slow," he said. "I spent most of it looking forward to coming here."

She grinned. "Wow. Where are you getting this stuff? Is there some men's magazine that tells you exactly what to say? I thought all they had were pictures of naked girls."

"If there is a magazine like that, I'd like a subscription," he said. "I'm always blurting out the wrong thing because I'm nervous. With you I just feel happy, so I don't get as messed up, I guess."

"Another good thing to say. Maybe I'll start a men's magazine and let you write for it."

"Have you thought about the job I told you about?"

"Not yet. I will, though. What is it?"

"It's support—a lot of filing and typing and answering phones. But in little companies you can make your own way quickly. You tear off as much work as you can do, and pretty soon that's your job, and they hire somebody else to answer your phone."

"How many people in the company?"

"Only thirty. Our section is ten. There are ten in sales, ten in administration. They're all young, and get along okay."

"Would I work for you?"

"No. You'd be in admin."

"I don't know. I'll think about it some more." She stood up. "Time to get dinner going. Just vault over the counter if you want to see me be domestic."

He followed her into the cramped little kitchen, and she said, "I promised you cozy. This is cozy, isn't it?"

"I like it, and I like what you've done with it."

She smiled. She had spent most of the day buying the prints that hung on the walls, the dishes and flatware on the table, the cookware and the food, the sheets on the bed and the bedspread.

The dinner seemed to materialize rather than be prepared. The lobster tails and the filets mignons were broiled and the asparagus seared, the wines poured. Judy had never been interested in cooking, so while she had lived in the apartment high above the lake in Chicago she had developed a few very basic meals that she could make by simply applying heat and butter. She poured the wine liberally, and drank sparingly. When they had eaten the main courses, she produced a plate of tarts and napoleons she had bought at a downtown bakery.

Greg had experienced so few occasions when any woman had even tried to impress him that he could barely contain his delight at each part of the evening. After dinner she walked into the living room carrying cognac in small snifters, but Greg said, "If I have this, I'm not going to be able to drive home."

She said, "Who said I wanted you to go home?" and sat on the couch to kiss him.

Later that night, she lay on her back in bed, listening to his breathing. Now and then a deep breath would end in a little snort, but she didn't mind. She knew that when she wanted to sleep, she would. She decided that she was satisfied with her progress. She had only picked Greg out twenty-four hours ago, and she knew that by now he would do anything she wanted.

The difficult part had never been getting a man interested in her. All men seemed to be doomed to hunt for sexual partners all the time, like restless, lonely ghosts. The problem was in choosing the right man, but she was almost certain she had chosen well in Greg. He appeared to be convinced that he was in the romance of his life, the one that made all of the conventional rules and precautions seem ridiculous.

The next morning, while they were eating the breakfast she had bought yesterday with the knowledge that he was going to be here to share it, he said, "I hope you'll take that job."

"I've decided against it."

"When?"

"Last night. At the same time when I decided you weren't going home."

"Why?"

"I hate complications."

"What complications?"

"If you and I break up, I couldn't stand to work there. If you and I don't break up, other people couldn't stand to work there."

He let it drop. She had to wait a whole week before he brought up the topic she was waiting for. He was taking her home after a dinner in a dark, romantic restaurant when he said, "You never tell me about driving anywhere. Don't you have a car?"

"No."

"Why not?"

"I'd like one," she said. "I know exactly the kind I want and everything. But I can't."

"Why not—money?"

"No," she said. "Can you keep a secret?"

"Of course. Let me tell you all of the secrets I've kept."

"Seriously. Do you promise?"

"All right."

"Well, I have a lot of tickets from when I went to school in

Boston. There was never any place that was legal to park, so I have parking tickets for all three years—about seven thousand dollars' worth. If you couldn't make it to class, you couldn't pass, so it seemed to be the only choice."

"So you're an outlaw parker?"

"Yep. I left Boston, and figured that was the end of it. But I found out that some judge had issued a warrant for my arrest. I tried to register a car in Colorado once, and my name came up on the computer. They wouldn't let me register a car unless I paid the fines. I didn't have that kind of money at the time, and so I didn't do it."

"I've never heard of anything like this," said Greg. "At least not for parking."

"Neither had I until it happened to me. But here I am. I can buy a car. I just can't register it or get insurance for it."

"Not to be too obvious, but have you thought about solving the problem by paying the fine?"

"Of course. At first I didn't take it seriously. It seemed like everyone was doing it. Then I got kind of mad, because it's just a way for the city to make money off all these disenfranchised students from other places. Then I figured I'd better pay it. But by the time I was in Colorado it wasn't seven thousand dollars. Those penalties had been growing for seven or eight years. It was up to about fifteen, and now that there's a warrant, we're talking about lawyers, and going back to court in Boston. They could put me in jail to make an example of me. Anyway, now you know why I don't have a car."

"It's a bad situation," he said. "Let me think about it."

"I'm not asking you to solve it," she said. "It's my problem."

Three days later, while they were on their way to a movie, he said, "Did I get it wrong, or did you tell me you have the money for a car?"

She shrugged. "Yes, I have the money. But big deal."

"I've got an idea. You give me the money, and I'll buy the car. I'll add your car to my insurance, which will also make it cheaper. Second cars cost practically nothing to insure."

"But then my car will be registered in your name. What happens if you get tired of having me around?"

"You'll be driving a car that's registered and insured in my name. What happens if you decide to drive it through the front wall of a nursery school?"

"I guess we have to trust each other."

She forced tears to well in her eyes, put her hand on his knee so he turned to look at her, and then kissed him on the rough skin of his cheek. "I think this is the best thing anybody ever did for me."

"So be nice to me forever. What kind of car do you want?"

"An Acura. Teal blue."

42

Catherine Hobbes stood in the outer lobby of the airport, her hand on Joe Pitt's arm. "I think this is as far as I go."

He said, "You're a cop. You could flash your badge at the security guys and they'd let you go to the gate with me."

"How about if we put you in handcuffs, and I say I'm escorting you to trial in California?"

"I wish you would escort me to California."

"Me too. But I can't leave here now. I've got three cases that are heating up and one that's getting cold, and that's scary. It's the one we're both interested in."

"The only thing about that case I'm interested in is you. My client let me go, remember? Then he replaced me with a professional psychotic."

"I haven't been replaced, and I'm going to do my job before I go anywhere with the likes of you. Stop stalling and go to your gate, or you'll miss your plane."

He held her and she put her arms around his neck and gave him a lingering kiss. "That's not going to make things easier," he said.

"Who said it was supposed to be easy?" she said. "Now move it."

She watched him as he turned and hurried up the escalator, taking three steps at a time until he came up behind a lady who was stopped on a step above him, then turned and waved. A moment later, he was at the top and gone.

Catherine walked out of the terminal and headed across the street toward her car. She had delayed driving in to the police bureau on North Thompson Street by telling the captain she thought she ought to drive Joe Pitt to the airport. It had not aroused his suspicion, but it had not exactly been honest. She had not said that since their collaboration was over she had been dating him.

For the thousandth time she had the same thought, that the words for the dealings between people of the two sexes were always wrong. She wasn't dating him. She had thought about him for a long time and then started sleeping in his hotel room with him and then rushing home every morning to get ready for work, or just spending the evening with him and driving home at one or two A.M. for three or four hours of unconsciousness. They didn't have dates. When one of them was hungry the other would say, "Let's go eat," and she would drive them to a nice restaurant, because Portland was her city. On three rainy nights when the restaurants had been near her house, they had slept there instead of driving back to his hotel.

The words were always wrong. If they kept getting along, then there would be a time when he would be called her boyfriend, even though he was over forty and already much more intimate than any friend, and she would be his girlfriend, even though she was hardly a girl and had already been married and divorced. The only time the words were right was when people changed their behavior to fit the words. When people were married they tried to fill the space made by the word, behaved the way they had sworn they would—all of them except her ex-husband, Kevin, anyway.

Was she going to marry Joe Pitt? When she had met him she had experienced the standard reaction. She had wondered, "Is he the one?" but she had gone to the Internet to learn about him, asked the older male detectives if anybody knew him, listened to what they said, and decided that he almost certainly wasn't husband material. But maybe that was just another case of the words setting up an expectation that wasn't real. Right now he was the one. That was the only word she could think of that described the relationship: the one.

She got into her car and drove through the early-morning traffic to North Thompson Street to get to work. She still went in as early as she could every day to work at finding Tanya Starling while her mind was fresh and she had solitude and silence. Today she was starting late. She could spend only a half hour reviewing the information she had about Tanya Starling and searching bulletins and circulars for anything that might relate to the case before the other homicide detectives began to arrive. This morning her in-box was full, but there were no signs in it that Tanya Starling had been seen anywhere.

Catherine had a theory about what was going on. Tanya would be living in a very quiet way in an apartment in a distant city, working at developing a new identity. She would probably be dyeing her hair again, making herself fake identification, and constructing a reason for being where she was. She would try to wait long enough for all of the law enforcement agencies all over the country to be buried in circulars about other people.

Catherine knew her, and yet the feeling of knowing was like being gagged. The things she knew weren't things that she could prove to anyone or translate into action. Tanya had been born with a reasonably agile mind, and whatever had made her into a killer—or maybe the actual experience of killing—had made her an avid learner. Tanya was learning at a phenomenal rate. Every day that went by while she was free seemed to make her better at staying free. Every time she killed someone she did it differently. The other detectives had all interpreted the range of methods she'd used as proof that someone else had been in charge all along, and Tanya was just the companion. Catherine had known since Los Angeles that it wasn't true—no man had been in Mary Tilson's apartment, and no man had been on the security tapes going into Brian Corey's hotel room. Tanya had no companion. Tanya's methods were new each time because she was learning.

Tanya had learned some things between Portland and Flagstaff that made her much more dangerous. She had learned how to isolate victims, she had learned that there were lots of ways of denying blood to the heart and brain, and then she had learned that she could induce other people to do the killing for her. Now anything could happen.

At ten, a fresh homicide case arrived on Catherine's desk. The previous night there had been a burglary in the house in Arlington Heights where Marjorie and Jack Hammond lived. When Catherine arrived at the house, Marjorie Hammond had been so carefully made up, coifed, and dressed that to Catherine she looked as though she had been sitting for a portrait. The responding officer's report said Marjorie Hammond was forty-two years old, but like some beautiful women, she seemed to be without age.

She had been present when her husband had shot an intruder in the dark house in the night, and they had tried uselessly to stop the bleeding until the ambulance had arrived. The downstairs entrance and hallway were still blocked off with tape, so Mrs. Hammond met Catherine at the kitchen door. Catherine sat in a spotless, cheerful sunroom at the back of the house while Mrs. Hammond brought tea on a Chinese lacquerware tray.

Catherine said, "I know it's hard to talk about what happened here last night, but you understand that we do have to be able to explain all of it."

"I understand."

"Do you mind if I record our conversation? It helps when I make out my report."

"No."

Catherine took the recorder out of her pocket so Mrs. Hammond could see it, turned it on, and said, "This is Detective Sergeant Catherine Hobbes. I am recording my interview with Mrs. Marjorie Hammond at . . . eleven-thirteen A.M. on October fifth." She put the tape recorder back into her coat pocket. "Let's see. You and your husband told the responding officers last night that you had never seen the intruder before. Is that right?"

"Yes."

"By the way, where is your husband right now?"

"Jack?" She looked shocked. "He's at work. I thought it would help him get through the experience if he went back to his routines right away. Men are creatures of routine, aren't they?"

"Are they?"

"Of course. Their work habits rely on it, and even the things they do for pleasure they do exactly the same each time. Once you've watched fifty football games, what can be new in the fifty-first, or the five thousandth? But it seems to give them some kind of reassurance."

"What about you? Are you getting through the experience?"

"I'll be okay."

Looking at her, Catherine sensed that it wasn't going to be that easy. She seemed too put together, too perfect. He should be here. "I guess I can interview him separately," said Catherine. Alarm signals were everywhere, but Catherine wasn't ready to decide exactly what they meant. "Tell me what happened."

"Well, Jack was working late last night. He had been in Seattle at a trade show. He sells power tools, mostly for the construction industry, and they were showing off a new line. I was upstairs in bed, asleep. Jack arrived home around midnight, came upstairs, and started to get ready for bed."

"Did he wake you up?"

"Yes. I heard him trying to undress in the bathroom, so I turned on a light by the bed and called out to him. That was when we realized that there was someone else in the house."

Catherine's eyes went to the doorway across the sunroom to the alarm keypad near the back door. "Was the alarm system turned on?"

"He turned it on when he came in. I should have done it before I went upstairs, but I forgot because Jack usually does it, and so I didn't think of it."

"Does he go away on business often?"

"Not really. There are conferences sometimes, or training sessions he has to go to so he can demonstrate new machines. Once in a while he goes somewhere to make a sale and stays over. It's only a few nights a year."

"What time did you expect him to come home last night?"

"Actually, I didn't know he was coming home. I thought he'd be home tonight. But he got his meetings in early, and he caught a flight yesterday."

"And when he goes away, do you usually forget the alarm?"

"I don't usually forget. I guess I was sleepy last night. That's all."

"Okay. So you said you realized there was someone in the house. How?"

"Jack was the one who noticed. When I called to him that I was awake, he answered, then started down the stairs. He had left his suitcase in the entry because he didn't want to wake me up clunking around with it, but since I was awake, he decided to go down to get it. When he reached the top of the stairs he heard something. He ran back to his dresser, where he keeps the gun. He told me to get ready to call nine-one-one, and went down to search the house."

Catherine was having the experience again of listening to someone lie, but not being quite sure of what the lie was. The secret that all police officers knew but that other people seemed not to was that truth and lies were not mutually exclusive. They were always mixed together in a kind of stew and had to be separated. Every person who told a police officer a story was lying. Sometimes they were only making themselves look braver or more sensible than they really had been in a crisis, and sometimes they were fabricating whole incidents to hide the fact that they had committed a crime. But while they spoke, Catherine always detected the same signs of lying in their faces and bodies. "So he went downstairs alone?"

"Yes."

"Where were you and what were you doing?"

"First I asked him not to do it, but he wouldn't listen. Then I took the phone off its cradle and brought it with me to the top of the stairs."

"Did you turn on the lights?"

"No."

"Why not?"

"We had heard someone making noises down here."

"What kind?"

"Footsteps."

"Walking or running?"

"Walking, at first, I guess. Then, when Jack came down, I think it was more like running. The man was trying to get into a good hiding place before Jack got there."

"What then?"

"When Jack got there he started looking around. The man jumped out of the closet at him, and Jack fired."

"How many times?"

"Once. No, twice. We called the police."

"Who did?"

"I did."

"And you told the responding officers that you didn't know Samuel Daily."

"Oh. That was his name, wasn't it? I remember the police officer looked at his wallet and said it. No, we didn't know him."

Catherine said very carefully, "Before your husband arrived, did the intruder touch you?"

"No," she said.

"Sometimes women don't say anything when something like that happens. I don't know if they're too traumatized to remember it clearly, or they block it out entirely, or if they have some misguided feeling that it must have been their fault. Maybe they're afraid their husbands will have the wrong idea. But nothing like that happened to you?"

"No. I already told you," she said. "I was upstairs asleep. He was downstairs."

"Do you have any idea what he might have been after?"

"I don't know."

Catherine was getting close to it, and she sensed that as Mrs. Hammond got more agitated, she was beginning to forget the tape recorder. "Sam Daily is the part of this that I can't quite get to fit," Catherine said. "He had no criminal record. He had a good job. He was a shift manager at a big supermarket. It's the Mighty Food Mart down on Tillamook." She paused. "Have you ever shopped there?"

"No."

"Are you sure? It might explain a lot."

"What would it explain?" She was confused, wary.

"Well, he doesn't seem to have stolen anything in your house, or even tried to. And he came here on one of the few nights when your husband was away. If he had noticed you in the store, he might have been stalking you. If you pay with a check, they have your name and address. He might have begun to watch you, seen your husband leave with a suitcase or seen that his car was gone, and come for you."

Mrs. Hammond's mind seemed to be working hard to evaluate the suggestion. "You know, I may have been there once or twice. It's not my regular store. But I'll bet you're right. I'm lucky my husband came home when he did." She was grasping for the story, trying to make it her own.

"It's a theory, anyway," said Catherine. "It's possible he wanted to incapacitate your husband or kill him, so he could sexually assault you. Some of them even like to make the husband watch."

"That's terrible," said Mrs. Hammond.

"You're right. We'll just have to wait for the rest of the information to come in and tell us which speculations are right."

"What do you mean?"

Catherine watched her face. "Don't worry. We'll try everything. We'll be looking at your financial records—credit cards, canceled checks, and so on—to pinpoint exactly when you were in that store, and then check the store's payroll to see if he was working those days. We'll be interviewing your neighbors to learn whether they've seen him hanging around. We'll ask his co-workers if he had any pictures of you, if he had any absences at odd times, like a few hours during the day when he might have been spying on you. We'll look at his phone records to see which numbers he might have called to find out your husband's travel schedule."

Marjorie Hammond looked sick. "What—what can possibly be the point? We know he was here, and he's dead. It's over."

Catherine was sure now what the lie was. She had to keep pushing. "Not for the police bureau. It's an open case. The forensics people were already here from twelve-thirty A.M. until around nine this morning, right? I haven't seen their report yet, of course. It will tell us a lot."

Mrs. Hammond said, "I want my lawyer."

"What?"

"Turn off the tape recorder. I won't speak to you anymore without my lawyer."

"Do you have a lawyer?"

"I'll get one."

"Okay. I'll read you your rights, and then I'll turn it off." She recited the warning, then took out the tape recorder, turned it off, and put it back into her pocket. She said, "And, of course, you'll have to come with me to the police bureau and wait for your lawyer so we can have the rest of our conversation." She stood up and took out her handcuffs. "Turn around, please."

Marjorie Hammond was shocked. "I didn't do anything."

"I believe you didn't shoot anyone," said Catherine. "All you were doing was spending time with Sam Daily. Your husband came home early and caught you together."

"No," she said. "It's not true. None of it is true. The whole thing is a lie."

Catherine switched on the tape recorder in her pocket. "You said you wanted your lawyer. You know that when I read you your rights it meant that you don't have to say anything to me at all, right? You'll have an opportunity to say whatever you want after your attorney is present."

"Yes. I know that. But I'm telling you the story you made up isn't true. I didn't do anything. There was nothing going on between me and Sam Daily."

Catherine knew Mrs. Hammond was walking right along the edge, and in a moment she would topple over. "Don't worry. If what you're saying is true, the physical evidence will prove you're right."

"What physical evidence?"

"From the crime scene people. They search for blood, hair, fibers, fingerprints. If they haven't found any DNA from Sam Daily in your room, your clothing or bedding, and they didn't find any of yours on him—hairs, saliva, and so on—or any traces of your makeup, then probably the case will be closed just as you said."

Catherine clicked the handcuffs shut on her wrists, and the voice came again, but it was changed. This time it was a whisper. "Sergeant. Please."

"What?"

"Please don't let them do that."

"Why?"

"I told you the truth. It's the truth."

"Do you mean it's what you want to have been true?"

"It's what happened. My husband didn't come in and catch us. He came home and started to get ready for bed. Sam really did hide in the downstairs coat closet, and when Jack opened the door, Sam did jump out at him. Jack's gun went off. It was an accident. Just a horrible accident."

"Do you mean that Jack didn't intend to pull the trigger?"

"No. I mean yes, I suppose he did. But it was because he thought Sam was a burglar, trying to kill him. It was dark, and how could he know that Sam didn't have a knife or a gun too? He thought he had to shoot—that he was protecting his life, and mine too. Neither of them had ever seen each other before, and neither wanted to hurt anyone. It was just a terrible misunderstanding. An accident."

"So your husband, Jack, really thought he was being attacked, and Sam thought he was about to be murdered and jumped out to defend himself?"

"Yes." Mrs. Hammond sat down on the couch, crying, her body bent over and shaking. "Yes. It was my fault."

Catherine looked down at her. The woman was so wretched that for an instant Catherine's strongest sensation was relief that she was not Marjorie Hammond. She was not this woman bent over and sobbing, crouching on the edge of the couch with her wrists cuffed behind her, unable even to wipe the tears that were streaking her face.

Catherine knew that she was about to do something foolish, and was violating department procedures. But she leaned down and used her key to unlock the handcuffs. She removed them, put them in her purse, and handed Mrs. Hammond a tissue. "Here."

Mrs. Hammond was rocking back and forth, crying steadily and silently. Almost inaudibly, she said, "It's so stupid. It's just so stupid."

"What is?"

"I always loved Jack. I love him so much. There was nothing wrong with us."

"Then why?"

"I don't know. It just happened. I used to see Sam at the store every week, and we said hello. Sometimes we talked for a minute if he was approving a check, or I was asking him where something was. It was nothing. Then one time when I was out in the afternoon, I stopped for coffee at a Starbucks downtown, near Pioneer Square, and he was in there. He came up to me while I was waiting at the counter, and we sat together. We were there for about two hours, and we talked in a way we never did in the store—about our lives, what we thought and felt. He said he always came there on his days off, Tuesday and Thursday, at one, right after lunch, when he'd finished his errands. About a week later, I was near there again, and I went in."

"Was it because he was there?"

"No, it wasn't. I didn't even remember it was Thursday. I happened to see the sign, and I remembered the place as pleasant. Then I got there and saw him, and I realized that the reason I thought it was pleasant was because of him. This time I went and sat with him." She stopped and cried some more. "He was just so nice. He was good, and smart, and he'd had such a sad life. He and I talked about everything, and then the afternoon was gone."

"How long did this go on?"

"For a couple of months. I would think to myself that having coffee with a man wasn't a good idea, so I would miss Tuesday. Then Thursday came and I would ask what the harm was, and it didn't seem like there was any. So I went, and he would look up from his paper and he'd say how pleased he was that I had come. He would notice things about me, and be able to tell how I was feeling. He was interested in everything I had to say. Pretty soon I would think about it ahead of time, look forward to going to meet him."

"Was he married too?"

"No. He had been engaged a few years ago, and then she'd changed her mind, and he hadn't been able to get over it for a long time."

"But he knew you were married from the start, right?"

"Of course. Jack was the center of my life, and so a lot of the time what I talked about was Jack and me. Sometimes I would tell Sam about fights or hurt feelings I had. And then one day I realized that I'd fallen into the habit of telling him things that I had not even told Jack. If there were problems he didn't always have answers, and that was a kind of wisdom, too, to know that if the answers were that easy, I would have found them myself. Or even if there was an answer, he knew that I knew it too, but that I wasn't ready to admit it to myself yet. At those times he would just listen and let me work it out. I tried to do the same for him."

"When did the relationship move out of Starbucks?"

"After a couple of months. That was my fault. I let that happen. I was feeling really good one day, and what was making me feel good was that Sam knew me so well and still liked me so much. When he saw how I was that day, I think the contrast may have been what struck him. He was kind of subdued and maybe depressed. I asked him what was wrong, and he told me. He said his life was empty and he needed more."

"More?"

"A real relationship with a woman. He said he didn't want me to ruin my marriage and break up with Jack. He knew that it was the most important thing in my life. He just wanted to be with me." She sobbed for a minute or more, while Catherine waited patiently. Then she looked up, almost pleading. "You understand? Jack and I were happy, and that was what he wanted, and I wanted it for him too. I just sat there at the table looking at him, and the words 'Why not?' came into my mind. I couldn't think of an answer that was real. The only answer was that I wasn't supposed to. He wanted to so much, and I did too. Sam knew that I would never leave Jack. So when I said, 'Why not?' this time, it was out loud. We went right from there to a hotel across Pioneer Square."

"That was the start. How long did it go on?"

"We still met on Tuesday and Thursday afternoons, at one. Sometimes we would go to his apartment. Sometimes we would drive somewhere, and he would have reserved a room. It's been about six months, from March until now. A couple of times, things just seemed wrong, and I would start to break it off. But then I couldn't."

"When was that?"

"A few times. I remember once, standing by the car outside a hotel in Fairview, and we were saying good-bye for the last time, and it was raining. I was crying because I cared so much about him, and we were both getting wet, and then I could see his face was wet too. It wasn't just the rain. And I took it all back and we kissed and went back inside, even though we knew we could be late getting home and I would have to make up a lie for Jack's sake. I knew I was using up one of my lies, because I knew I wouldn't have many of them. You can't lie to someone about why you're late on Thursday afternoons more than about twice, or they'll know. It would have hurt Jack so much." Saying it seemed to remind her of what was about to happen. She began to cry again.

"I'm sorry," said Catherine.

"Everything is ruined, and there's nothing to make any of it better. Sam is dead. Jack's life is ruined. My life is ruined."

Catherine needed her to get the rest of the story out before she stopped talking. "Was last night the first time Sam stayed over at your house?"

"No. There were a few times before. I couldn't go to his place at night, because Jack might call our house from his hotel. But this time Jack didn't call. He just came home to be with me. When Sam and I heard the car pull into the driveway, I was terrified. I looked out the bedroom window and saw the headlights on the garage door, and then the door started to open. I made Sam grab his clothes and run downstairs to hide, so as soon as Jack came upstairs, Sam could slip out."

"But Jack heard him?"

"Sam must have stumbled in the dark or dropped his shoe or something. I told Jack he was imagining things, but he wouldn't listen. I went to the top of the stairs and yelled at him not to prowl around—not just to persuade him, but to warn Sam too—but nothing worked. He opened the closet and Sam jumped out at him." She stared up at Catherine, her eyes red and swollen, her face a mask of anguish. "It's really the same as I said at first. I told you."

Catherine said, "I'm sorry. I'm really very sorry." She gently took her to the car without taking out the handcuffs again, and drove her to the police bureau to get her statement on paper.

By the time Catherine was finished with the statement and her report and had signed the transcript of the tape recording, it was too late to answer any of the telephone messages that had piled up on her desk. She used her cell phone to call Joe Pitt while she drove toward Adair Hill.

He said, "You're going home late. Solve another murder or something?"

"As a matter of fact, I did. Not a happy story, though." She told him what had happened, then said, "Oops. Joe, I need both hands to drive now. Sleep tight."

"Good night. Love you."

Catherine had started closing her cell phone before she

heard it, and now she cursed herself for ending the call. Had he really said that? If he had, what could it possibly have meant? It had sounded automatic, like a formula. She thought about it as she drove up the curving road. She decided to ignore it. If he really had intended to tell her he loved her, then he would do it again.

She stopped in front of her parents' house and went inside. "Mom?" she called.

Her mother appeared from the kitchen. "Hi, honey. Just coming home from work?"

"Yeah," she said. "I hadn't seen you guys in a couple of days, so I thought I'd come and brighten your empty lives."

"You mean you don't feel like making your own dinner?"

"That's right. Where's Dad?"

"He's upstairs. He'll probably be down in a minute. Want some leftover turkey?"

"Sure. Let me get my own." She walked into the kitchen and got herself a plate, then took the Tupperware container with the neatly sliced turkey breast in it, added some broccoli, and put it into the microwave.

Her mother watched her. "How is your new boyfriend working out?"

She turned her head in mock surprise. "How's your crystal ball?"

"It's not that hard. I called your house the last five evenings and you've been out late. So how much are you going to tell me?"

"I'll spill my guts. His name is Joe Pitt, and he was just here for a few days. I have absolutely no business going out with him. He's too old and too rich and has a bad boy reputation that I think he probably earned. Naturally I'm getting more interested by the day. I'll let you know when I need to come over and cry about how it ended."

"Well, that's nice," said her mother. "I'll set aside some time."

There was the sound of her father's heavy footsteps on the stairway, and then her father appeared. "Ah, the princess has returned."

"Hi, Dad."

He sat down in the chair beside hers, smiling. "Working late, eh?"

"Yeah," she said.

"Anything interesting?"

"Nothing you haven't seen a hundred times. Husband comes home early from a business trip. He trusts his wife, so he thinks the guy hiding in the closet is a burglar."

"Bang bang," said her father. "It's a rotten job. I told you that from the time you were a child."

"Practically from birth," she agreed. "This is good," she said to her mother. "It must have been nice to be one of the invited guests for its first appearance."

"Then answer your damned phone," said her father. "We tried."

"Sorry," she said. "I was busy trying to have a life."

"Anybody we know?"

"No. He was a cop for a while, then an investigator for the Los Angeles D.A. He's retired from that and working as a P.I. now."

"Sounds too old for you."

"He is."

"Of course, you're getting older by the day."

"Thanks for noticing. I guess the bloom is off the rose."

"The second bloom is more luxuriant than the first," he said. "You seem kind of down. It was that case, wasn't it?"

"You know how it is. Half the people you see are dead. The other half you're seeing on the very worst day of their whole lives. It makes you tired."

Her father stood up, kissed her on the forehead, and went out into the living room. In a moment, she heard the television.

She finished her dinner and rinsed the plate and silverware, then put them in the dishwasher with the ones from her parents' dinner. She talked to her mother for a time about the things that had been going on in her parents' lives. Then she and her mother both drifted into the living room and watched the meaningless activity on the screen with her father.

Suddenly she caught herself falling asleep. She stood up,

kissed them both, and drove the rest of the way up the hill to her house. As she pulled into the garage, she thought she saw something move, just beyond the reach of the lights on the eaves of her house. But she knew that sometimes that happened when a person had not had enough sleep for a few days—the mind supplied the monster that it feared.

43

Judith Nathan filled the small backpack with the quart cans she had bought, and then lifted it. She had not expected it to be this heavy, or this hard and lumpy. She took everything out, wrapped the cans in a towel, put them in the backpack, and slipped another folded towel into the space between the cans and her back. She put the straps on her shoulders to repeat the test, and the pack felt more comfortable.

Judith dressed in her black pants and her running shoes, put on her black sweater and her raincoat. She inspected herself in the mirror, then looked at her watch. It was just after two A.M.

She opened the cylinder of Mary Tilson's revolver and made sure all the chambers were loaded. She put it into the deep right-hand pocket of the raincoat and examined herself in the mirror once more to be sure it didn't show. She took six extra bullets from the box and put them into her left pocket. Then she went outside and locked her door.

She had always been able to make herself feel better by going out into the night. When she was about six she had sometimes waited until her mother and the current boyfriend were back from their evening at the bars and had fallen asleep. Then she would slip on some clothes, quietly open the front door, and go out. The first time, she started by just stepping out on the front porch, looking and listening.

The night was not black, as it had always seemed from inside the lighted house. It was made of gray-blues, deep greens, and the white moonlight. She could see the familiar trees, sidewalks, and houses, but all of them were now silent, and everything was motionless. The people had not just gone. In the deep night they did not exist. The world was quiet.

At first she crouched on the porch with her back against the front of the house, far from the railing and near enough to the door so she had a fair chance of getting to safety ahead of whatever might leap out of the shadows to eat her. She stayed there for a long time that night and on several others before she was sure that no such thing would happen, and then stepped forward to the railing.

After that she moved to the porch steps, and it made an enormous difference. The porch roof had kept her in the shadows and hidden her, but it had also hidden the stars and the sky from her, and blocked her from the gentle current of slowly moving air. What she could hear once she was away from the house was a silence that had a range, that came to her from a great distance, from everywhere the dark could reach.

By the end of summer she had moved away from the house to the sidewalk, and on into the world. By the time she was eight she was in the habit of sneaking out every night and walking the streets. First she walked the streets of her neighborhood and looked at the houses she had always seen in daylight. Then she got into the habit of walking to school. The night walk became a tour of all of the places where she had been during the day. It was a chance to revisit scenes where things had happened. At night, the places were only hers.

She would look down at a spot on the concrete steps of the school and remember it was where Marlene Mastich had stood and said Charlene's hair was dirty. She had stood right there to say it to the other girls, not an inch to either side. But now this spot, this step, this whole school, belonged to Charlene, and all other people were only memories, disturbances left in her brain from an ugly day. People weren't even real now, only the ground where they had stood. There was only Charlene in the night world. The trees were real, the dark stores with iron grates across their windows were real, and Charlene was real. That was all.

Charlene was Judith Nathan tonight, and it was time to move. She stepped around the building to the row of carports along the back. She wasn't worried that she would wake up any of the other tenants. Each carport had a cage at the rear of it where people stored things, and behind that was the laundry room. The first room where anybody slept was one floor up, and it was Judith Nathan's.

She drove her Acura far across town to the foot of Catherine Hobbes's street. Then she parked it a block away in a line of cars that seemed to belong to people asleep in a row of big old apartment buildings. She put on her backpack, walked to the foot of Catherine Hobbes's street, and began to climb.

The houses along the way were all dark and silent. After a minute of walking she began to feel again the peculiar sensation that had comforted her as a child, that the world was empty except for her. In the flat places downtown there were always people out and driving around, businesses with lights on. But up here on the winding, tree-shadowed street where people were all asleep, she was alone.

Judith had walked these same steps a number of times since she had arrived in Portland, but now the feeling was different. She was taking possession of the place. The neighborhood had moved into the few hours of late night when all of the people had fallen into unconsciousness.

She walked along comfortably even though her small pack was heavy. She was used to exercising and jogging long distances. The weight of the pack made her breathing seem louder to her own ears, but she took the extra weight in her thighs and calves instead of her back, so it wasn't a strain.

Judith reached the row of houses along the crest of the hill and sat down on the curb across the street to study them. She yawned to be sure her ears were clear and she was hearing every sound. It was two forty-five A.M., and the silence was still unbroken. When she felt ready, she stood and noticed that up here along the ridge there was a slight breeze. Good. That would help.

Judith walked across the street slowly, careful not to disturb the perfect quiet. She climbed the steps beside Catherine's house and walked around to the back door. She looked in the window at the kitchen. It was pretty. The color of the walls seemed to be a pale yellow, but it was difficult to tell the exact shade in the darkness. She could see that here, as in most houses, there were no smoke detectors in the kitchen, where cooking would continually set them off. Judith took off her pack, pulled out a can, opened the spout, and poured charcoal starter on the door and the wooden footing below it.

Judith poured the rest of the can of charcoal starter on the clapboards of the house, letting extra pools of it soak into the sills of all the windows. She put the empty can back in the backpack, opened another, and kept going along the side of the house, searching for the things she had noticed in previous visits. When she reached the narrow door set into the wall outside the house, she slowly and cautiously opened it to verify that it covered a gas water heater. She took the adjustable wrench out of her backpack, unhooked the gas line from the heater, and closed the door. Then she poured some charcoal starter on the door and the walls beside and below it.

She tried to keep a steady stream of charcoal starter going as she walked beside the house, soaking the lowest few rows of clapboards. Whenever a can was empty she put it back into the pack and opened another. She took her time, trying to be thorough. There was a front entrance at street level that she knew opened into a narrow hallway with a side entrance to the garage. From there an interior staircase climbed to the living areas on the upper floor. She had glimpsed it the night when she had watched Catherine pull her car into the garage and open the door to go upstairs. Judith poured a whole can of charcoal starter on and around the front entrance and another on the garage door.

Judith still had a couple of cans left, so she used them on the wooden clapboards along the side of the house as she made her way again along the steps up the hill to the back door. Then Judith put on her pack. It felt incredibly light now. She took out her matches, and listened once more to the world. She could hear nothing, not even a distant swish of traffic from the city below.

Judith wanted to do this in a particular way. She wanted the fires in the back of the house to burn unnoticed for a time. She would light them first, beginning with the one that would block the back door and eat its way into the kitchen, where there were no smoke detectors. After a time the fire would spread to the petroleum-soaked wood on the sides and front of the house, blocking the other exits. They were the lowest parts of the house and they faced the river, where the wind was coming from tonight. Once the back of the house was engulfed, the fire in front would run right up the stairs to meet it.

She struck a match, listening to the scrape and then the hiss as the match head flared. She dropped it into the pool of charcoal lighter that had dripped to the foot of the back door. The fluid lit and the flames began to flicker up the surface of the wooden door. She moved a few paces and lit the next match, which she held against the lowest clapboard where it met the concrete footing below.

The saturated boards began to flare up, and the flames moved along the back of the house more quickly than she was walking: Judith had overdone it. The flames were running along ahead of her now. She stopped, turned, and hurried along the back of the house the way she had come. She had no time to go the long way, because the little house was already ablaze. The flames were blistering and peeling the layers of old paint to get to the dry wood beneath, then blackening it and beginning to devour it.

Judith trotted down the steps beside the house toward the street. She could feel the breeze making the short hairs along her hairline move, and she knew she had to escape. The fire was moving too quickly. Judith reached the bottom of the steps. She had to block the front exits, or it would all go wrong, so she struck another match and dropped it in front of the garage door. She watched flames unfurl from it, rolling up the surface of the garage door.

Judith whirled and started down the street. The flames were bright and yellow now, and her shadow stretched ahead of her on the empty asphalt of the street. She began to trot. She needed to get away from the neighborhood before the fire trucks and police cars came up that road. She had trotted only a few paces before she realized that the faster she went the better she felt, so she broke into a run, pumping her arms and pushing off with the balls of her feet.

The sidewalk was too treacherous, a series of tilted blocks and cracks to catch her feet, so she moved to the middle of the street. She sprinted, dashing for the first curve that would get her out of the light of the fire. She made it around the first corner and the light was dimmer. She ran hard for a few seconds, but then the light seemed to get brighter again.

Judith turned to look behind her. It was a set of headlights brightening the trunks of trees. She could hear the car coming fast. The car stopped a few feet from her and the driver was out, crouching behind his open door. He had a gun in his hand. "Hold it."

She said, "What? What do you want?"

The man said, "You. I've been waiting for you, honey. I've been watching, and waiting, and here you are."

"Who are you?"

"My name is Calvin Dunn," he said. "Put the knapsack down and step away from it."

Calvin Dunn. That was the name in the newspapers, the man who had killed Tyler. She knew that she had no choice except to do what he said. She set the backpack down on the street and took a few steps away from it, stepping to the side to get the light of the burning house behind her, trying to see Calvin Dunn's eyes.

They were focused on her. He said, "All right. Stop there." She could see the fire's reflection in his eyes, the glow flick-

ering on the retina. Calvin Dunn took two steps from the car.
His eyes moved to the backpack.

Judith's right hand slipped into the pocket of her raincoat
and grasped the pistol. She sensed from a slight change in
his posture that Calvin Dunn's brain had registered his mistake. She saw the eyes flick back to her and his body begin to
tense, trying to raise his gun.

She fired through her pocket. The round hit his chest, but
he didn't go down, so she leapt to the side. He fired at her,
but she reached the barrier of a parked car. She heard Dunn
running too, so she popped up and fired. This time when she
hit him, he slowed as though the loss of blood was weaken-
ing him, so she fired twice more. He toppled to the pavement, and she stepped closer to fire into the back of his head.

The return of the silence seemed to waken her, and she
began to run again. She took a half dozen steps down the
center of the street, her gun still in her hand, before she remembered the backpack. She couldn't leave it lying on the
pavement beside Dunn's body. She turned and ran back,
snatched up her pack, and dashed down the street carrying it.
She saw the end of the street bathed in light from the streetlamps, and she pushed the gun back into her pocket and ran
toward the light. When she reached the bottom of the hill she
tried to slow down, but her legs refused to obey her. She ran
until she was around the corner and at her car. She fumbled
with the keys for a second or two, but got it started and
drove.

Catherine was in the midst of a dream she'd had many times.
In it she had bought a huge, rambling house full of long turning hallways, attics, and secret rooms. She knew there was
something in it that she had forgotten to take care of, something that was getting worse every second. She heard a shot,
then another. Her brain worked to fit the sounds into the
dream. Then there were three in a row, and she wasn't in that
dream house anymore. She was in her bed. For a moment she
felt the relief that awakening brought, the reassurance that
the impressions had not been real. But something was still
wrong.

She opened her eyes, and she could see there was light beyond the blinds in her room. She glanced at the clock, but it was only three-ten. Catherine sat up. The light in the cracks between the blinds was flickering and moving as though— She was up on her feet, and the air was thick and hot. She went down to the floor and began to crawl. As she did, the smoke detector overhead began to shriek at her, and she had to fight panic.

The lights were flickering beyond all of the windows. She had to get to the front of the house, where there were more exits. She crawled to the closet and pulled an armload of clothes off the hangers. There were a pair of pants—the silky black ones that were from her best suit—and a navy peacoat that she sometimes wore in cold weather. She put them on and crawled to the bedroom door. She reached up cautiously and touched the doorknob. It felt warm, as though it was beginning to heat up, but she could still grasp it. She turned it gingerly and opened the door.

She could see the sky through the greenhouse windows across the room at the front of the house, but there were flames moving along the walls on both sides of the room. The only windows still free of flames were the greenhouse windows, and they didn't open. Catherine rose to a crouch and rushed to the dining room table. She lifted one of the chairs and swung it hard into the greenhouse window. There was a crash and a spray of glass, and she pushed the chair rest of the way out.

She wrapped the tablecloth around her right hand and forearm, used it to clear the glass shards from the bottom of the window, draped it over the sill to protect her while she put her feet out, then slid her body out after them and held herself there. She extended her arms, looked down, then dropped.

44

Judith Nathan's alarm clock gave an insistent buzz. She reached across the pillow to turn it off, and sat up in bed. She had been asleep for barely two hours, but she had wanted to be awake at six. She walked out into her living room, turned on the television set, sat in front of it, and waited.

The local morning news began with a lot of oppressively energetic music, quick cuts of cars on highways, shots of office buildings downtown, and idealized stills of the couple who read the news.

The man said, "Good morning. Our top story this hour is an arson fire in the Adair Hill district that's linked to a murder." Judith stood up, the excitement building. Had she caught Catherine Hobbes in the fire? "Our Dave Turner was live on the scene with police lieutenant Joyce Billings this morning."

The image changed to a shot of a woman in her fifties wearing an uncomfortable-looking blue police uniform who frowned at a hand that thrust a microphone into her face. She said, "The fire at the house is now out. The firefighters say that the house will be a total loss, but they were able to contain the fire and limit it to the one building. Fire department investigators have already declared it an arson fire. There is conclusive evidence that accelerants were used."

The voice of the man holding the microphone said, "Is it true that this was a police officer's house?"

"Yes, it was. This happens to be an officer who has been involved in a number of high-profile cases during the past few months. We don't know whether this has to do with one of those cases or not."

"What can you tell us about the shooting?"

"At approximately three A.M. there were calls to report both the fire and, about a block from here, gunshots. The fire trucks arrived first, to find the street blocked by what appeared at first to be a disabled car. Firefighters got down to push the car out of the street and found a Caucasian male about forty years old lying nearby. A gun was found beside him. We believe that he was killed during a shoot-out with an unknown assailant. We won't release his name until after his family has been notified."

"Was he a suspect?"

"No," said the lieutenant. "He was not a suspect in the investigation." She turned away, and the camera panned quickly from the microphone up the arm to the face of the young male reporter who had been asking the questions. Behind him Judith could see Calvin Dunn's car, which was now pushed to the curb. There were cops milling around measuring things with long tape measures and talking. Among them was a shorter, possibly female figure in black clothes.

"This is Dave Turner, live for KALP News . . ." Judith kept her eyes on the figure in black. It was definitely a woman, but maybe only a curious neighbor. ". . . coming to you from the scene of a very mysterious fire." He gave his serious look, and the woman behind him turned to say something to someone. It was Catherine Hobbes.

"Shit!" said Judith Nathan. "How did you get out of there, you bitch?" Catherine Hobbes disappeared and the scene changed to the studio, where the news couple sat behind their desk. It didn't matter. Judith knew how Catherine Hobbes had survived. She had been afraid of it since the moment it had happened. It had been the shots. It had been that stupid Calvin Dunn.

He must have been sitting in his car somewhere above Catherine's house, waiting. She had walked past the house on several evenings before, but he had not been there. He must have known that Judith would come for Catherine late at night, when she was in her deepest sleep. Of course Judith would do it then. Catherine Hobbes was an armed cop, and she spent all of her days surrounded by other armed cops.

He probably had not seen Judith arrive. She had not seen his car, so probably it had been parked beyond the curve, where Catherine wouldn't see it either. But he had seen the fire. He had driven down the hill and seen Judith come away from the house in a hurry, and he had seen her running. The only thing all night that he had not seen in time was where Judith had carried her gun. He had thought she had it in her backpack.

Judith switched channels, going to each of the local stations to hear their versions of the same story. Some of them showed the same police spokeswoman from slightly different angles, and some had video clips of the burning house and the firemen.

At least Judith had shown Catherine what it felt like to be hunted. She had wanted her to know what it was like to be alone and afraid, to have to run for her life. She supposed that she had accomplished that much. It was a good start.

45

Catherine Hobbes hurried into the department store with the envelope full of cash. All of her identification, her checkbook, and her credit cards had been incinerated with her purse when the house had burned. The money she had now was from the bureau's cash fund for emergencies. It had taken the captain's written approval to get the loan.

She was still wearing her black silk pants and peacoat. Abby Stern, one of the other female detectives, always kept a spare blouse in the office, and she had let Catherine borrow it.

Catherine could have gone to her parents, both for the money and the temporary clothes. But she had been busy with the firefighters and the police investigators, and had barely had time to call her parents at seven to tell them about the fire before they saw it on television. She supposed it had been more a question of efficiency than actual time. She knew that her mother would insist on having her stay with them, and she knew that she didn't want to. There would be an argument, and her father would eventually reassert his ancient authority to make her stop arguing with her mother. That was something that could happen only if she did exactly as her mother said. The only way to avoid it was to rent an apartment somewhere before she allowed the discussion to begin.

She held a patrolman's radio in her hand as she shopped, because her cell phone had burned with everything else, and she needed to stay in touch with the bureau while the hunt for Tanya was on.

Catherine picked out some underwear and three outfits that she could wear to work. The requirements were that there be a coat that was slightly oversized so it would hide the gun she sometimes wore under it, and that the pants would allow her to run or fight if she had to. Beyond that, the outfit had to be fashionable enough so that she would not stand out in a crowd. The last purchase was the two pairs of shoes. They took longer than the suits, but she was finished quickly.

As she hurried toward the door of the department store, she decided the shopping trip hadn't been bad. When she had bought her first uniform in the academy, it had come as a shock to her that the uniforms were still all cut for men, and that the regulation shoes came only in men's sizes. When she had put on her first bulletproof vest she had learned that they weren't for women either, and wearing one loose was not a good idea.

She supposed she was still feeling a bit traumatized. Last night she had been absolutely terrified, and being afraid was never a good experience for her. It weakened her and reminded her that she wasn't what she wanted to be. Being burned out of her house was also a great deal of work, and it all came at a time when she needed to be doing her job. Tanya had been in Portland last night, trying to kill her. This was Catherine's chance to get her.

As she reached her unmarked car, she realized that the loss of her house had been a good mental exercise for her. She had suddenly been deprived of all the papers that the average person collected over a lifetime, and it had reminded her of how important they were. She had been unable to get money from her own bank account, unable to buy anything to wear, unable to rent a room to sleep in. Technically, she had driven over to the mall illegally, because she was not carrying a driver's license.

Tanya Starling had been traveling the country for months under a half dozen different names. She had been buying and selling cars, opening and closing bank accounts, signing leases, and she had done all of it without raising much suspicion. Catherine had known since she had become a police officer that the average person didn't really take a close look at anyone else's identification. They just glanced at the photograph, at most read the name, and accepted it, as long as nothing else made them suspicious. Tanya seemed to be getting better and better at making people trust her. She seemed to be immune to the nervousness that made people sense that something was wrong.

She was learning quickly, and that was frightening. Learning was one of the things some of the worst serial killers did. They got more efficient and expert at committing their crimes—did the things that mattered, and stopped doing the things that were useless and could get them caught—and the chances of catching them declined. As that happened, they seemed to lose restraint.

Their cruelty to victims wasn't personal; it was detached,

almost scientific. They studied their victims' reactions and their own, and as their studies progressed, the cruelty became more pronounced. A few months ago, Tanya had pulled a trigger and shot Dennis Poole in the back of the head. She had given him the easiest way to die—no fear, no time for the pain to reach the consciousness before the brain was obliterated. Last night she had tried to burn Catherine to death.

When Catherine arrived at the office, she saw that the first of the phone messages on her desk was from Joe Pitt, but she didn't have time to call him now. She had to work on Tanya's photographs. The one thing she had done that had shown any effect was to circulate Tanya's picture. Tanya had been recognized at least once in Flagstaff, and in Los Angeles before that. She needed to get the pictures out, and to be sure that the television stations that were running tapes of her house burning on the noon news would also show Tanya's photograph.

Catherine went to work preparing another set of circulars with the pictures of Tanya and the pictures of Rachel Sturbridge. This time, to the list of suspected crimes, she added arson and the shooting of Calvin Dunn. As she studied her computer screen, trying to make the pictures as large as possible, she became aware that someone was behind her. She turned, and saw the captain. "Hi, Captain."

"Hobbes. My office."

She saved the image and followed him to the big office at the end of the hall, then sat on the couch across from his desk where his visitors sat. He said, "I see you got some clothes with the emergency fund. Is there anything else you need?"

"I've ordered duplicates of all my papers. I've requested a new weapon and a new ID and badge. Nothing will come for a day or two."

He picked up the phone, looked at a list of numbers taped to the desk beside it, and dialed an extension. "This is Captain Farber in homicide. I have an officer here who had her house burn down last night in an attempt on her life. Right. Catherine Hobbes. I need to have her working cases, so I would like a new sidearm, badge, and identification card for her as of ten minutes ago. Can you possibly speed that up for me? Thanks. It's much appreciated." He hung up. "They'll bring it all to you in an hour. Who torched your house?"

"Tanya Starling."

"Not the guy who stuffed his wife in the trunk of his car?"

"John Olson? No. He's been denied bail, and he's a solitary nut with no chance of getting any money to pay anyone else to kill me. This was Tanya Starling. She is—or was—in Portland."

"Based on what?"

"I gave my business card to her landlady in San Francisco, and she gave my numbers to Tanya. She's used both my cell number and my home number to call me. I guess she converted the home number to an address. It's not hard. Anyone can do it on the Internet. Then there's the arson. The fire department investigators tell me it amounted to soaking the outside of my house with barbecue fire starter and lighting it up with a book of paper matches. She hasn't done any fires before. If it had been a professional there would be a timing device so he could have been a hundred miles away when the fire started, or it would have been set up to look like an accident."

"Do I need to say that's inconclusive?"

"There will be more. I think Calvin Dunn is the best evidence for the moment."

"What about him?"

"I was in the interrogation after he killed Tyler Gilman. Dunn said that he had been watching my hotel that night because he thought Tanya would show up to kill me. When somebody started firing at my car with a rifle, Dunn went after the shooter."

"So?"

"He went after the shooter because he assumed it was Tanya. He was hired to get her, and not to save me, so he didn't try. He didn't do anything to help me get to cover, and he didn't return fire to keep the sniper's head down. He didn't call the police. He wanted the rifle shots to continue as long as possible, so he could spot where the sniper was and get to her. Last night, I'm pretty sure he did the same thing. He saw that my house was on fire, so he drove off trying to find her."

"If that's true, then he should have succeeded. Have any idea how she killed him?"

"I might. It's possible that he saw the fire, then saw a woman running from it. He couldn't be sure it wasn't me. Maybe he hesitated to be sure he wasn't shooting the wrong woman, and she got him first. Or maybe he saw who she was but didn't know she had brought a gun on a trip to set a fire."

"I'm not sure I'm buying this."

"The point is, if anybody but Tanya—anybody at all—had burned me to death in my sleep, he would not have gone after them."

"Are you sure about that?"

"Yes. He and I already lived through this once in Flagstaff. You notice that last night he didn't do anything else—didn't try to save me, didn't call the fire department, didn't wake the neighbors. If I had managed to die, he would have gone to the funeral to see if she showed up."

He stared at her for a few seconds. "Would you like to be removed from the case?"

"What? No, of course not."

"Would you like to have someone assigned to work the case with you?"

"At the point where there's a fresh lead to follow, I'd like a task force. An army. But at the moment, all that can be done is to circulate her pictures to get people to recognize her while she's still in the area, or tell us where and when they saw her."

"What do you think the chance is?"

"I don't know. People have recognized her before, but every time she turns up she makes fewer and fewer mistakes. I have her fingerprints, but having them doesn't help me find her, because they don't match any that are contained in the databases. She's never been arrested, served in the military, or applied for any professional license. I think that if I ask enough people and circulate her picture enough, somebody is going to remember seeing her, and tell me exactly where she is." She stood up. "I've got to get her soon, Mike. She's killing people faster now, and she's getting better at it."

46

Every day at eleven, when everyone else had gone to work and the halls were empty, Judith Nathan put on a sweatshirt and jeans and went to her mailbox in the lobby of her apartment building. Today there was an ad for a dating service, a sheet of coupons for local stores that carried things like lawn furniture and garden hoses, and one big brown manila envelope. She took it out, read the return address, and hurried back to her apartment to open it.

The envelope was full of mail forwarded from her Solara Estates mailbox in Denver. She quickly shuffled through the junk mail and bills, and found one white envelope that she had been hoping for. She held it and let her fingers tell her that the answer to her application had been positive. She tore it open. There it was—her new credit card. It was the one she had ordered as a second card on the account of the young woman she had met in a club in Denver. And there was her name, embossed along the bottom: Catherine Hobbes.

It was a wonderful thing to have. The billing address was the Solara Estates mailbox in Denver, so nobody but Judith would ever get a bill for it. Nobody else would ever know it existed. Judith held the card in her hand while she searched the desk under her printer. She found the driver's license she had made to go with the credit card, and looked at it. There were some good touches on this one that she had added in the last batch of ID cards. This one had a little round sticker that said if she was killed she was willing to be an organ donor.

Judith had been preparing for this day for a long time. She had taken out a library card in the name Catherine Hobbes at the library in Lake Oswego, a couple of miles outside Portland, and opened a health club membership. She had made a social security card. Now she put all of the identification into a small wallet, so that the driver's license with her picture was behind the plastic window that was visible when she opened it. She practiced holding it open when she took out the credit card, so an observer could see several other cards with the name Catherine Hobbes embossed on them.

She went out during the afternoon to play with her new credit card. She considered the new name, repeated it to herself many times, and thought about the look she wanted. Judith drove to the mall and rode the department store escalator to the fourth floor, where the designer clothes were displayed, and was drawn to a tailored charcoal pantsuit because she had seen Catherine Hobbes on television wearing something similar. The only pantsuit she remembered ever owning was one she had bought to fly to New York once with Carl, and then never worn again. She had never worked in the sort of job where women wore suits. Most of her clothes had been dresses she had picked because they looked like they would be worn by someone she wanted to be—someone glamorous and feminine. During the day she had worn casual tops and pants. But as she stood in the dressing room looking at the four views of herself, she decided that she liked herself this way.

Catherine Hobbes was a cop, and she probably carried a gun on her somewhere. Would one of these suits have room for a gun? Where? She raised and lowered her arms, tried turning around to get a better view. Some male cops wore guns in shoulder holsters, but that would be an impossible look on a woman in a close-fitting, tailored coat. She supposed Catherine Hobbes wore a small pistol in a clip-on holster, probably at the spine, where the coat would cover it when she stood up, or maybe slightly to the right, where it was easy to reach. Judith looked down at the pants. She could even conceive of Catherine Hobbes with a gun in an ankle holster. There was room.

Judith kept trying on suits until she had found four that she liked. She selected the coats one size too large to give her extra room, then carried her purchases to the sales counter, where the girl at the cash register took her Catherine Hobbes credit card and asked, apologetically, to see her license. Judith opened her wallet and held it up so the girl could see it. The girl looked at it, said, "Thanks," and charged the purchases to the card.

Judith signed the slip, took the suits to her car, and went to lunch at La Mousse to celebrate her new card. Afterward she bought new shoes to go with the suits. She imagined that Catherine Hobbes would wear flats that were elegant but would allow her to run if she had to.

When Judith got back to her apartment, she turned on her television while she hung up her new clothes, and listened until the five o'clock news came on. Then she stood and watched. The newsman said, "For months Sergeant Catherine Hobbes, a homicide detective in the Portland Police Bureau, has been searching for a young woman who is suspected of killing local businessman Dennis Poole. Police now believe it was that young woman who set fire to Sergeant Hobbes's Adair Hill home last night and shot to death a Los Angeles private investigator. Here is the most recent photograph of her, taken a few months ago for a California driver's license."

Judith looked at the picture of Rachel Sturbridge on the television. The hair was long and looked almost black in the picture. The eyes were her original pale blue, and the face looked fat to her. The female half of the news couple said, "She is described as five feet five, one hundred and twenty pounds, with brown hair and blue eyes. She is to be considered armed and dangerous. If you do see her, police say, do not attempt to detain her. Just call nine-one-one, and the police will do the rest."

She watched with curiosity, but it was a detached curiosity.

She had changed her hair color to match Ty's in Arizona, so it was a sandy blond, and she had been wearing the blue contacts, so her eyes were a deeper blue. She had lost some weight since then and changed the kind of clothes she wore. She walked into the bathroom, looked in the mirror, and felt safe. She turned off the television and went to the telephone to call Greg at work.

"Hey, Greg. Are you working late tonight?"

"Not anymore. At least not if this is who I hope it is."

"Well, I hope it is too, because if it isn't, then you're hoping for somebody else," she said. "I'll tell you what. If you'll come right over here after work, I'll take you out tonight."

"Take me out?" he said. "You don't have to do that."

"Not have to, want to. You've been taking me everywhere for weeks, so it's my turn to take you."

"Well, okay," he said uneasily. "What do you want me to wear?"

"Whatever you have on now. I said I wanted you to come right from work."

An hour later, when he rang the bell, she said to the intercom, "Did you come straight from work?"

"Yes."

She pushed the button to unlock the front door and waited for him in the hallway. When he came up the carpeted stairs, she saw that he was carrying flowers again. She let him in and closed the door. "So, you raise flowers at work?"

"Well, no. They sell them on the way, though."

"You're not very sure of yourself, are you?"

"I guess I'm not," he said. "I keep wondering if I'll wake up and you won't exist."

"If you do, don't tell me. Come on. We're going to dinner."

She drove him to a restaurant called Sybil's. She had chosen it because it was quiet and the lights were dim. While Greg was in the men's room, she moved the candle away from the center of the table so the light would be off their faces, and studied the place. She had gotten into the habit of looking at the faces of people around her to detect signs of recognition. She was comfortable tonight, because it was too early to be crowded, and the waiters sat the first customers to arrive in the dim private spaces along the walls, leaving the center tables empty and the aisles clear for serving. Later the dining room would fill up.

She knew that Greg always felt best when the light was dim. As they ate, she judged that he was happy because they were at this remote table, and thought how pathetic it was that such a good person should be so self-conscious about his scarred face. She knew that he was grateful to her for keeping him out of the light. He probably thought she was the most sensitive, considerate person he had ever met, because she arranged to protect him without ever alluding to it. It would never occur to him that she had done it because she didn't want people looking too closely at her face, either.

When the check came in its leather folder, Judith palmed her Catherine Hobbes card, put it on the bill, and clapped the folder shut. The waiter snatched it up quickly and disappeared. A few minutes later he was back with it, she signed the slip, and she and Greg left.

After dinner they walked and she pretended to discover a club called the Mine, where promising music groups came to test new songs on a live audience. But tonight was a weeknight, so the band was an unenthusiastic, workmanlike group of middle-aged men who covered old rock hits. It didn't matter that they weren't inspired, only that Judith was out at night with a man who adored her, and she was paying for everything with a Catherine Hobbes credit card.

She ordered Greg a scotch and herself a martini. As they drank, she watched him, and decided she must get the maximum amount of pleasure out of him, even if she had to risk losing the use of him. As soon as they finished their drinks, she made Greg get up and dance with her. Like nearly all tall men, he was an awkward dancer, but at least his movements were only stiff and abbreviated. He was aware that his purpose was to provide a partner so she could dance, so he dutifully remained on his feet until she let him sit down and have another drink.

She drove Greg to her apartment, and then kept him for the

night. She loved being out so much that she forced him to go out every night for the rest of the week. She insisted that every second time she be permitted to pay, and when she did, she paid with her Catherine Hobbes credit card.

The following Tuesday, Judith went out and bought a pile of magazines. She drove home and spent hours looking at pictures of women until she found the right one. Then she cut the page from the magazine and took it to a hair stylist's shop. She had the stylist copy the cut and strawberry-blond color in the picture exactly. It was a three-step process and she had to endure the stylist's lectures about the damage that frequent dyeing had done to her hair. When she came out, she drove back to her apartment and stared at herself in the mirror for a long time, holding up a hand mirror so she could see from every angle. "Catherine," she whispered.

47

Catherine Hobbes's insurance company helped her rent an apartment not far from the police bureau. It was on Northeast Russell Street, about two blocks east of Legacy Emmanuel Hospital. The apartment building tenants all seemed to be young nurses, interns, and medical technicians. They used the place in shifts: no matter what time of the day or night she entered, there were people in medical uniforms coming in or out.

Catherine had not yet decided what she wanted to do about her burned house. The fire insurance would pay to rebuild it, but she was not sure if that was what she really wanted. At times she would awaken in the night and feel the same panic she had felt the night when she had seen flames glowing beyond the closed blinds. At those moments it felt good to her to be living in an apartment in a big building surrounded by people, and to hear the reassuring sounds of their footsteps in the hallway at all hours.

Catherine had been a cop for seven years now. She had seen traumatized people—witnesses and victims—suffer various kinds of aftereffects, and she recognized that hers was a very mild one. But she also knew that as long as Tanya Starling entertained some fantasy of killing her, it was not a great idea to rebuild the house and live in it alone.

When she had talked to Joe Pitt on the telephone about her burned house, she had started to cry. He had said, "What's the matter? Are you hurt or something?"

"No. I guess I'm crying about my house."

"What about it? Wasn't it insured?"

"Of course it was. I just miss it."

"So you'll rebuild it, exactly the same, except maybe fireproof and with a great alarm system."

"It won't be the same. And besides, I don't even know if I want to. It wasn't that great, objectively. I just loved it."

"So while you're thinking about it, I'll come up there and rent a house for a while. You can live with me."

That brought up even more complications. She had been holding Joe Pitt at bay. She had kept him from flying up to Portland the minute he'd learned that her house had burned. Every day he called, and every day he repeated the offers: they could rent a house or apartment together and he would protect her. She appreciated that instinct in men, that unfounded confidence that their sheer bulk and aggressiveness would prevent disasters.

Joe Pitt was the first man she'd had romantic feelings for in a long time, and she was cautious: she didn't want to suddenly collapse and become dependent on him, and she feared that artificial intimacy might be worse for the relationship than too much distance at this stage. She said, "As soon as you finish the cases you've taken on and feel like coming up, I'd love to see you in Portland. If I get any time off, I'll use it to fly to L.A. But I won't live with you right now. And I don't plan to go anywhere until I've got Tanya."

She had stopped calling the case "the Dennis Poole murder." It was now "Tanya Starling" when she thought of it, and she thought about it all the time. Tanya was evolving. She killed more easily, and with increasing frequency, but she seemed to be able to disappear afterward. She was going to keep killing until somebody stopped her, and stopping her was becoming more difficult.

Catherine stayed at the office late for the next two evenings, backtracking, making telephone calls to the witnesses who had met Tanya Starling in any of her guises. She called neighbors, people who had bought Tanya's cars, clerks at hotels. She asked them everything she could think of that might help her find Tanya. She was looking for quirks, for compulsive behavior, preferences and habits that might limit the search area or give her an idea of where to look and what to look for.

She spoke with homicide detectives in Los Angeles, San Francisco, and Flagstaff to be sure that any new information from the crime scenes was being sent to her, and asked them for any new theories they might have, any leads they might be following. When there was spare time, she would send pictures of Tanya Starling to businesses that might find themselves dealing with Tanya Starling under some new name: banks, car rental agencies, hotels.

At night when she came back to her apartment there were telephone messages. Each night she had to spend time reassuring her parents that she was all right, that she would not be better off living with them than in a small dingy apartment with practically no furniture, and that she was eating and sleeping regularly. Always she had to fend off Joe Pitt's offers of help, protection, and various kinds of comfort. She was becoming increasingly devoted to finding Tanya Starling, and increasingly isolated. Comfort was distraction.

On the third night after the fire, Catherine had just returned to her new apartment when an unfamiliar buzz startled her. It seemed so loud that it made her stiffen, but even as her muscles tensed she realized that the buzz was only the intercom on the wall near her door. She pressed the talk button. "Yes?"

The voice from the speaker said, "Catherine? Is that you inside this box?"

She laughed. "Joe?"

"I guess it is you in there," he said. "If this is a bad time I can come back at a worse one."

She pressed the other button, which released the outer door lock. "Get in here."

Catherine waited inside her apartment for a few seconds, then flung open her door, walked to the door of the elevator, and waited there. She was angry at herself. She had said too much to Joe on the telephone, sounded weaker and needier than she was. She had made him drop everything to fly all the way to Portland to hold her hand when they both had important things to do. She had used up a call for help, wasted one of her chances to say, "I'm in trouble and I need to be with you right now."

The elevator door opened and Joe Pitt stepped out. He was grinning, holding a briefcase in one hand and a long white box in the other. He kissed her on the cheek and handed her the box.

"Thanks. I don't suppose these are roses?"

"I'm a bit ashamed of that, because I'm usually more original, so don't tell any of the other girls, okay?"

"I'll keep it to myself." She led him to the door of her apartment and pushed it open. "I'd hate to see your legend crumble."

"I knew you'd understand."

She closed the door and locked the bolt, then set the box on the dining table and opened it. There were a dozen long-stemmed roses with pink and orange petals. She said, "They're gorgeous, Joe." She put her arms around him and gave him a deep, lingering kiss. After a moment she pulled away to look down. "Are you handcuffed to your briefcase?"

"I was being distracted by an erotic daydream and forgot." He set the briefcase on the table, opened it, and pulled out a salt shaker and a small freshly baked loaf of bread. "Somebody had to bring bread and salt to inaugurate your new place, so I got some on the way to the airport."

"Thank you," said Catherine. "You think just like my grandmother."

He turned in place and looked around at the sparse, utilitarian furniture and the bare walls. "And quite a place it is too. It's a lot like the apartments in L.A. favored by hookers from the former Soviet bloc. They like the no-frills aesthetic. I've only seen them on a professional basis, of course."

"Theirs?"

"Mine," he said.

"That's good," said Catherine. "I think like my grandmother too, and we have an agreement."

"I haven't forgotten," he said. "It's been kind of hard to be away from you."

She could foresee that he was going to bring up the idea of living together again, so she diverted his attention back to the briefcase. "Are you using that thing as an overnight bag?"

"No. I dropped my suitcase off at the hotel while I was waiting for you to get home from work." He reached into the briefcase and pulled out a thick stack of manila file folders. "These are just a few odds and ends I dug up for you. I stopped by Jim Spengler's office and picked up copies of interview transcripts from people who saw Nancy Mills in L.A. He also had some stills made up from security tapes at the Promenade Mall. One of them places her there at the same time as Rachel Sturbridge's bank manager from San Francisco, who got picked up there and killed. There's an analysis from a profiler, some reports from a blood-spatter expert and a ballistics expert."

Catherine looked at the thick stack of files, then picked up the profiler's file and looked at the first page. "This isn't from the LAPD. It says 'Property of Pitt Investigations.' You paid a profiler? This one says 'Pitt' too. And this one."

Joe waved his hand to dismiss it. "I had a few people I've used on cases before take a look at what we had, that's all. There isn't much there that you haven't already figured out on your own, and there isn't anything to tell you where Tanya is, but sometimes one little item in a report can give you an idea."

Catherine looked up at him. "Flowers and case files? What could be more romantic?"

He shrugged. "It's what we do, Cath. There's no use pretending you're somebody else, or that I am. We hunt down killers. I hope something here helps you get her."

"You're worried about me."

"Of course I am."

"Joe, this is my fault, and I'm sorry. I've been whining to you about the case, and about my house, and I'm sure I've played the whole episode for all the sympathy I could get. I guess I've felt so close to you intellectually and so far from you in miles that I didn't remember to use restraint. You were too far away to do anything about my troubles except listen. I talked my head off, but not so you would come and solve my problems for me. I just wanted to talk about them. You understand?"

"Sure I do. I was reacting to what happened, not to what you said about it. She's tried to get you killed in two different ways. I want her caught now."

"Me too." Catherine picked up the roses, took them into the kitchen, and started searching the cupboards.

"What are you looking for?"

"I just realized I don't own a vase anymore." She opened the refrigerator, took out a large jar that had a little Italian sauce in the bottom, rinsed it in the sink, filled it with fresh water, snipped the stems of the roses, and arranged them in it.

Joe watched her. "Very beautiful."

She looked at him for a moment. "I really am glad to see you, Joe. I mean anytime. I just didn't want to drag you all the way up here to be my caretaker."

"That wasn't why I came. I just grabbed any excuse I could get to see you."

"How long do you plan to devote to that?"

"I have a return ticket for Monday. I've got to meet with a guy who knows something about a case I'm working on."

"Three days. That's probably enough time."

"For what?"

She took his hand. "I'm going to your hotel with you now, and I'm going to do my best to make you really, really glad you brought those roses in person."

Catherine and Joe spent the next three days in isolation. It was really Catherine's isolation, but she had opened herself to let Joe into it. During the sunlit hours they went over the outside experts' reports together, compiling and evaluating possible avenues of investigation. In the evenings they ate late dinners at restaurants along the river and talked about their families, beliefs about love, theories of witness behavior and forensic evidence. Then they walked back to Joe's hotel holding hands and made love until they could hear the footsteps of the hotel's early-morning staff in the hallways.

On the last morning, Catherine drove Joe to the airport. As they stood beside Catherine's small gray rental car outside the terminal, he said, "Well? When is the next time going to be?"

"Whenever either one of us gets a chance," she said. "The second I can leave here, I'll be on your doorstep."

While she was driving to her apartment to get ready for work, she found that she was crying. She drove around the block while she dried her eyes, then left her rental car on the street in front of her building, took her overnight bag inside, and opened her apartment door. The first thing she saw was the jar of roses. The weekend with Joe had begun and ended so quickly that the petals were still fresh and a few buds were not fully open. If it had not been for the roses, she might have thought she had imagined it.

Catherine spent the next few days working more intensely than before, following the most promising leads and theories that she and Joe had developed, and then, when those failed, moving to the less promising leads. All of them served to verify evidence she already had. None of them seemed to take her to the next step, finding the place where Tanya Starling was right now.

One night about two weeks after the fire, she called the number of her bank and listened to the long menu: "For check orders, press four. For credit card billing inquiries, press five." She supposed that what she wanted was probably closest to five. After a pause, a woman answered. "This is Nan. How can I help you?"

"My house burned down about two weeks ago, and I called the next day and asked that my credit card be replaced. I haven't received it yet, and I thought I'd check to be sure that there's no problem."

"Your name please?"

"Catherine Hobbes, H-O-B-B-E-S."

"And your card was destroyed in the fire?"

"Yes. I ordered a new one right after the fire, and so it's been almost two weeks."

"Two weeks? That doesn't sound right. Let me check. Do you have your account number?"

"No. When my house burned, so did all the old bills and records."

"Social security number?"

Catherine recited the number, listened to the clicking of computer keys.

"I'm not sure what happened. It looks as though they tried to call you and verify your information before they mailed you a new card, and couldn't reach you. Do you have a new phone number and address to give me?"

"Yes." Catherine gave it to her. Then she added, "When I called before, I gave them my work number and address. I'm a police officer."

"I suppose it's possible somebody there answered the phone and said, 'Police,' and our person figured it was a hoax. Let's try to get this expedited so your new card goes out as soon as possible. It will have a new number on it. We always do that when the other one isn't in your possession."

"When should I expect it?"

"Tomorrow or the next day, if we can get it done without another glitch, and they're pretty rare. I'm very sorry about the mix-up. Have you ordered new checks and so on?"

"Yes, but if you have a way of verifying that that's being done, I'd appreciate it."

"Happy to do it. And one more thing. If you're a police officer, you've probably already thought of this, but I usually advise people to order reports from the three credit services to be sure all your cards really were destroyed and nobody picked one up. I can tell you that nothing has been charged to your account at this bank during that time, but you should still run the credit check."

"That's a good idea," she said. "I'll do that."

She let a day go by, and then another. Her replacement card came, and she forgot about the credit reports. But at the end of the week she remembered while she was in the office and called the three phone numbers to order her credit reports.

When Catherine came home from work two days later, the reports were in her mailbox in the lobby of the apartment building. She took them to her apartment, sat at the kitchen table, and opened them warily. For the past eight years, she had always been uncomfortable when she thought about credit. That was something she had gotten as part of the settlement after her failed marriage.

Kevin had been an optimist. When the marriage had ended, the extent of Kevin's optimism had become apparent. He had been running up the balances on his credit card accounts for a long time, on the theory that his future salary increases would make the overruns seem tiny. After Catherine divorced him, the credit companies had been quick to inform her that the growing balances on debts he had incurred before the divorce were her responsibility as much as his. It had taken time for her to legally separate her portion of the debt from his, get a second mortgage on the house she had bought in Portland, and pay off the credit companies.

It had been a painful process for Catherine, and not only because it was a time when she'd needed money, but because she couldn't keep herself from thinking about where the debt had come from. Kevin had assured her that he had gone into debt only to spend money on her. He had not been very specific, so she looked at two years of old bills. The credit cards had been used for lunches and dinners at restaurants where she had never been, and hotels in Palo Alto, the town where they had lived. Cheating on Catherine had been expensive.

Today, when Catherine read the three credit reports, she was relieved to see that her credit was extremely good. She supposed that paying off her half of Kevin's debts must have healed whatever wounds her marriage to him had inflicted on her rating. Maybe she'd gotten a few extra points for being a sucker.

She went carefully down the list of open accounts. There were a couple of department store charge cards that she had forgotten. She had accepted them years ago because they had been offering large discounts to customers who opened charge accounts. They had approached her when she was buying her first bed after the marriage. It had cost eleven hundred dollars, and getting the card had saved her about two hundred. The other occasion was when she was still in the academy and making practically nothing, and was forced to agree to go out to dinner with a visiting couple from the days when she had been married to Kevin. She had known that they were still in touch with him, and she'd needed to have them tell him that she looked magnificent, so she had bought a dress, coat, and shoes that she couldn't really afford.

There was one account that she could not remember opening. It was a Visa. She looked for the issuing company. The issuer was the Bank of the Atlantic. Her stomach dropped: Kevin? How could he have done that to her? She had already paid for his girlfriends. She repeated the question to herself. How *could* he have done that to her? He couldn't. It would have come to her attention at some point in the past eight years. She looked at the date. It wasn't eight years ago. The account had been opened a month ago.

She kept staring at the entry. It wasn't right. The social security number wasn't hers. And it said, "Additional card." What did that mean? Could this be somebody else's credit card that had been added to her credit report by mistake?

She looked at the reports from the other two services. The card was listed on all of them. The one from Experion said, "Primary cardholder SSN" and listed a second social security number. That explained the "additional card" business. The Catherine Hobbes Visa card was on someone else's account. Her eyes widened as all of the implications began to pass through her consciousness at once. A person on the run could get a credit card in her own name and an additional one in a false name. She could travel under the false name, and any business that ran the credit card would get the response that it was genuine.

Catherine reached for the telephone, then stopped, her hand in midair. It was too late to reach the captain anywhere but at home, and she wasn't sure what she believed, what she wanted to tell him. She decided what she was going to do, half-stood to go to her spare room to turn on the computer, then remembered that she wasn't in her house anymore, and the computer wasn't fifty steps away in that direction. She was in a small apartment, and the only computer was the laptop she had signed out from work. She went to the big briefcase she had brought in, unlocked it, and took out the laptop.

She plugged it into the telephone line, turned it on, and waited for the connection to the Internet. It took a very long time, then failed to connect, so she started the process over again. She was so impatient that she almost unplugged the computer to reconnect the telephone, but she forced herself to wait. It would not do to make a lot of fuss over what might amount to a relatively harmless credit reporting error.

She got connected, then found the Web site of the Bank of the Atlantic. She clicked on credit card accounts, then "Access your account," then gave the account number that was on her credit reports and the social security number of the primary cardholder. A box appeared that said, "Password." She swore under her breath, but then thought for a second. She typed in "none." A new page appeared, asking, "Would you like to create a password?" She had been right: there had been no password entered before. She clicked on the "yes" box. She typed in "Steelhead," the name of her first dog.

What appeared next was the current month's charges for the account. There were two women on the account, Laura Murray and Catherine Hobbes. Under "Charges for Laura Murray" there was nothing. Under "Charges for Catherine Hobbes" there was plenty: "Stahlmeyer's Dept. Women's Wear, $2,436.91. Sybil's, $266.78. The Mine, $93.08. Tess's Shoes, $404.00. La Mousse, $56.88." All of the charges had been made within the past couple of weeks. Catherine copied the bill into an e-mail and sent it to herself, then studied it one more time.

All of the stores were in Portland. They were all on the west side of the river, downtown. Catherine was sure she knew who this was. Tanya had made her mistake.

Catherine was operating now on an intuition. The part of it that was defensible was something that all cops were aware of and that the captain would understand: cops knew that coincidences existed, but not in the convenient numbers that people in trouble usually claimed. When coincidences turned up in the course of an investigation, they had to be viewed with skepticism. It was possible that even though there was no other Catherine Hobbes registered to vote in Oregon, and none besides her who had a telephone number, listed or unlisted, it didn't mean that one had not arrived in the past month. But that was unlikely.

The part of what she intuited that was not quite defensible would be difficult to explain to the captain, and it was the part that seemed most compelling. Catherine had a feeling about Tanya Starling. She had noticed that Tanya changed her identity more often than circumstances required. She seemed to change her name every time she arrived in a new city, every time anything happened that she considered unpleasant or unsuccessful. It reminded Catherine of the urge some people had to take a shower and change their clothes whenever they had a bad experience. Catherine was sure that she found it exciting, maybe even amusing. Tanya was getting very good at making or obtaining false identification.

Another thing that Tanya had done repeatedly was try to hurt Catherine Hobbes. Could a mysterious credit card in Catherine's name come up now and not be connected with Tanya Starling? It could, but it was unlikely. But how had Tanya done it? One possibility was that Tanya had been posing as the woman listed as the primary cardholder.

Catherine called the Denver Police Department and spoke with a woman who identified herself as Detective Yoon. The detective listened attentively to Catherine's story and agreed to find out whether there was a woman named Laura Murray

living at 5619 LaRoche Avenue in Alameda. If there was,
Detective Yoon would try to discover whether she had some
knowledge of how her record and social security number had
been used to get a credit card in the name Catherine Hobbes.

Detective Yoon called Catherine Hobbes the next afternoon at the police bureau. She said, "There is a Laura Murray, and she's sitting in front of my desk right now."

"She is?" said Catherine. "Is she somebody who might
have helped apply for the card, or just a victim?"

"She doesn't know anything about it. She's twenty-two,
with no criminal record—no record of any kind except two
old tickets, one for speeding and a parking violation. She's
got a good job, and has lived here all her life."

Catherine said, "Let me fax you a set of pictures. See if she
recognizes them."

Five minutes later, they were on the telephone again. "She
remembers her," said Detective Yoon. "They met at a nightclub about two months ago in Denver, near Larimer Square.
She says that when the girl in the picture danced with a man,
she asked Laura to guard her purse. Then when Laura
danced, the girl in the picture held Laura's purse."

"Thank you," said Catherine. "This is a big help. Do you
mind letting me speak with Laura?"

A moment later, a new voice came on the phone. It was
young and nervous. "Hello?"

"Hello, Laura. This is Detective Sergeant Catherine Hobbes,
Portland Police Bureau. I want to thank you for your cooperation. It's very important to us. I need to ask you now for a little more help."

"What do you need?"

"First, don't try to do anything about this credit card.
Don't call the company or try to cancel or anything. For the
moment we don't want to alert this woman to the fact that we
know about the card. When the investigation is over the card
will be canceled, and you won't be responsible for any debts.
Can I count on you for that?"

"Sure." Laura didn't sound sure.

"The other thing I need is to have you tell me everything

you can remember about meeting this woman, everything she said to you, the way she looked, what she was wearing. There is no detail that's too small to be useful."

48

Judith opened her eyes and listened to the rain outside her apartment window. She liked it when the rain came down for two or three days at a time. It always seemed to her to be the world cleaning itself of the dirt and dead things, the unhappiness and mistakes. It rained almost half of the days of the year here.

Judith sat up in bed and looked at the window. The rain was running down past it from somewhere above, and she could hear it hitting below, splashing like a tiny waterfall. She got up, pushed the button on the coffeemaker, then padded out to the bottom of the carpeted stairs, where the manager left her newspaper every morning, and brought it back with her.

She sipped the coffee, sat cross-legged on the couch, and ignored the newspaper. Sitting here listening to the water outside made her feel very warm and safe. It was a feeling that she had not experienced until she had grown up. She had never liked rainy days when she was just Charlene.

In Wheatfield it sometimes rained for days like this in the spring and fall. Her mother hated the rain, hated ever being cold or wet, so she never went out. She hated being trapped in the house too, so she would wake up already irritated. Her blond hair would be in a network of ringlets that Charlene could hardly imagine having happened in the short time between last evening when she had gone out and the very next day. It looked like an unraveled rope.

Her mother's pretty, childlike face would be warm and pink from being pressed against her pillow, and it would carry impressions from the folds in the pillowcase. She would get up and stand beside the percolator and scowl at the sight of the coffee gurgling up into the little glass cap on top. She would find the green-and-white pack of menthol cigarettes on the counter, light one on the stove burner, and leave it in the corner of her mouth while she poured her coffee and went to the front window to stare out.

Years later, Charlene had realized that her mother behaved exactly like a cat. Even though she knew it was raining—had seen the water streaming down the outside of the bathroom window, had maybe even been awakened by it as it poured from the gutters out the downspout near her corner of the house, she still had to go to the front window to see if it was raining out there too.

After a few minutes of silence while she glowered at the rain and built her mood, Charlene's mother would begin. She would look at Charlene with frank curiosity. "Have you rehearsed for the pageant next week?" Charlene would say she had spent most of the time doing homework, but she had rehearsed. Her mother would say, "Let's hear the seashore song."

Charlene would sing it, maybe not as well as she could, because she could see from the first seconds that her mother's expression was not admiring or pleasant. Singing for her was like pleading a case while walking up the steps of the gallows.

Her mother would hear the end of the song as a signal to respond. "How could I have spent thousands of dollars and thousands of hours of my time on you? You sound like a trained parrot. You dance like a cow. How can you possibly be anything but embarrassing by next week? God, I should see if I can get my entry fee back. And look at your skin. Have you ever thought of eating a vegetable instead of a candy bar? You look like the ghost of a ghost."

When she had talked enough about the next pageant, which she had trained Charlene to believe was the last boat out of poverty, she would move on to a variety of new topics. "Your room . . ." "Your clothes . . ." "Your . . ." As the morning got started, her voice would rise in pitch and volume until, during a pause for breath, Charlene would hear the current boyfriend creaking the springs in the bedroom, jingling his belt as he put on his pants. There would be a heavy thump as he put a toe in his shoe and stamped it to get his foot in.

A short time later he would appear, walking through on his way out, sometimes pausing to make some excuse, and sometimes just preferring the rain to the noise. Then her mother would blame her. "You always make me look like I'm the big bitch. I wouldn't have to raise my voice if you'd just listen and do what you're supposed to. My God, look at that hair. I spend hundreds of dollars on cut-and-colors, shampoos and conditioners, and you have to look like the bride of Franken-stein. I'll tell you, if you don't do well on this pageant—either Miss Hennepin County or at least first runner-up—I'm through with you. You can be your own coach and manager and teacher and maid and chauffeur. Then where will you be? Miss Nothing. Miss Ugly Little Zero." She would sit on the couch with her arms folded and put Charlene through a series of chores or a series of rehearsals, depending on her mood and the state of the little house.

Her mother would be distracted from her when the boyfriend returned, and there would be a fight. Usually the fight made it better for Charlene, but not always. She remembered one boyfriend named Donny, who was tall and thin and quiet, with long arms and legs. He was from somewhere in the South—was Tennessee right?—and he had an accent. He came in during one of her mother's tantrums on a Sunday, around one in the afternoon.

Her mother had heard the door and spun her head around to face Donny. She shrieked, "And you too. You worthless—"

Donny's arm moved so fast that Charlene wasn't sure whether she saw it or only heard the slap and her imagination supplied the abrupt motion, the forearm bringing the backhand across her mother's mouth. Her mother went backward onto the kitchen floor, either because she had seen the movement at its start and tried to save herself, or was actually propelled by the force of the blow.

She could remember Donny's face while it was happening. When he heard what Charlene's mother was saying he might have narrowed his eyes slightly, but otherwise his face remained impassive. The long arm just swung, and there was something in it of the routine. It was like a horse twitching its tail to brush a fly away.

Charlene watched her mother. After a second or two, she raised herself on one elbow, staring, her nose and mouth bleeding. Her expression of anger and contempt was gone. She just lay there blinking, her mouth open, eyes empty and surprised, no more ready for thought than a person who had been hit by a truck.

Donny kept going toward the bedroom, and Charlene realized that the whole episode had not interrupted his progress for more than two seconds. He went in and closed the door. After a minute, her mother managed to sit up. Ten minutes later Charlene could hear Donny snoring.

Her mother had withdrawn to the couch, lying there and crying for an hour or so, feeling sorry for herself. Charlene wanted to stand over her and ask, "What did you expect? Are you blind and deaf? Did you live with him, sleep with him, drink yourself sick with him, and imagine that anything but this could possibly happen?" But she did not.

Charlene had liked Donny better than most of the others, because he had a kind of forthright simplicity. He had none of the willingness to struggle for advantage that made the others pathetic victims of her mother's manipulation. For most of her childhood, her mother's rainy-day scenes were acted out with a boyfriend of the other sort: Paul, or Mike. She would turn on the boyfriend, practically spitting venom, and he would respond. He would act exactly the way she did, as though he were not another person, really, but just her mirror and echo. Within a few minutes they would be simultaneously shouting different versions of what had caused the argument, then a list of bad things that each of them had done on other occasions, then bad qualities and habits, and, finally, there would just be an apportioning of ugly names.

It would go on all through the long, rainy day and into the evening, because her mother would not go out on a rainy night. If the weather didn't clear, Charlene would get two days of it. Between attacks on the boyfriend, Charlene's mother would deliver harangues against her for everything she was and everything she should be but wasn't.

It had taken changing herself into Tanya Starling and moving into the high-rise apartment in Chicago with Carl to teach her that there were pleasures to a rainy day. Carl had been an expert at enjoying himself. On a rainy day, if he wasn't involved in a legal case that had something urgent about it, he would sometimes stay home. They would lie around in bed and make love.

It was only when they were really hungry that Carl would jump out of bed, throw on some pants, shoes, and a rain jacket, and head for the elevator. He would be back in twenty minutes with croissants, Danish pastries, doughnuts filled with cream and jelly, and special coffee from the bakery around the corner.

She remembered how, as soon as she heard the apartment door close, she would be up, trying to use the twenty minutes as efficiently as she could. She would quickly bathe, running the water while she brushed her teeth. She would do her makeup, brush her hair, put on something that looked good on her but maintained the pretense that she wasn't bothering today. As she remembered, she felt a sharp sense of loss, not for Carl but for the days with Carl. What was lost was the way she had felt and been.

She picked up the telephone and called Greg's house. She heard his voice answer, "Hello?"

"Hi," she said. "Are you planning to do anything important at work this morning?"

"Important, but not life-and-death important. Anything I can do for you on the way?"

"Yes. Come here instead of there, and spend a rainy morning with me. I'll make your dreams come true. One of them, anyway." She hung up. Then she went into the bathroom and threw off her pajamas. She got ready with the same efficiency that she had used in the old days when Carl had gone out for pastries. She knew it would take Greg about twenty-five minutes to drive here at this time of the morning in the rain.

Today Judith was determined to live the life she had willed for herself. It was precarious, because some stupid piece of bad luck could throw her into the hands of her enemies at any second, but that didn't matter right now. Maybe perfection was always supposed to be brief, just a limited period when everything was in its prime. The life she had imagined existed only if she was at her most beautiful and energetic, not a girl any longer but a grown woman, someone who had been loved enough to take all of the man-woman maneuvering lightly, like a dance, and not be overwhelmed by it or scared. The rest was eternal: the nights of drinking martinis with their icy, oily shimmer, even the shape of the glasses unchanging; the man, purely appealing because he was the man of the moment only; the dim, romantic lighting and the music; a day of soft sun filtered through rain.

There had never been anything in the fantasy about having the perfect moment go on into some decrepit old age, and it couldn't. For now, for this series of heartbeats—whether now lasted for a couple of years or now was already ending— things had reached a perfect pitch.

Judith savored her rainy morning, and in the afternoon she and Greg dozed peacefully on her bed, listening half-consciously to the steady rain. She roused herself twice, once to lift Greg's sleep-heavy arm and drape it across herself so she could press her back against his chest and feel the skin warming her. The other time it was to crawl off the bed and pick up the newspaper she had never gotten around to reading.

She took a pen to the ads for the nightspots, then looked at the ones she had circled and made a plan for the evening. They would start at the Ringside for dinner, because on a rainy night she didn't feel in the mood to ruin a pair of heels and get a good dress splashed. A leather booth in a steak house with big, warm dinner plates and a coat rack behind her felt right. Then she picked out a cluster of four clubs within a couple of blocks of one another, so she and Greg could move easily from one to another.

She made fresh coffee, drank the first cup by herself, and let the smell of it drift into her bedroom to wake Greg. When she heard him beginning to stir, she poured a cup and brought it to him. He sat up and took it, sipped it, and said, "I'm trying to sort out what part of this day was real."

"It's all real," she said. "The good parts have happened, or will happen, whatever they were."

"What time is it?"

"Time to drink your coffee and wake up. After that it will be time to take a shower and get ready to go out to dinner with me. You can do it all slowly, because I intend to."

"You sound as though it's all planned."

"It is. I want to walk in the rain so I can see it and smell it, but without getting too wet. I want to eat, drink, and dance a little. Are you up to all that?"

"Of course." He looked at her. "Did I tell you I like your hair that way?"

"I did get the impression you had no complaints," she said. "I'll take the first shower, because it will take me longer."

At nine they were in the Ringside, their umbrellas and raincoats hung on the coatrack beside their booth. Judith had not really eaten a meal today, just nibbled a few things from the refrigerator—a little cheese and fruit. She and Greg ate steaks and drank red wine, then sat and talked until they were ready for the rain again.

They walked to the Mine, listening to the drops popping on the fabric of their umbrellas. They stayed close to the storefronts, far from the curb, where a passing car might plow through a puddle and splash them. Once, Greg suddenly tugged her with him into an alcove outside a store entrance, and she thought he was saving her from a soaking. In a second she learned he had done it so he could kiss her in the alcove, where they were out of the lights and the rain.

The Mine was good tonight, the music all new work by a girl band called Danae. They had their own following, so the energy was all happy and appreciative, and the band tried to show itself at its best. Judith didn't mind that Greg's eyes lingered too long on the girls of the band. She might have resented the tight jeans on the bass guitarist, the ripped and abbreviated T-shirt on the drummer, but not tonight. It all helped to keep people's eyes on the stage, and not on her. She was enjoying a part of her perfect moment, and she didn't want to be disturbed.

49

Catherine Hobbes knew exactly how she wanted to conduct her hunt. The only success she'd had so far was the result of circulating the pictures of Tanya Starling and Rachel Sturbridge. This time she had printed five hundred flyers with the two color pictures, the physical description, and the list of murders. The words "armed and dangerous" were in larger, darker type.

During the early part of the afternoon, uniformed officers went to the businesses where the Catherine Hobbes credit card had been used, left flyers, and talked to salesclerks and waiters to find out what they could remember about the girl. Catherine had gone to Stahlmeyer's Department Store herself.

The women's-wear manager had checked the computerized record to find out exactly what purchases Tanya had made. As she walked Catherine to the right part of the fourth floor and began to show her the items Tanya had bought, Catherine felt the hairs on the back of her neck begin to stand.

Tanya had bought designer pantsuits. Two of them were almost exactly like the ones Catherine had bought at Stahlmeyer's a week before, tailored so the coats were not pinched inward to the waist but had a bit of drape. They were cut to hang from the shoulders, like a man's suit, so they allowed Catherine to carry a concealed weapon. Tanya was doing the same thing.

Catherine went outside to retrieve the digital camera in the trunk of the unmarked car, then carried one sample of each of the four suits Tanya had bought into a dressing room and photographed them. The blouses Tanya had chosen to go with them were conservative, very like the ones that Catherine had bought.

Catherine knew that Tanya must have seen her on television in Arizona and probably in Portland. It wasn't difficult to find clothes like Catherine's in a big city. But why was she buying them? What did Tanya hope to accomplish by imitating Catherine Hobbes? Did it have something to do with getting the credit card accepted?

Maybe Tanya was working up to doing a killing and then taunting Catherine. She might rent a getaway car in Catherine's name, or leave a charge receipt with Catherine's name on it at a crime scene.

The idea that Tanya might be making her killings into a game was not a welcome one. The list of killers who had begun teasing the police and leaving riddles for them was long and ugly. From the time when they began to taunt the police until the time they were caught, they became more active and prolific. Catherine hoped that whatever Tanya was doing, she was not getting ready to kill somebody just to torment Catherine Hobbes.

Catherine drove back to the bureau, downloaded the photographs into her computer, and made copies for the evening-shift patrol officers in the downtown district. Then she went to the second floor, to the vice squad office, and found Rhonda Scucci.

Rhonda looked up from a file she was reading, and said, "Hello, Cath. What's up?"

"Hi, Rhonda. I've got to go out tonight looking like somebody else."

"What are we talking—whore? Drug mule?"

"This is a single woman, maybe five years younger than I am, if the light is dim enough. She works nine to five in an office. She might be out with a female friend or two. She hasn't got a date. You know the Mine? Metro? That's the kind of place. All I have to do is not stand out and not get recognized."

"Yeah, there's a lot of that around this building. But don't worry. I know those places. You want what? A skirt and blouse? Shoes? Probably a raincoat tonight, just to protect our investment."

"I can use anything you can get me. But the part I need most is the wig. The hair is really important."

"So the suspect has seen your face?"

"Yes."

"Jesus, Cath. A homicide suspect? Is that what they ask you to do these days?"

"Don't worry. I'm going to be backed up."

"Just be sure it's close backup." Rhonda led her down the hall to a storeroom and unlocked it. It looked as though it had been a broom closet originally, but now it held shelves full of electronic equipment for stings—microphones, tape recorders, video cameras—and a wide array of clothes for men and women on hangers. Rhonda picked a few things off the rack and held them up to Catherine until they agreed on an outfit. Then she helped Catherine try on wigs.

The third one looked right. Catherine could tell as soon as she looked in the mirror. The hair was dark brown, long, and straight, parted in the middle. It wasn't eye-catching, and if she ducked her head a bit, it would fall forward to hide her face if she wanted it to. "What do you think?"

"What the hell do you care? It's to impress a killer. Want him to die excited?"

50

Catherine was on the street, walking the district where Tanya Starling had used the Catherine Hobbes credit card. Catherine had spent time in this neighborhood during vacations from college. Part of the attraction had been that the area had a bar scene full of young single people even then, and part of it had been that it had not been part of her father's precinct. She had been very careful to stay out of the parts of town where she might meet Lieutenant Frank Hobbes on business.

After that she had married Kevin and moved to Palo Alto. When that had fallen apart, and she had come home and become a cop too, she had not been assigned to fashionable places like this. She had spent her time as a patrol officer in the parts of town where people got robbed or killed, or bought ten-dollar bags of drugs.

The feel of the area had not changed, but it was much more crowded, much more expensive, and more stylish than it had been when she was in college. She supposed she could have said the same about all of Portland. It had spent the time filling up with the people who had ruined California.

Tonight was the third night of a persistent rain, and it was a weeknight, but it didn't matter. Men and women in their twenties and early thirties, some of them in suits and skirts from the office, were going into the restaurants and gathering at the bars, standing in knots while holding drinks in warm, wood-paneled taprooms.

Catherine needed to get used to the district again, and to develop a feeling for the spots where Tanya had used the credit card. She studied the entrances to the nightspots, picked out front windows where she might get a table to watch for Tanya, or where Tanya might be sitting right now.

All of Tanya's credit card charges had been between Eleventh Avenue and Fifteenth, as far north as Lovejoy Street and as far south as Glisan Street. The rain gave Catherine a chance to walk up each of the streets studying the buildings and the crowds, carrying an umbrella and wearing a hooded raincoat that hid her face. In Portland, rain didn't make anybody think of staying home, but Catherine's rain gear made it easy for her to study faces without much risk of being studied in return.

She patrolled systematically tonight, learning the traffic patterns. She began at the corner of Eleventh and Glisan and headed north to Lovejoy, then turned left and left again to go south on Twelfth. Each time she came to one of the places where Tanya had already been—the Mine, Sybil's, Metro, La Mousse—she lingered a few minutes, watching the doors, surveying the buildings.

One of the things she was trying to do was to evaluate the ambience and the customers. She needed to get a sense of whether the place would appeal to Tanya Starling or was somewhere she had gone once, had not liked, and would never revisit. Tanya seemed to like luxury—the bars in good hotels, nice restaurants—and the clothes she had bought in Portland were expensive. La Mousse and Sybil's were essentially the kind of restaurant that Tanya chose in every city, so Catherine was satisfied with them.

Catherine spent more time searching the parking lots and the nearby streets looking for Tyler Gilman's car. By now, Tanya might have sold it or abandoned it, as she had done with other cars, but until it turned up, there was a chance that she had kept it and might drive it to this district on a rainy weeknight. The little blue Mazda was just the sort of car that Tanya might convince herself would not attract any attention, and Tanya would not want to show up at a restaurant or a club looking like a wet rat. She would want to look good to attract the next man.

Catherine had not been able to find any record of Tanya's having done anything for a living but accept gifts from men. She seemed to have lived in the high-rise apartment building in Chicago for an extended period of time. The building manager had said he didn't know how long she had been around, but he remembered seeing her occasionally for years. The apartment had been rented by a man named Carl Nelson, and her name had never appeared on the lease or the mailbox. About a year ago, Carl Nelson had died of a heart attack during a trip to Europe.

After Nelson had died, Tanya had gone to Aspen and found Dennis Poole. He had supported her and given her money and expensive gifts. She seemed always to be looking for a man to take care of her, and always finding that she had to move on.

Tanya should have left Portland. She had made an attempt on Catherine and killed Calvin Dunn, so Portland could hardly be considered a safe place to stay. She should be in the next city by now, but this time something was different. The charges on the Catherine Hobbes card had begun after Catherine's house had burned, not before. Catherine had to act on what Tanya was doing, not on what Tanya should be doing.

Catherine kept walking along the streets, her hood up, staying in the shadows and moving quickly past the lighted windows, then pausing in the entranceways of closed businesses or under awnings near bus stops, where her presence would raise no questions.

Part of her consciousness was always devoted to watching for Tanya. Every time she came near a restaurant where a young couple was coming out, putting up umbrellas or trotting toward their parked car, she studied the woman. Whenever there was a woman visible through a front window, Catherine's eyes had to focus on her and find some disqualifying feature before she could release her from her gaze. When a car glided past her searching for a parking space, Catherine looked for Tanya inside.

She was also making mental notes about how to expand her search. The ideal way to do it would be to post a plain-clothes officer at the bar in each of the district's clubs and restaurants for a few weeks, doing nothing but watching the door to see if Tanya entered. It was impossible, of course, but she thought maybe she could talk her captain into sparing one team. If there was one cop in Metro, Sybil's, the Mine, and La Mousse for a few nights, all of them connected by radio to a control van in the middle of the district, something good might happen. If Catherine drew the right male cops, Tanya might even try to pick up one of them.

She decided that the parking lot behind Sybil's, on Four-teenth near Irving, would be a good place for the van. The lot was used by a bank and about three smaller businesses dur-ing the day, but at night the only one that was open was Sybil's. When Sybil's was packed, there were still at least a few empty parking spaces. A plain white van parked in the far corner near the rear driveway would look as though it be-longed to the restaurant or one of its suppliers.

She reached the Mine, at Fifteenth and Johnson, at eleven-twenty. There were no windows, but every time the door opened to admit more customers, she could see inside, where the crowd surged on the dance floor and the music blared and thumped briefly, and then was muffled as the door closed on it. The place was dimly lighted except for the stage, which she couldn't see from outside.

As she walked closer, Catherine had a subtle feeling that grew with each step: Don't walk past. Look inside. The Mine wasn't like a restaurant, where someone might make a sec-ond visit after a month or two. It was a nightclub. Tanya could go there every night. The place was crowded, and the lights were low and wavering. Catherine should get a better look. As she walked toward the door, the rain picked up slightly, so three girls who had been smoking outside headed for the door. Catherine pushed back her hood, closed her umbrella, and moved in among them.

The music was loud, and she could feel the pounding of the bass in her stomach. She glanced involuntarily at the stage, a simple reflex of the brain because it needed to know where so much sound was coming from. She noted that it was a girl band, and returned her eyes to the crowd.

The patrons were of the right age and the right style for Tanya. There were at least two hundred people of both sexes in the big room, their faces sometimes illuminated by the glow of the spotlights on the stage, sometimes held in the dark for long periods. As she scanned the faces—smiling, laughing, trying to talk to one another over the music—she felt a shiver of fear for them. They looked like Tanya, clean-faced and alert, between twenty-one and thirty, all with good haircuts and dressed as though they were employed in some white-collar job. Tanya could slip in among them and be so like them that she would be unmemorable and invisible, until one of them was dead. It could happen any night that Tanya felt the urge. It could be happening now.

Catherine began to make her way through the crowd, squeezing into the border between the dance floor and the outer ring of patrons lined up for a turn at the bar. She would move sideways a few feet, then extend a hand between two people and let the arm and shoulder follow, repeating, "Excuse me. Pardon. Excuse me" as she went, her voice just part of the mixture of voices to be heard trying to climb over the music but barely over it, so that she needed to be within a foot of the next person before he knew anyone was talking. Catherine slowly made it closer to the destination she had set for herself, the ladies' room.

She had known that in a crowd this size there would be a line of women waiting to use the ladies' room. No matter what else was true of Tanya, if she was here, she would have to wait in that line sometime. Catherine came within sight and began to move laterally in the crowd, studying the faces of the women in the line. Tanya was not among them.

Catherine devoted a few minutes to studying the layout of the Mine more closely. There were two fire exits at this end of the building, and probably another behind the stage. If there was a sighting of Tanya here, Catherine would have to remember to have those exits watched. She turned and began to inch her way through the mass of moving bodies toward the door. She was blocked suddenly as a tall man stepped into her path. "Excuse me," she said.

"Dance with me." He was handsome, but he knew it.

"No, thanks. Got to go."

"Come on," he said. His confidence grew until he became repulsive. "You know you want to."

To his right Catherine saw something that didn't fit, the flash of a face and then a sudden movement that went against the beat of the music. She saw a couple moving off in the crowd ahead of her. "Excuse me," she said as she tried to go around him.

He held her arm. "Please. I'm in love with you. The marriage is on."

She looked at his arm clutching hers, then up into his eyes. "Want a really nasty surprise?"

He let go, held up both hands, and stepped backward. She used the space that he opened between them to slip past him and make six feet of progress before the next obstacle formed.

"Excuse me," she said to a group of young women who had just come in. The nearest of the women turned to look at her, just an aura of blond hair to frame an expression that was utterly empty.

Catherine said, "You won't be able to get in unless you let people out."

The woman reluctantly stepped aside six inches. Catherine brushed by her and the next two, and was out the door. She squinted into the rain, then down the street the other way, but she could not see the couple. She had lost them.

She tried to analyze the impression she'd had. It wasn't that the woman looked like Tanya—she had not been able to tell what she looked like in the dim light. It had just been the impression of furtiveness that had made her want to get a closer look.

She began to walk again, this time heading for Metro. She had noticed something, and it had not quite reached her consciousness until a moment ago. Every place where the Catherine Hobbes credit card had been used had one thing in common. They were all very dim. She hoped that when the officers had gone around this afternoon they had asked the owners of the businesses to post the circulars where people could see them.

51

Judith was sitting at her favorite table in Underground. This was the bar where she had met Greg, and the table was the one where they had sat and talked for so long on that first night. She was drinking her second martini of the evening, and it was probably going to be the last. This night was precious, and she didn't want to get sleepy. It felt to Judith as though she had finally managed to hold together all of the elements of the life she had always thought about when she was a child.

She had not realized when she was eight or ten that what she was imagining was only a single evening that was repeated endlessly. She had determined that she would grow up, get away from her mother, and stop having to be Charlene Buckner. She had known exactly who she would be: a woman who wore beautiful clothes and held drinks in a manicured hand adorned with jewels that sparkled. She would dance with a tall, strong man who adored her.

Now she was a success. Charlene had grown up, and right now she was Judith and she'd had that special evening a hundred times. She leaned close to Greg and said, "I've wanted to go to the ladies' room since we were in the Mine, but I didn't want to wait in that line. I'm going now." Since she was that close to him, she kissed his cheek before she stood.

Greg smiled at her and shrugged. "I'll be here."

Judith walked to the back of the room near the bar, where there was a corridor. She passed the pay phone, then the door of the men's room, and then approached the ladies' room at the end. There was only one woman waiting ahead of her, so she waited too. She stood away from the wall, and pretended to look at the things that were written on it, glancing now and then in the direction of the telephone so she didn't have to make eye contact with the other woman.

She heard the door open and close, saw the girl who had been in the ladies' room move past, and heard the one ahead of her go inside. It was a relief to be alone. Judith waited, leaning against the wall. She hated being trapped anywhere with people who might have nothing to look at but her face. It had been about three weeks since the local television stations had shown the pictures of her old driver's licenses. People usually forgot everything quickly, but if just one person recognized her, Judith would be finished.

The door opened again, the woman edged past her, and Judith went inside. The room was small, like a half bathroom in a house, but it was clean and private. The walls were covered with copies of old movie posters, menus from forgotten restaurants, and travel ads, all pasted there like wallpaper. She flushed the toilet, went to the sink, and stopped.

Just to the left of the mirror, what she had thought was just another old poster wasn't. The pictures on it were the familiar ones of Tanya Starling and Rachel Sturbridge. But now there was a third one. Her face on the California license had been given a new hairstyle by computer.

Judith stared at herself in the mirror, then at the photograph. It had been doctored. The picture had hair like Judith's—hair like Catherine Hobbes's.

A dozen thoughts competed for her attention. Had those two women a moment ago seen the picture and recognized Judith? They had been in here, and they must have looked at the mirror. Could they have missed the pictures? What did the poster say? She read the print under her face. "Wanted for questioning . . ." That didn't sound like such a big deal. "Homicide, arson, auto theft . . ." That was worse. Maybe the women hadn't read that far. "Armed and dangerous." Could anyone not see those words? Could they have seen this and not connected the pictures with Judith?

She tried to calm herself. Maybe she had been lucky. Her pictures had been all over the western half of the country, on and off, and almost nobody ever recognized her. She had not talked to either of those women, had not even made eye contact. A bathroom line was one of the places where people hardly looked at one another. Nobody wanted to get caught staring and then have to stand around with the person for five or ten minutes. And Judith had been careful.

She pulled the wanted poster off the wall, prepared to throw it into the wastebasket, but changed her mind. Whoever had put it up could be the one to empty the basket, and they might just stick it back up. She quickly folded it three times and put it in her purse. No, that was the wrong place. It was covering the handle of her gun, just when she might need to reach for it. She pulled the folded poster out again, put it into the side compartment of her purse, took a last look at herself in the mirror, and opened the door.

There was another girl waiting. Judith kept her head down and slipped past her, walking fast. She approached the next door, with its blue cutout symbol of a man. What if the poster was in there too? If it was in the ladies' room, why wouldn't they put another one in the men's room? Judith was alone in the corridor, but her solitude might last only a few more seconds. She quickly opened the men's-room door, glanced in to verify that it was empty, went inside, and locked the door.

There was the poster. She tore it off the wall, folded it, and put it in the side compartment of her purse with the other one. She went to the door, opened it an inch, and saw that the corridor was still empty. She slipped out and began to walk, then heard the door of the ladies' room open behind her. She should already be gone from this corridor, and the woman behind her knew it. Had the woman seen her coming out of the men's room?

She was filled with terrors, imagining possible disasters that demanded her attention right now. She was going to have to walk past the bar. Who had put the poster in the bathrooms? The bartender, or a waitress, or that creepy man at the end of the bar who was at least forty, too old to be anything but the owner. She couldn't let them see her face, but she couldn't look in the direction of the girl who had followed her up the corridor either. At least the girl had not seen the poster. No, that was too easy. Who was to say this was her first trip to the ladies' room? If she had been in there before she would have seen it, and now she would know it had been ripped down.

Judith came to the end of the corridor. She hurried past the bar and headed toward the table where Greg waited for her, looking pleased to see her. His happiness was an unwelcome reminder that she had been happy too, five minutes ago. Now his presence was jarring, something she had forgotten about but had to tolerate. As she approached she planned her words. It had to be better than "Let's go." She didn't want to open a discussion, and couldn't afford one. She would say something that had a finality. "I need to go home right now." Something like that should do it.

She saw that while she was gone he had ordered new drinks. He was sipping a scotch and water, and there was a fresh martini sitting next to the one she had not finished. It was irritating. How could he be so insensitive? A woman her size shouldn't try to drink that much at any time, and tonight it was dangerous.

She said, "I need to go now."

"What?" He put his drink down and moved his chair aside to make room for her to sit.

"I want to leave right now." She picked up her coat from the empty chair, then the umbrella.

"Are you sick? Did something happen?"

He looked so pained, so stupid and slow, that she felt herself lose her feeling for him. He might be clever about business, but he had no instinct, no intuition. If he kept that concerned expression, he was going to be noticed. He looked like a big, foolish hoofed animal, ready to join a stampede, so she started one. She took a step toward the door.

"Wait. I've got to pay first." He picked up the check, took

out his wallet, selected a credit card, and tried to get the waitress's attention.

Judith snatched the check from his fingers, already reaching into the side pocket of her purse. She pulled out three twenties, set the bill and the money on the table, and kept going. At the door she slowed for a second and his long arm came over her shoulder to push the door open ahead of her. She was out.

"What is it, Judy?"

"I had to get out of there. I've had enough of that place." She was calmer now that she was out in the night. The beautiful darkness made her feel anonymous again.

"Did something scare you?"

"Of course not." She waited until he wasn't staring at her anymore, then glanced up at him.

He was gazing straight ahead up the sidewalk, his jaw muscles tightening and relaxing rhythmically. "Then what was the hurry?"

"I just had a bad feeling in there." She watched him. "I wanted to go there in the first place because it was where I met you and it was a really happy memory for me. But after we were there, it wasn't the way I remembered it at all."

His face turned down toward her, and she detected that his expression was false. Was it condescension, trying to pretend to take her seriously when he thought she was stupid? Maybe what he was feigning was any interest at all in what she said. Some men would patiently listen to all of the drivel a woman could say, biding their time until the woman seemed to wear herself out, free herself of nervous energy, and be receptive to sex. Was he hiding something worse?

Her heart stopped, then started again. How could she have forgotten? He had been in the men's room. He had gone in there right after they had arrived from the Mine. He had ordered their drinks, then gone into the men's room. He had come back quickly, before the drinks arrived. The waitress had accepted a tip, but begun to run a tab for the cost of the drinks. Judith tried to sort out the details, hoping to bring back a clear image of Greg's face when he had returned. Had he been concerned? Shocked? She tried to think clearly, but

the two martinis were making her brain slow and unrespon-
sive. Even the count was wrong, she thought. She had forgotten that at dinner she and Greg had both ordered wine.
Damn.

She forced herself to concentrate. He had gone into the
men's room. There was no absolute proof that he had seen
the pictures near the mirror and read the things that Catherine Hobbes had written about her. It was possible that Greg
had glanced at the reams of garish nonsense plastered over
the walls and seen none of it. Men stood to pee, so he wasn't
even facing the poster most of the time; he was looking at the
other wall, or maybe down at what he was doing. But how
could he not have seen the poster right next to the mirror?
Maybe his pitted complexion made him behave differently.
Maybe he was obsessed with staring at his own reflection
and didn't see things like the poster, or maybe he hated the
sight of his face so much that he avoided looking at mirrors.

She held him in the corner of her eye as she walked. "I
should have known not to go back to a place like that. It was
a nice memory, and I shouldn't have tampered with it."

"What was the problem?"

"It was just an impression. That creepy older guy at the bar
kept staring at me. Then I went to the ladies' room, and there
were these skanky girls ahead of me, waiting. And then I
thought maybe I was kidding myself. The last time I had
been in there, I was the one who picked up a guy. Then I had
sex with him on the first date. I wanted to remember the
place as romantic, but tonight the whole mess was—I don't
know—depressing."

"Then I guess it was a good time not to be there." They
reached his car, and he opened the door for her.

"Do you mind leaving?"

"Not at all," he said. "Where do you want to go next—
home?"

She reacted quickly, instinctively, and said, "Your place. I
want to go with you," and only then asked herself why. She
realized it was because she had to stay with him, to watch
him for signs. If he went off alone, she would lose control
over him. She didn't know if he had seen the poster, but if he

had, then leaving him alone to think about it would be a bad idea. She could imagine him spending some time trying to decide, then making the call: "I think the person you're looking for might be my girlfriend."

They got into the car and Greg pulled out onto the street. "My place? That's great. Of course, if I'd known you were coming, I would have cleaned up a little. You'll have to be tolerant."

"I'm reasonably tolerant. But if I find a girl in the bed eating potato chips and waiting for you to get home, we might have something to talk about."

"Nope. No potato chips."

"Then we're fine." She had been watching him, and she was almost certain that they really were fine. He wasn't a good enough actor to lie to her about anything this important, and she didn't think he had the audacity to try. He seemed perfectly normal now that she had told him why she had wanted to leave Underground. He had not seen the poster in the men's room; if he had, he had simply let his eyes pass over it without having anything register in his mind. If he had actually recognized her and read the text, what he would have done was lead her outside the bar, and say something stupid very slowly. He would say it staring straight into her eyes, holding her shoulders so she couldn't look away, talking with that maddening ponderous slowness that dumb men used when they were being serious. He would make some promise to stand by her.

What he wouldn't know, because people like him never seemed to know it until it was too late, was that his standing by her now was worth nothing. It was holding her hand while a tidal wave approached, its frothy top rising to a crest a hundred feet above them, bearing things like the hulls of ships and the splintered timbers of wharfs aloft for an awful final second.

One of her mother's boyfriends had been like that. His name was Michael. He had watched Charlene endure her mother's shrieking fits and whimsical punishments, and had tried to befriend her. He had said, "If you'd like to talk about it, I'm here for you." Charlene had been about ten, so she had taken him seriously. No grown man had ever offered her anything before, so she had assumed he meant he would hear what her problem was and then solve it. But he had only meant what he had said. He would listen to her for a while, then shake his head and say, "That's too bad." He had never intended to imply that he would, or could, make her mother stop.

Greg would be like the rest. The way she would learn he had found out about her troubles was if he told her he was here for her. It would mean he was here to shake his head in sympathy while she got crushed and ground up by Catherine Hobbes and the cops.

She gave herself more time to make up her mind about Greg. He was a gentle, affectionate person, and he had not seen the pictures yet. It occurred to her that she should appreciate his plight, because he was living in the perfect, fragile moment, just as she was. But he was going to know eventually. He lived in Portland, went to an office every day, talked to people, shopped, watched television, read the papers. The only reason he didn't know already was that Judith had been taking up so much of his time. He and his friends all worked sixty hours a week, and every second that wasn't occupied with work, Judith had claimed. She had made him come to her straight from work, and today she had not let him go to work at all.

Judith had kept him in an artificial vacuum with her, where no information had reached him. But as each hour went by, the barrier that had kept out the news became more brittle. He would have to go to work. He would have to open his newspaper, turn on his television. She couldn't save him forever. How long, then? If she tried hard, she might be able to preserve him until tomorrow morning. That was all.

She stared out the window of the car, watching the people on the street through the streaks of water. She wondered about them. If her picture had been in Underground, it had probably been in other nearby places. These people had seen her picture, and a lot of them had read all of the things that horrible Catherine Hobbes had written about her. Were they thinking about her right now, or had they just acknowledged that there was a poster—what was it this time, a missing woman or a woman who had taken off with her own child?—and gone on with their lives? She couldn't know. They were all potentially dangerous, all threatening to Judith. If they saw her face now, their knowledge might kill her.

She watched Greg, saw his eyes moving in their sockets, focusing on cars slowing ahead, cars rushing past him, the mirrors, the road. He was going to see the poster. He was going to recognize the pictures. He was going to be a problem. "You know, Greg, I think I haven't been as open with you as I should have been."

"Yeah?" He looked at her in horror. It probably sounded to him like the preamble to a breakup speech.

She was beginning to hate him. "I'm in love with you," she said.

He glanced at the road, then turned toward her and said, "I've been thinking that for a long time. I wanted to tell you."

"Why didn't you?"

"I was afraid it would seem too pushy, and turn you off."

Afraid, she thought. It was pathetic. He was so big and muscular. His flat, hard stomach and his thick hands and his success in business didn't seem to help him. He couldn't face the risk that if he dropped his protective timidity, he would find himself alone. "I'm not turned off. I think it's sweet."

"I should have said it first," he said. "I wanted to, but I thought I should wait a long time so you wouldn't think I was rushing you, or that it was too soon for me to love you."

"It's okay," said Judith. "Maybe I said more than I should have because we had such a beautiful day, or because the martinis loosened my tongue. But I'm glad I did."

"Me too."

Of course he would say "Me too." It was absolutely inevitable. Imagining him not saying it was like imagining him drumming only three fingers and keeping the fourth from tapping.

Judith let him drive to his apartment. She had been there only twice before, both times late at night like this, when they had been out all evening and his place was closer than hers.

He lived on the top floor of a commercial building on Northwest Vaughn in a space like an artist's loft that had high ceilings with steel girders and big south-facing windows. Since he wasn't an artist, he was freed of the responsibility to be tasteful. He had a basketball backboard and hoop at one end of the room, and at the other a treadmill, weights, and exercise equipment. The pictures on the walls were mostly advertisements that relied on near-naked girls in odd places. Two that were astride motorcycles. One, wearing an open blouse with the sleeves rolled up and short cutoff jeans, held a chain saw. Several others draped themselves like cats on the hoods and roofs of shiny new cars. He had a work area set up on a twelve-foot table, divided between computer equipment and piles of papers, schematics, and mechanical drawings. Behind a partition was a king-sized bed with a bedspread made of the fake fur of a bearlike animal.

Tonight the loft was in the usual state of disarray. Magazines, books, socks, papers, sweatshirts all mingled in a circular pile around the overflowing laundry basket. In the part of the big room that was supposed to be the kitchen, the counter held two-day-old dirty dishes, a few beer cans, and a bowl half full of soggy popcorn.

She watched Greg go to the end of the apartment and disappear into the bathroom. She wandered in the empty space and looked at it in new ways. She had removed all but a tiny residue of uncertainty about Greg, but there was still that last layer, so she stepped close to put her ear to the door of the bathroom to be sure he wasn't talking on a cell phone. There was no voice, so she returned to her study of the apartment.

Greg came out, tossed his wallet and keys on the long counter near where she'd left her purse, and began to make drinks.

"Don't make one for me," said Judith.

"Are you sure?"

"Yes. I'm tipsy enough already. Any worse and you won't be able to wake me up to take advantage of me." She watched his face as she talked, and she could see that he was happy, amused, but also calm and contented. He assumed that she cared for him sincerely—that maybe she really did love him.

He came to her, held her hand and gave her a very soft, gentle kiss on the cheek, then kissed down to her neck, where it tickled. She liked it, and she knew that she was going to miss him. When she thought about Greg, she felt flattered, but she also felt the same surprised, distant curiosity she felt about dogs. He really seemed to love her in the same way dogs did, wildly out of proportion to the near indifference she felt for him. He always seemed to be quivering all over the way they did, wanting to dance around with joy. It must be wonderful to feel that joy.

Greg walked her toward the screened enclosure of his bedroom, and kissed her again. She glanced at the bed. "My turn to use the bathroom. You see if you can make that mess look romantic, like someplace a girl would willingly go." He released her and watched her walk off.

She stood in the bathroom, looking at her face in the mirror. There was a ringing in her ears from the alcohol in her system, and her brain felt sluggish. The remnants of the smile she had forced for Greg were still there, making her facial muscles feel tired. She regretted the martinis again. Was she thinking clearly enough for this? There were so many details to consider, and she had to think of all of them right now. She had no choice. Tonight was the only night.

So far tonight she had touched nothing but the doorknob. Had she ever left any prints in this loft? Maybe she had, weeks ago, and Greg certainly would not have cleaned anything. Did Greg have any photographs of her? No. He had once said he would like to have one for his desk, but she had made an excuse and he had forgotten to ask again. Was there anyone who had seen them together? Thousands of people probably had, but they were all strangers, just the undifferentiated mix of people sitting in restaurants or theaters and walking down streets where she and Greg had been. She had resisted meeting any of his friends from work.

Poor Greg. He had not known what he was getting into. If he had been stronger, smarter, maybe she could have taken a chance on him. But now, it was already after midnight. In a few hours he was sure to go to work, to read a newspaper, to turn on a television set, to talk to people. Judith had to stop him. She had to keep Greg in his current state forever—it was like a snapshot. There would be a flash and he would freeze—ignorant, trusting, and happy.

She looked into the mirror and fixed the smile on her face. She opened the door, walked out into the loft, picked up her purse. As she came around the partition she saw that Greg was already in bed, under the sheet, with the bedspread folded down to the foot of the bed. She set the purse on the floor by the near side of the bed, lowered the lights, took off her clothes, and laid them out neatly on the chair. It gave Greg a long time to watch her doing it, and she knew he enjoyed that.

She went to his coat rack, took a scarf, crawled onto the bed, and slipped it under his head.

"What's that? What are you doing?"

"It's a blindfold. I'm blindfolding you. Don't struggle." She finished tying it and straddled his body.

"Is this an execution?"

She was taken aback for a half second. "It's something nice. Don't peek or you'll spoil it."

Judith reached into her purse and took out the gun. She drew the end of the soft, fake-fur bedspread toward her and wrapped it around the gun, held it there with her left hand, and pressed it gently to his head. When he felt the soft, smooth fur touch him, he smiled.

52

     Catherine Hobbes examined the blood-spattered screen beside Gregory McDonald's bed. The coroner's crew had taken his body out earlier, but this space was going to be the property of the visiting blood-spatter expert for a day or two, so Catherine had to stay back and look in from the opening at the side. She didn't need to be any closer. Catherine Hobbes, or any other experienced homicide detective, could stand at the end of the screen and see what had happened.

    Gregory McDonald had apparently been blindfolded with a scarf. The killer had wrapped the gun in the bedspread, held it to the left side of Gregory McDonald's head, and pulled the trigger. The blood had sprayed mostly from the exit wound on the right side of the head, and the blowback spatter had been taken mostly by the bedspread, but the killer had almost certainly been bloodied too. The upper end of the bed and the pillow under the victim's head had been soaked. Just from a glance at the bathroom, it looked to Catherine as though the killer had needed to clean up before leaving.

    Catherine stepped away and surveyed the loft. What she could see made the murder seem even worse, more wasteful. Gregory McDonald had been a well-paid software designer with an engineering degree, but the loft was decorated in fraternity-boy baroque, complete with a basketball net and a few empty beer cans. He had not had time to reach anything she would have recognized as adulthood.

As Catherine thought about the simple, unembellished facts—a single man found naked in bed shot once through the head, but no gun at the scene, and a killer who had cleaned up afterward—she began to have a sinking feeling.

Her cell phone rang, and she took it out of her purse. "Catherine Hobbes."

"Hey, Cath." It was the captain. "I'm moving my knights around on the board. Where are you?"

"Gregory McDonald's loft. Where do you want me?"

"You may as well stay there. This one is going to be yours too. One of the prints the forensic people lifted off the tile in the shower belongs to your girl."

"I was afraid of that." Instantly she wished she hadn't said that. The captain didn't need to be reminded that she had predicted this. He had given her as many people as he could spare to canvass the area where Tanya had used the credit card. She had to think ahead, not back. "Captain, I wonder if we could delay releasing the news about the fingerprint for a day or two."

"Why? Do you think if she hears it, she'll take off again?"

"I'm not sure, but it's a distinct possibility. I'm sure that she watches the television news."

"All right. Let's keep the print out of the press for the moment."

"Thanks."

She heard him disconnect, so she folded her phone and put it away. She raised her voice so all of the officers in the loft could hear her. "Attention, everybody. One of the prints on the shower tile has turned out to be a match for Tanya Starling. That is not to be released to the press for the moment. We've got a female perpetrator who sometimes dyes her hair. The minute you find hairs that don't match the victim, please find me or call me. I need to know what color Tanya's hair is this week."

She walked to the door of the bathroom and looked inside. The tiled walls, the sink, and the mirror were almost completely blackened with print dust. The crime scene people loved mirrors and tiles. Anything that got cleaned frequently and was smooth and glassy was made for preserving clear prints.

Catherine stood still and imagined the scene, putting herself in Tanya's place. Tanya had been in the bedroom area with Gregory McDonald. He had been naked, and so she had been too, probably. She had blindfolded him in some playful way. But she had done it because she had needed to have him lying still and not fighting her for the gun or ducking behind things. She had wrapped the bedspread around the gun to muffle the sound and then pulled the trigger.

The sound had not been as quiet as she had hoped. The gun must have sounded like a cannon in this loft. Catherine could almost hear the blast in her imagination.

Catherine imagined she felt the gun kick upward, heard the ringing in her ears. The bedspread had not muffled the sound. Tanya was afraid, and Gregory looked terrible now. She placed the pillow over what had been his face. She became conscious of her nakedness and felt vulnerable; the blood spattered on her was warm, almost hot, and the feel of it made her sick. She didn't know what to do. She wanted to put on her clothes and run, but she had Gregory McDonald's blood on her—on her face, in her hair, on her chest, her belly. She had been beside him, or maybe above him, straddling him, and now she rolled off the bed and crouched, the gun aimed at the door of the loft.

She stayed there for a long time, listening. Maybe it was ten minutes, maybe only five minutes, but it seemed to her to be much longer. She was waiting for a sound that would indicate that someone had heard. Cautiously she moved in the dark to the window and looked down at the street. Probably she knew that if a neighbor were coming to investigate, he would already have banged on the door. If the Portland Police Bureau had been called, their response time would not be this long. She reassured herself, because she knew the secret of shots fired in a city. When people heard one shot they told themselves it was a car backfiring or a firecracker. It was only when they heard multiple shots that they couldn't tell themselves that it was something harmless.

She went into the bathroom and looked at herself in the mirror. She was freckled with Gregory's blood, and she had to get it off. She turned on the shower, adjusted it to a bearable temperature, and stepped into it. She scrubbed herself, washing her hair and her skin, then stayed in the shower for a long time, being sure that the bright red blood was off her and the pink diluted remnant had long since washed off the tub. Maybe she was even aware that firing a pistol had left a residue of burned powder and heavy metals on her skin, so she scrubbed harder. She came out and dried herself with the cleanest towel she could find, then wiped the floor with it and the faucets and anything else she could remember touching. The one place that she missed was where she had touched one of the shower tiles and forgotten it: had she lost her balance for a second while she was getting out, or leaned against it to dry her foot? She took the towel back to his bedroom enclosure, stuffed it in the laundry basket beneath his clothes, or maybe tossed it in and then picked up some clothes from the floor and threw them in to cover the towel she had used.

Then she got dressed. If the gun was a revolver, she put it in her purse. If it was semiautomatic, she found the shell casing and put it in her purse with the gun. She went to the front windows again and looked outside to be sure the police were not visible in the streets below the building. Since they weren't, she explored the loft, probably with a flashlight. She was looking for money, or jewelry, or anything else that might be valuable. She took some time looking around, probably using something like one of Gregory's socks over her hand to open drawers. She bothered to do it not because she was desperate for money but because there was no reason not to, and the sound of a gun should not be followed by the sounds of someone leaving the building until a long time had passed.

Catherine knew that Tanya had learned that by now—that one reason people got caught was that they did not take time to think and prepare and act normally. They ran and they sweated and they looked suspicious. When she felt ready, she glanced outside once more, took Gregory McDonald's car keys, went down the stairs, and drove his car away. It had not turned up yet, but Catherine was sure it would later in the day, parked at a shopping mall or an airport or a public parking lot.

Catherine walked away from the bathroom and up to two of the forensic people who were dusting the long counter by the window. "If nobody's done it yet, I'd like somebody to take out the trap in the shower drain to check for her hairs. I'm almost certain the reason she touched a tile was that she took a shower after she killed him. Another good place to look is in his laundry basket. There should be a damp towel about halfway down."

Catherine walked down the stairs, not touching the railings, and stepped outside the building to look up at the windows of Gregory McDonald's loft. Nobody could have seen anything from down here, and the buildings across the street were lower. They seemed to still be used for some industrial purpose, not yet part of the gentrification that was gripping the neighborhood, but she would find out who occupied them and ask.

She hesitated for a moment, then took out her cell phone and dialed a Los Angeles number.

A woman who sounded younger than she was answered, "Pitt Investigations. May we help you?"

Catherine said, "This is Catherine Hobbes. Is Joe in?"

"No, I'm sorry. He's out right now, but I'll transfer your call to his cell phone."

"You don't have to do that," said Catherine.

"Yes, I do," said the young woman. Catherine thought she heard amusement in her voice. "He told us all that if he misses a call from you, then whoever dropped it is in trouble. Please hold for a moment."

After a few seconds she heard Joe's voice. "Catherine?"

"Yes," she said. "It's only me. Do you really threaten your employees?"

"Sure. Don't you?"

"I don't have any. I just called to give you more bad news. Tanya has done it again. I don't know why I'm bothering you with it, but I felt as though you had earned a right to a share of the misery."

"Who was it?"

"A young guy named Gregory McDonald. He was some kind of software engineer. He was shot in the head while he was in bed with her in his loft."

"So it's like some of the others—Dennis Poole and the guy in the hotel down here."

"That's what I've been thinking. I'm not sure yet if it was a one-night thing or a bad end to a relationship. I just got word a few minutes ago that one of the prints in the loft belonged to Tanya, so I'm just getting started. Nobody has checked yet to find out whether they were seen together, and so on."

"Would you mind if I flew up there tonight or tomorrow to take a look around?"

"Yes," she said. "I definitely would mind. This is my case, and my job, and you're the biggest distraction in the world. I've got to follow up the leads now, and then maybe later I'll talk to you about what it all means."

"It means she's still there," said Joe. "Be thorough, and be careful. I love you."

She said, "Why do you do that?"

"What?"

"Say 'I love you' when I'm just about to hang up. I could listen to you until my ears dropped off, but you never say it except at a crummy time like this."

"I don't think that's true. Is it?"

"Yes, Joe. It's true. The first time, I thought it was a bad cell phone connection. Now, is it just a figure of speech, like 'Take care,' or are you actually telling me that you love me?"

"I'm actually saying that I love you. I'll say it again. I love you."

"That's good," she said. "Because I love you too. Now I can hang up and have about a second of intense happiness before I go off to the coroner's and look at the young guy with the bullet hole in his head. Bye." She pressed the end button, put her cell phone in her purse, and got into her car, thinking about Joe Pitt.

As she drove toward the coroner's office, she prepared herself for the sight that she knew awaited her. Head shots were horrible, but she had to look at everything that Tanya had done or touched or left. Maybe this time Tanya had acted carelessly. Maybe this time she had forgotten to eradicate some detail that would tell Catherine where to find her.

53

Judith had stayed in bed almost all day. She slept for nearly twelve hours during the first stretch, letting the exhaustion keep her unconscious and the time pass so the sights and sounds would not be so clear and sharp in her memory. When she awoke she lay in bed thinking and remembering, but what she thought about was not last night. Once an unpleasant decision had been made, there was no reason to go over and over it.

What she thought about was that nothing ever seemed to work out for her. It never had, and it was because there was always somebody who didn't want her to be happy. The very odd thing was that the people who really wanted to hurt her were always other women.

Judith didn't expect much of men. They were indifferent and thoughtless. They were insensitive and selfish. A few even had some sexual issue, some program running in their heads that made them behave a certain way, and want her to behave in a certain, exactly complementary way. In fact there was a little of that in all of them—they thought about sex all the time, and every dealing with them had that as a part of it. Even if it was wildly impractical or even impossible for them to have sex with a particular woman, they wondered about her. All of those things were part of the world that was known. Nobody was hiding any of it.

Women had a lot of reasons to be on the same side, but they never seemed to be. They always seemed to be competing. In her life, men had been difficult or disappointing, but the people who had been real tormentors had all been female. Her mother had been the first.

Sharon Buckner had never been able to pull herself together and move to Chicago or Milwaukee to get a serious job. Every night from the time when she was about sixteen, she had managed to get dressed up and transported to one of those same big cities to dance and drink and have fun, but the idea of going there to work was too far-fetched for her.

Charlene had been about ten before she had learned where the name Charlene had come from. By then Charles Kepler had married and left town—been shamed out of town, Sharon Buckner said—but the rest of the townspeople had not left. That day Charlene had realized that since her birth, all of the adults around her—the neighbors, her teachers—had been looking at her and knowing the most private aspects of her life.

When Charlene was little and first went on the pageant circuit, Charlene's cuteness drew attention to Sharon. She got to be the pretty young mother of the pretty little girl. But when Charlene was in junior high school, the situation changed. Now the girls in the pageant were thirteen to seventeen. Charlene won Miss Junior Hogan County and Miss Junior Carroway County, both on false addresses, and finally Miss Junior Central Illinois. But her mother's pleasure wore out.

They were both ten years older by then, and the years looked better on Charlene than on Sharon. She was the one who got the attention; she was Sharon's competition, her enemy. Her mother began to make disparaging remarks about Charlene's weight, her hair, her complexion, her performances. She began to mock the answers Charlene gave to the emcee's questions. Charlene knew they were good, because there were only about twenty-five questions that all emcees always asked, and she had memorized the best answers of the winners over the years.

Charlene had to drop out of the pageants at the age of fifteen because her mother refused to enter her anymore. She was glad that she would no longer be forced into hours of close proximity to her mother, but it made her feel more vulnerable to the horrible girls at school. She no longer had the secret life where she got to wear fancy formal dresses—and, most of the time, a crown. When that world was gone, she had nothing.

The girls at school had always been cold and unfriendly, but beginning in junior high they were actively cruel. Anytime she talked to a girl she was told she was obnoxious and pushy. When she talked to a boy she was a whore. When she didn't talk she was a stuck-up bitch. When she did well on a test she was showing off and sucking up to the teachers. She ate lunch alone, walked from class to class alone.

As she thought about it today, she decided that if she had the leisure sometime, she would take a drive up to Illinois and see if she could find a few of those girls. By now Gail Halpren would be married and have a couple of kids. Judith would walk up to the house and knock on the door. It would open. She would say, "Remember me? I used to be Charlene Buckner. I thought you deserved to be thanked for the way you treated me in high school." Then she would pull out the gun. Or she would find Terry Nugent. Terry would probably be in Chicago, working as a lawyer or a stockbroker. She would wait for her in a parking garage. "Aren't you Terry Nugent, from Wheatfield? Yes, it's me. But let's not talk about those days now. We can talk about them forever in hell." Pow.

After she moved in with Carl, the other women were the wives and girlfriends of important men. None of them had liked her, but now the reasons were clearer. The parties in that social set had been beauty pageants too—women parading stiffly around with fake immovable smiles and wide, scared eyes. She had been more convincing at it than they were, and so they'd hated her.

Now the police were hunting for her, and the one who was

causing it was another woman. She hated Catherine Hobbes, but she knew that part of her hatred was just outrage at the unevenness of the competition. Catherine Hobbes had the right look, very erect and tailored. She had a cool, imperturbable demeanor that made her seem wise and knowing. And behind her was all that power.

Judith got up from the bed, looked out the window at the clear day, went into the bathroom to shower, then came out and dressed. She wore a smart skirt and sweater as though she were going to work in an office somewhere, but she put Tyler Gilman's old baseball cap and his jacket into her backpack and took them with her to the car.

She wished she knew whether the police had found Greg by now. She supposed she could find out if they had by driving past his apartment and looking for their cars, but she didn't want to go there. She didn't know whether the police believed that old adage about killers returning to the scene of the crime. If they believed it, they would be watching for her.

She drove north and east across the Broadway Bridge, toward the police bureau on North Thompson Street. She found a parking space for her Acura on North Tillamook and walked around the block. As she approached the building, she tried to take in everything about it. She saw a number of cars, some of them police cars, coming and going from the lot beside the building. It was a busy place, and she was not the only pedestrian. She had noticed other times that the people who came and went from police stations always looked hurried and preoccupied, never happy. This afternoon, none of them seemed to have much curiosity about anyone else.

Long before she reached the building, she saw what she had been looking for: beneath the building was an entrance ramp. She guessed that there must be some kind of underground garage where the police parked their personal cars. She walked past the entrance, looked inside, and made a decision.

She followed the ramp down into the lower level. The cars here had to be the ones that belonged to the cops, but as soon as she was there, she began to lose hope of figuring anything out. There were so many cars, and she'd begun with only a theory about Catherine Hobbes to help her.

She had believed that Catherine Hobbes was so sure of herself and of her tastes that she would have replaced the car she had lost in the fire with one exactly like it: the car would be a new teal blue Acura, paid for by her fire insurance.

Judith walked purposefully between two rows of cars, looking hard at them, but she saw no Acura, and no teal blue cars of any brand. She reminded herself that it was always possible that Catherine wasn't at work today, or that she had parked on some nearby street as Judith had, or that she was out right now using her own car instead of a police car. All of those things were possible, but possible wasn't the same as likely.

Judith kept looking, walked to the end of the aisle, then turned up the next aisle and headed back. She sensed that she had spent all the time she could down here. She heard a sound, and looked up to see a male driver in a Ford Explorer come down the ramp and turn into an empty space. He was obviously a cop—short-haired and beefy with a mustache— and he was in a hurry. He stepped down from the driver's seat, reached back into the vehicle to take out a hard-sided briefcase and a jacket, and looked at Judith.

"Can I help you find something?" He was like all cops. He was trying not to look suspicious, and he had no reason to be suspicious, but he couldn't help it. She could tell, however, that he had the wrong crime in mind. He didn't recognize her. Maybe he would recognize her later, when she was long gone.

She said, "This is the police station, isn't it?"

"Yes, it is. But you can't park down here. You have to go up to the ground level and come in that way. There's visitor parking up there."

"Thanks. I parked on the street," she said. She kept walking, her heart beginning to beat hard only after the danger was over. She was nearly to the ramp before she realized that she might have seen the car while he was talking. There was a gray Dodge Neon with a license-plate holder from Enterprise Rent-a-Car on it. Catherine might not have replaced her

car yet. She might still be driving a rental. Judith knew she
couldn't go back and look at it more closely. She came up out
of the parking area and headed for the front door of the station, then at the last moment went past it and walked quickly
up the street.

She reached her car and drove off. She came back to North
Thompson Street at five and parked where she could watch
the driveway from a distance. She saw a steady stream of cars
come out just after six, but Catherine's car was not among
them. Judith judged that the shift had probably changed, but
Catherine was Detective Sergeant Hobbes. She didn't have
to keep the same hours as the traffic cops. She saw another
group go at eight, and a third at ten, but she didn't see the
small gray Dodge Neon.

She conceded that she could have guessed wrong. Maybe
the rental car wasn't Catherine's. Some other cop could have
his car in the shop for repairs and be driving the rental until
it was ready. She might be wasting her evening. She was getting bored and hungry, and she needed to use a restroom. She
started her car and angled the wheels away from the curb.
As she prepared to move up the street, away from the police
bureau, she glanced in the mirror to be sure the street was
clear. The Dodge Neon was moving up the ramp and turning
toward her.

Judith waited and let the Neon go by. She could see that
the driver was a woman, and the woman seemed to have the
right kind of hair, but the face was in darkness. Judith gave
the Neon a head start, then pulled out after it. She followed
at a distance, waiting for a few seconds before she made the
right turn to follow it onto North Tillamook, then waited
until two other cars had gone by before she made the second
right up North Interstate Avenue.

Judith followed as the car made another right turn onto
Northeast Russell Street. She managed to keep one of the two
cars between her car and the Neon as they drove past the big
hospital on the left side of Northeast Russell. Then the Neon
signaled for a left turn. Judith went past on the right slowly,
studying the driver, and saw that it was Catherine Hobbes.
Judith went down the street for a block, and watched the car in

the mirror as it turned into the driveway beside a modern brick apartment building.

As soon as the car was out of sight behind the building, Judith turned around, came back, and parked where she could watch the windows. But as she watched, Judith saw two women in scrubs walking from the direction of the hospital turn up the sidewalk toward the front steps. One of the women was fishing in her purse. She pulled out a set of keys. But before she could use them, a young man in a similar hospital uniform appeared in the lobby, came out, and held the door while they went in, then released it and headed for the hospital.

Judith saw Catherine come up from a set of stairs into the lighted hallway, apparently having come in from the back of the building. She walked past the elevator and stepped into the stairwell.

Judith got out of her car and walked closer, watching the side of the apartment building. After a few moments the lights in a row of third-floor windows came on.

54

The next evening, Catherine drove up Adair Hill and parked her rental car across the street from her parents' house. She walked up the porch steps and tried the knob. It was locked. She had been hoping it would be, but she couldn't help feeling a cold, sad sensation as she took out her key and opened the door.

"Hello?" she called. "Anybody home?"

"Where would we be?" It was her father. He came around the corner from the kitchen and let her kiss him on the cheek.

"I don't know," she said. "You're old enough to make your own decisions, and to live with the consequences."

"Thank you, dear," her mother called from the kitchen. "Nice of you to come by. Did they close the police bureau and kick you out?"

"No, I left voluntarily." She came into the kitchen, followed by her father. She kissed her mother, once again surprised by the incredible softness that her mother's cheek had developed in the past few years, and savoring the faint scent of gardenia soap she had smelled since childhood.

Catherine sat at the kitchen table and accepted the cup of coffee her father set in front of her. He sat down with a glass of water and eyed her as he would a suspect. "Hard day, kid?"

She shrugged. "I don't know anymore. Since we found that guy yesterday and Tanya's fingerprint in his shower, nothing much else has turned up. Maybe that's good. We're not up to our armpits in new bodies. But it doesn't feel like we're winning."

"It never does until it's over," said her father. "I was betting she would be recognized by now, though."

Catherine's mother seemed to be more and more agitated as her husband and daughter talked. She said, "How about your life outside of work? Anything interesting happening?"

"Not that I've noticed. I seem to be the same bitter divorcée I've been for years."

"We haven't seen you much. Has Joe Pitt been around?"

Catherine's father seemed to remember something else he had to do. He took his glass of water with him to another room.

"A couple of weeks ago. He's back in Los Angeles doing his own cases. We call each other a lot."

"What do you talk about?"

"Meaning what?"

"Oh, I don't know. I think I mean, are you serious about him?"

"Or is he serious about me."

"Both ways."

"Headline: Mother Wants Daughter to Settle Down."

"Or not," said Martha Hobbes. "Maybe you're getting too settled as it is. Is being a cop all you ever want to do?"

"Is that such an odd idea?"

"It's a big joke on me, I can tell you. I spent twenty-five years waiting for your father to get to retirement age without any holes in him. And now I worry about you. Marriage might not be so bad compared to having murderers burning your house down around your ears."

"I was married, remember? That's how I realized I should be a detective. I detected that my husband was screwing everybody he could reach."

Her mother stared at her. "Is that funny to you?"

"Funnier than it used to be," said Catherine. "Believe me, I've come a long way toward your way of thinking in the past few weeks."

"You mean you really are serious about him?"

"Yes, I'm very serious. But I'm not making plans for any weddings. I wasn't going to go out with him at all until I purposely forgot everything my mother had told me about men."

"He lives in Los Angeles, doesn't he? What would you do if he asked you to move there?"

"He hasn't."

"That doesn't mean you have to put off thinking about it until he does."

"I don't get it. Have you decided you want me to move to L.A., or that you don't want me to?"

"I want you to be happy."

"Good. I'm happy."

"I mean really happy."

"Mother, make yourself happy. Make Daddy happy. I'm not in a position to be 'really happy' right now. I have a reasonable facsimile of a boyfriend. We're seeing where it goes, but at the moment it's not going anywhere. Long-distance relationships are everything they're cracked up to be, which is horrible. We tell jokes and say 'I miss you.' Half the time when I talk to him I'm sure he's watching some game on television with the sound off."

"There. Was that so hard?"

"What?"

"Telling me what I asked you in the first place."

Catherine closed her eyes and took two deep breaths, then opened them again. "No, I guess it wasn't."

Her father came in, carrying a newspaper. "Have you tried the emergency rooms?"

"Huh?"

"She killed this big fellow, right? Sometimes while they're killing somebody, they get hurt. Wood or glass chips fly, people you think are dead aren't. She could be hurt."

"She's not. This one was blindfolded, lying naked in bed. All the blood in the apartment is his."

"Oh," he said. "How about parking tickets? I picked up a few suspects by seeing what cars got ticketed near the scene. There's a description of the car and the license number on the summons."

"Tried it."

"How about security videotapes? That apartment is in a neighborhood that's mostly commercial."

"Tried that too."

"That's my girl." He wandered off again.

Catherine's mother said quietly, "Does he ever make any sense?"

"Always. He's trying to think of a way to shortcut this for me."

"Well, that's a relief," she muttered. "It's hard to tell if you're just humoring him."

"I'm not, but I would."

Her mother put a piece of cherry pie on a plate and set it in front of Catherine. Catherine cut it in half and returned half to the pan without comment. Then she ate the other half and listened to her mother talk about the past few days in the neighborhood.

The stories were a peculiar comfort to Catherine. They calmed her and reassured her that the rhythms of the real world were intact. The sun dried the rain-soaked gardens, the roses bloomed, and Lydia Burns put a letter in a mailbox and accidentally dropped her car keys in with it.

At eleven Catherine went into the living room, where her father was watching the local news. He looked up. "Have you had uniformed officers circulate her picture to the mom-and-pop stores?"

Catherine said, "What am I missing?"

"She's got to buy food and toothpaste somewhere. Supermarkets are full of people standing in line staring at one another, and four or five assistant managers watching customers. Maybe instead, she shops at one of those little stores run by immigrant couples who can't tell one young American woman from another, or are afraid to cause trouble."

"I'll give it a shot. Thanks, Daddy." She kissed his cheek.

He said, "Are you going?"

"Yeah. I've had my free slice of pie, so I guess I'll be on my way."

"I drove by to check out your apartment building."

"And you hated it?"

"I don't work for *Architectural Digest*. I like that it has a locked door with an intercom and a lot of people around. Looks like a lot of doctors."

"They're all interns," she said. "The ones that are old enough to be keepers must all have houses."

"When you park in that lot behind the building, look around before you get out of your car, and then watch your back."

"I always do," she said. "Good night."

"Good night, kid."

She went out and stepped onto the porch. Her eyes took in the configuration of trees and houses that were so familiar to her they were the landscape of her dreams. She could see it was all as it had been for as long as she could remember, and there was no shadow that she had not memorized. She walked toward her car slowly, looking up and down the quiet street.

The day after Tanya had burned her house, Catherine had requested that a plain car be posted a hundred feet below here, on the curve of the road, so that an officer could get a close look at the face of anyone who drove or walked by. After a week there had been no adequate justification for keeping a car any longer. There had been no indication that Tanya had looked for Catherine's parents, but tonight something felt wrong.

She continued her walk to her car, stopped beside it, and reached into her purse, pretending to search for her keys while she watched and listened. There was no unfamiliar sound, no sign that anything was out of place. She stood there a bit longer, waiting, giving Tanya a chance to move. Nothing happened.

Catherine got into the car and started it, then turned on the lights and drove farther up the hill. She turned around in the spot where she would have hidden if she had been Tanya, just on the uphill side of the Tollivers' high hedges. Then she coasted down the road, turning the wheel slightly now and then to shine her headlights on the best hiding spots along the narrow street.

She kept encouraging her mind to feel its discomfort, trying to let it intensify so she could identify what it was. If she had seen something too subtle to interpret, it was gone: no troubling image formed in her memory. As she reached the bottom of the hill and turned left toward the bridge, she realized what it was: timing.

She had listened to the stories of her father and other old cops and had read files from hundreds of cases of serial killers. Serial killers were almost all male, and most of them seemed to be acting out some fantasy that was a mixture of violence and sex. Many appeared to search for a particular kind of victim. Others seemed to be trying to reproduce exactly some scene they had concocted in their imaginations. It was not clear to Catherine what Tanya was doing when she killed someone. It seemed to Catherine that it had something to do with power. Maybe in some part of her past, Tanya had been powerless, and had been harmed or abused in some way. It seemed to Catherine that with the killings she had created a method of making herself safe.

Tanya seemed to be driven by fear. Every time she killed someone she had more to fear, so she had to kill again to feel safe. Whenever Tanya felt she might be losing control, she proved she wasn't by killing somebody. What was bothering Catherine tonight was that she had become accustomed to Tanya's rhythm, and it seemed to Catherine to be time.

She pulled her rental car into the parking lot behind the apartment building, and her father's advice came back to her. She turned the little car in a full circuit of the perimeter, letting the headlights shine on the low brush that came to the edge of the pavement. She selected a space in the middle and got out of her car, her left hand holding her purse and keys, and her right hand free to reach for her sidearm.

Catherine took a last look around her before she unlocked the back entrance of the building, stepped inside, and closed it behind her, listening for the click of the lock. She walked up the hall to the staircase at the front of the building instead of riding up in the elevator. When she was inside her apartment on the third floor she locked the door and flipped the latch across it. Then she headed for the shower.

55

Judith lifted the package off her bed and worked at getting the heavy plastic wrapping off. She went to the kitchen and got a steak knife, then came back and made a slice along the top. The package said, "Hospital Scrubs, size S, OSHA Compliant." She held the pants up in front of the full-length mirror and looked at them critically. Were the legs going to be just a bit long? She had bought the scrubs this afternoon at a uniform store that specialized in medical clothes, and she had not wanted to spend much time shopping or ask any questions.

She had just picked up the package, paid cash for it, and gone. She took off her jeans and T-shirt and put on the scrubs, then stared in the mirror. They felt like starched pajamas, but she liked the way they looked on her. She turned halfway around to look over her shoulder, then kept turning until she was facing forward again. She was very pleased. The only essential part was that the fit be good: no nurse would have scrubs that weren't her size. Judith made a very attractive nurse.

She had chosen the maroon color because she didn't want to be too visible in the dark. Some of the men and women she had seen walking up Russell Street from the hospital wore bright white coats or pants, and when a car came around the corner they seemed to glow in the headlights. The ones who wore dark blue or maroon were almost invisible.

Judith put on the pair of walking shoes she had chosen and checked the pant length again. The pants came right to the top of the shoes and rested there with only a half inch or so of overlap. That was just right. She lifted the loose pullover top and looked at her bare stomach. That was the only place for a gun. The loose top would cover it.

She stared into the mirror. She made a serious face, as though she were a nurse hurrying down a hallway to a patient's room. Then she tried an empty face, and decided that was the right one. She wasn't going to be clapping a defibrillator on somebody's chest. She was just going to be a young woman coming off a long evening shift.

Judith used an elastic band that matched her scrubs to tie her hair in a ponytail, then put on the clear glasses she had bought in the hobby shop. They were for protecting people's eyes when they worked on crafts, but they looked just like regular glasses. She looked smart in them.

She took off her top and picked up the roll of adhesive tape she had bought. She wrapped it around her waist twice, then twice more to hold Mary Tilson's gun so it rode comfortably above the waistband without tugging on her pants. Then she put on her loose top and checked the effect. The gun was invisible.

She put on the hooded waterproof jacket she had bought when she had arrived in Portland, and decided the effect was right. It could rain in Portland at any time, and she had seen that the people she wanted to look like all wore jackets at night.

Judith examined the fabric purse with the long strap that she had carried in Denver, and tried it with her work outfit. She could fit the adhesive tape and the steak knife in it easily.

Judith looked around her small apartment to assess her preparations. She had already packed her suitcase. If she needed to run, she could. The place looked neat, nearly empty, and clean. She carefully folded her jeans and T-shirt, put them in a paper sack, and brought it with her suitcase.

She had a feeling of elation as she stepped out of her apartment and went down the back stairs to the outside. The night was clear and calm, a little like the late nights she had loved when she had been a little girl. There was a silent, private emptiness. There was nothing for a block or two that was moving, and the lights from the big busy streets to the south were blocked by apartment buildings.

She put the suitcase and the clothes in her trunk and started the car. She looked at the clock on the dashboard. It was eleven-fifteen, time to be moving. She let the car drift quietly down the alley behind the building, then accelerated gradually as she moved up the street.

Judith drove across the Broadway Bridge to North Interstate Avenue, then turned onto Northeast Russell. She could see the big shape of Legacy Emanuel Hospital as soon as she made the turn. She pulled over on the street near the east end of it and parked.

Judith looked at the car clock again. It was eleven forty-five. When she had followed Catherine up this street to her apartment building she had noticed that the activity picked up around midnight, which she assumed must be when the hospital shifts changed. She wanted to be ten minutes ahead of the change, so people would be leaving Catherine's build-

ing when she arrived. She got out of the car, put her keys into
the pants pocket of her scrubs, and looped her purse strap
over her shoulder.

She walked up to Catherine's apartment building just as
a young man in green scrubs appeared in the lobby. She
looked down into her purse as he hurried out of the building
past her, but then she lunged ahead, caught the door before it
could swing shut, and stepped inside. Her heart was pounding. She had made it past the first barrier.

But now Judith was in the lighted lobby, where people outside could see her, and anyone who came downstairs to leave
would have to walk right past her. She stepped quickly to the
row of mailboxes and read the Dymo labels stuck above
them. There was one that said HOBBES. It was apartment 3F.

Judith opened the door to the stairwell and began to climb
to the third floor. At least while she climbed, while she was
in the deserted stairwell, nobody was looking at her. But
when she reached the third-floor landing, she became tense
again. She opened the door to the third-floor hallway a crack
and listened. There were no voices, no footsteps, no sounds
that indicated that anyone was awake. Judith moved cautiously into the hallway. She had never been in this building
before, and so she had to think as she walked. She stepped
along the hallway scanning, searching for any opportunity
that would permit her to do what she wanted, and listening
for someone who might stop her. As she came to 3D, she
paused and listened for the sounds of people awake, then
stopped at 3E and did the same, but there was nothing. She
went on more slowly and quietly until she came to 3F.

When she had followed Catherine home last night, she had
seen a whole row of windows light up. Catherine's apartment
had to be big—at least three rooms along the side of the
building, probably with the bedroom in the back, away from
the noise of the street. But Judith couldn't know for sure.
Catherine might be standing right on the other side of that
door. Judith's hand went to her belly, and she felt the hard, reassuring shape of the gun under her shirt. She leaned close
and pressed her ear to the door. Catherine's apartment was
just as quiet as the others.

She prepared herself, then carefully touched the door handle at apartment 3F and tried to turn it, just in case Catherine had forgotten to lock it. The handle didn't budge. She looked closely at the lock on the door. She didn't need to try to slide a credit card between the door and the latch, or try to pry it open with the steak knife. She could see that the hardware was the heavy and expensive kind that was fitted tightly and would be sunk too deep into the receptacle to be opened.

She resumed her walk along the hallway. There was an unmarked door, so she tried it. The door opened. Inside were a set of circuit breakers and a supply of cleansers, carpet cleaners, mops, and rags. She stood with the door open and thought. She could pop the circuit breakers. People would come out of their apartments, and one of them would check the panel and flip the breakers back. But that wouldn't work unless the one who did it was Catherine. If she was asleep, she would never know it had happened. What would rouse her? Pulling a fire alarm would do it, but that would bring firemen and cops. She closed the door to the little room and moved on.

The only barrier that kept Judith away from Catherine was a single wooden apartment door. She had to think of a way to get past that door. Was there a way around it? Was there a way onto the roof? Maybe she could find a rope or make one, tie it to something solid—the central-air-conditioning unit, a pipe—and then lower herself down outside Catherine's window. She could look in and see her lying in her bed asleep. She could stay pressed against the window like a night creature. And then, when she was ready, she could fire through the glass. No. That was far too athletic for Judith—crazy.

She kept going, looking closely at everything she saw. The windows at the ends of the hallways opened, but that didn't seem to her to do any good. She studied the ceilings. They were made of plasterboard. If she'd had a ladder, she could go to the ceiling outside of Catherine's apartment, cut a hole in the plasterboard with her knife, climb up, and carve a hole into the ceiling on Catherine's side so she could climb down.

It was crazier than the first idea: far too loud, and too likely to get her caught.

The doors were beginning to look less substantial. After all, they were made of wood. Maybe, in an hour or two, she could carve a hole through one of them with the knife, reach through it, and turn the handle.

If she had to, she could simply stay here—maybe in the third-floor storage closet across from Catherine's apartment—until dawn. She could wait and watch until Catherine came out. She recognized that as the first sensible strategy that had occurred to her. She had done the hard part, gotten in past the outer doors without being noticed. If she just stayed in the building, her chance would come. She decided to finish her tour of the building before she gave up and hid in the closet.

She reached the stairwell again, went back down to the lobby, and looked at the triple row of mailboxes. If the Dymo labels told her where people lived, then maybe an empty one would tell her which apartments were vacant. If she could find one, maybe she could break into it and wait in safety.

"Is something wrong?" It was a male voice from behind her.

She turned, her body instantly tense and ready to fight. He was in his fifties or sixties and he wore a uniform, but it wasn't medical like hers. He was balding and chubby. He looked like a janitor. She said, "I forgot my keys."

"Your apartment key?"

He didn't seem threatening now, but she knew it was an illusion. She couldn't make a mistake. "Yes. I thought it was in my purse, but here I am, and it's not there. I'm hoping I didn't lose it permanently."

"How did you get into the building at all?"

"As I was coming up the steps somebody else was going out. He held the door for me. I didn't know I didn't have my key until I got up there."

"Do you have your ID?"

"Sure." She was making a plan. It was just a series of pictures in her mind, a flash of images. She would fire, and step around him to go out the front door. She would dash back along Northeast Russell Street to the hospital. If she was being observed, she would go into the building as though she were late for the midnight shift, then come out of the hospital at the parking lot entrance with whatever stragglers were left, make her way to her car, and be gone.

She opened her wallet and held it up so he could see the Catherine Hobbes driver's license and the credit card. She pointed at the mailboxes. "See? That's me—Catherine Hobbes." She let her hand linger near the pistol she had taped to her body.

The man held out his hand. "I'm Dewey. I do the handyman work for these apartments and three others that the company owns."

"Pleased to meet you," said Judith. She managed a sad smile as she shook his hand. "We'll probably see each other a lot while I'm sleeping in the hall."

"Don't worry," said Dewey. "I've got a grand master key for the building. I can let you in."

"You can?" Her eyes widened, and her smile became real and grew. "Oh, that's wonderful. You don't know how awful I felt. Thanks so much."

"Don't mention it. What's the apartment again?"

"Three-F. But there are six or seven interns on my floor, and at least half of them will be trying to sleep off a forty-eight-hour shift. Do you think we'd be quieter if we took the stairs?"

"It's okay," he said. "I've had all kinds of calls to come here in the middle of the night, and the elevator never wakes anybody up. When it's a plumbing thing on an upper floor you've got to get up there quick, or it's going to start coming through the ceilings. You a nurse?"

"Hmm?"

"A nurse. Are you a nurse?"

She tried to think of something he would know nothing about. "Yep. A surgical nurse." She was fairly sure that anybody who'd had surgery would have been unconscious.

"You mean like when the surgeon says 'Forceps,' you're the one who says 'Forceps' and hands them to him?"

"That's me. Only sometimes I hand him the monkey wrench or the pruning shears for fun."

Dewey chuckled. He looked at the numbers lighting up above the elevator door: 2, then 3.

She had to get whatever talk there was going to be out of the way before the elevator door opened, and she needed to head off trouble. She reached into the pocket on the side of her purse and pulled out a twenty-dollar bill. "I'd like to give you something for helping me out."

He said, "It's nothing."

"Please," she said. "I insist." She had to hold him off this way or he would expect to come in, have a soft drink, and be sure her faucets weren't leaking. She had to keep this under control and foreclose all chances of a mistake.

The elevator stopped and the doors slid open. She tiptoed to the door of apartment 3F, almost pantomiming the act of being quiet.

Dewey slipped his key ring off his belt and tried a key, but the lock on Catherine's door wouldn't accept it. As Judith waited, the noise of the keys on the ring seemed to her to be terribly loud. What if Catherine heard that jingling right outside her door? Even if he got the door open Judith might step inside and see Catherine standing there with a gun in her hand. Dewey held up his key ring again, picked another that looked like the first, and tried it. He pushed the door open, but Judith stepped forward and held it open only an inch. She leaned close, whispered, "Thanks," then slipped inside and closed the door.

It was dark. There seemed to be no sounds of movement in the apartment. Judith stood absolutely still, listening. She heard Dewey's heavy feet move off. After a few more seconds she heard the elevator doors open, then heard them slide shut. The last barrier was gone. She was in.

56

Judith felt relief, but it was only tentative. She was not yet sure that Catherine had not heard her enter. She listened and waited for a long time, and then began to orient herself in the darkness. This was a big open space, and ahead of her was the large window she had seen at the front of the building. She was standing in the tiled entry where Catherine had left a pair of shoes that must have been wet from yesterday's rain.

Judith stepped over them and onto the soft carpet, across the room to the window. She took her time, not rushing to the bedroom. It was only twelve-fifteen. There were probably day-shift people in the building who had not even gone to bed, and some of the night-shift people might leave late for the hospital.

She stood at the window and looked down at the street. She could see a white van down there that must belong to Dewey. It had steel screens in the back windows, probably to keep thieves from breaking in and taking Dewey's tools while he was inside some apartment building fixing a hot-water heater or something.

Judith knew that when this was over, Dewey's description of her would not be of much use to the police. It would make them lose a day finding all the female tenants Dewey didn't know and letting him see them, then showing him the identification photographs of the female employees of the hospital, and then probably interviewing the clerks at the stores where a person could buy hospital scrubs. It would all be a waste of time.

She wanted to wait until Dewey had left the building. She didn't see any need to harm him, and she knew that she would have to if he returned. She watched for several minutes, and then several more. Cars went by. The neighborhood had reached the hour of night when there were no pedestrians out, everyone's dog had been walked, and the hospital's visiting hours were long over.

Dewey's foreshortened, wide body appeared below the front window, coming down the front steps in a little dance. She watched him reach the bottom, walk down the sidewalk, step off the curb, and cross the street to his van. When he got inside she saw the van shake a little as though he were walking around in it, but then the taillights came on. The van slid forward, away from the curb, moved up the street, and disappeared. Dewey was gone.

She stared down at the street for another minute. Dewey did not return, and no one came to take his place. She looked at her watch. It was still well before one. She turned away from the window and studied the darker parts of the apartment.

It was sparsely furnished, just like the one Judith had rented on the west side, across the river. Catherine had not even added any pictures. She was treating her apartment like a hotel room, just a place where she came to sleep. Catherine was undoubtedly planning to rebuild her house very soon, and she would save her decorating ideas for that. Judith hated the thought of it—an insurance company paying to build Catherine a better, newer place. Judith had risked her life for that.

She walked slowly from the window across the room to a narrow hall. Her eyes were now accustomed to the dark. Every shape, every line was clear to her, but it had been cleaned of its color. Time had changed for her too: if she took a single step and did not take another for fifteen seconds, it made no difference. There was no need to risk making a succession of rapid sounds that did not fit with the slow current of the night. Soon enough she was standing in the doorway of Catherine's bedroom.

She could see Catherine curled up in the middle of a queen bed. She was smaller than Judith had thought from the television shots. Or maybe it had been the telephone conversations. She had always sounded big, authoritative, like a strict teacher. But Catherine was one of those people who looked like children when they were asleep, the closed eyes pressing the eyelashes against the cheeks, making them look longer, the skin on the forehead and around the eyes smooth and relaxed, the body curled on its side with the covers pulled to the chin.

Judith spotted Catherine's purse on the dresser. She drifted silently to it and reached inside. Her hands felt Catherine's wallet, a small leather case that seemed to be filled with business cards, a thin leather identification folder. She would go through all of that later. She didn't want to let her eyes stray from Catherine.

From this angle, she could tell that Catherine had left some things under the bed on the side where she slept, away from the door. She could see a long, black four-battery flashlight, a pair of slippers, and Catherine's gun, stuck in a tight little holster that barely covered the trigger guard and two inches of the barrel.

Judith drifted quietly to the bed, bent her knees, and picked up the gun and flashlight, then rose and stepped backward two paces. The pistol was a semiautomatic, and Judith had to get to know it by touch. There was a safety catch, so she clicked it off, then raised the pistol to aim at Catherine's head. "Catherine," she whispered.

She watched Catherine's face as the whisper reached her brain. Her body flinched involuntarily, her eyes snapped open, and her head gave a quick side-to-side motion that was like a shudder while she found the shadow near her bed. She started to sit up.

Judith turned on the powerful flashlight to blind her. "Sit still, Catherine," she said. "Don't move."

Catherine said, "Hello, Tanya." Her voice was a bit raspy

from sleep, but she was making an effort to keep it artificially calm.

Judith knew Catherine was afraid. She could see Catherine's heart beating, making the thin pajama top quiver—*see* it. "I'm not Tanya. I haven't been Tanya for a long time."

"Who are you now?"

"Lie down again, this time on your stomach."

"You don't really want to do this."

"You really don't want to make me angry. You know that I wouldn't mind pulling the trigger."

Catherine lay down again and rolled onto her stomach. "You don't get anything for doing this. That's what I meant. I've been trying to help you come in safely for a long time. Breaking in here doesn't help your cause, and it's dangerous."

"Hands behind your back. Cross your wrists."

She watched Catherine do as she had ordered, then leaned over and pulled up the blankets, keeping Catherine's arms and hands on the outside. Catherine said, "You came here to talk to me, didn't you? Well, I'm happy to listen, and I'll try to do what I can for you."

There was silence. Catherine was beginning to feel heaviness coming on her. There had been a few seconds of hot panic, when she had heard the whisper in the dark, and then seen the shape that proved it had not been just a nightmare. But now the heat and the urgency were gone, and the cold fear had begun. Fear was bleeding her muscles of strength and making her nerves slow to transfer signals. Fear made her arms and legs weak and heavy. She concentrated on controlling her voice. She knew she had to keep talking. "What can I call you?"

"Nothing." The voice came from behind her now, beyond the foot of the bed. That was a very bad sign. Dennis Poole had been shot in the back of the head. The banker in Los Angeles had been shot in the back of the head. Gregory McDonald had been blindfolded in bed and shot in the head.

Catherine tried again. It was easy to kill someone who was lying facedown and silent. She had to keep talking to stay alive. "If you were just planning to kill me, you wouldn't have needed to wake me up. You took a risk, so you must have wanted my help. That was a wise decision. Coming in to the bureau with me voluntarily to answer questions is the best thing you could do."

"Answer questions?" The voice was bitter, angry. "Are you still pretending that you just want me to answer a few questions?"

Catherine knew she had fallen into a way of speaking that could get her killed. She had to be extremely careful now not to offend her, and not to appear to be lying. She had to keep the same tone, not retreat. "I'm a police officer. What I say and do have to reflect what the law says. You haven't been charged with anything. You're still wanted for questioning—here and in Arizona and California—so that's what I have to call it."

"And when I'm done, I'll be able to walk out, right?"

Catherine spoke as carefully as possible. "I think that you almost certainly won't. You're a suspect, and so you'll probably be detained. You can wait to answer questions until a lawyer is with you."

"I'm not here for questions."

"Why are you here, then?"

"I'm here for you. I'm what you asked for."

"I asked you to come in to save yourself."

There was a small, voiceless laugh, like a quiet cough that Catherine heard coming from the foot of the bed. She waited for the shot, the pain. But instead, it was only the voice. "If I came in to the office with you tonight, the way you asked, you're saying you wouldn't get any benefit out of it?"

"Of course I would."

"What kind of benefit?"

"Some people I respect would be proud of me."

"Who?"

"Other cops. One in particular. He's retired, but he'd hear about it."

"That's it?"

"Whenever a person in trouble can be persuaded to come

in peacefully, it makes everybody safer. And no cop had to do anything that gives him nightmares."

"God, you're such a liar," said Judith. "You'd be a hero. They'd promote you, and they'd show the mayor on television pinning a medal on you. That would be my life. You could pin my life on the front of your coat. Each time you wore it you could remember me."

"That's what I've been trying to prevent—you losing your life."

"Shut up, and don't move until I tell you." Catherine heard her step in the direction of the closet. There were sounds of hangers scraping on the pole, then other sounds like the sliding and swishing of fabric. There were more sounds of hangers moving on the pole, a couple of dresser drawers opening and closing. Finally, after a very long time, she said, "Very good, Catherine. You didn't move. Now listen carefully. Roll over to the center of the bed onto your back. Do not sit up."

Catherine had been listening carefully to the sounds, but she had not been able to devise a way to take advantage of any possible lapse in Tanya's attention. Lying on her belly under the heavy blankets with her hands crossed behind her had prevented her from making any kind of quick move, and any move might be the wrong one. Now, as she rolled onto her back, she freed her arms, swept the blanket off her, and looked for Tanya. She was still standing at the foot of the bed, where Catherine could not hope to reach her before the gun went off. Tanya had learned a lot in a very short time.

Catherine saw the throw, and winced in advance, but what landed on her was an old white sweatshirt with the University of California seal on the front.

"Put it on."

Catherine held it up with both hands, used the seal of the university to find the front, slipped it over her head and arms, and tugged it down in back. She knew she had to start talking again to keep herself human in Tanya's mind. "Why do you want me to wear this?"

"For fun."

That made Catherine feel the heavy, passive kind of fear again. Maybe Tanya had turned that corner too. Sociopaths talked that way. Things struck them as funny. Another bundle flew through the air. This one landed on Catherine's stomach, and she flinched. She touched it and felt denim. It was a pair of blue jeans. As she slipped them on, still lying on her back, she decided that Tanya had made a mistake. Clothes made her feel stronger, less vulnerable and helpless.

"All right. Sit up."

Catherine sat up. The light came on, and she saw Tanya. She felt her breathing stop for a second, as though her chest wouldn't expand to take in the air. Tanya was standing at the foot of the bed, holding her gun. She had taken off whatever she had been wearing, and now she was in one of Catherine's suits.

Tanya smiled. She opened the coat. Catherine's badge was pinned on the belt, where Catherine wore it sometimes. "I'm Catherine," she said. "Maybe Cathy. I think I'll be Cathy."

Catherine knew that she should have anticipated this. All this time, Tanya had been lost, trying to invent a person to be. Each time she had tried it she had succeeded for a time, been discovered, been chased. Of course this was what would happen. At last she had decided to stop being the runner. Now she wanted to be the pursuer, the one with the power and authority. "Don't," said Catherine. "Don't do this."

"You don't think I make a good Cathy?"

"It's not a name you can take, because it will get you caught, and maybe killed. People would know that something had happened to me."

"Then what? They would search for me? They're searching now."

"You've got to start thinking clearly about how to end this."

"I have." She was Cathy now. There was nothing that she needed to decide. "All right, Catherine. Listen carefully. You and I are going out. We're going to walk together about a block to the west, and get into my car. There will be no talking along the way, and no noises. If I think you've made a noise that might wake people up, I'll wake them the rest of the way by killing you."

"Where are we going?"

"I told you. My car."

"After that."

"We're going to go for a ride. Or I'd like to. Obviously, if at any point you cause me trouble, I won't be able to bring you any farther. You'll stop there."

"Why are you doing this? Do you think I'm the only one who's been looking for you? I'm one little cop in one town. Police forces everywhere are searching for you right now."

Cathy raised her gun and aimed it at Catherine Hobbes's head. Her expression was cold impatience. Catherine waited for the shot. From this distance Cathy could hardly miss her forehead.

Catherine wanted to close her eyes, but she knew instinctively that closing her eyes would be a bad idea, a signal of resignation and readiness. She forced herself to keep her eyes unblinking and focused on the eyes of—she had to accept the new reality—not Tanya, but Cathy. She tried to keep the fear and anger out of her eyes, and show only calm. The two women stayed that way for several seconds, an age, while Cathy decided.

Cathy lowered the gun a few inches. "You're right," she said. "I did come to talk. I need to make a decision about how I want this to end. It will take time to make a decision and time to come to an agreement, and we can't do it in this apartment. Being here is too dangerous for me. We're going to my car now. Remember what I said. No talk, no noise." She gestured toward the door. "Stand up. Put on those slippers and walk to the door."

Catherine looked at the closet. "My sneakers are right there. Do you mind if I wear those?"

"Yes. Do what I said. Quiet."

Catherine stepped into the slippers and began to walk, the slippers flapping at each step. Cathy was lying. She wanted Catherine to wear the slippers so she couldn't run or fight. Cathy had no interest in talking. She had become so much more sophisticated at killing that she now knew how to make the victim help her. She had learned that anyone she held at gunpoint would help her fool him. The victim might detect the false tone, but he would choose to believe it because it bought a few more minutes of hope, a few minutes when he could still be a person who was going to live and not a person who was about to die. It occurred to her that Cathy might be trying the lie for the first time. Everything a killer like Cathy did was a kind of experiment. She was learning now, preparing for the next person.

Catherine walked to the apartment door and stopped in front of it. From this moment on, she had to force herself to stay calm, to see every spot of the world around her with immediacy and accuracy—with her eyes and not her mind—and try to construct an advantage. Accepting this woman as "Cathy" had been a first attempt to acknowledge the fluidity of events. Each second from now on, she would need to do it again.

Things were not as they had been, and not as they should be. They were what they had become. Catherine stood still and let Cathy open the apartment door. Catherine was thinking like a police officer again, and not like a scared young woman who had been dragged from her bed. She wanted to make sure that if she died tonight, there would be fingerprints here to tell the forensic team who had killed her.

She watched Cathy's left hand clasp the doorknob and open it. Then Catherine stepped out into the hallway. As Cathy pulled the door shut, Catherine watched surreptitiously. Cathy had taken a tissue with her from the box in the bedroom, and now she wiped the doorknob clean.

Catherine walked toward the elevator, but Cathy touched her arm and shook her head. They walked to the stairwell. Once again, Cathy used her left hand to open the door, and kept her right hand on the gun. Catherine had to step into the stairwell, then stand in silence while Cathy closed the door with her left hand and wiped off the knob. There was no reason to wipe off the fingerprints unless Catherine was going to die.

The two women walked down the two flights of stairs to the ground floor, and Catherine stopped. She considered the possibility that this was the place to make her stand. It was a lighted, closed vertical space with only cinder-block walls and a set of steel steps, so no bullet would go through a wall

and kill a sleeping neighbor. She took too long to think abou
it, and the moment passed. Cathy had the door open, and she
was waiting with the gun aimed.

For a second Catherine felt anger at herself, but that passed
too: the opportunity had to feel right before she took it. An
intuition was not magical; it was a conclusion that came
from a hundred small calculations made at once—distance
between her body and Cathy's, momentum and balance, eye
motion and focus. If the conditions had been right, she had
not detected it. The moment had not yet come. Catherine
stepped out into the lobby.

She walked to the front door and waited. Cathy pushed on
the crash bar and guided her out. They walked down the steps
to the sidewalk. "Keep going," Cathy whispered. "Cross the
street."

Catherine's eyes swept the route ahead, still trying to find
a feature she could turn into an advantage. Could she use
something ahead as a weapon? A distraction? Was there a
dark place where she might be able to slip away and outrun
Cathy? On this side of the street she saw only a broad sidewalk, a few young trees too thin to hide behind, a few parked
cars. She longed for the comfort of a plan. When she realized
that her desire was for the comfort, she abandoned it. She
had to keep this difficult, not comforting. She had to keep
searching, identifying, and evaluating, second by second. The
moment would come, and she simply had to recognize it and
act instantly.

She slowed her walk and turned her head slightly to get a
view of Cathy, then immediately turned her head forward
again to keep from alarming her. She felt a panicky shortness
of breath. The sight she had glimpsed was unsettling. Cathy
was not only wearing one of Catherine's new suits, with the
coat unbuttoned, so that Catherine could catch a glint of her
own badge at the belt; she was also carrying Catherine's purse,
and her hair had been redone to resemble Catherine's style.

Cathy was walking along, planning to kill Catherine and
take her name, identification, weapon, look—her place. The
sight of it in the light of a streetlamp made it seem worse

han just dying. This was a total obliteration, not like being killed but like being devoured.

She looked ahead to see if she could spot which of the cars parked at the curb would be the one, and her breath caught in her throat. It was a new, teal blue Acura. It was exactly the same as Catherine's car, the one that had been burned in the fire.

Catherine knew now that Cathy had stepped off solid ground, and then kicked reality to pieces behind her. There was nothing holding her to the world anymore except some perverse interest in playing in the spaces between things—moving, fooling people, hiding, changing herself.

Catherine could see where this was going, as though simple foresight were clairvoyance. Cathy had made herself look enough like Catherine so she could flash the driver's license or the police ID and get most people to think it was a match. She had probably become good enough at manipulating strangers to convince them that she was a police officer: people who met a cop weren't suspicious of the cop's identity; they were defensive about their own, anxious to get the cop's approval.

What was coming was handcuffs. The handcuffs were in the purse, and Cathy had been using the purse to shield her gun from sight. She must have seen or felt the leather case with the handcuffs. She couldn't hope to drive Catherine anywhere without them.

The handcuffs introduced a time limit. Cathy would walk her up to the car, and only then take out the cuffs. She would restrain Catherine's wrists behind her, and put her in the seat. Catherine had to make a move before that happened, before they even got near the car. Cathy was smart enough to know that rather than being restrained and put in a car, Catherine would take the chance of dying in a fight.

Catherine stared ahead to detect an advantage, but it wasn't there. It was still the broad, flat sidewalk, a few widely spaced saplings, a few parked cars. There were no garbage cans, no pieces of loose metal or wood, nothing she could snatch up and swing. The teal blue Acura was only forty feet away.

Catherine pivoted and swung hard. Her fist grazed Cathy's

chin, slid off, hit her neck and collarbone. Cathy staggered
back, and the gun fired. There was a ricochet sound as the
bullet chipped the pavement at their feet and flew off into the
night.

The gun came up fast. Catherine had no time to strike it
away, so she charged under it and plowed into Cathy's mid-
section. Cathy's left hand tangled in Catherine's hair, tugging
at it to pull her off, but Catherine kept pushing, digging in hard
with her feet, and Cathy fell backward. Her back slammed
into the door of a parked car, and the gun fired again. She
couldn't get the barrel of it around to aim it, so she pounded
it down on Catherine's head.

The pain exploded into a red flash in front of Catherine's
eyes, and she could feel it growing, blossoming. She punched
at Cathy's belly, and her hand hit something hard. She knew
the feel—a gun. Cathy had taped a gun to her waist under her
clothes. Catherine hit at Cathy's face with her left hand and
used her right to snatch the gun out of the tape, bring it upward, and pull the trigger.

Catherine Hobbes stepped off the airplane at Los Angeles
International, hurried along the concourse carrying her
overnight bag, and joined the gaggle of people stepping one
by one onto the crowded escalator. She could hardly wait for
it to take her down to the baggage area, where Joe Pitt would
be waiting for her.

There was a tall man on the step ahead of her, so she had
to look over his shoulder to see down through the glass wall
below the escalator into the waiting area. She smiled when
she spotted Pitt standing a distance away beneath the television sets that displayed flight arrival times. She could see
him in profile, talking to someone. Catherine craned her
neck to see the other person.

Beside him was a young blond woman clutching the extended handle of a small suitcase. She was clearly charmed
with Joe Pitt. She reached up to touch her hair twice, her
eyes widened as she looked at him, and she leaned forward
to laugh at something he said. She gracefully reached into

er purse, took out what seemed to be a business card, and
eld it out to Pitt. He took it.

Catherine's stomach felt hollow, and her mouth was dry.
She sensed that she was watching her time with him ending,
 just as she had watched the end of her marriage—Catherine
was once again on the outside, looking into a room, seeing
what she was not supposed to see. She knew that Joe had
probably not even intended anything like this. He had come
to the airport to pick her up, and while he was waiting, he
had found himself in a conversation. He was simply being
Joe Pitt. One of the reasons he was fun to be with was that he
liked women. He had a cheerful, mildly cynical view of things
that made them laugh. She was sure he had not searched for
that young woman. He had simply found her—probably
looked at her appreciatively, or said something friendly—
and she had liked him.

There would always be women like that, and they would
always like Joe Pitt. If Catherine was with him, moments like
this would always be part of her life. They would happen
over and over, and she would always catch herself wondering. She had known enough to understand this from the beginning, and she had decided she could live with the feeling.
But this was more than a feeling. How could she have picked
another man who would not be faithful to her? Somewhere
there was a man who would be satisfied with just Catherine
Hobbes, but Joe Pitt wasn't the one.

Catherine looked over her shoulder, up the escalator. Maybe
she could slip between the other passengers, make her way
back up to the concourse, and exchange her return ticket for
the next flight to Portland. She could call him on his cell
phone. She would say, "Joe? You know, I've decided not to
fly down to Los Angeles after all. Something's come up and
I can't get away." What was she thinking? A woman—an
armed woman, at that—scrambling the wrong way up the escalator would be a breach of security, and they'd probably
close down the whole terminal while they arrested her.

Already it was too late to do anything. She reached the foot
of the escalator, looked down, and stepped off. She could not
even pause, or she would cause other passengers to pile up

behind her. She looked up and spotted him again, now standing alone. She walked directly toward him, and watched him
recognize her. He grinned happily and bounded forward as
though he was going to hug her.

She veered to stay an arm's length from him, walking beside him toward the door to the street, and said, "Hi, Joe.
Sorry if I'm late. I hope you didn't get too lonely waiting
for me."

"No," he said. "I happened to run into a woman I knew
from the days in the D.A.'s office. She's a crime reporter for
the L.A. *Times,* the one who covered Tanya's killings here."
He reached into his pocket, produced the business card that
Catherine had seen him take a moment ago, and held it out to
her. "She asked me to give you her card. She wants to interview you about the case."

Catherine glanced down at it, then stopped and faced him.
She said, "Aren't you going to kiss me or anything?"